LEGAL INFORMATION

Published by Tri-Quill Publishing Limited 2014

Concept & Story of *The Kinship Chronicles*:
Copyright © Cassie Kennedy 2014

Cover Artwork, Illustrations & Poetry
Copyright © Brigid 2014

Tri-Book® is a registered trademark of Brigid, Tri-Quill
Publishing Limited 2014

Disclaimer: All characters, names and places appearing in
this story are fictitious with the exception of 'The
Empress'. Any resemblance to real persons, living or
dead, is purely coincidental.

E-Book ISBN: 978-0-9930330-0-1
Hardback ISBN: 978-0-9930330-3-2
Audiobook ISBN: 978-0-9930330-6-0

D1615382

THE KINSHIP CHRONICLES
Tri-Book®

ACKNOWLEDGEMENTS

Creator-Owner:
Cassie Kennedy
The Kinship Chronicles Tri-Book®

Creator-Owner:
Brigid
The Kinship Chronicles Tri-Book®

Professional Psychic & Medium in Residence:
Prophecies & predictions given for certain characters,
events & places by 'The Empress'
www.psychicdenise.co.uk

Reader in Residence:
Margaret Thomson

Formatting, Typesetting & Graphics by Mayfin Design
www.mayfindesign.com

Edited by Bright Writing www.brightwriting.co.uk

CULTURAL & DESIGN REFERENCES

Fantasia on a theme by Thomas Tallis by Ralph Vaughan Williams (1872-1958)

Gold key image downloaded from www.dreamstime.com

Invictus by William Ernest Henley (1849-1903)

Maori border designs
Purchased from www.keyimagery.com
Arohanui

Ultimate Book Cover - Kaperua

Book 1 - *The Feathered Roots*: Patiki
Book 2 - *Scatter of Kin*: Koiri
Book 3 - *The Binding Veil*: Ngaru

Snow Patrol
www.snowpatrol.com

*Every effort was made to contact Cultural References prior to publication for professional acknowledgement purposes. If acknowledgement needs to be sought retrospectively please contact the Creator-Owners at **tqpublishingltd@gmail.com**.*

DEDICATIONS

Mum, Dad, Neil, Nicola,
Alex & *the* George

Thank You.

I Love You All.

In memory of my beloved Nana,
Evelyn Jessie Young (1927-2014)

I'll miss you forever.

CK x

Dear Daddy

It took me a while but now I understand,
Why you had to depart
this earthbound land,
Helping me more than
you ever could from here,
Rest assured Daddy,
I shed heaven-sent tears,
Through the challenges I have yet to face,
I trust my heart to find
it's rightful resting place.

In memory of my Dad,
David C Fraser (1944-2009)

Love you always, B x

'The Empress'

In The Magic Garden, that beautiful
summers day,
Three lives entwined, in a story yet to
say…

The Time is Now, all endeavors are done,
Thankful to your gift & John, our
Blueprints begun,

The world must now re-evaluate,
A prophecy for our planet, The Empress
shall make...

Dear Reader,

Three books bound together in one,
Your Tri-Book journey has nearly begun,
Thankful for your trust & faith,
Turn over the pages,
where a new world awaits...

PROLOGUE

"The eternal battle begins,

A binding cast dwells within,

Good versus evil beyond the veil,

Here we begin our faerie tale..."

...on behalf of Archangel Michael

Archangel Michael

MAP OF SENSIO

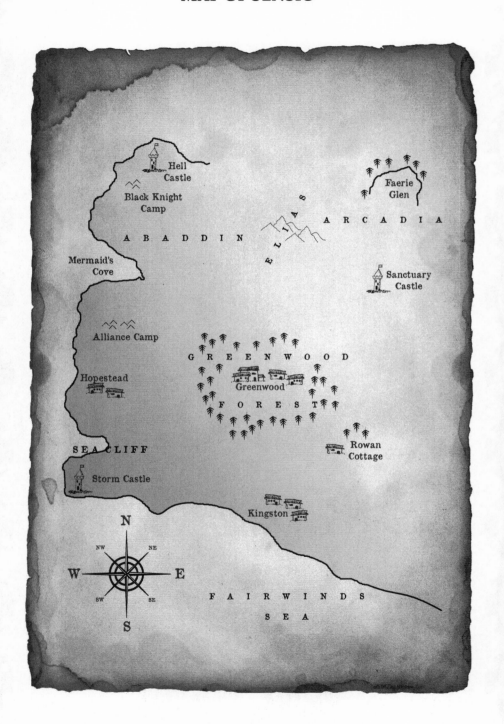

THE KINSHIP CHRONICLES

The Feathered Roots

CASSIE KENNEDY

Air

Earth

Fire

Water

4 elements
3 parts
2 sides
1 last chance
0 the time is now

Illustrations & Poetry by
BRIGID

RIPPLES

Lauren Lockwood

I winced as Rora clenched my hand. "This isn't that bad" she smiled optimistically; trying to convince herself that all the horror stories had been concocted or exaggerated. Having lived in the village of Ravenswood all our lives, Rora had been approached by many well-intentioned women; most described it as the quickest pain to forget and had smiled at her reassuringly. It was only now that she knew the real truth. Childbirth is a brutal and bloody business and no one can prepare you for it. I knew it had to hurt like hell. I stayed silent, tenderly placing a cold cloth on Rora's glistening forehead and tried to look calm. As a nurse, I knew this was only the beginning.

As the contractions became stronger and more frequent, Rora faded from her surroundings. Her hands tore and clutched at the sheets with each new wave of pain and I would have done anything to make it go away. Rubbing Rora's back I wished I could help her, a worry that had plagued me since she came home six months ago. I'll never forget her lost, haunted expression when I first saw her.

Little by little, she entrusted me with her broken heart, left in fragments after she had fallen hopelessly in love and been left alone and pregnant. My childhood friend had never had it easy, first losing her parents and then losing her Nana, the last of her family, two years ago. But she was not alone, she had me, her family, and I would do anything for her, as I know she would for me.

I placed the cloth back in the bowl and went into the kitchen, running the tap until the water turned cold. Looking out of the window, I saw the now familiar dark figure standing like a sentry at the gate, the puff of his warm breath threading like ribbons into the frosty night air. Daniel Darkings arrived yesterday just as Rora's bump had begun to distinctly descend. It was hard not to be intimidated by his appearance. He was man of great stature, well over six feet, with hawk-like features and piercing blue eyes. His jaw had been clenched in determination as he tried to gain entry to the cottage. I only granted entry when Rora greeted him like an old friend, appeasing my initial reservations.

"I've come to protect you," he had said, hugging her, smiling at the large bump between them. She smiled back, clearly happy to see him.

Once I'd shown him to the spare room, I asked Rora to tell me what was happening and who he was.

He worried me. His clothes were made of a material in a curious mixture of greens and browns that I'd never seen before. He was hyper vigilant, checking the security of the cottage and constantly looking out of the window, making me wonder if he had a military background.

But she never got the chance to tell me, because at that very moment her waters broke. Rora screamed. I ran back to the bedroom and saw that the baby had crowned. Daniel ran in behind me.

"I heard the scream outside" he said.

Sitting on the bed behind Rora, she rested against him like a pillow, smiling gratefully. I took my position in front of her. She didn't have long to go now. She grew weaker and weaker with each agonising contraction, until at last, screaming loudly, she gave one final push and the baby's small, slippery body slid into the towel I was holding. I cut the cord and gave Rora her baby boy. His cries filled the room.

"He sounds healthy enough." Daniel chuckled.

I examined Rora and said, "This isn't over. There's another baby coming."

Daniel and I exchanged a worried look knowing how weak she was.

"I can do this." Rora whispered, kissing and stroking her baby, before she gave him to Daniel to hold. Daniel propped Rora against some pillows and held the baby, close to her so she could see him clearly. The second baby, a girl, arrived quickly. She was slighter than her brother and cried softly, as if unhappy to leave her mother's body. I held the baby close to Rora, knowing she was too weak to hold her herself. Rora looked at her babies, her love for them lighting up her face.

She smiled weakly at Daniel and said softly, "I wish he'd been here."

Turning to me, she motioned to the bureau drawer: "My journal – it will help you understand. Trust Daniel... please do as he asks."

I looked at my friend's ashen face and felt the full force of stricken panic. I shook my head in disbelief.

"Is this why you wanted a home birth? Rora, you can't…"
My words faltered as I cried out in anguish. Rora's face
gradually became serene as her breathing stilled and finally
ceased.

The room fell to absolute silence, apart from my rapid,
shuddering breaths. Then the babies began to cry, as if they
understood that they had just lost their mother. I turned to
Daniel. He was too calm. He had known exactly what was
going to happen.

"Why didn't you tell me?" I whispered, hot tears running
down my frozen face.

"I had hoped…" he faltered, then stopped himself. "I'm
sorry." His arms tightened around the tiny baby boy, cradled
in his arms.

"I don't know what to do." I shouted, infuriated by his
calmness.

"We need to separate the babies," he said looking at me
unflinchingly.

Overwhelmed, I stepped away from him, and tightened my
grip around the baby girl. "What are you talking about?
Rora's just died," I sobbed. What's the matter with you?" I
shouted releasing the confusion, anger and grief tied up
inside me.

Disturbed by the noise, the babies momentarily stopped
crying and then began to cry even louder as they sensed the
tension. I forced myself to calm down.

"Lauren," Daniel said, - "Believe me, I understand. Rora

was my friend too. "My Maggie loves..." he hesitated "loved her like a sister."

I saw his features soften and glimpsed genuine grief.

"Do you think I would be suggesting this if there was any other way?" he said, his voice sharp with frustration and anger.

I scrutinised him, trying to make an objective decision based on my medical training, his reaction and Rora's last words. He looked back at me without flinching.

"No, you don't have a choice." I whispered understanding this was the truth.

He nodded, calmer and the tension drained away.

"We need to go now. We don't have much time."

He placed the boy in a Moses basket and removed two large bags and another Moses basket from the cupboard. I gulped back tears as I realised Rora had prepared for twins. He walked to the bureau where he rummaged around, found the journal and tucked it away in one of the bags. I placed the baby girl into the empty Moses basket and looked to him for guidance.

"Ready?" he asked. "Ready?" he asked again.

Standing silent, I swayed, everything around me suddenly taking on a grey fuzziness. Daniel grabbed my arm urgently, and I re-focused again.

"Not now, she needs you," he said, nodding to the baby, now sleeping, her body turned towards her twin brother, only a thin veil of woven fabric separating them.

Tucking a blanket around the baby girl, I picked up the basket and followed Daniel out to the back of the cottage towards a 4x4, invisible in the darkness to the naked eye. I buckled her into the car seat, as Daniel placed the bags in the car.

"You knew this would happen." I whispered.

He nodded. "Listen to me, Lauren. Drive and don't stop until it feels right. You need to look after her. You need to do this for Rora."

At these words, the adrenalin started to kick in. I nodded.

"Where will you take her brother?" I asked, touching the soft skin on the sleeping baby's forehead. He stirred and whimpered in his sleep.

"Back home. He'll grow up with my Mate and boy. We'll look after him. Daniel said. "And don't worry, I'll take care of Rora too."

I nodded again and climbed into the vehicle. I trusted him. I trusted the vow he had made.

"Keep her safe," he said softly, looking tenderly at the baby. "Now go." he urged.

I held his gaze as I slammed the car into gear. Within a mile I knew I was lost from his view, but despite the blackness of the night I felt his watchful eye follow us. As I drove, the rain fell, caressing the windscreen, as tears rolled down my cheeks. The baby woke up and cried softly. I looked into the mirror as she moved then settled against the blanket around her. Then I remembered the name Rora had picked for a girl.

"Amber," I vowed, "I promise I'll look after you."

We drove on through the night, into the dawn, towards an unknown future.

14 YEARS LATER...

DREAMS

Amber Lockwood

As long as I can remember I've never had a peaceful night's sleep. Just one night with puppies or kittens is all I'm asking for. I wish I knew what the dreams were about. I've even tried to write them down in a notebook to make sense of them. It did not take me long to realise that its hard to make sense of something you can't understand.

I was five when I became aware of how different I was. I had started primary school and thinking that everybody had dreams like that, I had excitedly told my new, best friend Amy about them. We had met on the first day of school and I told her everything. I still remember the conversation that Amy's parents had with Mum. They were tense and beseeching as they tried to make her understand that it was nothing personal, but they really didn't want Amy to have contact with a little girl "with such an overactive imagination."

I can still feel their awkward glance in my direction as they led Amy, smiling sadly, to the next classroom. As I saw her leave, I started to cry. Okay, I know that sounds pretty dramatic, but I was only five years old and she was my first, real friend. I had met her two weeks before on our first day of school.

But what I remember the most was my Mum's reaction. As Amy's parents spoke she adopted what I now know to be her 'professional nurse' mask. I remember thinking that she was paying them as much respect as the conversation warranted, but that her full attention was on my reaction. When I began to cry the professional mask slipped, she stretched her arms out and hugged me close.

"Don't worry." she had said, wiping my tears away with the back of her hand. "It's going to be ok."

An expression I didn't understand had flickered across her face as she stood up, before she concealed it with a smile.

Back at home, Mum said, "It's okay to have dreams Amber, but not everyone will understand them."

I wouldn't be allowed to play with Amy again but that was not my fault. "Promise me you won't mention the dreams again, will you Amber?" She repeated until I nodded.

It didn't occur to me to question her. I only wanted to please her. There were some things that we simply didn't talk about. Like when I was four and wanted to know who my Dad was, because everyone else at nursery seemed to have one. Mum had paled. "You'll always have me," she said, pulling me into a tight hug. That's the last time I ever asked about my father.

So here I am at fourteen waking up from another dream-filled night. I wish I knew what they were about. All I ever remember is a kaleidoscope of coloured images moving through my head at such warped speed that I can't hold onto one before another appears. Sometimes they wake me, leaving me shaking with fear like I'm being chased by some unknown entity. On these mornings, I truly think I'm going mad. Other dreams are soft and comfortable, and make me feel like I'm being cradled by a large warm body. On those days, I'm don't want to wake up.

Last night was a bad one. When I woke up my hands shook as I covered my face and tried to steady my breathing. Pulling on my robe, I walked into the kitchen to get a glass of water. Mum was sitting at the table reading a newspaper.

"Hi." I said as I drank the icy cold water and rolled the cold glass against my hot cheeks.

"Morning," she replied.

I felt Mum watching me over her newspaper. I put the glass in the sink and looked outside the kitchen window. The trees in the nearby woods sparkled red, gold and brown in the autumn sunlight. Frost sparkled on the grass. It was a perfect day for running.

Mum broke the silence. "You still have the dreams, don't you?"

I turned round to see her face before I answered. I needed to see her reaction to my words. Her face was open and tense. I knew she was vulnerable to my answer.

"Yes." I said. Maybe if she knew how bad it was she would want to help me.

Mum recoiled and a ghost of an expression flickered across her face as she swallowed and tried to control her emotions. She looked as if she was going to say something, then the moment passed, until she composed her features into her impenetrable professional mask.

"Are you going for a run this morning?" she asked.

It was my turn to recoil. My eyes filled up with tears and unable to speak, I nodded as I walked out of the kitchen. Whatever I was dealing with, she'd made one thing clear. I was on my own.

The leaves crunched below my trainers as I ran through the woods. I had starting running regularly by accident. A couple of years ago, following a particularly bad dream and went for walk early one morning to get some air. Within minutes my fast walking had developed into a steady pace. Being in the open space, near trees and water seemed to calm me. At Mum's suggestion, I joined the school's running club. I loved being surrounded by nature and the peaceful silence in my head as I ran. My teacher and fellow pupils believed I had a natural talent. All I know is that you run faster when you have demons chasing after you, even if they were your own. As I covered the first mile, my body fell into a natural rhythm, my muscles relaxed and my mind cleared. Finally, I saw what I had been too confused to see before. What had been right in front of me the whole time. Mum's fleeting expression. I remembered it. When I was five and I'd told Amy about my dreams. Her expression this morning was exactly the same.

It was fear.

CURIOUS

Amber Lockwood

Even at 15, I knew opportunities should not be wasted. "See you later." Mum called from the front door. Moments later I heard the key turn in the lock and her footsteps fade down the garden path. To supplement our income, Mum provided private nursing care to the elderly Mrs Taylor a couple of nights a week. I checked the clock and I had an hour before she came back. I went into her bedroom and closed the door. The bed was well made and ready to pass any stringent hospital inspection. The oak furniture was well worn but sturdy. The bedroom window looked out towards the small garden surrounded by the secure six-foot fence. I know this room like the back of my hand, but I didn't have a clue of where to begin searching.

As I stood there, I was transported back to being ten again, determined to find my Christmas presents. I had known they were in the closet, because Mum had shooed me away as I was about to open the door. I sneaked in later to search and found the pink jewellery box that had been at the very top of my Christmas list. But Mum quickly found me. With hindsight, I should have waited until she did more than go for a cup of tea before I began my scavenging. Mum had sat me down and explained how special it was for her to watch my expression as I opened my presents on Christmas Day. I felt so guilty that I never attempted to look for presents again.

I felt the same childish guilt trip, as I prepared once more to snoop where I'm not supposed to. I knew exactly why I was here. I simply didn't know what else to do. I was devastated the day I told Mum I was still having the dreams. She didn't offer me the help I so desperately wanted and needed. I was devastated. I am her daughter. She could see I wasn't sleeping, struggling, hurting. She watched me fall apart and did nothing to stop it.

I was angry for a long time. I retreated to my bedroom in silence. I refused to eat my dinner. My grades dropped. I quit the running club and decided instead to go out on my own. I became a loner. In short, I no longer cared about anything that once mattered to me. To be fair she took it on the chin. She accepted my anger as though it was her due. She met every selfish, attention-seeking act with a calmness I couldn't break, no matter how hard I tried. I looked at the clock and galvanised myself into action. Thirty minutes later, I struck gold. Finding a faded black bag with a shiny gold lock at the very back of the closet. As I picked it up, to confirm my suspicions, something inside it moved. It felt like a square object. I tried to open the bag, but the lock wouldn't budge. What could Mum be hiding in an old bag that needed a secure lock? I checked my watch. Realised I only had fifteen minutes to get the room back into shape before she arrived home. I committed the hiding place to memory and closed the closet door. I will check again as soon as I get another chance.

When Mum arrived home I was in the kitchen making a pot of tea. She smiled gratefully at me. A shiver of guilt ran through me. But I steadied myself. I was doing what was necessary.

A few hours later I woke up to darkness and there was a cold stillness to the air. Pure blackness filtered through the window and though the night was still, the house sounded awake. Hearing a noise, I crept quietly from my bedroom to investigate and hissed as the coldness of the wooden floorboards penetrated my bare feet. I peeked round the living room door and saw the lamplight cast a glow over Mum as she sat on the couch covered by a worn woollen blanket. She had a small brown book open on her lap. The cover and pages were worn and looked as if they could disintegrate at any moment. Gasping, I realised the noise that had awoken me were from Mum. She was crying, balling up a tissue and pushing it against her mouth to stifle her sobs. My natural instinct was to comfort her, to say sorry for being such a spoilt, selfish brat over the last few months. Instinctively, I knew my presence would not be welcomed. My upset would revert her back to her Mum role and she would offer me comfort instead. I did not belong where she was. Her body may be on the couch in our living room, but her mind was elsewhere. She was living in the world of words held within the little brown book. And wherever that was, it was a world of pain.

I crept back to bed and stared into the darkness, more awake than I have ever been before. Little by little, the anger and resentment I had harboured over the last few months faded until it disappeared. Rubbing my hands over my face, I felt agitated, mostly at myself. Despite my recent dramatics, I was still in the same position. There was a secret Mum didn't want me to know and it was hurting her like hell.

What could be so bad? Despite the fact that I wanted the truth, part of me was scared to face it.

A week later I got another opportunity to search again and was in the closet before Mum had closed the garden gate behind her. I knew the book that Mum had been reading was the object in the black bag with the gold lock. I pushed the boxes and bags out of the way and looked at the back of the closet and saw nothing. Crying in frustration, I desperately searched under the bed, behind and on top of the wardrobe and in every single cupboard and drawer. Mum had moved it. It was gone. Along with all the answers I had been searching for.

Where could I go from here?

THE PRETENCE

Lauren Lockwood

I moved the bag below the floorboards. I didn't know what else to do. There is no rulebook, no medical procedure to follow for a situation like this. It seems the last time I thought clearly I was driving north in a black 4x4 with a newly born baby girl who'd just lost her mother. My only thought was to do as Daniel said - to go somewhere I felt safe and look after her. Sometimes, I wonder if I was duped. If my shock at losing my best friend, my family, had left me so traumatised that I wasn't capable of making a rational decision.

The only reason I ended up in this small village was because my father stopped here for an ice cream on a childhood holiday. It was only after we found the cottage and we had settled into some sort of a routine that I read Rora's journal.

What I read still haunts me. Am I up to this task? Do I have enough strength to do this? I know Amber is curious. I would be too. All those unanswered questions and half answers. Then I look at her and see Rora, the shine of her auburn hair, that cheeky smile, and I feel comforted. Her mother was the strongest person I have ever known.

One thing I do know. One thing I am absolutely certain about. When I looked after that tiny, vulnerable baby in those early, emotional days I did more than change nappies and feed her. I fell completely and utterly in love with her. As far as I'm concerned, she is my daughter and I'll do whatever it takes to protect her.

Even, if it is from herself.

"Confused and lost, compass broken,

Words & thoughts never spoken,

Will I find a way to navigate?

For now, I'm bewildered and hesitate"

…Amber

Amber

VINTAGE

Amber Lockwood

My friend Elaine does not believe in coincidences. Call it fate, kismet, destiny or serendipity. She sees every person or opportunity as something that is meant to be. The same goes for car parking spaces, meeting people and most of all romance. She meets 'the one' at least once every few months. It starts off with the essential 'textual chemistry'. If they make it past the first month, it's true love. Unfortunately, by month two, they invariably reveal some fatal character flaw and the relationship comes to an abrupt end. To Elaine's credit, her absolute belief that she will meet her one true love never wavers. As the boy wanders off into the sunset wondering what the hell happened to him. She has already begun dreaming of the next perfect romance.

I on the other hand, am yet to experience a stirring beyond affection. I just don't feel that way about romance. Sure, some boys in our year are cute, but when I look at them all I feel is friendship. As a result, I've got a lot of male buddies at school. Sometimes, I wonder if there's something wrong with me? Is my wiring faulty? Is there someone special out there for me? Despite our different approaches to life, Elaine and I have been best friends since primary school and she has never wavered in her efforts to convert me to her way of thinking, claiming that not everything has a logical answer.

She knows the whole story about Mum, the book, the

mystery Dad and the dreams. She knows when I desperately need to talk about it, even if I don't want to. She stops me from going mad. We've debated all the possible theories after the disappearing book incident. Is my Dad a master criminal whose past may catch up with us? Am I the result of a relationship with a married man? Our theories range from the sublime to the ridiculous.

We both turned eighteen a few months ago and are midway through our sixth year. A year where we must make decisions that will affect the rest of our lives. But how can I make any kind of decision when I have no idea who I am or where I come from? I don't even look like Mum, so does that mean that I look like my father? Five foot seven, long auburn hair, green eyes and curves. Do I look like him?

I snap out of my reverie as Elaine's yellow beetle draws up and I shimmy myself into the seat beside her. I look at her outfit, laugh and think again that she is my absolute opposite. Her long blond hair is tucked under a fedora hat and her skinny jeans are covered in a vintage cape. She looks like a young Jane Fonda on her way to a war protest. I'm more like a fifties model without the pencil wiggle dress. It's Saturday and she's hoodwinked me into going to yet another vintage fayre in the next town.

She gives me a hug and her excitement is contagious. "I'm on the lookout for some bargains today, Sis. I can feel a pair of vintage Jimmy Choo's coming on."

I laugh but don't have the heart to tell her that Jimmy Choo only started selling shoes in the mid 1990s.

As we reach the community centre we go our separate ways

and agree to meet up in half an hour. I stifle a giggle as I watch her striding purposefully towards the jackets. Unlike Elaine, I'm not particularly bothered about clothes or shoes. It's people watching that I enjoy. And vintage attracts a fascinating crowd, from middle-aged women reminiscing about what they wore in their youth to teenagers laughing at the flares and bored-looking men being dragged around against their will with their wallets open. I could sit around for hours watching and listening.

The one thing I do love is vintage jewellery. I pick up a bracelet and romanticise about its origins. Where did it come from? Who did it belong to? Perhaps a soldier from the trenches gave it to his sweetheart before he left for France? What was their story? It's all so intriguing. I pick up and examine other pieces, looking at the rich colours and different textures, metals and semi-precious stones. Then I become aware of something sparkling, twinkling out of the corner of my eye and I turn around to see what it is. It's an amulet. When I look at it, it blends into the other jewellery, as if it's hidden from everyone else. Like it's only me who is meant to see it. I pick it up and scrutinise it. The design is unusual. A chain of intertwined strands of bronze, with four glittering, precious stones of a vivid black, white, red and pink hanging from the front. I'm transfixed and I've never seen anything quite like it before. When I try it on, it feels comfortable, like it's always been mine.

"That fits perfectly," the lady stallholder says eagerly, keen on a potential sale. "I like that," Elaine materialises by my side and studies the amulet. She's got two huge bags in each hand and obviously thinks it's time for me to buy something.

I smile at the stallholder and say, "I'll take it, thanks."

As we drive home, I mentally kick myself for forgetting to ask for the amulet's origin. My mind wanders as I magic up a romantic story to explain how it arrived at that stall.

Its turning dark by the time Elaine drops me off and we promise to meet for breakfast the next morning. Mum is on a night shift tonight, so I'm careful not to disturb her as I open the door. During the evening, I can't stop feeling the amulet tucked safely below my shirt. I feel drawn to it. By ten, Mum has left for work and my eyelids are heavy. I head for bed. Today's run must have taken more out of me than I realised.

For years, my dreams have been grey and undefined. Tonight, this all changed. The visions before me are sharp, vivid and real, like scenes from a film. I can slow them down to examine them properly. I can speed them up until they are a blur. For once, I don't want to wake up. The montage stops and I'm in another place and another time, like a star floating serenely in the moonlit sky, with no fear of falling. I can move right to left and up and down at will and I laugh with sheer delight at my power and freedom. I swoop down so that I'm touching the top of the forest. I pull a pinecone from one of the tallest trees and smell the green, fresh scent of the sap. It begins to rain. Soft droplets fall on my hair, skin and I'm borne along by the wind. My body feels soft and comfortable as I give up my free will to the elements surrounding me. Closing my eyes, I relax as my body falls gently to the earth and I come to rest in my bed.

I wake up and my eyes widen as I take in my soaked jeans, jumper and trainers. I had gone to bed in my pyjamas. Stumbling about my bedroom, I changed myself, my mind whirling. Too exhausted and disoriented to consider the implications. I returned to bed and for once fell into a peaceful, dreamless slumber.

THE AMULET

Lauren Lockwood

I panicked when I saw every light in the house was on. What had happened? Have they managed to find us? I run through the front door, along the hall and into the bedroom. She's sleeping on her bed, waves of auburn hair covering her face. My breathing slows and relief floods through me. Moving to the bed, I gently push the hair back from her face. My eyes fall upon the amulet in her hand. I look at it closely and still.

The last time I saw that amulet Rora had been wearing it. Rora said it was a special gift from the man she loved. Then one day, without explanation, she donated it to a charity shop.

I try to prise the amulet from Amber's hand, but she tightens her grasp on it and turns over, away from me. I know suddenly, instinctively, that something has changed. The countdown has begun. Danger is coming and I have no way to stop it.

It's time for Amber to know the truth.

WATER

Amber Lockwood

I dream of water. I float on waves. I feel the spray on my face and the coldness imprinting onto my veins, but the freezing temperature registers no pain. I am a single droplet in an entire ocean. I am insignificant. My will is no longer my own. I follow the path along the river towards the Hermitage. My feet crunch along the carpet of honey brown autumn leaves on the forest floor. The dawn sun filters through the trees, highlighting the natural path I need to follow. The air is crisp and I breathe warm puffballs into the cool morning.

I reach a clearing and stand in the centre of the trees, straining my neck to look up at the kaleidoscope where forest and sky become one. I stumble, dizzy, and fall to the ground. I feel the water before I hear it. It pulls me to my feet and draws me towards its spell. This is where I am meant to be. I reach the shore of the River Braan and feel its strength flow through me. The water flows on its journey, no resistance, no misdirection delaying it from its destination. This is where I am meant to be. I close my eyes and hear the whisper of the wind through the trees. I feel the smoothness of the pebbles and the tug of the water as it ebbs and flows.

I hear the words that both free and haunt me: "Call to the water..."

The energy begins as a tingle, but spreads through my limbs until I am taut, in suspension. I hear the break in the water's flow. I open my eyes to see that the water is flowing around me and behind me, missing my body and no longer touching me. I see the light pink nail varnish on my toes, sparkling in the dawn light like expensive pearls against the brown pebbles below my feet.

I look up and understand that my lapse in concentration will have a consequence; that all laws of nature have a balance that must be restored. I feel the power of the water coming towards me, focusing solely on me. For I need to pay a toll for my indiscretion. Panic floods my body. Closing my eyes I accept my fate. Voices whisper and I become aware I'm no longer alone. As I fall into unconsciousness, arms pull me back and hold me. They stay with me as I fall into oblivion.

As I wake up in my bedroom, blinking in the sunlight, aware of the stiffness of my limbs. I stretch my legs and groan in discomfort. This is the third night of the really weird and wonderful dreams and, as fascinating as they are, I acknowledge my departure from normality. I have to admit that it really isn't normal to dream of flying and wake up looking like I've been dragged through a hedge backwards, or dream of water and wake up shivering with wet hair. And don't get me started on the voices, not just one but a whole bunch of them. For years, sleep hasn't provided the sanctuary it promised. Now that the images in my dreams are defined my mind can at least begin to make some sense of them. But the strangest thing is, none of this scares me.

I put on my robe and leave the bedroom. Coffee has always helped clear the cobwebs and is essential. The aroma of French blend reaches and cleanses my nostrils. I walk into the kitchen and the words, "Hi Mum." die on my lips.

The man leaning over the worktop and looking out of the kitchen window is definitely not my Mum. Taking in the tall, hulking figure wearing black jeans and a jumper I watched fascinated as he raised the mug to his lips and took a drink. Who was this stranger? More to the point, what was he doing helping himself to my coffee out of my favourite mug? Assuming that he was a guest of Mums, good manners came to the fore. Then I remembered Mum is at work. Before I could say anything, the man puts the mug down, turns towards me and smiles. He walks over and I retreat until my back hits the wall.

He puts one hand on either side of my head to stop me escaping and studies me intently. I study him back and see a wild thatch of black hair, cobalt blue eyes with strong eyebrows; a well-defined face and a strong determined jaw. Taller than me and gauging him a few years older, I knew this was no boy before me. It didn't occur to me to be scared. I was beyond curious.

"Who are you?" I whisper.

"Yours," he whispers back, slowly moving his mouth over my face, placing the softest of kisses on my neck.

I close my eyes and shiver.

I don't know this man, but my body certainly does. He tucks my hair behind my ear and gently traces the line of my jaw with his thumb. Then he pulls away abruptly.

"Take care of the arm," he says, as he straightens, opens the kitchen door and leaves the house.

I stand in shock for a minute and then the absurdity of the

situation kicks in and I start to laugh. I notice the bandage on my arm for the first time. What on earth was that all about? I have to speak to Elaine about this craziness. I grab my mobile and we agree to meet for a coffee as soon as I'm ready. I'm just about to put my coat on when the front door opens and Mum calls my name. I scoop up my bag and scarf and go into the living room. Mum's sat on the couch, her skin as white as her uniform.

"Are you okay?" I ask. I don't like the look of her colour.

"Not feeling great to be honest. I managed to get my shift covered." I re-adjusted the shoulder strap on my bag. "I was just going to head out. Why don't you go to bed and sleep it off?"

Mum looks at me and says, "I need to speak to you, Amber."

I sit on the couch, my heart thudding, waiting for whatever it is she has to say.

"Amber, I don't know where to...." she suddenly stops, presses her hand to her mouth and runs to the bathroom.

MESSAGE

Lauren Lockwood

I'm not surprised I was sick. My heart has been in my throat for the past week. How do you tell your daughter she's not yours? Part of me was almost relieved I couldn't talk. Then Amber left and the opportunity was lost. I can't wait any longer. We don't have much time left. I can feel it.

Shaking, I get out of bed and take the bag from under the floorboards. I shiver as I walk through to Amber's room, with its messy bedcovers and discarded clothes. The normality mocks my intention. I open the bedside drawer and put the journal inside. I know I'm a coward, but some words are just too hard to say. I close my eyes and pray silently that help will come when we need it. I can do no more.

COLLISION

Amber Lockwood

I wake up buzzing with excitement. Yesterday's events have thrown me into a tailspin. Elaine and I spent hours discussing possibilities and theories over one too many lattes. By the time I arrived home, caffeine-high and as excited as a five year old, I had missed dinner and went straight to bed. It was the early hours before I finally fell asleep.

In the morning I pop my head into Mum's bedroom before I head out for my run and see she's still asleep. I gently shake her and point to the glass of cold water I've placed on her bedside.

"How are you feeling?" I ask. Mum nods, barely awake. "I'm just going out for a run, ok?" As she falls asleep again, I stroke her hair.

I begin the two-mile run to the Hermitage. As I reach the edge of the River Braan, my surroundings beg for silence. My pace falls to a walk as I approach the Falls, my chest rising and falling as I listen to the roar of the water. It's a truly majestic. Leaning over the bridge, I decide to take a short rest before I head back home, thinking a disco nap might be in order.

The dull throb creeps from my shoulders and reached my head before I became fully aware of its presence. Then, just as the pain becomes intense, I hear a dull crack. Whirling around, I look for the source of the noise. I'm alone. The pain becomes unbearable and I drop to my knees and shout but only silence comes out. A couple walking their dog pass by and look at me with concern. The ability to form words has left me and I can feel myself sweating as I lose control of my body. Reaching up I push my hair back and touch something wet. I look at my hand and see my hand and see it covered in moisture. I'm sweating blood. I try to scream, but I can't. Gripped by panic, I shout for someone. Anyone to help me. Just as I think I can't take any more, warmth spreads through my body and the pain begins to recede. I stand up, shaking, and begin to breathe more slowly. My mind clears and I become aware of my surroundings. A feeling of dread slowly burns in my gut. Instinct told me to get home. Fast. Something was wrong. Something was wrong with Mum.

I pick up pace and run as fast as I can. I hear Mum crying. I feel her pain at the edge of my consciousness. Another voice demands my attention, telling me to stay away, to stay safe. The torture in my head continues as the sky turns from blue to a dark indigo. The rain begins, tiny droplets at first, then becomes heavier and heavier, with large splodges drenching me. Leaving the forest, I run towards our house noticing a shadow around it, as if it's been shrouded by darkness. I push the door, but it doesn't move. I can hear voices, getting louder and louder. I keep pushing as hard as I can. I become frantic. I have to help Mum. She needs me. I feel energy surging up from my feet to my arms, and I push the door with everything I have. The wood begins to splinter and the door finally yields and I hurtle into the hallway.

Terror floods though me when I see Mum lying on the floor, a knife pointed at her stomach. Dried blood has formed around a wound on her head and her jaw has a large purplish bruise. A huge man towers above her. He is wearing black plated armour that pushes against his muscles and has greasy black hair. He grins as he teases the knife along her stomach, relishing the act of torture.

"Get away from her!" I scream.

He looks at me, licking his lips. "See" he says to Mum in a soft, silky voice. "Was that so difficult?"

She opens pain filled eyes and moans softly.

"Come here and I won't hurt her anymore" he says to me, holding my gaze as he pressed the blade against her skin.

Beads of crimson seep through her white nightgown. I look into his black eyes and see no soul. He'll break whatever promises he makes. I act instinctively and push my arms in front of me to ward him off. I feel the energy flowing along my veins, it glows red as I point my hands towards him. I see his expression change and he turns around, ready to move.

Without warning he turns on his heel and plunges the knife into her chest. My energy ebbs away and I'm flooded by tiredness. My will to fight dissipates. He senses this and stalks towards me. Dimly, I hear a rush of footsteps behind me, as strong warm arms surround me and pull me back. He roars in frustration, falls to his knees and in the next second transforms into a large black crow. He swoops past the two men standing in front of me with swords drawn and flying out of the door, soars into the air until he joins a large flock of birds that ascend higher and higher and disappear into the clouds.

Exhausted, I collapse into the arms holding me.

ACCEPTANCE

Lauren Lockwood

I do not and never will regret the choices that have brought me here. I would do anything to save my daughter. Hearing my name being called, as if from a great distance, I turn my head to see Daniel, years older with the same serious face and intention. He grimaces as he puts a hand on my stomach. I smile at him. I knew the truth of my situation.

"Mum..." I hear Amber say, looking at me in anguish, bloodied, hair awry.

She is being held up by a young man. I gesture for her to come to me. She moves slowly, reluctantly, not wanting to face what is happening.

"Trust Daniel" I whisper.

She nods and looks at him nervously. He covers her hand with his larger one and smiles at her reassuringly.

"The journal...it's in your beside cabinet."

Amber's eyes widen momentarily and I look at her, hoping she knew what she meant to me.

"Please Daniel," I beg. I don't want her to see this."

He nods and the two men lift Amber, kicking and sobbing from the room. Her eyes lock onto mine until she disappears through the door and it clicks shut. Daniel's hand takes mine. I'm glad I'm not alone. I have no regrets.

Closing my eyes, I finally let go.

LEAP OF FAITH

Amber Lockwood

Fighting against the arms that hold me back I cry out in pain. For the first time I recognise that the man holding me is the same man who was in the kitchen yesterday. In my head, I hear Mum's shallow breathing. Then nothing. The silence is overpowering. Awful.

"She wanted to spare you that," he whispers.

The other man, with the black beard strokes my forehead, tentatively, before walking to the window and looking out. The man holding me, gently pushes my hair from my cheek, and I feel his lips graze my forehead. I don't know what to say.

"It'll be okay Amber," he whispers.

The door opens and the man that Mum had called Daniel walks through. He's built like a Titan with dark hair and hawk-like features.

"Amber, listen to me. I know you are confused and upset but we need to leave." His voice is calm and steady but authoritative.

"But I… I don't know any of you." I cry out, bewildered.

"My name is Daniel and this," he nods to the man holding me, "is my son, Duncan." "And this," he points to the man walking towards us from the window "is my ward, Aiden." "Lauren has trusted me with your safety and I'm going to honour her promise."

My mind is a blur. What do I do? Call the police? What can I tell them? That some Black Knight has attacked us, but that I first felt it two miles away when I began to sweat blood? Mum knew this man and she had told me to trust him. She'd asked very little of me. This is the least I could do for her.

Daniel takes my silence as agreement and issues a series of instructions to the men. Duncan helps me to the bedroom and asks me to pack some clothes and anything that's important to me. I sit on the bed and open the bedside cabinet. Isn't it ironic? Just when I lose everything, I finally find the one thing I've been looking for. I pick up my rucksack and put the book inside, then spot a framed photo of Mum that had been taken a year ago and put that in too. A happy moment, frozen in time, it hurts to look at it now. Duncan finishes zipping up the black bag. He looks up, holds his hand out to me and smiles reassuringly. I take it without hesitation. I look around the room one last time and memories flood back, words whisper and laughter rings, imprinted here forever. We walk into the living room where Daniel and Aiden are waiting.

"We took care of her. She's at peace." Daniel reassures me. I nod, silently.

"Ready?" Duncan asks, tightening his grip on my hand. Pulling me to the door, we leave the cottage and walk into the forest, our trail hidden by a burst of fog and darkness. My trainers squelch into the grass, holding briefly before I move on. I follow the men into a clearing. I see the familiar shape of trees, their view now sharpened as I take in the shapes of the branches and dusky haze of the wood. My eyes focus on the white birch tree central to my view.

Reaching the birch, I look up, seeing the crest of the branches fading into the sky, highlighted by a molten purple light. I stand transfixed, appreciating the delicate beauty of the colour, until Duncan points to stone steps, peaking up from the grass just past the large base of the tree. The white of the birch glows against the darkness casting a light over the stepping stone path. It revealed a flicker of a symbol etched into each stone, rising up a whisper into the air, a dust of magic freed from a secret.

Light filters through me, and for a moment, as they float off into the air, I want to follow them.

"Amber, follow Duncan." Daniel said. Taking the same steps as Duncan, I feel the symbols push from the stones, through the soles of my shoes, seeping into my skin, warming and lighting a spark within the bone. Shaking my head, I watch Duncan complete an intricate patterned dance from one step to the next, missing one or two, reaching for three; applying a runic coded route to our passage.

In my mind's eye, I see the circle shimmering with beads of light, the figures and forms of our bodies shift into an indistinguishable mass. A hum begins. Cresting, little by little, until I don't think I can stand it any longer. Then everything falls silent and still.

Duncan tightens his grip on my hand and whispers "Open your eyes."

I open them and gasp in wonder. We are in a clearing in the middle of woods. Light orange sunlight filters through the trees spilling around the lush green grass below my feet. The wind rustles the branches and leaves above. The birdsong is clear and sweet. But it's the sky that holds my attention. Instead of a vivid blue, it's a deep purple, and there are two moons, one slightly larger than the other. I shake my head as though the image would right itself with the movement.

At the edge of the clearing there's a crowd of people gathering, watching us with interest. A small woman pushes through them and walks quickly towards Daniel. He picks her up like she weighs no more than a bag of sugar and kisses her soundly on the lips. A younger girl joins them, smiling and chattering excitedly. Out of the corner of my eye, I see that Duncan is watching my reaction with interest. I hold his hand tightly, needing his familiarity in this strange, confusing place. Then I feel a hand on my other arm and turning around, I look at Aiden's face, his thick hair and his brown eyes. Then I see an amulet, the mirror image of mine around his neck.

"Welcome to Sensio, sister," he says.

RETURNING

Maggie Darkings

Even after all these years, he still makes my heart race. Now, twenty years after we were mated, I still get excited at the thought of seeing him when he returns. My Daniel has always been serious and responsible and as Greenwood's Protector, it's part of the job description. I know that later when we close the door to the outside world, he will relinquish his responsibilities for a while and smile and laugh with me. That is the person I fell in love with.

The village is buzzing about the latest trip to the other realm. They want in equal parts to go and see what all the fuss is about and stay here with the familiar. I have never had any such desire. Sensio will always be my home. In our world, we all have a role to play. For my part, I do my council duties as necessary. But my heart does not beat for politics or strategy. My concern is keeping my family together, in a world that has fallen away from the Natural Laws we once held so dear. For some time, Sensio has moved towards a point of no return.

Looking at our first born, I see the image of my Mate. Duncan followed his father as soon as he could walk and began training as the next Village Protector at the age of ten. He wants to play his part. As his mother, I struggle to reconcile my acceptance of his desire to protect his people, whilst equally, I don't want my boy hurt. It's a constant battle I face. I look at Aiden's sister, her skin is covered in dry blood and she is deathly pale. She looks like a breath of wind could knock her over. Her hand clings to Duncan's and I'm happy their bonding has already begun.

I turn to look at Rose, my youngest and always my baby. I know she is frustrated by the constraints on her freedom. Like her brother, she is determined to play her part, just as we're determined to keep her safe. It's a constant bone of contention. Daniel squeezes my hand as I let it go and walk towards Duncan and Amber. She's looking at Aiden in shock and I know my arrival is timely. Aiden is our "ward," part of our family, but not of our blood. It's not a term I'm fond of. When Daniel brought him home to me as a baby he became my son, pure and simple. He has always known about Amber and we hoped he understood that they had to be separated. Even as a young boy, Aiden was alone in a crowd. I could see him fall away from the other people around him. The longer he was away from his twin, the more lost became. A compass without a steady north. But as my mother always said, fate will take you exactly where you are meant to be. Just as I have been destined to Mate with Daniel and have my three children. I know I'm meant to protect Amber, who has no idea of what's to come. Rora, my childhood friend, would expect nothing less of me. She knew I would protect my family and hers like a tigress would her cubs and God help anyone who ever tries to hurt them. Daniel might use a physical sword but my talent is just as unforgiving. I will use it without hesitation or conscience to protect those I love. Just because I'm only a little over five foot doesn't mean to say I'm powerless.

I walk up to Amber and smile, to put her at ease. I don't think she can take in any more information. Duncan introduces us and she nods shyly.

"Amber, I know this is a lot to take in. Why don't we get you home and cleaned up?" I offer.

She looks at Duncan, unsure about making the decision herself. He smiles and nods encouragingly and we begin to walk out of the clearing, towards our house. As I walk behind them with Aiden, I wave the small crowd of onlookers away. I pass Daniel and he smiles at me.

Sometimes, you don't need a sword to get the job done.

"Take a moment & cast a spell

Into Greenwood's wishing well,

When you think all hope is lost...

Be glad of the coin you humbly tossed"

...Wishing Well

Wishing Well

BONDING

Aiden Darkings

Okay, maybe I shouldn't have come out with it quite like that. Perhaps I should have waited a little longer. But when you have been waiting for years to say that one sentence that could somehow make your world become right, you don't have a lot of patience.

We all begin to walk through the woods to the village. The evening sun filters slowly through the trees and throws their branches and twigs into sharp relief. It highlights the green mossy undergrowth of the path created through years of walking to the clearing. The two moons have risen and by the time we reach the village the dusky purple sky has deepened to a liquid black. I'm glad. Sometimes, darkness is safer. As we reach the village, Amber looks around in amazement. To the casual observer, Greenwood looks like any other small village on Earth, although our structures are more rustic than decorative and we use stone to blend in with our habitat. We pass the wishing well and I see Warwick, Head of the High Council, watching us. He nods in approval as I throw a coin into the well and wish that what is to come will pass. I've no doubt Amber will make his acquaintance in the coming days.

The houses are arranged in a semi-circle. We walk through them to the edge of the village. As Village Protector, Daniel's home is placed strategically between the outside of the village and Greenwood; the village he's bound to protect. It also reflects his status on the High Council.

Despite its symbolic nature, Maggie has always made it a warm happy home. But our roles can't be left at the door and picked up again when we leave. After all, it is who we are. Maggie takes Amber's arm and leads her upstairs to wash and change. I'm glad of the respite. I sit before the dwindling fire, taking a moment to work out what I want to say.

"Are you ready for this Aiden?" Duncan asks, as he sits beside me.

"I have been for years, or at least I thought I was. But now the moment is here I find myself…daunted."

I look at him. As my older brother he has always been my example, running into dangerous situations without fear or hesitation, with an absolute belief that whatever happened was meant to be.

"She's stronger than she looks." Daniel says quietly as he passes me a cup of brew.

I feel the twist of the alcohol and I feel calmer, more aware of what I want to say. I remind myself to thank Warwick for the fortification the next time I see him. Silence falls in the room, interrupted only by the snap and crackle of the fire and the lonely howl of the wind outside. Turning, I see Maggie and Rose guiding Amber into the room ushering her into a seat beside the fire. She is dressed in clean trousers and a top, her long hair is curling as it dries in the warmth. Maggie gives her a bowl of soup and Rose encourages her to eat it. She tries a little, more out of politeness than hunger. If she's anything like me, her hunger will disappear when nerves hit. She looks around, tense and agitated, unsure of us and her new surroundings. Her body is like a tightly strung bow. I wonder if a night's sleep might help her take in what I have to say. Maggie senses me hesitating and shakes her head in silent disagreement. It's never a good time to tell the truth. Amber puts down her spoon and thanks Maggie quietly. Maggie sits beside her and takes her hand. Everyone turns and looks at me expectantly.

I begin to speak.

ANSWERS

Amber Lockwood

A m I somewhere between asleep and awake? I concentrate on the words Aiden is saying, but before I can get my head around one sentence, he's moving onto another revelation that is tearing my life in two. Part of me is glad that I am finally hearing the answers to all those unanswered questions. The other part of me wants to run away and hide in some black hole and never come out again. It hurts to hear the truth of your life. The effect your creation has had on the people around you. This isn't the moment I'd so richly anticipated. I was so sure that all the answers would move the fragmented pieces of my jigsaw life into perfect alignment. Instead, all I know is being ripped apart and I'm powerless to stop any of it. I feel numb. Looking at the face, so like mine, I try to focus again on his words and fight the dangerous emotions that threaten to overwhelm me. Gripping Maggie's hand tightly, I try to bring myself back to the room distancing myself from the dizziness on the edges of my consciousness. The words race and repeat as I try, once again, to process them.

"I am your twin. You were born a few minutes after me."

"Our mother was Rora Ravenswood."

"She died not long after we were born."

"Daniel thought it was best to separate us."

"I was raised in Sensio by Daniel's family...your family."

"You were raised by our mother's friend, Lauren Lockwood."

"The amulet you are wearing is one of a pair. Your amulet belonged to our mother. We knew where you were as soon as you put it on."

"You have potential you don't realise."

"Have you been having strange dreams?"

That one hits home. I look up in disbelief. The only person who knows about my dreams is Elaine. Now in this world, that seems so strange yet so familiar, these images make perfect sense. There is no need for me to answer the question. My reaction is enough. My nerves finally snap as my body gives up the fight.

I fall into the darkness.

"The infamous Knight's pawn,

My existence lies between life & death,

I'll make my move and forgo my last breath,

My heart still beats but frozen,

The price to pay for all I have chosen,

When the game is over, be it King or pawn,

All fall the same till the battle is won"

…Aiden

Aiden

THE CHOICE

Amber Lockwood

Jumping, I recoil from the hand on my shoulder. Maggie is hovering over me, looking concerned. She's done that a lot since I arrived in Sensio a month ago.

"I'm sorry," I say feeling guilty at being such a burden. "I can't bear to be touched."

Maggie sits down on the bed and puts her hand on mine. We sit in silence, the warmth of her hand keeping me fixed in the present, away from the past and the revelations that haunt me. We don't speak about the nightmares that wake me up, sobbing, every night. We don't speak about me going through the motions but not feeling any emotion. We don't speak about me being too frightened to leave this house.

My arrival in Sensio has given me the opportunity to do what I've always wanted. To finally discover who I am. All the answers are there for me to explore, if I am brave enough to take the first step. This choice seems frightening when I can hardly get out of bed.

"Everyone I've ever loved has died because of me," I say, almost to myself.

I can feel Maggie looking at me as I study our joined hands. The guilt is overwhelming. My Mum died giving birth to my brother and me and Lauren died trying to keep me safe. I shudder as I replay the moment when the Knight plunged the knife into her chest. I was powerless to stop it. Did my hesitation to give him what he wanted – me - encourage him to make his choice or was this already settled in his soulless mind? Would I feel better if she had fallen asleep one night and just never woken up? I torture myself with endless scenarios. Coming back to the present, the guilt lingers and the unanswered questions are making it worse. I need to understand why.

The sun filters through the brightly coloured but worn curtains and casts hazy purple shadows on the rustic furniture. I squeeze Maggie's hand, get out of bed and walk to the window. Looking out, I can see random people scurrying about the village carrying baskets, looking like busy worker bees tending to the demands of their Queen. I can't remember the last time I looked at the sky and noticed what colour it was. Turning back, I see Maggie watching me with interest. I can hardly blame her; this is the most she's seen me move in a month.

Turning round to face her, I ask, "Can I take a bath and then help you with dinner?"

"Of course" she smiles and walks to the door. "I'll see you downstairs."

Sitting in the warm, soapy water, idly watching the steam rise, I know that I have to make a choice: continue to hide from the world or get out there and make sense of what has happened. One thing is for sure. Anything is better than feeling like this. I dry my damp hair and twist it into a ponytail. It's time to start living again. I take a deep breath and go downstairs.

Daniel, Aiden and the mysterious Duncan have not seen

hide nor hair of me for the last month, and they keep sneaking curious glances at me over dinner. The atmosphere is tense and awkward. Rose fills the uncomfortable silences with nonsensical chatter, asking me, about clothes and music from "my world." Already, I liked her and her unguarded enthusiasm.

I put my cutlery on the plate, squeeze my eyes shut and pinch the fold of skin between my eyebrows, stealing myself to speak and mutter, "Look, thanks for giving me time to get my head round this. It's been a lot to take in."

I look to Aiden and he grimaces. "I needed to know, I understand that, but you need tell me more. I don't know who I am. I don't know this place."

I move my hand theatrically trying to help them understand the staggering effect of the revelations on me.

"I don't know my place here; you need to tell me more."

I look at Aiden again.

"You say we're twins? I can see the physical similarities but I…you…you're a stranger to me. You need to give me a chance to get to know you."

I sense Daniel watching me, and I turn to him.

"You knew my mother, didn't you?" "You knew… Lauren. How? Why?"

"And you…" I turn to Duncan in exasperation. "I don't understand why you appear in my dreams or my home, and I don't get whatever this is," I say, gesticulating theatrically again, trying to explain the chemistry between us.

He smiles a crooked smile and swings backwards and forwards on his chair, looking pleased with himself. Rose stifles a giggle and I immediately regret my honesty.

"Maggie and Rose, you've both been very kind. But I know you're busy and I want to help you."

Rose claps her hands in childlike enthusiasm and Maggie nods, relieved that I am opening up at last. Suddenly I'm desperate for space, desperate to be left alone.

"I'm going to get some air," I blurt out. In my peripheral vision, I can see Aiden get up to follow me.

"Leave her." Daniel says.

I feel the stares and hear the whispered conversations as I walk through the village. Realising I must look like an oddity to these people. I wish I'd asked Maggie if I could borrow some of her clothes. Jeans and a tank top just don't fit in here.

The old man I noticed when I arrived is standing at the wishing well, watching me with studied interest. Beside him is a tall, thin, blonde-haired man with what looks like a permanent scowl. I nod to them politely, and they return the salutation with some hesitation. Looking ahead, there's a clearing in the trees, and I break into a run towards them. My body quickly adjusts as I follow the path I travelled along four weeks before. The wind rustles in the trees and if it weren't for the purple sky and two moons, I could almost convince myself that I'm running through the Hermitage. Who am I really kidding?

I'm running from myself.

THE RULES

Boon Cuthbert

The wee missy made an appearance this afternoon and not before time, I might add. Does she not understand how much danger our people are in every time they go through the portal? As my Dot says, its not like you're going next door for a cup of brew, you are visiting another realm. My Dot says I'm far too impatient, and she should know. We've been mated nearly 20 years now. My woman knows me better than I know myself.

Daniel should have laid down the rules before she got to leave the boundaries of the village. That type of clothing might be acceptable in her world, but it certainly isn't here. Anyway, we'll see what the wee missy has to say when she comes to the High Council meeting tomorrow night. Then I'll make a few things clear. She'll need to know our history. She'll need to know that the High Council has kept this village safe for a long time, but that times are changing. Sensio is governed by the four elements of Earth, Air, Fire and Water. We exist to address the imbalance created on Earth by the actions of man. The greedy desires of man on Earth are infecting our world and the balance of the Natural Laws are in danger. What a mess they've made.

There are even whispers about the Knights who were appointed to guard Sensio, keep the peace amongst the villages and protect the borders. They say they've been treating villagers, particularly women, badly. I've even started to feel it here in the village where I was born. My Dot tries to get me to stop talking about it, but I know she agrees with me. As young Duncan walks past us, he thanks Warwick for the brew. The man makes a good keg. Many times over the years, I've tried to get the secret recipe from him, just so I could help him make it, but he just taps his nose and smiles. I'm confident I will find out the truth. I always do.

So, we'll see what the little missy has to say tomorrow and if necessary I will set her on the straight and narrow. It's my responsibility. As my Dot says, I always try to take pride in a job well done, might as well start how I mean to go on.

WOODLAND

Amber Lockwood

My hearts beats wildly as I run through the trees. Being used to running a few miles every day, I'm paying dearly for my month of inactivity. Instead of settling into a rhythm, my body is telling me to give up. I slow to a walking pace as I try to get rid of the stitch forming in my side.

I wander on until I find myself in a small clearing of trees and vegetation. Plants in a variety of wild colours spring around my feet and the grass looks lush and as soft as a comfortable blanket. I feel weary enough to fall asleep on it.

I feel around in my pocket and take out my mobile, surprised to see that there's a smidgen of battery left. Suddenly, I wish I could phone Elaine, because if there's anyone in the world who'll appreciate the inexplicable sights around me, it's her. But instead, I select Snow Patrol. Leaning back against a tree, I close my eyes and let the music wash over me. Time disappears, events recede and the emotions of the past melt away. Then the music stops. I open my eyes and see the battery is now dead and with it my last tie with home has been severed. I want to cry.

"You shouldn't go so far into the woods." Whirling towards the voice, I see Duncan leaning back against a tree watching me.

"There's a surprise." I bite out sarcastically.

He raises an eyebrow and says nothing. I almost smiled.

"Let me recap the last month of my life for you. I watched my Mum, who was not really my Mum, get killed by some freaky Knight, who then turned into a crow. My long lost twin brother whisked me away to some strange land where the sky is purple instead of blue. I can't phone Elaine. I can't even listen to music because my phone just died. But let's not forget that I shouldn't be going into the woods. Are you kidding me?"

Anger and frustration bite as I throw the phone against the tree, right next to his head. It smashes open. I want to stomp my feet like a five year old. Closing my eyes to wish the world away, he takes my face in his hands and looks into my eyes. His body crowds mine against the tree.

"Are you done?" he asks calmly. I nod, feeling contrite. "Good," he says and lowers his lips to mine.

I've been kissed before, but it always felt well…awkward. I never got lost in it, never abandoned myself to it. And to my shame, my mind always wandered away to think of what I had to do or who I had to see, whilst trying to end the moment of intimacy in the easiest and quickest way possible. But this kiss… This kiss makes everything else disappear. If he didn't have his hand twisting in my hair, anchoring me in place, I think I would float away. He pulls back just as the wind around us settles into droplets of rain. Duncan laughs and takes my hand, pulling me back along the path towards the village.

"I think I might have got lost on the way back," I confess.

"No, you would've been fine. I was just behind you."

I look at him, not really surprised and strangely comforted. "You do realise this is our first conversation Duncan," I begin.

"I know." He stops walking, and looks at me. "Some things are just meant to be."

"That's another half answer."

"And have you retreat like you did weeks ago? No way, Miss Lockwood, you're just going to have to trust me."

"And like I said before, I don't know you; you can't presume what I feel."

He pulled me back into walking and we fall into silence. Gradually, I begin to take in the fading light, the subtle shadows and wild array of colours of my surroundings. Sensio is beautiful. I catch a buzzing sound and stop suddenly to look around.

"What's that?" I ask.

"Ah. You should find this interesting." Duncan walks us over to an upturned tree trunk and we sit down.

I'm still looking for the source of the noise, but I can't find it.

"Look down." Duncan whispers.

I do as he says and see a small figure, the same size as the palm of my hand. I bend down to get a closer look and a little pointy face with tiny ears and a mass of long, brown hair with a golden crown on top looks back up at me. His tiny body is clothed in what looks like leather trousers and a waistcoat and he has delicate body length wings coming out of his back. They flutter constantly, like a hummingbird. We study each other curiously and then I suddenly giggle as I felt myself being measured and most definitely found wanting by this little creature. He leans forward and winks cheekily at me.

"Who are you?" I ask him, aware of Duncan watching our interaction with interest.

"Fingle, Prince of the Faerie's" he replies proudly in a surprisingly strong voice for such a small figure.

"A faerie? As in Tinker Bell?" I look incredulously at him, then yelp in pain as I feel a sharp sting on my hand. Fingle folds his arms and looks at me with disdain.

Duncan leans over and whispers, "They get pretty fed up of people from Earth comparing them to Peter Pan's sidekick. They find it quite insulting."

I lean forward in earnest. "Apologies Fingle, I'm Amber. I'm happy to meet you."

He nods, appears to accept my apology and looks at Duncan.

"Is this your Mate then?"

"Yes" Duncan laughs, as I rolled my eyes.

"The trees are whispering again, with darkness from past the water," Fingle suddenly says, nervously. "The Knights are breaking their oath. This can't go on."

"We have a Council meeting tomorrow. I'll pass on your

news and your concerns."

Fingle nods, satisfied that he's completed his task.

"Duncan, Ms Lockwood, it's been a pleasure."

Fingle bows theatrically, winks at me again and flying from my knee, disappears as quickly as he arrived. Duncan stands up from the tree trunk and holds out his hand. I take it and as we begin to walk once more. I review the events of the day, shaking my head. Surreal doesn't even begin to describe it. Darkness descends as we walk into the village.

We pass the wishing well where a few families have gathered, hearing laughter and snatches of banter as we pass them. It looks like an open-air pub. I see Maggie sitting with Daniel, with Rose and Aiden pushing at each other and laughing. Maggie waves to us and I walk over to the table to join them. She pats my hand silently, welcoming me back, her cheeks pink with happiness. I look around for Duncan. He's speaking in hushed tones to a girl around my age, who is pulling persistently at his arm. Licking my suddenly dry lips, I take in the scene and it's implications. I try to look away but I can't. A quickening of white-hot anger floods and floors me at the same time. As unexpected as it was unfamiliar, my hands clench involuntarily, as I realised I was feeling jealousy for the very first time. Rose catches my attention and I lean towards her, hoping I've managed to hide my emotions.

"It wasn't serious," she whispers. "As soon as Duncan felt you. He ended it." I look at Rose, so young and innocent, speaking of events and emotions that seem so beyond me. I nod, the ability to form words having left me.

I feel Duncan slide in beside me, the heat of his body filtered to mine, cold and frozen by what I had seen. I shiver involuntarily.

He pulls me towards him and whispers "I'm yours" in my ear. "Yours."

I carry on staring at the girl as she walks away; back ramrod straight, her blonde hair shimmers in the hazy darkness. It stands out almost like a warning signal. Uneasiness washes over me.

For the first time, I lean towards him and kiss his lips softly, voluntarily and with a full awareness of what I was saying to him without words. I had told him earlier not to assume my feelings.

I know enough to admit when I am wrong.

AGENDA

Rose Darkings

I am so excited. I finally get to attend a High Council Meeting. Megan has made me promise to tell her every single detail and of course I will. She's my best friend. We tell each other everything. It's dark by the time we leave home and walk down past the wishing well to Warwick's home. I can't wait to see Amber's reaction to the Great Hall. I've heard all the stories, so I know what to expect. It's been good having another girl in the house to chat to. It's kind of like having an older sister without having to put up with all the aggro that goes along with it.

Since Amber arrived there has been no more of those whispered conversations that stop when I entered a room. I love my family but do they really think I am stupid? I'm going to be 17 soon, but I've known for a long time how to listen quietly without people being aware that I'm there. Among my group of friends I'm known as the one who knows what's going on. If the adults become suspicious, I just smile and giggle and they assume that it's Rose, a silly young girl, who is indulged and protected. Don't they understand that the secrets make me want to find out more? Why can't I have the same chance as Duncan and Aiden to contribute and prove myself? I thought Dad was going to have a fit when I suggested going through the portal with them to get Amber. It's so unfair. Once I find my talent, they'll have to take me more seriously.

"Rose, come on now, stop dreaming." Mum calls.

I run to catch up with them, and Warwick winks as he shuts the door behind me, we must be the last to arrive. He walks to the door at the back of the house, pulls it open and we walk down the stairs in single file. My heart flutters excitedly at the thought of seeing the Great Hall for the first time. We are here because Dad is introducing Amber as a member of our family. I'm here because I get to be a witness. I stand at the entrance and look around carefully so I don't miss any details. The fire lit sconces at regular intervals along the walls of the massive room give it a warm, welcoming glow. The stone wall is covered with swords and shields, their bronze and silver glinting against the flames. The room is dominated by a table shaped like a horseshoe with a lectern front and centre, so that those attending can make a statement to the High Council, as Dad has done before.

The High Council members are already sitting down. Warwick sits at the top in the centre, looking very distinguished, with his greying black hair, all brushed into place, and his thick, caterpillar-like moustache. To his left is Boon Cuthbert, a village mentor. His job is to advocate the Natural Laws and keep our lessons in line with them. Next to him sits Morgan Rose. He's our representative to the other villages and it's also his job to look after our interests at the Kings court, so we don't see a lot of him. On the far left is Ruth Gentles. She's the mother of Caroline, Duncan's fleeting girlfriend. Ruth is a widow and has another daughter, May. She's the 'moral' authority of Greenwood, and she really likes to give her opinion.

The room goes quiet as Dad takes his place at the lectern and clears his throat.

"I stand before you tonight, as Daniel, head of the Darkings clan, to introduce Amber Lockwood to the High Council as a member of my family."

The Council members turn to look at Amber standing beside Duncan. She withers under their scrutiny and I feel sorry for her. Duncan puts his hand on top of hers and squeezes it in silent comfort. I have noticed that they can't stop touching, like they can't bear to be away from each other. I don't understand it, but I think it's sweet and I wonder if I will be like that with my Mate when the time comes.

Dad continues "Her mother Rora Ravenswood entrusted me with her and Aiden's safety as babes. We managed to find her before she was taken."

"Has she put us in danger?" Ruth asks sharply.

Dad visibly bristles, annoyed at the interruption.

"There's no evidence to indicate this. I am more concerned with why they wanted her."

"Who tried to take her?" Morgan leans forward, eager for an answer.

"It's not clear, but they brutally murdered the woman who raised Amber to get to her."

Now that's interesting. Amber has been shouting in her sleep every night for weeks about a man hurting her Mum. Dad knows this, so why is he being so evasive?

"May I continue?" Dad looks at Warwick, who nods, and

continues to gnaw on his pipe.

"I would like to request that instruction is offered to Amber to help her find her way in this new world," he says, moving back to await their reaction.

"I'm not sure if such a teaching would be appropriate for this young lady," Ruth says. "Her behaviour wouldn't suggest that she has the proper moral background. And we all know who her mother was."

Mum immediately steps forward. Duncan is also about to jump in, but Mum holds a hand up to stop him, and he sits back down, angry red flushing his cheeks.

Mum says clearly, "The High Council judged her mother appropriate for the teachings at a time when we could trust few. I'll vouch for Amber's character as a member of my family and as my son's future Mate. I don't believe it's appropriate to make judgements without giving her a chance to prove her worth."

"You're correct, Maggie Darkings," says Warwick.

"I, for one, would be interested to see what the little missy has to say for herself," says Boon, impatiently.

Amber looks pale and bewildered by what's happening and I will her on to get some gumption and prove to the Council that she deserves to have her place with us. She takes a deep breath and steps forward. "I would like to thank the Darkings for supporting me at this meeting. I want you all to know that I'm willing to work hard and learn all that is needed," she says quietly.

"Surely we should take this under advisement?" Ruth stares challengingly around the table, looking for support.

Boon answers firmly, "No Ruth, you need to leave your pride at the door. We are here to serve Greenwood; not your personal agenda. I'm happy to mentor Miss Lockwood."

Morgan and Warwick quickly agree, leaving no room for any further debate and Warwick draws the meeting to a close. Ruth thrusts her chair back, noisily screeching the wood against the stone floor. Gathering her shawl and throwing it around her shoulders, she marches out.

Morgan and Warwick begin to speak about Sensio politics and Boon walks forward to speak to Dad. Maggie breathes out a sigh of relief and asks Amber if she's okay. Amber smiles and nods. Aiden and Duncan are talking amongst themselves.

Boon walks up to Amber in his no-nonsense manner and says "Right missy, we start tomorrow. You work with your family in the morning and then and I'll meet you after lunch for lessons. Don't be late."

"I'll be there, thank you." Amber says.

Boon nods briskly, saying he had promised Dot he wouldn't linger tonight and leaves. We bid Warwick and Morgan goodbye, leaving them to their pipes and politics. On the walk home, I can sense movement at the windows of the houses as the gossips note our departure from the meeting. Gleefully, I secretly hug myself. I can't wait to tell Megan. Greenwood gossipmongers can speculate all they want.

I know the truth.

"Lessons learned all my days,

Natural Laws lighten the way,

Love for my Mate, Sensio & beyond,

For two worlds, I'll always be strong"

…Boon

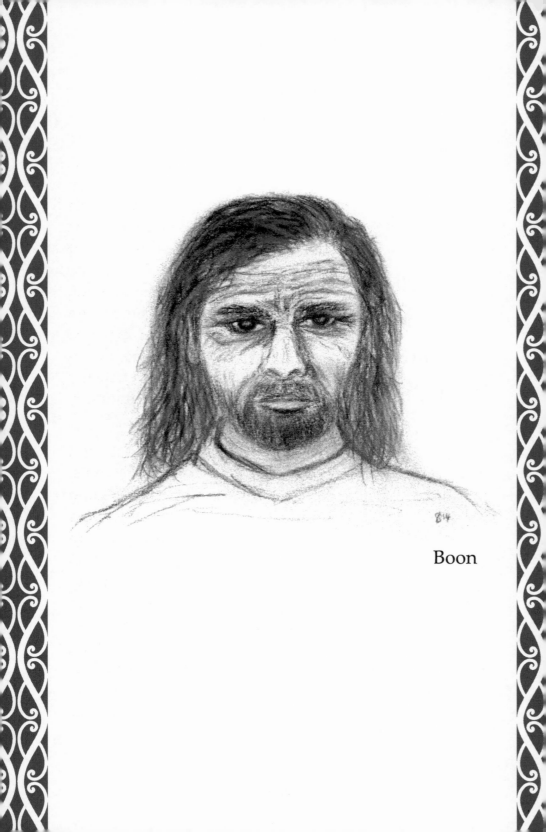

Boon

DARKNESS

The Stranger

Hate courses through me like a fire out of control. I've fought for months against this onslaught of emotions. It's left me weak, unable to eat, unable to be who I know myself to be. It's hard to keep up the pretence and do what is expected, to do what is right, or what I used to believe was right. But most of all, I miss clarity. I miss the instinctive desire I have always possessed, whether via nature or nurture to look at the facts and make a decision without emotion. To the outside world, I appear to be fine. But I'm the shell of my former self, a mannequin that speaks and acts like me but feels no emotion. All my energies are concentrated on keeping up this performance, but now I am just too weak to fight anymore.

Today, sitting in the woods hiding from those I love, I surrender to the negative emotions and to the hate. Warwick is the only one who knows, who can see beyond the performance. My hands shake as they resist carrying out the actions the voices tell me to. They tell me to give into the devil hiding inside me. I listen to lessen their kicks on my body. The harder I resist the more they hurt. Today, they take hours to recede, leaving me even more numb than before. I steel myself. I only need to get through dinner before I can be alone again. The façade is slipping irrevocably and it's only a matter of time before I surrender to the force consuming me. My only hope is that when the time comes I have the strength to do the right thing. Before it's too late.

"If she happens to cross your path,

Grant safe passage, her mission is vast,

Without her, no plants or air to breathe,

Respect this dutiful Queen,

our loyalty she must receive"

…Queen Bee

Greenwood's Beehives

LESSONS

Amber Lockwood

Months have passed since I arrived in Sensio and yet there are still things that I learn about this new world that fill me with a mixture of bewilderment and sheer wonder. My lessons with Boon started the day after the High Council meeting. I was really nervous about what those lessons entailed and more than a bit apprehensive of the gruff, scowling man who was to teach me. In the afternoon, Rose walked me to Boon's house. She knocked on the door and waved goodbye. Moments later the door was opened by a small woman wiping her hands on a dishcloth. Her dark hair was pulled back into a tidy bun, her cheek had a dusting of flour on it, and her brown eyes sparkled and crinkled at the corners, like she laughed a lot.

"You must be Amber?" she smiled at me. I nodded silently, and smiled hesitantly. "In you come then, love. I'm Dot, Boon's Mate. It's good to meet you. Maggie's been telling me all about you."

She showed me to a seat and asked me if I wanted a drink. I thanked her, and sat at the kitchen table, which was piled haphazardly with wooden blocks, an abundance of fruit, nuts and bowls of flour.

"Can I help you?" I asked, familiar with the baking rituals of a household.

In Greenwood, each home cooks and shares with the whole

village, so if Maggie was baking apple pies, then all of the families in the village, nearly thirty of them, got one too. I often wondered how it all got organised. It was one of the Natural Laws to share food amongst your fellow villagers, so that no family had more or less than another. When I first learned of this, I thought about the poverty on Earth and how welcome and effective this simple approach could be.

"That would be good," Dot said, "but have your drink first. Oh, there he is."

Boon shut the door and walked towards us. He took the cup that Dot was holding out to him and tenderly wiped the flour from her cheek with his thumb, his habitual scowl disappearing and his features soften as he looked at her. Dot passed me a cup too and I sipped at the delicious sweet honey and mead concoction. Boon sat opposite me, taking in my appearance. That morning, Rose had proudly presented me with a set of clothes and although they weren't made of the denim I was used to, the trousers, boots and jacket were flexible and comfortable. Sensing his approval, I waited for him to speak and placed my cup down on the table. To give me something to do, I moved the chopping board in front of me, picked up a knife and began to chop fruit. Then Boon and Dot began to speak. And so we established a comfortable routine. I would arrive, have a cup of brew and then help Dot with the baking. While we whisked and chopped, baked and cooled. Boon would tell me about the history of Sensio; how the very creation of the world had grown from a need to counterbalance the damage done to Earth by man – whether through war, poverty or politics – had required another realm where the balance could be restored. Boon and Dot are the fifth generation of Sension's to be responsible for preserving the way of life set by the Natural Laws and finding the balance that couldn't survive on Earth. Occasionally I would interrupt and ask why they held a particular belief. Boon would simply explain that some beliefs were just meant to be.

Remembering the angst of my previous life on Earth, I had to agree it seemed an ideal way to live. However, because of who I am and where I come from, I couldn't help but want to know what, how and why. Boon and I began to take walks around Greenwood, where he introduced me to all the villagers we came across. Meeting the Raven and Mossen families helped me to understand my place amongst this society. We walked through Greenwood Forest, around the outer edge of the village, past the apiary, a collection of ancient beehives, surrounded by a flurry of worker bees pledging devotion to their Queen. Dot explained that most families were connected through marriage and I came to realise that Greenwood was populated by one big family who lived, loved, fought, cried and stuck together. The Natural Laws were mentioned so many times, I eventually asked Boon if they were written down, so I could study them.

Boon stopped walking and asked, "How could you understand the Natural Laws unless you think about them, understand them and live them? The people of Earth did that, but they've forgotten."

Boon explained the Natural Laws of Sensio originated from the ancient tribes and cultures scattered across the four elemental corners of the world living in harmony with nature, only ever taking as much as they needed. But as man's desire to conquer Earth's land and oceans grew, these cultures retreated, continuing their tradition of oral history and their respect for the Natural Laws. "Some came to Sensio, but they are wary and were mistreated and we have yet to earn their trust."

From then, Boon and I studied one Law per lesson, to help me understand and appreciate what it meant and how it applied to life on Sensio. Today we are walking a circuit of the village while Boon questions me about everything we have discussed during the last few months. Sometimes I hesitate before answering each question, so I can find the best words to give a proper reply.   "

Just say what's natural Amber, you're not being graded." Boon laughs.

As we walk from the clearing a fluttering of the leaves in front of us draws our attention.

"Hey little missy, hold up now." Boon walks in front of me, pushing me behind him and taking out his sword.

My stomach flutters with nerves as I watch him walk forward. Then suddenly small chirping noises erupt from the vegetation. I walk forward, more curious than afraid. Boon reaches down and carefully moves a plant backwards to reveal the source of the noise. I look over his shoulder, and see two birds in a nest, one larger than the other and covered in sparse brown and grey feathers. The noise was coming from the smaller bird who protested as he was being pushed out of the nest by the older one.

"It's only a Dodo nest," Boon says replacing his sword.

"Dodo?" I repeat, remembering the pictures I had seen once on a school trip to a museum.

Boon ushers me back towards the trees, away from the nest, which is now exposed to the predators of the forest. The older chick has succeeded in pushing the smaller one out of the nest. It gets up, and walks slowly and uncertainly, whimpering in protest.

"Dodo's are extinct?" I say incredulously.

"On Earth they are. The last few were brought here to save them from human-induced extinction. From what I understand most have flourished since they arrived."

I look at Boon in amazement. Rustling leaves catch our attention and I watch in wonder as an adult dodo walks towards the nest. The frail little bird begins to chirp noisily as it recognises its mother. The dodo stands at least a metre tall and looks down regally at its chicks. It has brown-grey feathers, yellow feet and a naked grey head with a green and yellow beak. The dodo looks at the smaller chick, then at the other chick in the nest and comes to a decision. It steps over the smaller chick and feeds the stronger one.

I gasp at the callous decision, whilst hypnotically watching it feed and settle the older chick and ignore the cries of the more vulnerable young. Turning to Boon, I inexplicably want to cry.

"That sometimes happens. Survival of the fittest and all that," he said quietly.

What will happen to it?" I look at the little bird desperately struggling to get the attention of its mother.

Boon sighs and as if to confirm the inevitable, the Dodo gets up and walks away, followed by the older chick. Silence. The abandoned bird chirps weakly.

"I'll take it." I say, taking off my jacket.

"Now Amber, nature must take its course," Boon says.

I walk gingerly towards the little bird and using my jacket, I scoop it up into my arms. It chirps shrilly and struggles to get free. Noticing the crusted skin where its right eye should have been, I understood why the mother had chosen its stronger sibling. This baby dodo had been deemed unworthy of a chance of survival. My resolve strengthened. I place my hand over the bird's small head, stroking it gently, wincing as it nips my finger with its beak.

"I'm not standing here, watching someone else die and not doing something about it." I say, staring Boon out.

He groans and throws up his arms in acceptance. "Ok. Come on then, Dot will have some fruit, no doubt."

Firelight signals the arrival of dusk as we walk back to the village. We make an odd comedy trio: the scowling man, the orphan and the extinct bird. But I now understand the Natural Laws that says all inhabitants of Sensio should have a chance to prove their worth and contribution to our world, even if they are only a little baby bird.

"Forever frozen to a page in a book,

A consequence of man & the liberties he took,

Amber saw past my lack of sight,

Hope shines despite diminishing light"

...Dodo

Dodo

FAMILY TIES

Amber Lockwood

Some people think it's impossible to forget your birthday, but I can honestly say it is very easily done. At home, time is marked by the ticking of a clock, marking off each hour, day, week, month and year. At home, time dictated how I lived my life: get up, get ready for school, eat lunch, finish school, come home, eat dinner, go for a run, be back home by curfew, go to bed and then start the whole process all over again the next morning. You knew exactly what time it was and what you were supposed to be doing.

In Sensio, time is completely different. You know it's time to get up by the brightness of the purple morning sky, and you know its end of the day by the illumination of the two moons against the black sky. No alarm clocks ring: everyone seems to have an internal clock set to just the right time. It's a novel way to live and once I accepted this was the place I was meant to be I fell into its rhythm. Here, time is marked by activities; helping Maggie and Rose bake in the morning; my chats with Dot before my lessons with Boon begin; conversations with the other villagers as they take time to discuss the Natural Laws with me; Duncan's hand in mine as he meets me for the slow walk home; the banter and laughter around the wishing well in the dusky evening and the stolen kisses outside my bedroom door as we say goodnight.

So when I come home tonight, I'm totally surprised to open

the door to cries of "Happy Birthday." I'm 19 years old. I accept hugs from Daniel, Maggie and a huge hug from Rose. Aiden and I are ushered in front of a birthday cake and blow out makeshift candles in unison.

I'm suddenly flooded with memories of previous birthdays. Mum somehow managed to make sure she never worked on my birthday and we always celebrated with a meal out - a rare extravagance – where a small cake was always presented with a flourish at the end. Mum would smile proudly as I blew out the candles and we would laugh and joke as we dug into large slabs of cake. Looking back now, I always remember a moment during that day when a sad expression would momentarily cloud Mum's face. I know now she was thinking of my real mother and her dearest friend, Rora.

I accept my previous life is over. Looking around, I see my village around me. Dot and Boon are chatting with Maggie in the corner. Rose is holding Peck, the name affectionately given to the baby dodo I rescued months earlier. Peck has taken to life in Greenwood like a duck to water. He was given his name for a reason: if you don't give him enough attention, he'll use his beak to let you know about it. He makes small chirping noises as Rose patiently feeds him an apple, his favourite treat. Ruth Gentles gives me sidelong glances from the corner as she speaks formally to Daniel. Warwick stands to the side, listening quietly.

As I watch the people of Greenwood around me celebrating my birthday, I feel a sense of belonging rest upon me that is at once both conflicting and soothing. My mysterious background had always left me feeling out of place. I belong here. Now I have a compass and I know where I am. Duncan's hands slide around my waist and bring me back to the present.

"Happy Birthday," he whispers, softly kissing my cheek.

I smile, and turn to face him. Out of the corner of my eye, I see Aiden.

My twin brother, part of me, but still a stranger. I suddenly need to connect with him. I promise Duncan I'll return, go quickly to my room and then follow him.

I shut the door behind me. The light that floods the courtyard throws two figures into sharp relief. Warwick and Aiden are speaking in raised voices. As I draw nearer, Warwick suddenly looks up and sees me. He whispers to Aiden and leaves quickly. Since the High Council meeting we haven't spoken directly to each other. Sometimes when I'm walking through the village with Boon, I'll catch his eye and we'll look at each other, curious, but we've never had the opportunity to have a conversation.

Aiden looks at me. I can tell he's desperate to get away. It's ironic, but as time has passed I've grown closer to his family, my family, but more distant from him. Today of all days I want to reach out to him.

"Happy Birthday Aiden." I said, holding the worn, brown journal out to him extending it like a talisman.

He steps back immediately. I haven't yet read the diary. It would be wrong to do that on my own – I want to share its revelations with my brother. Pulling the journal back, I held it delicately in my hands. Holding his gaze, I spoke hoping to breach whatever held him back.

"My Mum… Lauren gave it to me. It's Rora's journal. I think it will tell us more…what we need to know." I spoke quietly.

"Do you think that knowledge will help Amber?" he says.

Dumbfounded, I step back, shaking my head in confusion. "We're still strangers aren't we? I've been here for months I'm offering to give you the answers. This is our mother."

Aiden's face is defiant, but he stays silent. Suddenly, Duncan's hands are on my hips, pulling me back against him.

"Brother or not Aiden, I won't have you upsetting my Mate."

Aiden turns to walk away. I call after him, and he turns to look at me, his face conflicted, but silent and defiant.

"Who's our father?" I whisper brokenly. "Can you at least tell me that?"

He looks down, as though contemplating his answer. Sensing his hesitation, Duncan pulls me closer to him in silent support.

"I don't know. I'm sorry Amber," he says, walking away.

I've had years of half-answered questions, and the anger wells up suddenly, knocking the breath from me.

"The journal might tell us Aiden. Why won't you try?"

He carries on walking, encapsulating the answers I had always yearned for but never found. A feeling of bittersweet acceptance fell over me as I accepted the irony of this day, in this land where time was marked so differently. Now at 19 years old, I understand that people, even family members, can't give me what I want. The ability to know who I am, where I came from and what my place is in this world. The brother I never knew has turned out to be a stranger, while an adopted family and friends have given me a sense of belonging I never knew I needed.

Isn't that just the definition of irony?

"She visits in dreams, but never when called,

I feel I know her, yet bond not formed,

How will I know if the Heaven's align?

Perhaps when my heart is no longer mine...."

…Duncan

Duncan

DUNCAN

Amber Lockwood

I never thought I could feel this way about another person. My relationships with the opposite sex were based on friendships I had with boys at school. We laughed, we teased and they sometimes annoyed me. That was the sum total of my experience. I didn't have Elaine's flirtatious nature to capture their interest. Her vision of the perfect romance was as alien to me as a father figure was. I always imagined that if I had a Dad that he would be my ideal of what a man was supposed to be, what a potential partner should live up to. So I looked at my friend's relationships with their fathers with a mixture of bemusement and envy. Elaine and her Dad bickered like they were playing a verbal tennis match. Having said that, I never once doubted his love for his daughter. Sometimes, I would catch a whisper of a smile as he looked at her, the image of him, delighting in the sparring match. She was the object of such devotion and love.

So here I am, in what appears to be a serious relationship, with no reference point from where to begin. For, at twenty-three, Duncan is no boy. He walks with the confidence of someone beyond his years, of someone who has proved himself to his people. He is a man who knows who he is. I, on the other hand, behind the mask I present to the world, I'm just one big boiling pot of emotion. Which begs the question – what does he see in me? I struggled to find an answer, so I decided to gauge the topic of Mates with Maggie the next time we were alone. Once I fell over my words and manage to string a coherent sentence together, Maggie smiles at me and begins to explain:

"Life here is really quite simple Amber. You're with your Mate because that is exactly where you are meant to be."

"How did you know?" I asked incredulously.

"I was twelve when I had my first dream about Daniel." Maggie smiled at the memory, her features softening. "I was nearly eighteen when he understood. Men develop their abilities later than women," she whispered, "but we mature a bit faster."

"So has Rose…." I asked.

"She hasn't said anything, but she'll come to me when the time's right."

I feel nervous speaking to Maggie about my relationship with her son and swallow nervously.

"I don't understand my relationship with Duncan. I've nothing to compare it with." I say.

"But you've never felt anything like this before, have you?" she asked

"No…never." I looked up, my face hot. Maggie throws her hands up in a 'there you go' gesture.

"Amber, I know you've lost Lauren and I wouldn't dream of trying to take her place. But I do have some advice, for what it's worth. Trust your feelings and your instincts."

I smiled at her, appreciating her kindness. I wonder if she knows how much my relationship with Duncan has changed in last few months.

To begin with, it felt like he was the lion and I was his prey. My status was assumed and my feelings unconsidered. Now it's different. Time passed and somewhere between the handholding and stolen kisses I began to understand my feelings for this mysterious man. Then came the dreams filled with stark erotic images. Now we can't be in the same room without reaching out and reassuring ourselves of the other's presence, his hand on mind, my arms round his, his fingers gently pulling my hair behind my ear and kissing my neck softly. It's like an invisible thread exists between us ensuring a live connection at all times. And my feelings for Caroline, Duncan's ex-girlfriend, are a minefield. Whenever I see her, I'm consumed by a white hot jealousy that crashes through me. It's an illogical feeling for a girl I have yet to have a conversation with.

Watching Aiden walk away, my only living relative, Duncan's arms tighten around me, holding me, bringing me back to the present. I wave my hands in frustration and suddenly realise that this action has caused some stones to rise into the air – as if I'm a conductor and they're obeying my signal. When I stop they drop to the ground.

"What was that?" I cry out.

"I think we might have found your potential," he says, turning me around to look at him.

For once I don't want to know more. Seeking the truth so many times and having it thrown back in my face was beginning to smart. I want to enjoy the now. I look into his dark blue eyes.

"Whenever I think I'm going to fall, you're always there to catch me." I whispered.

"Now she notices." he grins.

I touch his cheek softly with my hands, then reach into his thick dark hair and pull his face towards mine. When it came, the kiss was an explosion of emotion, I desperately wanted to show this man how much he meant to me, my actions would translate the words I could not yet say. He trailed his lips across my cheek up to my ear.

"Come with me?" he whispers. I look at him and realise the last few months of my life have led me here.

"Yes."

I took his hand, certain in my choice. This is what I want. This is what I've wanted since I met him, but I didn't understand before. Pulling me into his arms, he holds me close to him as we walk into the darkness towards the building at the bottom of the garden. He opens the door and we go inside. My breath creates halos in the coldness of the room. I sit, shivering, on the bed while he snaps his fingers and lights the candles and the fire. He sits beside me and I lick my lips, shaking and nervous. He takes my hand, and places it against his heart.

"Be my Mate, Amber? Be mine?"

His eyes held me, unwavering and sincere. I mirror him, pulling his hand to my heart.

"Yes," I whisper, flooded with happiness. "Yes."

For a moment he grins like a boy and kisses me softly. Standing up he placed my hands on his chest encouraging me to unbutton his shirt. Concentrating on the small movement, I feel Duncan's hands on my sides and heat rushes through me. The firelight flickers over him teasing me with a glimpse of muscles and his concave stomach.

Duncan hangs his shirt over a bedpost and begins to kiss me as he takes off my jacket, trailing his hands up my arms to my shirt, the little pearl buttons tiny against his deft fingers. Our breath is loud and overshadows the silence of the room. The scream is so unexpected, we spring apart. Duncan stiffened his arms around mine, sighed and reached for his shirt. I buttoned my shirt, touching a finger to my swollen lips.

"I don't suppose you'll stay here?" he asks.

I shake my head, rubbing my arms as we leave the now warm, fire lit room. He sighs, snaps his fingers to extinguish the candles and the firelight. We walk towards the front of the house and see a circle of people forming, whispering nervously in low voices. As we get closer, we hear moans of pain. My gut is churning. In the middle of the circle lolls Morgan Rose, his face and body almost unrecognisable beneath the blood and bruises. Daniel tries to pull him upright. Duncan kisses me, takes me to his mother and runs over to help. Maggie hugs Rose and me, and I'm grateful for her comfort. Warwick and Boon are talking quickly and quietly. The tension from the crowd gathered. The feeling of foreboding is palpable and I know instinctively that danger is coming. Except now I have nowhere to run.

PROMISES

Maggie Darkings

I have been here before. I lean against the wall and silently watch the High Council gather to discuss and decide. Decide the future of Greenwood. Morgan Rose survived until the early hours of this morning. His injuries, were unlike anything I have ever seen before. Someone had sliced his stomach systematically, long indiscriminate slices of varying degrees of penetration, with a sword. It looked as if the sword bearer was torn between playing with him and punishing him. The cruelty of it will haunt me forever. By the time he reached Greenwood, Morgan had developed a fever and was whispering frantically, hoarsely, trying to make his message heard. He said the same two words over and over.

"They're coming. They're coming."

It was heart breaking to see this once elegant, articulate politician struggling, fighting against death to warn his people of the danger they were in. As I watched the High Council take their seats, Warwick glances briefly at Morgan's empty chair. Daniel's eyes constantly find mine. Ruth Gentles looks uncommonly nervous and Boon sits quietly. I thank the two moons that Morgan was able to warn us of the danger and has given us a chance to protect what is ours. Warwick clears his throat, and the murmuring stops. He begins to speak quietly about the events that have brought us here. I look at the opposite wall. Perhaps if I can concentrate and block out the words, I can pretend this situation doesn't exist. Dot and I share a glance and our thoughts mirror as one. Dread. We've both been here before. We had each been only mated for a couple of years when the last war took place.

Before the King's family came to the throne, there had been many rivals, who had seen the opportunity to rule as a prize too tempting to pass. Daniel and Boon had left with their fathers to protect our village and our way of life. They returned a year later, bloodied, bruised and weary of war. Daniel had missed a year of Duncan's life. Since then we have lived in relative peace. The old King re-issued the scroll of the Natural Laws to all village representatives. Morgan's first visit to Court had been with his father to be presented with the scroll on our behalf. Looking at it now above Warwick's head, it's writing elegant and intricate, it seems to mock our purpose.

People start to move around me and I realise that the meeting has ended. It does not take long for your fate to be decided. Daniel takes my arm and I look up into the face I know as well as my own and hope that I have the strength needed for the days ahead. Even small separations from him have a cost, like a needle thread pulled too taut, the strain and tension pulling my body to the point of pain. Later, the village meets for our last gathering before our men leave in the early hours of the morning. Some will stay: Warwick, Boon and Aiden have been tasked with protecting Greenwood. I feel happy for my friend Dot and glad that one of my boys will stay safe. Fiddles play long-forgotten tunes and I watch Daniel and our Rose dancing quietly in the firelight. I know my daughter will have good memories of her father to help her in the times ahead. Looking around my village, my people and my family, I feel teary at the thought of our way of life ending. This feels like it could be our last time together.

Back in the house, I sit on the staircase taking a moment to collect myself. For as much as I'll grieve in private, my family deserves my happiness tonight. I hear the voices upstairs.

"Why do you have to leave? I don't understand Duncan."

He is unable to placate her and I remember all too clearly feeling exactly the same as Amber, resenting having to let him go, unable to understand that Greenwood's and my fate were intrinsically linked.

The early dawn comes all too quickly and casts an orange glow over the village. We say our goodbyes and watch silently as our men walk away. Tears are rolling down Amber's face as Duncan disappears from sight. Rose puts an arm around her to comfort her and I remember my own tears, all those years ago. But no matter what the cost, we must honour the promise they have made to us, as a Mate, son, cousin and friend. Silence falls on our village as we each return to our way of life with a whispered hope that those we love will return to us safely.

DUTY

Amber Lockwood

Of all the duties I expected to attend to today, a lesson was not one of them. "Right little missy, gather your jacket." I looked in askance at Boon. The man can't help but see my swollen eyes and red nose. After learning the nuances of his personality over the last few months, I know he is in in one of his better moods. Knowing that argument isn't an option, I pick up my coat and follow him.

We walk our usual circuit, giving Boon a chance to reassure villagers. Boon's sword is more prominent today than in the past. I watch the worried faces of the people around me, searching my face for the reassurance and understand why he wanted me to accompany him. As a member of the Darkings family, it is my role to reassure Greenwood they will be protected. Remembering how Lauren would have acted in a similar situation, I smile and make positive comments, despite the whirling vortex inside me.

As we leave the village, I see Warwick and Aiden arguing, their body language is tense as my brother turns and walks away. Moments later, Rose follows him. Boon watches the exchange but stays silent. I think about Rora's journal, sitting unopened and unread on my bedside table. A can of worms I still have to deal with. We walk into the woods, the wind whispering softly among the branches above us. Our feet crunch into the ground. I wish away the silence. It makes me remember what's missing. Emotions swirled as I remembered last night.

"I don't want you to go Duncan."

"Do you really think I want to leave now we've found each other?" he had said quietly.

Alternatively shocked and frustrated by the events of my life that have made the people I care about leave me, I fell to anger. It was not until the light began to move in quick circles above us that I realised I had to calm down.

Taking me in his arms Duncan laughed, "I hope you never get really angry at me." and hugged me to him.

I sighed as the anger ebbed away: the dancing lights above me stopped. Winding my arms around him, I hoped he knew that when he left, my heart would go with him.

I snap out of my reverie and return to the present, I follow Boon. We leave the forest and walk along the shoreline, where the water is a rich white colour instead of blue. Foam from the waves teases against our boots as the tide ebbs and flows. I can see lights fall across the water and wonder vaguely what they are.

Boon turns to me. "Duncan says your potential is beginning to show."

I react instinctively at the mention of his name.

"Boon, do you really think this is the day for more revelations?"

"Yes, little missy. We don't have the luxury of time anymore."

I watch him as he stretches his hand out towards the water. A liquid sphere emerges from the waves and he uses his hand to control it, as if it's some kind of animal he's trained. As he raises his hand higher and higher, the sphere rises higher and higher. He makes a circular motion with his finger, and the sphere responds by spinning round, faster and faster, in time with his command. He looks at me, challengingly and without thinking I raised my hand and push it towards the sphere. It immediately distinguishes and splashes back into the water, spraying our trousers as it does so. I'm stunned by what's just happened. Completely stunned. I fell to silence, the churning in my stomach now resembling a spin cycle.

"You have potential you don't realise. What others would do anything to possess," Boon whispers.

I close my eyes, remembering the water at the Hermitage, the energy that had flowed from my hands towards the Knight, the moving stones and the dancing lights.

"You have strength you don't realise. Don't doubt yourself…"

I opened my eyes as Boon stops and suddenly looks across the shore. Following the direction of his stare, I realise the dozen vague lights I had noticed before were boats. They looked like toys moving at the will of a master. Shadowy figures move around on board as large black oars dipped in and out of the white water. A black cloud hovers over them. Dread overwhelms me.

"We need to warn the village." I shouted.

We run, stumbling, dodging trees, until we reach the village. We bang on doors and shout, telling everyone to run to the Great Hall.   Then from the other end of the village, I hear screams and smell wood burning as they arrive, ransacking, smashing and burning as they go.   Maggie is running around frantically, calling Rose's name. Then I watch, as if in slow motion, as Aiden strides towards her, pushes her roughly to the ground and she looks up at him in shock. Taking out his sword, he places the point of the sword to her heart.   Aiden is going to kill the woman who raised him.   I run to stop him, waving my arms, and a stone flies up and hits him on the head. The force of it makes him fall down. He lies there for a moment stunned.

"Maggie run, I'll get Rose." I shout. She scrambles to her feet and runs.

I run home, chaos all around me. Houses bellow with fire, swords clash and blood-curdling screams fill the air. I run upstairs, two at a time and find Rose on her bed clutching the sheets, tears streaming down her face, her body quivering. I pull her roughly to her feet and we run downstairs, her small hand tight in mine. We come to a sudden halt. Around the Village Protector's house is a circle of Black Knights, swords in their hands, sweat and blood covering their bodies, fevered lust dancing in their eyes.   Rose whimpers and begins to shake. I instinctively pull her behind me.

"We meet again."

Looking to the voice, I found myself looking into the smiling, black soulless eyes of the Knight who killed Lauren. Black hate liquefied and travelled along my veins. Before I can react, I turn and see Aiden walking slowly towards me. Rose hides her teary face between my shoulder blades, her slight body quivering. I look into his eyes – eyes so like mine. Now black and without any emotion. He roughly pulls Rose from behind me. I try to stop him and he draws back his hand and in almost slow motion, slaps my face. The movement, so quietly violent, I fall to the ground, blood spraying from my mouth onto the ground. The Black Knight laughs softly. Aiden pulls Rose in front of him, holding her small hip roughly within his large hand and points a knife at her neck and she swallows in fear. The shocked faces of Maggie and Boon, look on in the distance, terrified and helpless. The Black Knight walks slowly towards me removing his black gloves elegantly, the hands beneath covered in whitened scars and thickened grime. I try not to shudder.

"So here we are again my dear. I wonder what choice you will make this time?" he spoke calmly, like we were speaking over coffee at a church fete.

I look at the Knights surrounding us and at Aiden, smiling maniacally. I see Maggie and Boon watching my reaction. I see Rose, shaking, and so vulnerable to my choice. Slowly, I pull myself up from the ground and stay still, not wanting to give them a reason to hurt Rose.

"I'll do what you ask." I answered.

The Black Knight, smiles.

"Aiden, bring your sister," he commands, turns and walks away.

Aiden turns; pushes Rose to the ground and with his back to us thrusts the knife down violently. Rose whimpers and is then silent. Tears fill my eyes as I watch Boon frantically trying to smother the screams being wrenched from Maggie. Aiden walks towards me and ties my wrists with rope. I looked into his dead eyes and asked the question running through my head.

"Why?"

He shrugs nonchalantly and pulls the rope keeping us together.

"Move." he says, pushing me forward roughly.

The Black Knight, throws his head back and laughs triumphantly. I hate him with every fibre of my being.

As we walk away, Greenwood witnessed my tragic departure. I remember the nights around the wishing well, the friendliness of the villagers, their reassurance and how they had welcomed me, a stranger, into their fold. Guilt overwhelms me as I realised I had brought this blackness to their door. As we enter the forest, the heavens begin to weep fat droplets of rain. Grieving for me, for all of us and our fates.

ALONE

Amber Lockwood

Even in my wildest dreams I never thought that my life would end this way. Needles of freezing rain fall relentlessly as we leave Greenwood. Without protection, its runs freely coating my hair, face and filters through my clothes, until I am numb and feel no more. My hands are bound together and my twin brother is pulling me behind him, like an animal. I feel the same numbness inside me as I did when Lauren died, my body so achingly tired it seems as if I have to wade through treacle. Being alone never bothered me before. Mum was solitary and didn't socialise because she didn't want anyone asking awkward questions about our background. So apart from Elaine, my friends were sparse. Now Lauren's gone and I don't know if I will ever see Duncan again. I am truly alone and I'm terrified.

"Move." Aiden tugged the rope violently, pulling me to the ground.

I push my hands onto the wet mud to break my fall, but my knees jar against the ground. He turns to look down at me and I feel very much like a pawn in a game where I don't know the rules. I never got to know my brother as well as I had hoped but I know he never looked at me with such a lack of emotion, like I am some inconsequential stranger he can use to serve his purposes. I think of Rose with her small, elfin face and her huge smile and I can feel the tears well up as I look at the man who murdered her.

"Why did you kill her?" I ask.

For a moment he pauses and a ghost of an emotion flickers across his face, like a memory he can't place, before he moves determinedly, pulling me up and ahead of him. The Black Knights laugh loudly, and the man they call Luther watches our exchange with a twisted smile.

I smother my anger and compose my features. Eventually we come to the sea where I had stood with Boon only a short time ago. Two things are clear from my exchange with my brother. Aiden, as I knew him, is well and truly gone and if I needed help it wasn't going to come from him. As we reach the shoreline and I look out to the white water, froth bubbles on the surface at intermittent pauses, reacting to the violence around it. The long black boats I had seen earlier are moved quickly and efficiently into place along the shoreline, like a dozen black pencils. Aiden pushes me forward to the front of the boat. A feeling of foreboding fills me and I begin to fight against him. I had a horrible feeling that if I get into this boat I would never be able to escape.

"I'll help ye restrain her."

A brick house of a man with a gruff voice moves in front of me. He has thick, greying black hair that covers his head and flows over his chin into greasy stubble and his lips are covered with a film of spittle. I shuffle backwards as far as I can go, but he brings his face close to mine and stares at me with his soulless, vacant black eyes. Clumsily, he pushes my wet hair back with a huge bear claw of a hand and then he slowly traces the outline before moving it slowly down my collarbone. I squirm away and as his eyes follow the contours of my body beneath my wet clothes.

"Amber don't move, will you Sister?" Aiden's voice slithers near my ear.

I swallow hard and try to block out the raucous laughter and bawdy comments. I moved myself backwards as far as I can go and hold my body rigid and hope they can't see my fear. The crowd around us laugh. The boats set off from the shore and I feel like a kidnap victim in a modern day Viking tale. The ships and their oars move swiftly and rhythmically through the water.

"Boon never brought you here did he?" Aiden asks. "That's why."

His arm points to the large-boned head breaking the water's surface, inky black eyes searching for the source of the noise. Another one emerges, then another and another, until the boat is surrounded. Unable to hide my shudder, the men in the boat laugh heartily and look at me with pity like I was precluded from some obvious joke.

"I'll protect you lassie," Brick House laughs.

The shoreline looms closer and closer and I know it won't take us long to breach the shore. The further away they take me, the less likely it is that I'll have the chance to save myself. It's just a matter of time before they hurt me and the fear of their form of torture was growing by the minute. We reach the shore and Brick House lifts me bodily and throws me onto the hard wet sand. Winded, I pull myself up and gingerly rub the mixture of blood and sand away from my legs and arms. My only hope is to act meekly so that they watch me less vigilantly. Aiden pulls my rope and we set off once more, heading away from the shore into dense woods. I keep my head down, letting my eyes adjust to my new surroundings.

Dusk descends, silhouetting the branches and leaves of the trees. The noise of the crickets cuts through the silence, broken only by the Knight's quiet conversations and heavy feet. We reach a natural clearing surrounded by trees where a camp has been set with tents and blazing fires. Women, dressed sparsely in ragged clothing, wander around preparing and cooking food. I idly wonder how long this camp has been in place and if this was where Aiden had come to plan his betrayal. I turn to look at him and the expression on his face confirms my suspicions. He pulls me towards an overturned log, then forces me to sit down on it, loosening the rope a little around my hands. I rub my skin and wince at the pain in my wrists, watching small groups of Black Knights gather, chatting and pulling cooked meat from spindles and stuffing it hungrily into their mouths. My stomach churns. Brick House holds a jug to his mouth and takes long, sloppy gulps of the liquid, as splashes fall from his mouth and coating his thick, black beard. His eyes land on me and hold me stiff and terrified. Luther's voice rises above the crowd.

"Gentleman." he exclaims, while a laugh rings through the crowd, "To the victors go the spoils."

The men move in unison through the camp women grabbing them randomly. They scream as they are picked up, small fists pummelling ineffectually against the shoulders of their captors. Brick House gets up from the tree log, throws his jug to the ground and begins to stalk towards me. On instinct, I turn towards Aiden and find him laughing, amused at my predicament, before he turns his back on me and walks away with Luther. A small part of me hoped that he would save me. Watching him walk away, something inside me died, never to return. I know this is one experience I won't recover from.

I never thought that my life would end this way.

RUN

Amber Lockwood

The voices inside my head tell me to run. Warring emotions tumble through me as I fight the desire to close my eyes and pretend this is one of my bad dreams. A woman's scream wrestles me back to reality as she is picked up and taken away by one of the Black Knights. Recovering, I see Brick House is now flanked by four other men and unless I want to willingly submit to the fate he has in store for me, I need to make my escape now. By sheer will, I wrench my wrists free of their bindings and run, stumbling on my frozen legs and feet towards the opening to the dense forest.

"We've got a race on our hands lads!" Brick House roars.

My heart beats violently, his words making the hairs on the back of my neck stand up straight and the adrenalin pumps through my body. I quickly find the natural path that brought us to the clearing and I try to remember the quickest route back to the beach. Despite my damp clothing, my body quickly adjusts to my pace. I daren't look behind me, but I can see the image of five large men in pursuit of me. I see the violent intention on their faces, I see their swords ready to cut and slice my flesh and I see their desire to break my soul.

The path intricately winds around the trees and up and down over the forest floor, like a rollercoaster. I feel the curves of the corners and the wind whips my hair, as fear and nausea threaten to overwhelm me. To distract me, I focus on my movements and find myself remembering back to a year ago, when I had entered a 5k race around our village that ended at the Hermitage. I set off that day, thinking about it as nothing more than an ordinary run. I was running steadily, but as the finishing line came into view, a glimmer of white caught my eyes and I saw Lauren watching for me in her uniform. She knew about the race, but I'd never expected to see her. I was so uplifted by the sight of her, cheering and shouting my name, that my pace increased and my competitive streak emerged with a vengeance. I finished third that day for her and for myself, because as much as there was distance between us, I needed her. As the footsteps thunder behind me and I hear the exertion of harsh breath, time falls away and all I hear is Lauren shouting at me to run faster and harder than I've ever done before. The noises behind me slowly receded to dull thuds on the edges of my consciousness only overtaken by the sounds of waves. I am nearly there.

As the water comes into view, I have no choice but to stop and look round at the devils chasing after me. My feet sinks into the soft wet sand as I raised my eyes, my breath harsh in my ears, as I faced my reality. Brick House walks nonchalantly towards the grassy bluff overlooking the beach, his eyes gleaming with triumph. Two Black Knights, their eyes sliding over me while they draw their swords, the sharp edges pointed directly at me, flank him on either side.

"By god, that was fun lass" he jeers at me, one bear club hand resting at his hip. I could see I was being surveyed like a prize already won. They look at me like I am their prey. "Lads, do you remember the last girl?" he asks his companions. The men laugh heartily, sharing the private joke. Nerves gnawed as I was forced to listen. "She ran too and it really got her nowhere," he explains patronisingly. "Come now. We'll make it easier on you."

Brick House replaces his sword, in an apparent act of faith and waits for my answer. Revulsion and anger rip through me like a tidal wave. Is this my only choice? Hell will freeze over before I surrender willingly to be abused. The anger becomes a burning sensation, like an electrical current that flows down through my spine to my legs and arms. My vision blurs red and I drift out of my surroundings into unconscious awareness. I take a step forward and Brick House smiles at what he thinks is my surrender.

"No." I shout.

Fire fell from my fingertips like flowing water, covering the edge of grassy knoll in front of the men, shooting and spitting at them, setting the grass in front of the men alight, making them retreat.

I held Brick House's gaze and blazed a fire path between us, wanting him to understand that if I so choose, I can aim the fire at him. The stream of fiery lava stops. I come back to myself and drop my hands to my sides. Rubbing my thumbs over my fingernails, now hot to the touch, I find myself remembering Boon's words "You have more potential than you know." Brick House and his men appear to collect themselves and preparing to move towards me as the fire burns itself out. Turning to the sound of the waves and the unknown creatures within its depths, I take a breath as I run into the water.

I make my choice.

OBLIVION

Amber Lockwood

The last time I was in open water, I was dreaming. Now, in reality, the coldness penetrates my skin, through my nerves and deep into my bones. My body heat plunges to icy cold until it reaches my head and my ability to think freely is taken from me. Vaguely, I hear voices from the shore calling me back. The different pitches and tones merge into one monotone voice calling my name. Despite my disorientation, I know they can't be trusted. The hell I am trapped within is one of my own choice and it's preferable to my fate on the shore. As my body is tossed haphazardly at the will of the sea and the moons directing it, I'm pulled back to a distant memory.

"What does Sensio mean?" I asked Boon on one of our walks.

"What do you think?" he asked, "given the lessons we have had so far?"

We walked quietly as I pondered, my mind assimilating what I had learned so far. From what I saw, Sensio represented a need for balance that Earth could no longer meet. Earth had been infected by war, hunger and oppression but neither politics or intervention could counter balance the damage. The balance had altered irrevocably to a point where another existence had to be created. Sensio was the platform upon which the balance could be re-established.

"I think it means natural balance," I said slowly looking at Boon for an indication of whether my thoughts were correct.

"Exactly," he smiled.

I fight for breath as another wave lifts me up and then pulls me under. In desperation, I wonder where my current situation fits into the definition of natural balance. I have never felt sorry for my circumstances but the facts remain clear. My real Mum has gone. Lauren too. I was not brought here by my own choice. My Mate has left to fight a war. My presence has brought pain and suffering to a family and the village who took me in. My brother has betrayed me to be vilely abused by strangers. I asked myself one question. How much more can one soul take? The toll that I have paid so far is not a reflection of natural balance. As my mind shuts down and body gives up the fight, my soul cries out for the retribution that has escaped me in life. For if Sensio is the place I imagine it to be, it will deliver what it has promised, whether I live to see it or not.

PERCEPTION

Aiden Darkings

To live without a conscience is a heady thing. My previous existence pales into insignificance; one of servitude, orders and the unequivocal expectation of unwavering loyalty. I'm surprised my mask has lasted as long as it has. I will be happy when Luther delivers what he's promised. The woman sitting atop of my naked body is beautiful. Wide spaced blue eyes watch my reaction, recording for future reference. Wild tangled blonde hair falls down her naked back. Pictures filter at the sides, shadowed and evasive. When I try to concentrate on them, they race away into the darkness, before returning at regular intervals to tease once more. The picture of a girl's anguished face with tears flooding down her cheeks. My mind tries to place her without success and gives up as I push her away.

I feel her lips trail down my body, close my eyes and give in to the lust that brought me here in the first place.

BELONGING

Amber Lockwood

A ll of my life, I have yearned to belong. Growing up without knowing my origins, without knowing my history and finding myself surrounded by others who do, I question where I belong.

For now, the purple sky pins me in place, I see the clearing, the road to Greenwood and the lush forest that surrounds it. I see the wishing well with villagers scattered around it. In the distance, I see Maggie waving to me and feel Duncan's hand in mine pulling me forward. As I smell the fire, I stop. Duncan walks away from me, unaware I'm frozen. The scent of hot, tarred sulphur reaches my nostrils and clogs them. Opening my mouth to warn them, I hear only silence. I wave my arms, frantically, but no one stirs. They whirl around on a revolving cinema screen, moving and laughing at the same jokes like a remote control on constant rewind and play.

Suddenly the picture changes. The village is in darkness, flames consume blackened dilapidated buildings. The Black Knights rampage through the village, destroying homes at will with fire torches in their hands. My eyes are drawn to the small figure lying on the ground, deathly still. My head is filled with the screams of her mother, who shakes her as though sheer will alone will bring her daughter back to life. Her head turns towards me, her blackened face streaked with tears running uncontrollably down her face. She sees me and stands up slowly on shaky legs. Walking towards me and stopping in front of me. She looks back at her dead daughter and around the burning village and looks at me steadily with a hate-filled gaze.

"You brought this upon us." she shouts.

I frantically try to speak to Maggie, but my words are silent. Trying harder, I gesture wildly with my hands trying to say how sorry I am and how guilty I feel. In the distance, Rose's lifeless body taunts me. The villagers gradually surrounded me, screaming and pointing at me, their insults stabbing my heart like invisible knives. The fire surrounds us all, heading towards us like a tsunami. Exhausted, my last act is to warn the people who taunt me and when my body finally begins to burn, I welcome the pain. A child's voice whispers insistently as I suddenly wake up, roll onto my side and cough up the salty seawater clogging my throat. My body is taut, my head aches and my limbs are heavy.

"She's awake," a little voice says excitedly. Looking above me I see a thick stone ceiling. Large rocks surround the walls and light filters through them at different angles, suffusing the room with a soft, romantic glow. Beneath me, the rock floor feels smooth, softened by years of lapping water. In the middle of the room is a pool of water, dark and luminous, like a gate to another world. I look towards the voice.

"This was a mistake Ero."

"We couldn't let her die, Moren."

Stretching carefully, I sit up gingerly and moan as my limbs unlock from their frozen state. I move towards the darkened pool. Two small heads and shoulders float above the surface of the water looking at me intently. The faces have delicate human features, small lips and a nose. They look like young girls. It's the eyes you notice. Their pupils are fully dilated, stretched to accustom to the water. Their heads are smooth and hairless and stretch upwards into a boned crown at top of their skulls. They lean forward hesitantly, as interested in my appearance as I am in theirs. They hold the side of the dark pool with elegant fingers, webbed with dark skin.

"Look at all that hair Moren, it must be annoying."

"I don't know why you're so impressed Ero, I don't like it."

I hear the conversation although I don't see them use their mouths, and I realise that I can hear their voices telepathically. For the first time, I think there's a possibility I might actually have died.

"Don't be silly, of course you didn't." says Ero, bobbing about in the water excitedly.

"I'm sorry. I don't know where I am," I ask in my head.

"Our secret cave," Ero replies, swimming towards me.

Moren remains where she is, looking at me cautiously. "You're to stay here, eat the food, until we take you back."

I nod silently. Moren turns and sinks back into the dark water. I wave my hands, trying to attract Ero's attention. "Wait." I shout "Why did you save me?"

Ero looks back at me like I have asked her a silly question, tilts her little head to one side, her brow furrowed.

"Amber, you asked for help."

Without waiting for my reply, she jumps up and launches herself back down into the pool. The small fin of her tail rises just above the water and splashes me cheekily as she leaves. I laugh out loud in disbelief. I've just met a mermaid.

The days that followed take on a dream like quality. Twice a day the mermaids arrive with small fish or mossy seaweed for me to eat. I was able to generate enough sparks to create a fire in which to cook the food and keep myself warm. Ero is as curious about me as I am of her and she asks endless questions about life above the water. She reminds me of Rose.

"You can't tell anyone about us," she says to me one day.

"Of course, but why is that? Are you a secret?" I reply.

"We survive because we hide from humans" she says, her face sombre.

Remembering Peck, the little Dodo I had saved, I reluctantly agreed. Humans are not good at co-existing with other species. Moren is more reticent. She drops the food at the corner of the dark pool before quickly turning tail back to where she came from. Slowly my strength returns and my broken spirit begins to heal. I've dealt with so many soul-destroying events and I'm only just 19 years old.

One afternoon I sit in front of the fire. The light filters

through the cracks in the rocks and illuminates the cave wall with a soft haze. I hear a splash and turn to see Moren at the pool. This time, instead of disappearing, she lingers and points to the seaweed she has placed at the edge of the dark pool.

"Make sure you eat that," she says, looking at me meaningfully to ensure I understand the message.

I nod vigorously, quickly pick up the food and place it in front of me. Another splash and she's gone, I look around me and wonder what's going to become of me. All of my life I have owed my safety to others and even when I thought the game was up, something whether human or mythical, has intervened. Deep inside, I burn for the power to look after myself and control my own destiny. I think about this, and where I'm going to go while eating the food. My only choice is to return to Greenwood and hope that as many people have survived the attack as possible. What if the Black Knights have returned? If I go back and walk right into the village would I put everybody in even greater danger? A plan starts to form in my head. I finish my meal and climb down to the soft rock below me. I look lingeringly on the lights suffusing the rocks around me and listen to the water lapping gently around the dark pool, lulling me into the darkness of a heavy sleep.

In my dreams, there are arms around me and I feel water lapping backwards and forwards, moving my body with the rhythm of its pull. The light gradually fades until only inky black darkness exists. I wake up grabbing at clumps of wet sand. My clothes and body are wet from the ocean and the tide has moved up to my ankles. I'm surprised by how easily I stand up. Whatever is in that greenery is definitely good for you. I turn around to face the ocean and scan it for any sign of my rescuers. Moren sees I'm upright and returns to the sea, believing her obligation to be complete. Ero lingers for a moment and I hold her eyes, one species to another and placed my hand on my heart, hoping she understood the depth of my gratitude. She breaks the surface and rises out of the water, majestic and beautiful and dives back in with a splash, her tail fin disappearing out of sight.

I turn my back on the ocean and begin to walk towards Greenwood. At first I'm unable to guess the time, but as the purple sky fades and shadows appear, I realise that it's early evening. This is the time that Boon completes his nightly circuit around the village. I walk quickly, getting closer and closer, my heart thrumming with nerves. There's no noise. But then I reach Boon and Dot's cottage encouraged by the smell of fire and smoke piping through the chimney. I hear footsteps coming towards me. A hunched figure moves haltingly along the path. As it gets closer, I see a face and eyes haunted and etched with shadows so deep I don't know where they begin. Boon emerges, like a shadow of his former self. His eyes meet mine not in greeting but with caution, and his words cut me like a knife.

"You don't belong here anymore Amber."

AFFINITY

Amber Lockwood

Since childhood I've always had an affinity with animals. Peck wriggles as he watches the shadows cross the bedroom ceiling, then he settles down and rests on my elbow. I rub his little bald head, pulling a finger over his tiny beak and back along his body. His yellow clawed feet rest upon my arm, my body providing the substitute nest he craves. As I hold the little orphan bird, he offers silent comfort, accepting me without question. As much as I pleaded, Lauren never yielded to my pleas for a pet. I thought that was because of our limited finances. With hindsight, I know that if we needed to run, an animal was an extra responsibility we didn't need. Instead my friends' animals became my own. Elaine's dog Pilot had a soft spot for me, for when I visited I always brought a treat for him. He would meet me at the door, sit quietly and look at me with his big chocolate brown eyes, absolutely trusting that I would never forget the dog bone I always brought with me. My love of animals goes back to being told to stay away from Amy in the first few days of Primary one. I didn't have to pretend who I was around animals. I didn't have to forget the dreams and pretend that their drain on my emotions didn't affect me.

Now, after surviving a near rape and drowning, I find comfort not in people I thought I knew but in an orphaned dodo. I swallow back the lump in my throat at Boon and Dot's reaction to my arrival. Despite my worst fears that everyone I loved would be taken from me, I had developed a soft spot for Dot, and particularly for Boon. The gruff old warrior had spent time with me, teaching me about the Natural Laws and giving me part of himself in the process. Nostalgia pulled me back to Dot, unselfconscious with the smear of flour across her cheek, her eyes sparkling as she smiled and laughed and my daily walks around the village with Boon, remembering when life was simpler and without danger. How they looked at me when I arrived will haunt me forever. Their eyes are smudged with black shadows, testimony to many days without rest. They looked haunted by the devastation around them. They are polite, but nervous. They usher me quickly to the kitchen, sit me down, lock the door and shut the curtains.

"I'm sorry. I had no idea of where to go," I mutter awkwardly, pushing my tangled hair behind my ears.

Boon forces an awkward smile. "It's ok, little missy, you did right coming here."

He walks off, muttering, into the other room, leaving me alone with Dot. Silence descends, interrupted only by the wind outside and the snap and crackle from the fire in the hearth.

"How's Maggie?" I whisper, almost afraid to ask.

Dot looks at me, then looks away, her eyes brimming with tears. My mind replays the image of Boon holding his hand over Maggie's screaming mouth as we helplessly watched Rose die. My eyes fill with tears and I try to find the right words to express my sorrow. None are adequate. Boon comes back into the room and passes me my backpack. He tells me that each of the 30 families has lost loved ones in the raid. When Boon sends me away to the bedroom to rest, I welcome the respite, but sleep comes with difficulty and when my body eventually gives in, my mind hurtles between Earth and Sensio, the images from each eventually blur into a kaleidoscope of colours, underlying my overwhelming guilt at the destruction my arrival has wrecked here.

Boon shakes me awake. "Amber, it's time to go."

I get up and get dressed in the freezing darkness of the bedroom, my breath fanning circles into the air. Peck is wakened by the noise, and squawks in protest. I walk into the fire-lit kitchen, sit at the table and eat the bread and brew Dot passes to me. She gives me the backpack and squeezes my arm for a few seconds. If it wasn't for the shadows under her eyes and the frailty of her limbs I could pretend that this is just another lesson day. But the time for pretending is long gone. Boon hugs Dot and she looks at him as if she's memorising every last feature. I look down, feeling guilty again. "Right missy. Time to go," Boon says with false cheerfulness. We leave the house and I peek quickly into the bedroom, the dodo spots me and squawks, happy to see me.

My heart aches as I realise that Peck will be the only one to truly miss me.

THE LAST LESSON

Amber Lockwood

For the first time in my life I'm truly and utterly alone. It's been a week since we arrived at Rowan Cottage. I remember our journey as we headed out of Greenwood, in the early hours of the morning. I noticed that even the outer edge of the village had been affected by the destruction of the Black Knights. Buildings were blackened by fire, abandoned, windows boarded up. In my mind, I see them as they were before, filled with light and life and people. I grieve for them. I had no idea where Boon was taking me. Was he sending me home? Had the damage been so devastating that the only way to recover was to send me away? My anxiety heightened as we reached the clearing, circled around, then walked into the woods and darkness. He strode ahead, his walking stick tapping against the ground in a steady rhythm. His figure became like a ghostly silhouette on the edge of the darkness as he walked further and further in front of me.

The early morning sun gradually filtered through the trees, casting sword-like shards of light on the ground. Sounds of the night gave way to sounds of the day: birds chirp, animals move in the undergrowth, wind rustles and water trickles in the distance. Finally, we reached a mass of trees that at first appeared too dense to walk through. Boon walked back and forth, muttering, as if he was trying to identify a particular spot. Suddenly he stopped, walked forward and pushed against one particular tree branch. It gave way as if it had been opened with an invisible key. He turned round and he looked at me for the first time in hours, grinning from ear to ear, obviously pleased with himself for remembering the answer to the puzzle. The smile was so at odds with the last few hours that I felt nervous, unsure of how to react. Pushing back against the branches, he motioned to me to go in front. I walked through brief blackness into brilliant light and gasped. Trees formed a tight intricate circle, two or three thick. They gave the impression the barrier is impenetrable. From the inside looking out, they blocked the light and cast long shadows across an overgrown pathway.

We followed the path to a small clearing, where the light fell on a brick and mossy thatched cottage with a chimney. It looked small, built for one or two people and was constructed of hundreds of small solid stones. It had a faded wooden door and windows at either side. It was surrounded by a sea of wildflowers. On the left, was a stack of logs ready for its next occupant. But it had an air of abandonment. I opened the door into the living room. In the middle was a fireplace flanked by two chairs. To my right was a small kitchen and at the back of the room was another door which, I assumed, led to a bedroom. Boon put the bags down. The silence seemed to stretch endlessly and became uncomfortable.

"I'm sorry for all the trouble I've caused, Boon," I said desperate to connect with him in some way.

"I would have been disappointed if you had not come to me," he said quietly.

In the bedroom he opened the heavy curtains, sending a layer of dust into the air and light flooded in revealing a large bed with ornate shapes carved into the headboard. We walked back into the living room, where we sat in the chairs.

"This is your last lesson Amber," he said. He spoke to me for the next hour without interruption. Boon told me that he had faith that I would do what I must.

As the sun went down, I dozed off in front of the log fire. I felt a blanket cover me, then a rough hand stroke my hair, before I heard the door shut. The room was in hazy darkness when I woke apart from the orange glow of the flames. I stretched, moving my stiff muscles and looked around for Boon, realising he had gone just like he said he would. I got up, opened the door and looked out at the clearing just as his silvery silhouette moved through the path. Instead of calling him, I accepted that for the first time in my 19 years I was truly on my own. What did fate have in store for me now? Even as a young girl unsure of her roots, I knew I possessed a strength that would help me face what I had to.

It was time for me to learn to do it on my own.

THE PRICE

Aiden Darkings

Blood trickles down the large man's face as Luther punches him without mercy and without pause. This performance is being provided for our amusement and I watch it without any emotion. I catch a glimpse of long blonde hair out of the corner of my eye and I'm flooded with memories of the girl I spent last night with. I will have her again. Luther begins to hit the man with less force now, but I know this is due to boredom rather than the effort it requires. He deserves no sympathy. Anyone who allows a slip of a girl with no potential and little knowledge of Sensio to escape deserves all he gets. He won't kill him. Luther keeps all his pawns on the chessboard until they serve their purpose. Then and not a minute before, will he sacrifice them. I wonder idly when my moment will come. We have used each other and for the time being I'm content to wait to make my move.

When I was growing up, I knew I was different from my friends. They all pinned their hopes on a particular talent from the elements. By ten years old, I had understood and mastered all of them. My life is about more than just keeping a natural balance in order. I was given these powers for a reason. I'll get what I want. I always have. The large man slumps into unconsciousness, his face pulped like a burst tomato. Luther walks without pause to the next man and begins the process again. I conceal a grin, thinking that Amber has unintentionally gained what I never thought she would. My respect. I no longer care whether she's on her way to the burnt out husk of a village that is Greenwood or floating lifelessly in the water. She has served the purpose she was meant to and I have no further use for her - sister or not.

ROWAN COTTAGE

Amber Lockwood

I have always been known for my even temperament. Elaine was always the spitfire of the two of us, raging passionately about any subject that mattered. I, on the other hand, do not stir so easily. It takes a lot to make me lose my temper. I just don't think it helps in most situations. Today is different. No matter how much my head tells me to calm down, my heart just isn't listening. I'm so angry my body is shaking. I can barely cope with the pain I'm feeling. Tears so near to the surface I can feel the moisture pool in my eyes, but through sheer will, I refuse to release them. Last night, a film reel of images played on constant repeat while I was sleeping. Lauren's murder; the destruction of Greenwood; Aiden's attack on Maggie; his murder of Rose; my capture; my near rape; my unwelcome appearance in Greenwood and my banishment to this unknown place. The reel played through again and again.

I walk towards the trees and into the forest beyond, unconcerned with my destination. As I walk along, I realise that I now finally understand the secret whispers, the emotions that filtered across the faces of strangers when they saw me. In Sensio every person has a potential; a talent to influence one element of nature, whether it's air, earth, fire or water. I'd been given clues: Duncan snapping his fingers to start and extinguish a fire and Boon controlling water in a circular swirl to his whim. But Aiden and I are different because we can influence all of the elements. Boon couldn't give me a reason for this, only that it was meant to be. We are both lucky and vulnerable. Is this the price of having power? If so, I never asked for it. How many people have died trying to prevent Luther from capturing me? The price is too high. Before he left me Boon warned me of the extremities of emotions I would feel. That's why I am angry, to be filled with such negative vile feelings is the price my soul has to pay. This is not justice. This is not what Sensio is meant to stand for. All I am left with is pain, overtaking my body and spewing from my soul and I badly want someone to pay for it.

I notice a river and walk briskly towards it. I've always felt particularly drawn to water. Closing my eyes, I try to imagine the familiar view of the Hermitage. Instead, I see a river in full glide, gurgling and gushing towards me while I remain still. Without hesitating, I push my hands forward to stop it. The water stops immediately, in full flow, as if someone has magically thrown up an invisible brick wall. The feeling of satisfaction is immense and I revel in the knowledge of my power and the realisation that I can use it whenever I choose. For a moment, I get a glimpse into Aiden's psyche and I panic. But then I remember Rose's murder and his disregard for my safety and I immediately calm down. I know I'm completely different. I know I don't want have his murdering black soul. While I've been thinking about all of this, the water has risen into a wall of liquid so high that I have to tilt my head to see it completely. It pushes against the invisible force that is holding it back. I look to my right and I can clearly see the bottom of the riverbed, littered with debris from several small, wrecked fishing boats. Fish are thrashing about, gasping for the last residuals of water. Contrite, my hands fall lifelessly to my sides. The water pours back into the river, drenching me with freezing cold water from head to toe. One of the fish jumps and slaps me soundly on the side of the face before plunging back into the water. I laugh out loud, rubbing my cheek. Nature shouldn't have to suffer for my excessive use of power.

I think about this as I'm walking back to the cottage in my sodden smelly clothing. I really need to understand how to use my powers without disturbing the balance of nature. My punishment for not doing so was a soaking and a slap on the cheek from a fish. Aiden and Luther, had caused immense damage to the world around them. What would their punishment be? My fantasies of revenge fade as I realise that justice will be done. I wouldn't have to seek it.

Nature will do that for me.

POTENTIAL

Amber Lockwood

I have powers I never knew I possessed. I know Boon told me months ago, but in my heart I didn't dare believe him. I've certainly had plenty of clues. Whenever I have experienced emotional turmoil, my abilities have taken over. Until now, I've been in denial about them. In the months since I arrived, Rowan Cottage and its surrounding area has become my home, my territory, and the place that I feel safe. Walking towards the door, beams of sunlight fall along the wooden flooring of the living room. I leave the cottage and break into a steady run.

I began running again the day after my unexpected river shower and subsequent fish slap. Running has always been my outlet. It doesn't chase away the nightmares, but it helps me to cope with the life I have now. For the first time in my life, I am truly alone. At home I always had Lauren and Elaine. In Greenwood, my adopted family always sheltered me. Even my relationship with Duncan cast me as the vulnerable young girl and him as my protector. The first day I had gone for a run since I arrived at Rowan Cottage was the day it all began to click into place for me. Before that I had kept the powers within me a secret. I feared the implications of setting them free. I had returned to the cottage, my body warm and lethargic. Lingering in front of the fireplace and without thought or intention, I snapped my fingers just like I had seen Duncan do in the past. Instantly the fire flickered to life crackling in the silence of the room. Intrigued, I experimented next with the pile of logs beside the fire. I focused on them and everything else faded away. I closed my eyes, breathed slowly and calmly and visualised the logs rising steadily, almost gracefully, rotating and spinning in the air. I controlled their movements at my whim. When I opened my eyes, my heart leapt, what I had imagined was happening in front of my eyes. I stared in wonder before my concentration lapsed and the logs ricochet back onto the floor with a clatter. I obviously needed practice. So that's exactly what I did every day. Triumphs were small and well earned. And if I overdid things, then nature reminded me, be it with a slap from a fish or a heavy rainfall. I would constantly remind myself of Boon's last lesson. "Don't rush it missy, you need to find your centre. It's different for all of us. Find that place that calms you."

I remembered his calm, serene expression as he made the water from his cup rise into the air and then drop back in again without spilling a single drop. When I look for my centre I think of Duncan. I imagine my body fitting snugly into his, my head below his chin, my hands round his waist, his arms around me, two halves of one whole separated until now by space and time. Destined to be joined together. I still ache when I think of him, but the ache allows me to do something extraordinary and that dulls the pain for a short time. In the afternoons, I venture outside the circle of trees that hide me from the world. I collect water, rummage for food and fish from the river. Boon brings supplies from Greenwood once a month in the dead of night. He barely lingers during these brief visits, keen to return to Dot before the morning light arrives. I don't seek to delay him, despite the fact I miss talk and companionship, and I've even offered to walk part way to lessen his journey. He refuses the offer politely each time I suggest it. I like my own company, my routines and my way of life at Rowan Cottage, and as time passes I realise I have left much of my former mollycoddled self behind. I am travelling the path I was meant to. I was never meant to rely on anyone but myself. It's taken me 19 years to understand that I am in control of my destiny. This realisation is both extraordinary and liberating.

Now I understand my power and my potential.

HAUNTED

Aiden Darkings

I wish the witch would leave me alone. She haunts my dreams - crying, pleading, tears covering her cheeks. It wouldn't be as frustrating if I could actually hear what she is saying. Her mouth shapes the words, but all I hear is silence. As if she is tuned into a frequency I can't hear. The dream wakes me every night and if it wasn't so annoying it would actually be boring. The blonde continues to visit me every night and in the morning I see her rubbing the bruises on her wrists. I have no idea how they got there. Her welfare is none of my concern. I'm not even interested enough to ask what her name is.

Luther warned me there would be remnants of my previous life that would take a while to be erased. I can only assume that my little witch doesn't care for the change in my personality. But she still returns every night for our silent exchange. It's interesting and a useful trick to know that she responds to my words as if she'd been physically struck. It's always useful to have power over somebody. In the meantime, I will use one woman to exorcise another.

Sensio should appreciate the karma in that.

PACK

Amber Lockwood

The small animal in front of me freezes and begins to pant in panic as I draw nearer. By now, I'm used to the unusual in this new world, so I can take this unknown animal well in my stride. I've already encountered a dodo, mermaids and I've heard grey wolves, so this unknown animal in front of me should not cause too much concern. I reach for the small blade at my hip and remind myself to stay calm in case I need to react quickly. In the last six months, I have accepted my abilities as another part of me, respectful of the damage I could inflict if I choose. The animal's feline eyes look at me warily as I approach. Its small, muscular body is shaped like a dog. It has four paws, with tiger like stripes around the bottom half of its body. Its paws are trapped in its mother's pouch, making it easy prey for any passing predator. It tries to snuggle into her body, seeking warmth and safety. But all the life, warmth and safety has already seeped out some time ago from ragged, bloody slashes across her stomach. I vaguely remember hearing the distant howl of wolves and wonder if they were responsible. Remembering my childhood visits, I recall something about an extinct type of tiger from Tasmania that was hunted into extinction. Ruefully, I wonder what other animals I am destined to encounter next.

Reaching into my pocket, I take out a small piece of chicken that I cooked over the fire last night. My allowance of meat from Greenwood was sparse but as my diet mostly consisted of vegetation and fish, some protein was needed.

For a moment, I remember the roast chicken that Lauren used to cook on a Sunday and remember the taste of soft mashed potatoes and soothing gravy. Slowly, I hold it out to the animal. It smells the food and hunger overcomes caution as it leans forward to take the meat from me. I drop it to the ground. The animal sniffs the meat, grabs it with its small, sharp teeth and swallows it ravenously. I manage to get closer to the mother's body and see the paws still trapped within the pouch. Throwing another piece of chicken, I quickly take out my knife, slice the pouch open and free the animal, which growls like a tiger. Now that it's on all fours I can see that it's the size of a small dog. I'm glad it's free, if it had stayed trapped for much longer it would have had little chance of survival.

Holding my hands up, I accept its wrath as it yelps in my direction, indignant at my audacity, looking like a West Highland Terrier having a temper tantrum. I start to laugh and tiger stops yelping, quirked out by the strange noise I'm making. I walk back to the cottage and when I go through the turnstile of trees, I hear branches snap and turn to see the tiger following behind me at a distance. Over the next few weeks, we established a routine where tiger hangs around the cottage, following me at a distance, and accepting the occasional titbit. And as for me? I no longer resemble the girl who had arrived in Sensio in either appearance or spirit. My daily runs have left my muscles taut and my body slim and efficient. My hair has grown down my back into long thick curls that I pull back into a ponytail. My surroundings no longer scared me. I feel at peace here. My growing confidence in my talents has made me believe in myself. I can look after myself. When Boon visited last month he asked for a demonstration. I did it without hesitation, thought or question. My gifts have become so much a part of me that that I use them naturally.

Dusk begins to fall as I move from the river back to the cottage and I begin to hear the noise. When I arrive, tiger is standing in front of a large bush watching me, while a slightly larger dog is watching him, barking persistently. I stand still, watch the interaction and I'm taken by surprise when tiger begins to approach me, both confident and wary. He stops a few feet from me, leans forward and sniffs the air around me, as if trying to sense my mood. Taking his actions as an act of faith I offer my own and slowly extend my hand. He sniffs it curiously then, he licks my finger with his coarse, rough tongue. He turns and runs towards his companion, and they both head off into the trees. I watch him leaving, knowing I would never see him again. Despite our tentative efforts, we will never be true pack mates. He belongs with his own kind, just as I do.

Instinctively, I know that it's nearly time for me to return to my own pack.

PREDETERMINED

Amber Lockwood

My mind and body awaken instantaneously. The dawn light filters through the bedroom curtains and I can see my breath form dragon shaped swirls into the sharp cold air. The stillness is interrupted only by the sound of the wind whistling through the trees and cries of a lone wolf. The hairs on the back of my neck rise as I feel the presence of another drawing ever closer. My heart starts to thump as adrenalin courses through me. I jump out of bed and run to the front door and onto the porch, searching the darkness for the source of my fear. I hear footsteps coming towards me and my heart thunders in my ears. A figure emerges from the trees, but I can't see it properly because there isn't enough light. My eyes gradually adjust and I see thick dark hair and a chin now covered with a beard. Dark blue eyes meet mine and I release a sob of relief as Duncan reaches me, grabs me, holding me against him.

He lifts me up, strides into the house and kicks the door closed. I'm trapped willingly between his body and the cold hard wood of the door behind me. My hands move over him, reassuring myself that he was really here and this is not another cruel dream. He leans his forehead on mine; his beard is soft against my lips and he whispers my name, searching for my mouth. We stumble into the bedroom and I close the door with a flick of my hand. He smiles indulgently, snaps his fingers to light the fire in the hearth, casting a soft glow over us. Walking me back until the back of my legs touched the bed, I watched silently as he removed his clothes one by one, my hands stayed at my side, yearning to touch him but unsure of where to start. He strokes my face and I pull his body against mine and he takes my mouth, claiming it, intense, deep. I moved my hands over his chest and feel the edge of a bandage on his lower abdomen, looking down I see dried blood.

"It's nothing, it doesn't matter," he whispers, trailing a finger down my cheek.

He gently pulls my nightgown over my head and lets it sweep soundlessly to the floor. Shyness sweeps over me as I stood in front of him bared as I have never been to another. Duncan takes a sharp breath and pushing me back into the bed moving over me, his arms at the side of my face, caging me in. As his lips move down my body, I think I stop breathing, my body becomes languid, melting to his touch. My hands caught in his hair and pulled him towards me impatiently he chuckled at my efforts to distract him. Returning to lie above me once more, I look into his eyes, his gaze intense but soft as he looked into my soul. His large body tense and dominating. He threads his fingers through mine and whispers "Mine" into my ear as we join together. I cry into his mouth as the pain appears and fades. In this one precious moment, my world alters forever. Duncan pauses, searching my eyes and pushes into an unknown rhythm that sweeps us together until we lay together, our bodies glistening with sweat and looking at each other in wonder. Duncan props himself up on his elbow and leans over me, a smile playing about his lips.

"You're mine now Amber," he whispers, trailing a finger

down my cheek and across my bottom lip, until I catch it, biting softly into the fleshy padded finger.

"You're mine too," I whisper, pulling him closer. He laughs as he kisses me. Then he pulls me to him and loves me again.

We talk through the night, into the day and into the early hours of the next morning. Most of the men who had left Greenwood had perished in a battle with Black Knights a month ago. Duncan, his father and others have formed an alliance with the other villages and species. Returning to Greenwood when word reached them of the attack on the village, Boon had told him where to find me.

"We need you to come home," he says determinedly.

I remain quiet, conflicted, and nervous about going back. Greenwood is no longer the home I once imagined. Duncan curves his body around mine as we sleep, his face buried in my hair, our bodies breathing as one. Morning comes too soon. My insides churned as I collect all my belongings from the cottage that had become my home. Hitching my bag over my shoulder, I take a last look at the sparse furnishings, knowing I will miss my uncomplicated existence here. We chat easily on the way back, sharing myself with him has only strengthened my trust in him. But there's a shadow that crosses his face from time to time and because I suspect that Aiden is the cause I keep my own counsel.

Greenwood is busy but subdued when we arrive. Duncan's hand holds mine tightly as we walk past the crowd, my cheeks burning. The once friendly faces are now wary and resentful. I understand. My Mate is alive and well whilst they have lost a family member. Aiden and I had brought the Black Knights here.

When I walk into the Darkings home, I feel as if I'm stepping back into a very old memory. Daniel and Maggie sit quietly near the fire. My mouth dries up. What can I say to them to make up for the loss of their daughter? Then I notice the small, slight figure in the chair beside them. Sable dark hair that was once thick and shiny hangs limp against her shoulders and the once healthy cheeks are thin, the very life and soul ripped from her.

"Rose, you're alive..." I broke off on a sob.

Rose turns to look at me with pain-filled eyes. "Amber, you don't understand. Aiden saved me."

SIBLING

Amber Lockwood

The room erupts. Daniel and Maggie rush towards Rose and talk over each other. Maggie cries as she stokes her daughter's cheek. Rose stands on wobbly legs and tries to move towards me. I help her to sit down and kneel beside her.

"What do you want to tell me Rose?"

"Aiden took it off and gave it to me."

Reaching into her pocket, she pulls out his amulet and passes it to me.

She says earnestly, "You need to give the amulet back to him so he can come home. That day...he whispered to me to stay quiet, cut his own hand on his knife and smeared it on my clothes to make it look like he'd killed me."

When I recovered from the shock of her revelation, I slipped his amulet on beside mine and suddenly everything became clear, everything changed.

"We need to help him," I announce to the silent room.

The loud crash when it came is unexpected and makes everyone jump. Turning, I see Duncan remove his hand from the wall, covered in splinters of woods and blood.

"Like hell we will. Aiden told me he left you to get raped or worse. He didn't know if you're alive or dead, not that either result mattered to him."

I couldn't back down. "He released my bonds Duncan. He gave me a chance to run."

He whirls, pulling his shirt up, revealing the bandage, covered in fresh blood.

"Who do you think gave me this?" He turns his back on me, dismissing me and joins his family, leaving me to stand isolated. Alone. I walk into the bedroom I had once occupied. A film of dust covers the furnishings, making it clear that no one had entered the room in my absence. The amulet grew warmer as I picked up the small journal on my bedside table, the symbol of my mysterious beginnings. I opened and read the message inside. 'Amber, it's time for you to read our mother's journal. I hope you understand. Please stay safe, Aiden.'

When I go back downstairs the Darkings look at me cautiously, fearing what I'll bring upon them next. My heart sinks as I look at Duncan, leaning against the wall, his arms folded.

"Look at it," I ask him, holding the journal out to him, beseeching him to look at the message that I knew could make him understand.

He remains immobile, his jaw set, refusing to lift his hand.

"I'm not interested Amber. The cost has been too high."

Stock still I look at him, my heart processing the words. He refuses to try. He doesn't believe in me. I know, as far as I'm concerned, this is a moment that will define us. Am I the girl who arrived in Sensio all those months ago, who thought others knew better and allowed them to make her decisions?

Or am I the person at Rowan Cottage, a woman who knows her own mind and stays true to herself? My throat constricts with suppressed tears as I bend down to Rose and whisper in her ear. She nods and holds my hands for a moment before I smile at her and squeeze hers back. I put my bag over my shoulder, and turn to look at everyone one last time.

"Thank you for everything."

I avoid looking at him. It hurts too much.

I walk out of the door, and he follows me.

"Amber you can't leave. How will I keep you safe?" he said, frustration lacing his tone.

My heart sank. He really had no idea what he had done. Was that what our relationship had become; his responsibility for my safety?

"You'll never let me follow my own path will you?"

Duncan's face is taut with hidden emotion, his eyes blazing. He stays silent, trying to find the words to make it right. He doesn't understand. It's already too late.

"I love you Duncan. If I can't believe in myself," I placed my hand on my heart, "how can I expect you too?"

I take a deep breath and force out the words that will break my heart.

"I release your oath to me. You're free to pursue another Mate."

An image of Duncan and Caroline suddenly flashes into my

consciousness, and I am overwhelmed with jealousy. I feel sick to my stomach. But I carry on walking. Duncan strides towards me, grabs my shoulder and pulls me towards him.

"No Amber, I don't release you. Last night changed everything." He pours his soul into the frantic kiss and my body sags, loving him, wanting him, my heart breaking. I tear myself away from him. I can't stop myself from stroking his cheek and looking deeply into his dark blue eyes. I walk away and feel his body calling mine, pulling mine back to him. I ignore it and walk faster. Part of me desperately wants to surrender and stay with him, but I know that I won't be able to live with myself if I ignore what my heart is telling me to do. I have to trust my own instincts and follow my own path.

The residents of Greenwood stare at me silently as I leave. It no longer matters. My twin has called to me. He is my blood and I have to follow him and find him, wherever it may lead.

THE KINSHIP CHRONICLES

Scatter of Kin

CASSIE KENNEDY

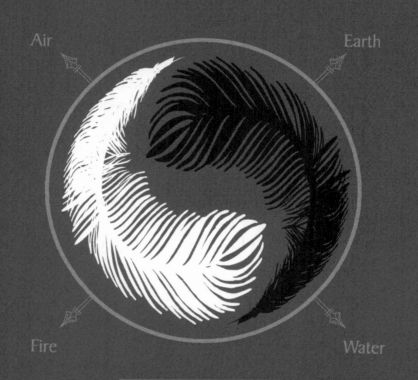

Air

Earth

Fire

Water

4 elements
3 parts
2 sides
1 last chance
0 the time is now

Illustrations & Poetry by
BRIGID

"Make a wish on a breath of air,

Pray the wind to carry with care,

Scattering of kin, so necessary & needed,

for without it,

those wishes would never be seeded."

…Scatter of Kin

Scatter of Kin

HISTORY
Amber Lockwood

I am so scared. I knew when I left Greenwood that my journey would have its challenges. But I hoped that my bravado in the face of Duncan's doubts would remain a viable and permanent part of my character. The whispers of self-doubt began at dusk on the first night. I'd found a disused building, home to numerous bugs and mice and I got a small fire going, warding away the dirty musk permeating the air.

"You brought this upon us."

"The cost has been too high."

Now, three days later I keep hearing these words, the images circle around my head, a visual manifestation of my doubts. I keep seeing the look on Maggie and Duncan's faces. I keep remembering Rose's listlessness, the life sucked from her. I close my eyes and put my hands over my ears, as if the physical act will push away the sounds and images. Stop them. Silence them. But it doesn't work. Instead, they wait in anticipation, planning their next attack. I must stay strong, if I have any chance of saving Aiden and live up to the belief he had in me, I must banish these thoughts. Forever.

I try instead to think about Rowan Cottage: the lush greenery, the calming melody of the river and the image of Duncan walking out of the dark towards me. My chest tightens at that image and I try to push it away. It hurts too much to think of him.

I look up into the darkness. Tonight, my home is a small cave. Snow is falling delicately and persistently, as if it's being sieved through the sky and I decide to take cover inside. A small fire is burning and casting flickering, hypnotic shadows on the walls and I pull my blanket around me, gradually thawing out. I'm desperate to believe in something, to hear a voice of encouragement that will help me move forward with any sort of fortitude. I clutch the journal with its worn binding in my cold clammy hands. This little book has represented the questions I've been asking for years and if I were able to read it everything that seemed grey would finally lock into black and white. If only I possessed the courage to open the first page. As the whispers began to speak once more, I silence them by opening the journal. My heart hammers as I study the elegant handwriting and as I begin to read I realise I'm no longer alone.

I'm meeting my mother for the first time.

PURPLE SKIES

Rora Ravenswood

I've never kept a journal before. You can't really count jotting dentists' and hairdressers' appointments on Nana's cute animal-adorned calendar that hangs in the kitchen. Yesterday, I put the calendar in a box, along with most of Nana's other possessions. It's hard to pack someone's life away. To put away treasures lovingly placed on the mantelpiece away from sight. Every ornament has a memory that reminds me of how much she meant to me. I still can't believe she's gone.

Nana never seemed old. She was spritely, exactly as she'd been when I first came to live with her after Mum and Dad died in a car crash. I was only 12. But despite losing her only son and her daughter-in-law less than a week before, she still put the radio on and danced around the kitchen to make me smile. It's hard to understand that someone so full of life and laughter could go to sleep one night and not wake up the next morning. She's been there all my life, the invisible support system I took for granted until it was taken away. I feel so alone. Lauren tells me that she and I will always be family, but my heart aches with loneliness. It's the right time to leave for another world.

My forays into Sensio began accidentally a year after I lost Mum and Dad. I was 13, grieving and full of angst ridden hormones. I sought sanctuary in the dense forest at the back of our cottage for a few hours, losing myself within nature, until I came upon the stepping-stones past the white birch tree, and followed them, curiously. It wasn't until I found myself in a clearing with a purple sky and two moons that I realised I'd gone too far. Certainly, the shock on the face of the girl who stumbled upon me definitely confirmed it. But the fact that we lived in different realms only encouraged Maggie and I to become friends. She'd gone for a walk that day to lose herself as well. Daniel, her future Mate and the boy she loved had no idea she existed.

She makes me laugh. You know that laugh that starts in your belly and just makes your whole body shake silently, and makes the tears roll down your face? That's what I remember of my teenage years. If Nana and Lauren noticed a difference they didn't mention it. I couldn't tell them about Sensio. I made a promise to Maggie and I had to honour it. Boon says it's time for me to make a commitment. He believes I'm upsetting the natural balance by living between two worlds. I can't explain it but it feels right to go now. Just as I know it feels right to start writing in the brown journal I came across yesterday. I feel like I'm being pulled down a road where the ending is uncertain but irresistible and I want to record what happens. Lauren and I said goodbye this afternoon. She thinks I'm going travelling around Europe for a year or two. Little does she know I'm leaving for another world. At least there I won't be alone.

SHADOW

Rose Darkings

I look at my reflection in the mirror and don't recognise the person staring back at me. I only ever used the mirror for ten seconds at a time; a quick glance to make sure my hair was in place. Where is the thick dark hair that used to gleam and hang past my shoulders? Where are the cheeks that used to glow with health as I ran from one adventure to another? That's how I saw my life, as one big adventure to be experienced, aware that if I needed help, all I had to do was ask for it.

That perception changed forever six months ago. That's when I had my first dream of him. I knew him, better than I knew myself, but that night changed how I saw him. I remember touching his hand, something I did naturally without thought. But this time was different. It excited me. I looked at him as if for the first time and saw the real man – the thick lashes framing his brown eyes and the lock of thick dark hair on his forehead that I had to stop myself from pushing back into place. I looked up at my family, sitting around the shadowy room. They were smiling, nodding, and supporting the emotions I was trying to hide from them. That's when I realised I was dreaming of him. My Mate.

When I woke up the next morning, I felt only excitement. I looked in the mirror as I brushed my hair. The girl looking back at me had sparkling eyes and cheeks glowing with excitement. All I could think about was being with him.

When I was dressed and ready, I opened the door and

looked around. I spotted him immediately. He and Warwick were walking away from the village towards the forest. Curious, I followed. In the quiet of the woods, I was able to hear their voices.

"I can't do this anymore Warwick," Aiden said.

"You have to lad, we're so close."

Aiden turned suddenly, and I hid behind a large bush. He looked different, pacing backwards and forwards over the same patch of woodland, repeatedly dragging his hands through his hair, his cheeks flushed red with agitation, and his brown eyes laminated in the shadows.

"It's been months. I don't know who I am anymore," he bit out.

My heart ached for him and I yearned to take away the pain of whatever was hurting him.

"You just need to breathe lad. Go to the Great Hall and get it into perspective. You know why we're doing this."

Aiden walked off without saying goodbye to Warwick, who headed in the opposite direction. Hiding in the shadows I felt exposed as he walked past, but the direction of his stare towards The Great Hall was absolute. I stood still for a moment, deciding what to do. I waited until everything was quiet and headed back towards Greenwood. I walked through the village, walking amongst people I'd known all my life, but this was first time I ever felt separate from them. Seeing Warwick's front door slightly ajar, I took the silent invitation and slipped inside, and crept silently down the stairs. The flickering sconces lit the way casting an ethereal glow all the around me, and I felt nervous as I neared him. At the bottom of the stairs, I saw Aiden hunched over the lectern, his hands clenches into the element, sharing his burden with the wood. Edging closer, I saw him actually shaking with an effort to control himself, like the slightest push would tip him over a precipice he'd never come back from. Without thinking, I put my hand on his shoulder. He whirled round and pushed me back against the stone wall.

"Rose, what are you doing here?" he bit out, when he realised it was me.

Looking up into his anguished face, I said the words I promised to keep to myself.

"You're my Mate Aiden."

The colour drained from his face. He ducked his head away from me and wouldn't meet my eyes. "I'm not fit to be anyone's Mate, Rose. Look at me."

I said nothing, unconsciously leaning closer, breathing in his scent. I moved my hands to circle the muscled arms at either side of me. Awareness trickled through my limbs and curled languidly in my stomach.

I put my arms around him and held him to me. The effect was electric. At his touch, heat coursed through my body. I looked up at him and saw him not as Aiden, the family ward, but as Aiden the man.

He jumped away from my touch, as if I'd burned him. "Rose … please go before I do something I regret."

I ignored the warning and pressed on. "I don't want to go Aiden. You know we're meant to be together."

I tried to pull him close, but he tensed up, and when he finally raised his head and met my eyes, he seemed different. Feral. Pulling me against him, his hands gripped my hair, his mouth searching my face until it found my mouth and he began to kiss me softly at first, until he plundered my mouth roughly. Just as quickly, I was released to stand on shaky limbs, feeling lost. Confused. As Aiden stalked away and violently kicked the lectern and pushed it to the ground, then walked around the table and threw each chair against the wall until it broke into splinters. One chair dislodged a ceremonial sword from its case, and it fell clattering onto the stone floor, the ringing of the metal reverberating loudly around the room. I looked at Aiden, bewildered. He stared back at me and, as if in slow motion, I watched him pick up the sword and walk towards me, pointing the blade straight at my face.

"You better run before I get you Rose," he whispered, narrowing his eyes.

I stared at him. I didn't recognise his voice. I didn't recognise him. What had I done? Tears fell as I saw my Mate move towards me with the sole intention of hurting me. I ran, scrambling back up the stairs and all the way home without stopping or looking back. A sob broke from my throat as I opened my eyes to the present and looked at my reflection in the mirror. I don't recognise the person staring back at me. My hair hangs lifelessly down my back, black shadows haunt my eyes and my face is wet with tears. Six months ago, I looked like a young girl in love. And now? Now I've become a shadow of myself.

SILENCE

Rose Darkings

Why can't they understand I don't want to talk about it? I still function. I get up in the morning, I bathe, I get dressed, I eat and I drink. I go to bed and do the same thing the next day. I do what I must to survive, but I'm not alive. My former life is like a hazy memory, a dual existence that teases me but floats away before I can grab hold of it. I feel Mum watching me. She talks to me as if we're having a conversation, except my part is spoken in silence. I haven't spoken since that day. I want to, but I can't. Sometimes, I will the fire that used to light my belly to spark and come alight. But the effort is futile and exhausting. I tried to speak yesterday after Warwick visited, bringing Mum a medicinal version of brew. She was so pleased, so hopeful. But then Warwick left and her façade and hope faded. She sat beside me, took my hand and pleaded with me to come back to her. Her hand tightened on mine holding me in place whilst she sobbed out her grief, pleading with me to return to world where she and life existed. I desperately want to answer her, to give her some hope. But how can I leave this place inside me that protects me, hides me from the images that hurt whenever I think of them? It would be too painful.

Swallowing, I try to push the words past the broken glass trapped in my dry throat. I open my mouth but only silence comes out. I close my eyes and wish Mum would disappear, taking her grief and disappointment with her. Instead sounds, images and feelings from that day overwhelm me again.

I see myself running away from the Great Hall towards home, tears blurring my eyes. I hear the lick of flames, swords clashing, men shouting and high-pitched screams of the women. I crash into my bedroom, my sanctuary, only to be dragged off my bed and told to move. I feel Amber pulling my hand, insisting we leave. I see the Black Knights circling us, I feel Amber pushing me behind her to protect me and then I saw him, the one who destroyed me, and I buried my face against the back of Amber's jacket to hide from him. Aiden walked towards Amber like a skilled predator and I heard the slap as he hit her, like a crack from a cannon, so loud in the absolute silence, broken only by the Knights who surrounded us. Then he pulled me into his arms, but not to love me or kiss me, his hands were hard and bruising and bit into my skin, as he held the knife to my throat and gently across my skin until I felt a warm trickle of blood wet my hair. In that moment, my heart shattered into a thousand pieces. My soul mourned for what would never be and my heart filled with a passionate hate I never thought I was capable of.

The memories usually halt there, but today, they persist, determined and relentless. I'm on the ground, coughing dust. I can feel the villagers watching me, unwilling witnesses to my execution. I stop fighting and give into the inevitable. A harsh intake of breath makes me open my eyes and I see Aiden cutting deep into his palm with the blade. His blood flows all over my clothes and body and he whispers, pleading, "Keep still." He plunges the knife into the ground beside me and the crowd gasps in horror. He locks his amulet into my hand and whispers, "Give it to Amber," before getting up and pushing me roughly away with his foot.

The shock of these memories hits me like a sledgehammer and my body finally gives up. When I wake, Amber is standing over me, saying my name, her face pale and pinched in the warm firelight. I look around and see Mum, Dad and Duncan, watching me anxiously. The words rush through my throat knocking away the broken glass trapped within. My voice is small and rough.

"Amber, you don't understand. Aiden saved me."

Then all at once it's mayhem. Mum rushes towards me, sobbing, Dad sits down on the floor and his face crumples and Amber and Duncan start to argue. Somebody offers me a cup of brew and I swallow it gratefully. I hear Amber and Duncan leaving the house, their rising voices outside. I try to get to my feet to placate them, but Mum holds me still. I sit quietly and remember Warwick's visit from yesterday. His innocent questions to Mum about me, about what I'd told her. Then I remembered the conversation that Aiden and Warwick had before Aiden changed. What was the argument about? What made him behave like that? I'm consumed with curiosity and I need to see Warwick to find out the answers to these questions. If nothing else, I've earned the right to ask them.

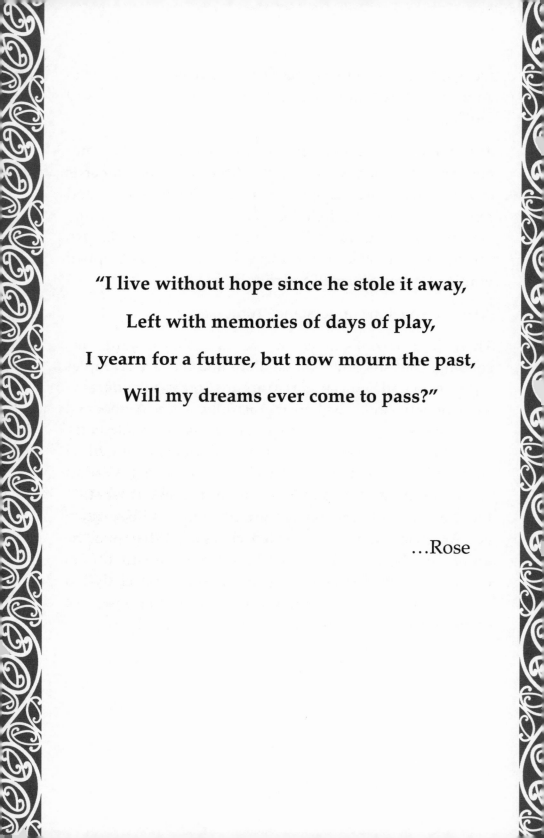

"I live without hope since he stole it away,

Left with memories of days of play,

I yearn for a future, but now mourn the past,

Will my dreams ever come to pass?"

…Rose

Rose

NEW LIFE

Rora Ravenswood

I have settled quickly into my new life in Sensio. The decision to leave was made for me. All the elements that held me on Earth disappeared leaving open a path to Sensio. Nana is gone and Lauren is at nursing college. I'm alone, apart from Maggie. I still remember Nana's funeral. I didn't cry all day. I watched, numb, as the casket holding the woman who raised me was lowered into the ground. Back at the cottage, filled by lifelong friends and neighbours, I handed out cups of tea and sausage rolls exchanging words of gratitude for words of condolence. Then everybody left, darkness fell and the cottage became still and silent.

I walked into the kitchen and was overwhelmed by a memory of my first day at the cottage. Nana and I had sat at the worn wooden table and to break the silence, she had lifted down one of the dozen teapots that decorated the top of the kitchen cabinet and proceeded to demonstrate proper tea etiquette. I still remember it. Tea should always be made in the pot, not in the cup and a lady always adds a drop of milk after the tea, which must first be brewed to caramel colour perfection. Once she had served the tea in bone china cups, she began to speak quietly but positively about my Mum growing up, how she met Dad, the day they came here with me as a baby and how she watched me grow first into a toddler, then into a little girl. As she spoke, she smiled, her memories genuinely happy. She promised I would feel like this one day, once I stopped feeling so sad. She was right of course and through all the years I lived at the cottage, not a day passed without us sitting at the same table, with a different teapot, speaking of school, friends, college and boys.

That night, after everyone was gone, the sight of the worktop strewn with teapots that symbolised the life we shared, brought home to me that it was gone forever. Nana wasn't going to be there to pour the tea any more. Tears blurred my vision as I faced the truth of my life. I was now alone. Moving away from the hurt, I ran towards the door and into the woods, tears streaming down my face. I reached the white birch tree and past it, to Sensio, where I was loved and wanted and could be happy. When I got to the clearing, I collapsed on the ground, lungs burning and body shaking uncontrollably.

I was vaguely aware of Maggie's small but strong arms holding me, as she whispered, "Rora, it's going to be okay, I promise."

The next thing I knew I was being carried in Boon's arms, and Maggie was walking beside him. The villagers watched us in curious silence, accepting of my presence but not yet fully welcoming it. Boon had discovered our secret friendship five years before. The first time I met him, he scared me senseless. He was an intimidating figure, standing lean and tall, with shoulder length blonde hair. He peppered Maggie with questions asking why she was consorting with someone from the other realm, studying me with a scowl that appeared embedded into his face. Now after years of knowing him, I understand this behaviour. For Boon is a man with a keen sense of right and wrong. He believes that the Natural Laws of Sensio are absolute and should be followed with unquestioning loyalty. He reported our friendship to the High Council, and volunteered to be my mentor, monitor my visits and teach me the Natural Laws. He also, quite unexpectedly, became a friend into the bargain.

I stayed in Sensio for two days before I returned to the cottage, seeking sanctuary in this world that had found me. It was during that time that Boon told me I had to make a choice: he was worried about the effect that living my life in two worlds would have on the natural balance. The decision was easy. My family was gone. Lauren had a full life at nursing college. My existence was unnecessary. Here in Sensio, I could play a role and share responsibilities. So once more, Boon went to the High Council, accompanied by Maggie and her Mum Primrose, to advocate for me. My choice to stay here indefinitely was accepted and Boon remained my mentor. The villagers slowly accepted my presence and the questioning silence has for the most part been replaced by a nod and a reluctant smile. Some are still resistant and very vocal about it. Ruth Gentles is no fan of mine. I tried to talk to her once, but she just walked past me, like I wasn't even there.

So here I am, a month into my new life and still a creature of habit. Some habits stay with you forever. Just as I sat at a table with Nana and shared a pot of tea, now every day I take a long walk. Every day, I make my way to the clearing from the edge of the village and wonder through the woods. This is my favourite time of day; it calms me, fills my head and lungs with fresh air and helps me review my lesson with Boon. Every day it's just me, with the whispering of the trees and the pull of the wind. Today my surroundings are silent with an eerie twinge. I pull my jacket tight around me, listening, watching and waiting for something unknown. A heavy snort made me jump. Whirling around I freeze. In front of me is a huge animal, its coal black coat shimmering with sweat, its reigns are fringed in a luxurious, heavy gold and royal blue fabric. As I look up at the rider, my view is partially obstructed by a single, horn emerging from its head. It dawns on me that this majestic, beautiful animal is none other than a mythical unicorn.

Still trying to wrap my head around the reality of a piece of folklore living and breathing in front of me I looked up and found myself caught by ocean blue eyes fringed with thick dark lashes, a sharp nose and firm, full generous lips. He has thick, dark wavy hair, and his chin covered by a beard that's looks silky to the touch. My hand tingles with the desire to touch it. Languid energy smoothed and scintillated, running from my smallest toe to the top of my head, making me feel relaxed and poised for something I couldn't identify. He smiles like he understands the effect he has upon me. Mentally shaking myself, I step back, interpreting his smugness for arrogance and I feel my usually even temper rise. I turn away and walk off, masking my confusion with action. He laughs – a deep, rich laugh – like I was performing a comedic act for his sole benefit. I whirl around but the unicorn is trotting steadily away and disappointment I can't fathom washes over me. I walk back to the village, trying to make sense of what has just happened and dismissing it because I can't. But I'm certain of one thing - this charismatic rider and I will meet again.

PLAYING

Aiden Darkings

For as long as I can remember, I've always played a role. As a child, I was conscious that when I was in an environment with particular people, I would adopt a personality that helped me to fit in. I had to. You need to learn to adapt when you're the child of a woman from another world and a father who has abandoned you. My only legacy is a woman's amulet, hardly worth the metal it's made with. I have to rely on my own skills and so far they've served me well. Now I'm playing the role of the bastard who betrayed the village that adopted him. The prize became too tempting to resist, the chance to have more power than I ever dreamed of. I can almost touch it, like a mythical cup just out of reach but never fully within my grasp. Luther and I use each other. When we struck our deal he was very clear about what he wanted, just as I was. He wanted Amber.

The Black Knights started off as a noble cause. After the old King came to power they were formed to keep the peace within the villages and to prevent any further resurrections against the throne. Then Luther joined their ranks and they became infected with evil and cruelty. And he was very good at explaining away his actions whenever the whispers of unjust violence reached the King's court. They would be noted, dismissed as necessary, and then no further action taken. The exploits of the Black Knights filtered through to Greenwood via Morgan Rose, our representative to the King's court and I fantasised about joining their ranks and finally having the status that was my right, that truly reflected my talents.

I've never been taken seriously in my own right. I was always Daniel's ward. I was the fortunate boy who became Maggie's lucky adopted son and Duncan's younger brother. And in the last few months, I've had the indignity of being Amber's twin. They'll all rue the day they judged me unworthy of what I'm due. They'll remember the name Aiden Darkings. Duncan certainly won't forget. Not after what happened two weeks ago. I came across him in the woods. I knew he'd bonded long enough with Amber to sense something was wrong with his Mate and he wouldn't rest until he found her. I knew he would only stop briefly before he planned to be on his way again. Duncan is like his father and thinks strategically in any situation. I watched him for a while, washing his hands and face in the river, then I called his name. He looked up, startled, pleased at first, and then confused to see me so far from my sworn duty in Greenwood.

"Aiden … What are you doing here?" Duncan said.

He stared at me, bewildered. Then his eyes narrowed as he looked at my shiny black armour and I waited for the jigsaw pieces to click into place. I smiled when he reached for his sword and started towards me.

"So the penny's finally dropped. Don't you want to know about Amber, brother?" I taunted.

He stopped immediately, my words cutting him deep just as I knew they would.

"I'm trying to remember the last time I saw her … Oh yes. Now I remember… She was running away from five Black Knights who wanted to show her a good time. I wonder what on earth, excuse the pun, happened to her?"

I watched the words chip away at Duncan's resolve. His body shook slightly at war with taking me to task for my words and running off to make sure his Mate was safe. Duncan was always the victor in our sword fights as children. So assured of his position as the son of Greenwood Protector that he's become arrogant in his abilities. I got satisfaction from bringing him this low by distracting him with a few simple words. Pressing the tip of my sword into his belly I nicked the skin with its blade. Blood immediately spurted from the wound and almost simultaneously flames licked along the sword blade and began to consume the handle, melting my thick black gloves until I had no choice but to drop the sword and remove them. Duncan mounted his horse and turned to face me. His blue eyes darkened as we stared at each other, aware of the chasm that I just opened between us. We were now soldiers for different allegiances.

"That's just for starters Aiden," he shouted, as he spurred the horse into a gallop. "I'll see you soon."

I laughed as he disappeared into the distance. Now I know his true weakness, I won't hesitate to use it again. When I returned to camp, I had already removed the mask of the jealous brother and replaced it with that of the bastard betrayer of Greenwood. As I rubbed the burns on my hands, I anticipated the pleasurable distractions that Sierra would provide. After all, I have earned it. Later that night, I fell asleep sated, with a genuine smile on my face.

Playing any good part well is truly exhausting.

FATED

Rora Ravenswood

I have always known Maggie would make a beautiful bride. The reason we met that day in the clearing was because the boy she loved, Daniel, had no idea she existed. I can still see her. Arms hanging listlessly from her small body as she walked in indiscriminate circles, wiping tears from her face and sniffing loudly to clear her nose. That was the day I found out about the Sensio approach to love. Everyone has a predetermined soul mate, selected before you're born and their identity is revealed through dreams. The night before we met, Maggie had had her first dream about Daniel. But when she saw him the next morning, breathless and in the throes of young love, she came upon him kissing another girl and ran to the clearing and into my life. I can't help thinking that some sort of serendipity was at work on that day. Taking me, a grieving orphan, to another world at the same time on the same day that Maggie sought refuge in the clearing. All I know is that Maggie is more than a friend: she is like a sister to me. She's intelligent, fearless and loyal, a cog in the wheel of my adopted family along Nana and Lauren.

The first time I walked through Greenwood I remember feeling truly intimidated. Everyone stopped and stared at me, the village falling to an incremental silence so still I had to fight the desire to run away. Maggie on the other hand, drew her barely five foot self up to her full height, stood with her hands on her hips and shouted.

"Does everyone have a problem? Come on! Speak your peace then!"

When silence was the loud reply she pulled my hand and hauled me into her house, slamming the door so loudly, the noise echoed round the village for several seconds. I still laugh the memory of her stalking round the kitchen, bristling like lion infuriated that someone had dared to threaten one of her cubs. Not surprisingly, I met Boon for the first time ten minutes later.

As the years passed by and I visited the village on a regular basis, Greenwood gradually began to accept me. I'm not surprised that they looked at me as if I was an alien on that first visit. My appearance on that first day would have been disconcerting to anyone who'd never seen flared jeans, a white tank top and platform boots. So from then I kept a bag of clothes at the back of my wardrobe that I dubbed my 'Sensio uniform.' Maggie confided in me regularly about her feelings for Daniel. She would follow him with adoring eyes as he strode purposely around the village. When he flirted with a pretty girl Maggie would visibly shrivel up and look the other way, hiding the sheen of tears in her eyes. I hoped Daniel would come to his senses but Maggie warned me that Sensio men only realise who their Mate is as they grow older and she would have to wait until he was ready. The boys in the village were friendly, but none stirred my interest. Sometimes, I found myself wondering if there was someone out there just for me. Then I would witness a dip in Maggie's emotions and feel contrite; fated Mates experience high emotions.

One morning after I'd been living in Sensio for a while, we

were in the kitchen baking for the village, up to our elbows in flour, when the front door burst open, banging against the wall and making us jump. Daniel stood in the doorway, his large frame almost filling the space, silhouetted against the sun. Without saying a word, he walked quickly towards Maggie, picked her up and kissed her passionately. Shocked but delighted, she quickly responded, pressing her small flour covered hands into his thick dark hair and holding him tightly. I giggled, exited discreetly and left them to it. I wasn't surprised when later that evening, Daniel and Maggie announced that they were going to be formally mated.

A month ago, Maggie had rarely spoken to Daniel. Now she can't take a step without him following her with his eyes. A situation she's delighted with. He loves her deeply without wanting to change her or temper her spirit. I can only hope that if ever fall in love I am as fortunate. The mating ceremony is similar to weddings on Earth, with wedding clothes, a Sensio version of a bridesmaid and best man, and the wedding guests, in this case, the entire village of Greenwood. Maggie even insisted we have a Sensio version of a hen night where we consumed far too much brew and had to get a special potion from Warwick the next day to help us recover.

Snapping out of my reverie I concentrate on adjusting Maggie's dress. I walk behind her down the makeshift aisle, my feet crunching against leaves and small pieces of bark. As she and Daniel meet at the top of the aisle, I look up into the face of Daniel's best man, the childhood friend he'd spoken off so fondly, the one that arrived late last night.

Rooted to the spot, my heart thumps against my ribcage, as I find myself looking into deep blue eyes fringed with thick black eyelashes, the thick, silky dark hair and the beard that had been recently groomed. His mouth twisted into a smile in recognition as he pinned me with his stare.

His hair had been brushed back tidily only but I could see the wind pulling it into waves and his beard had been recently groomed. Looking away, I contemplated the circumstances that found me in the company of the mysterious rider I'd met months ago and he's staring intently at me, his smile twisting in recognition and laughter dancing in his eyes. The effect is disconcerting and I fight the urge to flee the steely intent behind them. I flush self-consciously, and concentrate all my efforts on listening to Maggie and Daniel taking their vows. But I can still feel him looking.

He knows.

INTRODUCTION

Rora Ravenswood

I want to escape. It's early evening, the bright purple has now faded to a dusky hue, casting shadows into dark places. The dancers are thrown into relief by the glow and flicker of the firelight, their silhouettes jumping and twirling to the music. Chortled laugher at different volumes spills from the tables gathered in a circle around the wishing well. The village is relaxed and celebrating. The mating feast, prepared and cooked by all, has been enjoyed, consumed and is nearly depleted. Today has been a joint celebration: Daniel has been confirmed as successor to his father as Greenwood's Protector, meaning that Maggie will be moving to the large house at the end of the village. Greenwood is happy and relaxed. I wish I could share that emotion. I've felt his eyes on me all day. Maggie introduced us when sat down to begin the feast.

"Rora, have you met…"

"Will Thornton," the rider said to me, extending his hand. "Good to meet you."

His voice was deep and cultured, like rich dark hot chocolate. He held onto my hand until I tugged and won it back again. Daniel looked at him curiously and leaned forward to speak to him. I quickly turned away and offered to help Maggie rearrange the curls that had escaped from her headdress. Moving away quickly, Maggie and I walk towards home and unable to help myself, I turn round and look at him. Daniel is asking him something, but instead of answering he lifts a cup of brew to his mouth and swallows it, watching me all the time. I shiver involuntarily. No one has ever made me so … nervous.

"He's rather intense isn't he?" Maggie asks.

I can feel her watching my reaction. Unsure of exactly what I'm feeling I decide to distract her.

"So how does it feel to be Maggie Darkings then?"

Maggie blushes, her face lighting up with her smile. "Oh Rora, you've no idea" she says, giggling, like a teenager.

As she talks, my mind wanders. I think about Will and the strength of my reaction to him. I just don't understand it. After months in the village, I'm used to the company of men. At school and in my brief few months at college before Nana died, I made as many male friends as female. Daniel and his peers are gentlemanly in their conduct. There are whispers of one person's involvement with another but gossip is not generally encouraged or fostered by the Natural Laws. My contact with men has been cordial and platonic – until now. I've never felt so flustered in a man's company that I had to get away from him as soon as I could. I never looked at a man and wondered how his lips would feel against mine - until now.

Later in the evening, I stand on the periphery of the celebrations, watching Daniel and Maggie dance slowly in the dying firelight. They fit naturally together, despite the fact he is so tall and she so petite. I see Ruth Gentles shimmering blonde hair out of the corner of my eye. She walks towards Will and starts to talk to him animatedly. Her arms move expressively at her sides like she is conducting a silent symphony, the movement against the firelight almost hypnotic in the shadows. I force myself to look away to quell the nervous flutters dancing in my stomach.

"May I have this dance?" I turn to see Morgan Rose bowing down theatrically in front of me.

Laughing, I return the gesture and I'm swept into a dance. Since I first came here, Morgan has always sought me out, asking endless questions about the world I came from and telling me about Sensio in a way I can understand. As he is taking over from his father as Greenwood's representative at the King's court next year, he visits the court regularly and tells me funny stories about all the characters, their opulent clothes and their methods of seeking favour with the courtiers. Morgan is charming and engaging company.

"May I cut in?" We stop and turn around.

Morgan bows graciously. "Will," he acknowledges deferentially and walks away.

Pulled against a strong muscled body; he holds me tightly against him, his hands holding mine firmly, not giving me the chance to pull away. I try to focus on something, anything, but find myself fascinated by the whorls of dark chest hair that peek through the top of his shirt. I want to lean into him to feel the heat and smell his skin. I want to touch his hair and find out if it's as soft as it looks. Laughter from one of the tables brings me to my senses. What on earth is wrong with me?

"Am I going to have to kiss you to get your full attention?" I look up, and his blue eyes are filled with laughter.

For some reason, I become irrationally annoyed. This man has been smiling, staring or chuckling at me all day long. Pulling out of his arms, I whirl around, ignoring the stares that follow me. Rationally, I know my response was unreasonable. But my usual calmness has deserted me. I escape down the alley of a cottage, trying to hide in the darkness. I hear footsteps behind me, before arms band around my waist and I'm pulled back against his chest. Stilling, my heart thudded in the silence. My breathing ragged as I fought the twin desire to stay and run away. He circles my waist with his arms, turns me around and holds me tightly; placing a long finger under my chin he raised it, forcing me to look at him. In the darkness, I could still make out his features; imprinted in my head for all time. There's nothing to do but be quiet. There's nothing to do but listen to the blood pounding in and out of my heart, listen to my ragged breathing, and to his.

"You scare me," I whisper.

He relaxes and kisses my hair gently. "Don't be frightened. I won't hurt you."

My emotions swirl, unpredictable and heavy as they push, threatening tears. This man has the power to do what no one else could; he could break my heart into tiny unrecoverable pieces that would never fit together again.

He sighs, as if he can read my mind and then gazes down at my face. "You're mine, little mouse. We're Mates. You need to understand this."

Before I can say anything, he bends down and kisses me, his mouth taking mine, taking over my soul. My mind fights briefly before I gave in, as sensation drifts from my lips and down my body. Closing my eyes, I fall into the tempest; aware I would curse myself later for my reaction. Like an illicit piece of chocolate, I continued to feed my addiction understanding all too easily that the illicit always tastes good and always leaves you wanting more.

AWOKEN

Rose Darkings

Warwick won't see me. I've visited, enquired and near enough stalked the man in the last month, and yet he still manages to evade me. When I ask Boon or Ruth where he is they either say they don't know or tell me airily he's on "council business" and shut the door in my face. Do they know about his plan with Aiden and are covering it up? Or are they ignorant of the entire scheme? The only way I'll get an answer is by asking him.

I never sought to possess a particular potential but I was always very curious about when and how my talent would reveal itself. As I was walking through the village yesterday delivering bread to all the families, I suddenly became aware of hearing what I never have before. Villagers went about their normal everyday business, however, I found myself listening to conversations on the periphery; the whispers between friends; the open maliciousness concealed by kindness. I'm drawn in, listening intently to the whispers, greedy for information about my village, that's changed into something else whilst I was away.

I spot Megan on the other side of the village, speaking animatedly to a group of our friends, or they had been until I withdrew from life. I can't remember Megan visiting, maybe Mum sent her away, but I've haven't seen her since I got better. As though sensing my thoughts, she waves to me quickly but then returns to her conversation. I hear laughter a few seconds later and I know it's about me; that I'm the subject of some witty quip that entertains the masses.

Then, as clear as a bell, although her mouth wasn't moving, I hear the words: "Rose used to be so normal? What happened to her? Dad says her whole family is strange."

My face flushed with shame and anger, spinning around, I try to hide my reaction. Angry tears burst from my eyes and I wiped them away as hurt and shame battled for supremacy, as I realised that six months ago, I would have thought exactly the same. Shock reverberated as I realised my talent was second sight, the ability to read thoughts and predict events. A rare talent I wasn't sure I wanted or was prepared for.

"People are scared of what is different Rose,"

I turned at the small voice, and looked down to see May Gentles studying me, her small elfin face open, almost hidden with a mass of thick blonde hair, her delicate hands clutching the arms of her wheelchair. How did she know what I was thinking? Of course she did, May had lived her life in the shadows, behind the larger-than-life personalities of her mother and older sister.

"Peck's losing the sight in his other eye Rose. He's going to miss your smile."

Pushing on her wheels of her chair, she moved away, before looking back and giving me a sly smile and a cheeky wink, and saying; "What's normal anyway?"

May, born with spina bifida and underestimated by those closest to her, had also been gifted with second sight not with us mere humans but with animals, a talent so extraordinary I'd never heard of another possessing it. As she disappeared into the crowd, as she has all her life, I watched her in awe and admiration. If May with all of the challenges she faced could do this, then so could I.

I walked away from the village to a small alcove of trees, and leaned my back against a large oak. The bark smoothed over years of use provided a solid base to lean upon and I tried to make sense of it all. I no longer recognised my village. Greenwood, once made up of one large family, now had an underlying layer of cruelty within it that rotted out from its core. Is this what happened to Aiden? Had be been infected? Is that why when I offered him my heart he broke it into tiny pieces before he gave it back to me? My mind swirled and nausea and dizziness hit. But still the thought persisted, there is another layer existing within Greenwood that's yet to proclaim its agenda. The Natural Laws are meant to protect our world. This force, insidious and frightening, is in no way natural.

Since I woke from my self-induced coma, I see the truth of my life; not the hazy tinted hue of before. Those close to me sense my shift in perspective. Mum still hovers afraid that the slightest wave will send me back to my silent prison. Boon studies me like I'm another problem he must fix, and the village looks at me like I am a puzzle yet to be solved. They don't understand that I had to retreat because my mind couldn't cope with the horrors I witnessed. I'm still the same person underneath but to get better, I had to become another version of myself. I understand their reluctance. I was broken, so damaged I feared I could never be fixed. I feared for my sanity; paralysed by the notion that I'd never gather the courage to break free, and until the moment I saw Amber, I didn't realise that underneath all the layers I had the strength all along. I'd just forgotten I did.

Now I feel alone in a crowd. My life, so carefully planned and anticipated has changed forever. That's what I did in my silent prison; I mourned. I grieved for the life I thought I would have with Aiden; for the children we would make and watch grow. I missed the strong arms that I dreamed of holding me every day of my life. How do you learn to live again? I wake up every day and I believe I can. For now it's enough - to get up and move one foot in front of the other in the hope it will take me where I'm meant to be. Today my purpose has been made clear. I need to find the core of the rot that's set in Greenwood. I must have second sight for this reason.

Pushing myself away from the tree, I moved back to the village, it was time to experiment with my talent. At least now I know why Warwick is avoiding me.

He already knows.

EVIL

Aiden Darkings

I've become what I desperately tried to avoid. Gratification floods through me as I slowly slice the man's flesh from chest to navel. The effect is immediate as the blood spurts from the wound, leaving a crimson path that permeates his clothes. His cries fill the air like a high-pitched fiddle song that pierces as it plays. Closing my eyes, I savour his pleads for life and almost tell him not to waste his last words seeking my mercy. Then I hear that last delicious grasping breath before its stutters and finally stops. Vacant lifeless eyes stare up at me; demanding acknowledgement. In answer, I draw back a bloody boot and violently kick the man's head. The audience of Black Knights roars wildly. I roll the body over with my foot, take my gloves off and walk away. I don't acknowledge their applause. I don't need anyone's approval. The memory of the kill has already left me.

"Well done Aiden." Luther watches me with pride.

I am a good apprentice. I am a killer without conscience. Today, to stem boredom we've been instructed to fight each other to the death to retain our place in his ranks and I have beaten each opponent. Nobody can match me.

"Who's next?" I ask, matter-of-factly, replacing my gloves and picking up my sword again.

I stand and wait for my orders. Turning back to the crowd of Black Knights, I survey my future quarries. Dismissing my competition, I turn back and wait in silence. Luther takes his time deciding. He gets annoyed by outbursts of emotion; seeing it as a weakness. In my dealings with him, I speak only when necessary. He believes he's grooming me in his image and I don't tell him any different. He will offer me up to pay for Greenwood at the first opportunity. In the meantime, I use him as he uses me. Luther points languidly towards another Black Knight and I move forward and do what I must. The image of the sobbing girl suddenly flashes in front of me, her voice pleading with me to stop. I push the image away, turning my venom towards the other Knight. Plunging my sword into the soft pliable flesh, I push away the voice that screams for me to stop. Finally, I smile and savour the dying cries of the weaker man. I kill therefore I am.

I'm killing myself.

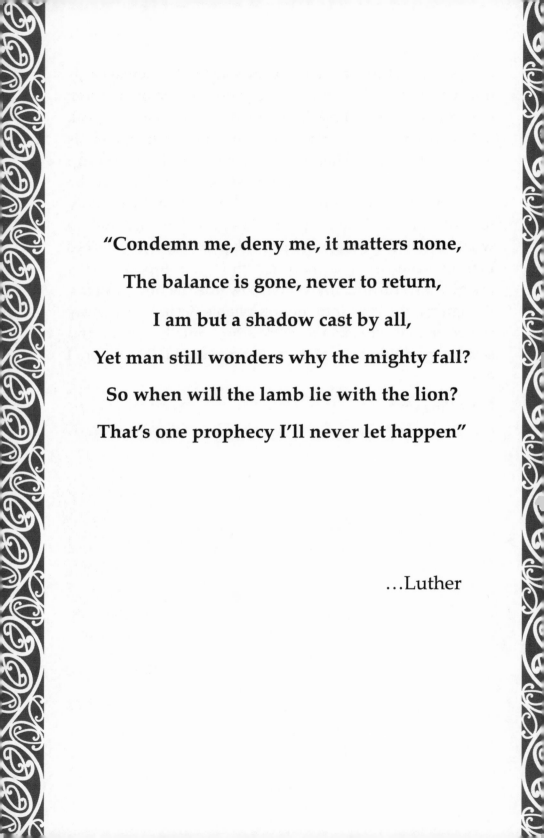

"Condemn me, deny me, it matters none,

The balance is gone, never to return,

I am but a shadow cast by all,

Yet man still wonders why the mighty fall?

So when will the lamb lie with the lion?

That's one prophecy I'll never let happen"

...Luther

Luther

DISTRACTION

Amber Lockwood

I live in a dream world. Each day I walk for miles, keeping well away from villages and people who could be working for Luther. In my last lesson, Boon warned me that Sensio has been infected. People have become too focused on their own needs and are willing to do anything to get what they want. He warned me not to trust anyone with my name or my purpose. Unfortunately, if I'm going to find Aiden I'll have to ignore his advice. I also need to rest and eat and although I had to scavenge for food when I stayed at Rowan Cottage, I also had help from Greenwood to sustain me. Now I must live on my wits to survive.

I watch people from a safe distance as they go about their daily business. I yearn for company but I rely on my instincts and don't go near them. The gut feeling that told me to run home to Lauren, the gut feeling that told me Duncan was coming to the cottage, is a sense I trust, when I trust very little else. Part of my reticence is fear. My trust in people has been shaken since I came to Sensio. I get to know someone, give them a vital part of me, trusting their words on a measure of faith. I get comfortable with them; trust them with a vital part of myself and then they reveal an aspect of their character that's so fundamentally different from what I believe that person to be that I can't help but feel betrayed by their deception. Duncan. How can I still feel his hands on my body, his fingers moving slowly down my naked back and his mouth on mine? He didn't believe in me. That truth hurts the most. He didn't understand that during my banishment from Greenwood, I became a different person. I came to believe in myself, and in my own talents. I came to believe I had a voice that deserved to be heard. I still remember his angry words as I left and I know I did the right thing by walking away. I had to follow my own path. No matter what the cost to my heart.

Until now my search for Aiden has been fruitless. The smoked trail of devastation usually left by the Black Knights has quietened. I hear rumours all the time. I walked through a busy village yesterday. I felt safe; aware the villagers were too distracted by a visiting fete, to notice me walking among them. I stayed in the shadows avoiding eye contact with people for fear of inviting questions. It was then that I overheard a conversation between two elderly men. The village had been ransacked some months before and the men had been given a choice: join the Black Knights or die. Most had joined up but some had refused. It seems that the Black Knights are currently recruiting men and holding them at a camp north of Sea Cliff, where the King and Queen Consort rule. It was then I realised I was meant to wander into this village so I'd know where to go next.

At night, I am no longer alone. I have the company of Rora. Reading her words, paints a picture of her in my head. Tugging a memory from childhood of when Lauren once asked me to get some money from her purse. Searching the compartments, I lingered over a picture hidden within. It was faded sepia at the edges, showing three women huddling close together, laughing in the sunlight as one held the camera. The sun cast them in a warm glow, their smiles happy. A precious memory locked in time forever. Lauren had snatched the photograph hastily from me before I had a chance to ask who the people were. Curious, I stayed silent, aware that some questions would never be answered. But now I know that that the images were of Rora, her Nana and Lauren. As I walk north, her words give me the strength to continue. My feet depress into the grassy undergrowth. Wind blows through the trees and branches move to its song. The purple sky brightens and fades. I note this, move onwards but don't participate.

I drift into a dream world because it helps me to cope with my reality. I dream of saving Aiden and being close to him. I dream about the people of Greenwood accepting me for who I am. I see myself being held by Duncan, accepted as his equal. I dream of our children. I dream of a golden future, where I've become the person I'm meant to be. I dream because I can't live without hope. Nurturing and fostering the belief that all the death and destruction might actually be worth the future that I dream of. Have I finally gone mad? Have events been so catastrophic to my psyche that my only way of coping is to dream of an impossible future? I don't know anymore. All I know is that I must have hope to go on, to keep walking, to keep believing somehow, everything will be work out in the end.

Something sharp pierces my back and I regret my decision. Holding up my hands in surrender, I turn round slowly to see my captor. My heart leaps as I look into the black soulless eyes of a Black Knight. Grimacing, I chastise myself and learn that living in a world of dreams has a cost. I dream of saving Aiden and now I have an opportunity. I pull the knife quickly from my boot, stepping backwards and give the Black Knight my most charming 'come hither' expression. He smiles and walks toward me. I have to fight for what I believe in. All dreams have a price.

Now I'm paying for mine.

MESSENGER

Rose Darkings

I wait in the shadows of the Great Hall. Firelight from wall sconces highlights the horseshoe table, the lectern centre now abandoned in a corner in large broken pieces; the result of Aiden's anger. Swords and artefacts that had fallen to the ground have been tidied away, and on the surface the room is as grand and austere as it's always been. But something has changed forever – here and in the village. Something has broken in Greenwood.

It's thanks to Boon that I'm here tonight. I followed him at a safe distance as he took his daily walk this morning through the village. I could hear his thoughts as he reviewed his tasks for the day and my ears piqued at the mention of a High Council meeting. This was the opportunity I needed to confront Warwick.

Under the cover of darkness, I hide myself in one of the deep dark corners that the firelight never reaches. The cold stone seeps through my clothes and goose bumps litter a trail over my skin, triggered by the cold, nerves and sad memories. This is the place where I gave my heart to Aiden. This is the place where my life as I knew it came to an end. I only have to close my eyes to lull myself back to the whisper of memories. Hearing voices, descend down the stairs. I pull myself away from the past. I have a purpose tonight and don't need an emotional trip down memory lane.

"Warwick man, what's happening to you? I've never heard you talk like this." Boon exclaims.

Chairs are scraped back as both men sit down at the table and face one another. Firelight flickers over Warwick's face and I stifle a gasp. His eyes are black-ringed and red from lack of sleep, his cheeks are sunken and his face lined with worry. His grey hair hung listlessly and even his moustache was flattened against his top lip.

"I encouraged him Boon," he whispers. "I thought I was protecting the village. All I did was encourage The Soothsaying. I've set events in motion we can no longer control."

"Warwick, you have to listen to me," Boon says, grabbing his shoulder. "Aiden was willing. He knew the dangers. Neither of us anticipated he would be so seduced by their darkness."

"Amber has his amulet. If she is able to reunite them, it might restore his balance."

Boon rubs his eyes with his fingers, then turns round to where I'm hiding and clears his throat loudly. "Rose – why don't you come and join us at the table?"

Gulping in the silence, I tried to stop my shuddering breath from invading the room. Warwick turned his head swiftly, squinting in to the dark trying to locate me, belying his apparent weakness. I step forward, hesitant and shame-faced at being discovered, and join them at the table.

"You meant to bring me here tonight." It was a statement, not a question.

Warwick nods slowly. "You will have your part to play young Rose. If Aiden has any chance of redemption he will need his Mate."

Hope burned through me like small flame seeking purchase. We look at each other searchingly, taking each other's measure, and then Warwick says, "You are not the only one with second sight Rose."

Hope is quickly replaced by searing anger as his words sink in and everything suddenly clicks into place. Pushing myself against the table, my chair snaps back against the stone floor. I began to pace the room in frustration and anger.

"You knew about this and yet you left me in hell for months. Why?" I shout.

My voice reverberates loudly round the walls of the chamber.

"You just weren't strong enough or mature enough then, Rose. But now you are. Now you understand what we do." Boon says quietly.

The anger fell away, leaving me feeling calmer and more rational.

"So Greenwood is infected," I say as I pick up the chair and sit down once again.

They both nodded solemnly

"What do I need to do?"

Remembering the medicinal brew Warwick delivered the day before I remembered everything. More pieces of the puzzle slot into place.

"You needed me to tell Amber about Aiden."

"It's better if I show you Rose," Warwick says as he closes his eyes.

I nod in agreement, and focus with all my will until the room recedes, Boon disappears and the room and everything in it fades away. Then the images begin. I feel horror in the pit of my belly as I see burnt and devastated landscapes, piles and piles of bodies, stretching endlessly into horizon, animals squealing and running for cover. I see Greenwood consumed by fire and then flooded by water. I see a cyclone rip up earth, buildings and trees tossed into the air as if playing with them, and then hurling back down violently on the ground. I see an image of Sensio and everything, every person, every living thing, is gone.

Tears fall down my face as I try to push the images away, lock them out of sight, but I can't. They're seared into my mind. I had seen the death of my world.

"The darkness is killing Sensio isn't it?" I whisper brokenly, numb. "How do we stop it?"

We talk long into the evening, and by the time I get up to go home, the light has faded from the sconces. It seemed appropriate. The light had faded everywhere. When I get back Mum is sitting beside the fire, working on some embroidery.

"I've nearly finished your dress," she says excitedly, holding up the material for me to admire.

I run my fingers over the soft, yellow material and the intricate needlework, committing it to my memory.

"Megan's asked me to help with baking tomorrow. I'll be away early, if that's ok?"

Mum nods happily, relieved that I've been more sociable recently. I sit on the floor beside her, and cuddle into her, breathing in her unique, sweet smell. She puts down the dress and strokes my hair gently, just as she did when I was a little girl. A lone tear slips onto my cheek and falls onto my arm. I feel like my heart is being clutched and twisted. Moments like these so common in my life that they assail me at once. I let go and enjoy the moment. I can't be dissuaded. I have to do this.

Dawn comes all too soon. Condensation runs down the windows as I look out over the dark village, trying to imprint it into my memory in case I never see it again. I pick up my bag and walk quietly out of the house before I change my mind. Boon is waiting for me at the clearing. Mist cloaks the village, making it disappear from my view.

"There you are, Rose. We've been waiting for you."

I look around to see who Boon is referring to.

"I'm here, Rose." I turned round to see Bramble, Finge's Mate, at my shoulder. Her little, fey body is covered with worn clothing, and the wings on her back flutter nervously. She moves every few seconds: she literally can't stay still. I looked into her tiny face with its pointy ears, peeking through thick brown hair. Her normal glowing skin was pale and her cheeks were flushed. I know I have a similar expression.

"Does Fingle know you're here?" I ask her. Her Mate is

conspicuous by his absence.

Boon clears his throat. "You can support each other on this journey." I hitch my bag up over my shoulder. "Mum thinks I'm with Megan."

Boon nods "Don't worry, Rose. I'll look after her. I promise." he promised. I offer my shoulder to Bramble and she settles herself against my hair, just as she did when I was younger. I salute Boon silently, and then turn and walk away. I look around me at the lush green fields and I pray for our future. I think of Aiden. I think of hope and the promise of another future.

I walk away from the darkness and I walk towards love.

"No conscience to consume me,

No soul to feel remorse,

Free to accept my fate,

True redemption, too little, too late?"

…Aiden

Aiden

CONFIDENCE

Amber Lockwood

Everything I've learned so far has been for nothing. The Black Knight smiles slowly and points his sword at me. His black eyes held mine, amusement dancing around like ants impatient to reach their destination. He's playing a game that I don't know the rules of. We move around in circles like a violent version of ring-o-roses. But before I have the chance to gather my thoughts, plan my next move or even raise my arms, I am flung backwards and fall with a squelch onto the soggy ground leaving me wet and mud-caked. Distracted, I don't register the rope until it tightens around my wrists. I'm so angry with myself and appreciate the irony of being the one with all the elements at my disposal, but I was at the mercy of the Black Knight because of a smile and a bit of mud. I can almost see Boon shaking his head at me. My captor pulls me upright and looks at me with an amused expression.

"Don't get used to this." I lash out at him. Even while it apparent to everyone, including the trees, I was an amateur in a world full of masters.

He picks up my backpack and pulls behind him, completely ignoring me. I have no other option but to follow. As I stumble along, I think about Rora's diary in the backpack and occupy myself with how I'll get it back. Darkness begins to fall and we carry on walking at the same steady pace, with me occasionally slowing down or pulling at the rope and him yanking me back in line.

When I stayed at Rowan Cottage, I honed my skills and trained diligently for this very situation. But I never had the chance to train with another person. My invisible opponents took the face of whoever I was angry at on that day. Luther. Aiden. Luther. Aiden. Alternative hate-filled images spinning like an uncontrollable cyclone. When you're alone anger comes easily. It whispers poison into your soul; so seductive and welcoming in the silence that you don't understand the depth of its disease until it's too late. Convincing myself it was a good training tool, imagining my enemy and using all the skills I possessed. Walking back to the cottage, covered in grime and sweat, I caught my reflection in the mirror. My hair tangled wildly, a film of perspiration leaving droplets on my dirty skin and my eyes darkened. My green irises now covered with a thick layer of black. Is that what happened to the Black Knights? Did their evil permeate through every layer of skin until it changed the colour of eyes they were born with? At that moment, alone with only my reflection for company, the only emotion I felt was shame. Is this what I'd become; a feeder for hate? I was no better than Luther. I may as well have raised the sword and killed Lauren myself. Looking in the mirror with his dark eyes looking back at me, I saw the result of allowing hate to settle and take up residence within my soul.

Taking a steadying breath, my heart stopped thundering in my ears and returned to a silent steady pace. The crushing silence between my silent captor and me let the voices recommence.

"You don't belong here."

"You have brought us nothing but pain."

"You're worthless."

The insidious whispers continued and overlapped, feeding my fears that I didn't belong or have a part to play, in Sensio, Earth or anywhere else. Learning about my elements had given me a sense a hope. The months of silence gave me the confidence to believe in my talents and myself. But my confidence bubble had burst epically; the residual shudders still leaking all over me. Tears of frustration threatened and I pushed them away, refusing to give into emotion. Instead, I focused on action. In the area of combat I was definitely lacking. That was something I'd need to rectify.

At last we come to the woods and walk into a military camp, where small groups are gathering around campfires. I scan the camp quickly, preparing myself for the mass image of black armoured male bodies radiating malevolent violence, but to my astonishment, there aren't any. The atmosphere is jovial and relaxed. Some of the groups are even laughing and joking. Small gatherings of varying body shapes were silhouetted in the darkness; my arrival was spared a curious glance before the voices began again, intercepted only by the occasional gulping laughter.

We entered a tall hexagon tent and stop in front of a table with cloth maps. Firelight met shadows, casting a hazy glow over the tent showing a bed against the corner and a stockpile of weapons, crossbows and swords. I try to concentrate on what the men say, but the voices from outside drown out their words. Whoever they are, they were fully concentrating on the task in hand. The Black Knight put the backpack at my feet and motions me to stand still, then clears his throat to gain their attention. They straighten immediately and I take a calming breath as they turn to face me, reminding myself I'd been prey of Black Knights before and survived. I could do it again.

"Release her now," a voice says sharply.

The rope is cut and I massage my wrists to get the blood circulating again. When I look up, I find myself caught in Duncan's sharp gaze. He takes in my worn clothes, rumpled and dried with caked mud. For a second, I think he's going to walk towards me, but he changes his mind and leans back against the table, folding his arms across his chest. Naked, uncontrollable emotion surges through me and my stomach rolls over. I stay silent and shiver.

"Marcus was a Black Knight. He has since joined The Alliance. You've nothing to fear from him. I hope he didn't scare you?" Daniel's voice is solicitous.

I shake my head to acknowledge. I was unhurt, only my pride dented. Just then, Fingle appears, buzzing around my head, contorting his little face, wiping his nose and looking me up and down pointedly. I burst out laughing, relief ebbing through me. I look down at the state of my clothes.

"I have looked better Fingle I must admit."

Daniel walks forward and takes my chilled hands into his warm ones. For a moment, Duncan is blocked from my view but I still feel his eyes on me.

"Fingle will take you to your quarters Amber, so you can clean up and rest."

I pick up my backpack, and Marcus steps aside for me. As I walk past him, he winks at me. Devilment flirted and takes hold. Pushing out my hand, and using my talents, I pull some air towards me before directing it towards him and knock him flat on his back.

"Next time it'll be the mud for you." I wink back, and smile down at him.

He looks at me for a moment, stunned, then laughter rumbles deep within his chest and reverberated loudly within the tent. "Understood Miss Lockwood," he says "Welcome to The Alliance."

"Fingle, shall we?" I say.

Without waiting, I head towards the door of the tent. The small pieces of my dented pride moving slowly back together; congealing chipped shards into solid stone.

Just as I'm about to leave, I hear Duncan growling. "Forget it Marcus, she's mine."

The words and his tone take me back to another place and time, but I'm not confident enough to turn around and go back to him. Everything I have learned hasn't been for nothing. If I'd gotten away from Marcus I would never have found The Alliance. They are following Luther who has Aiden with him.

In true Sensio tradition, I have ended up exactly where I am meant to be, even with my pride restored.

SHADOWS

Aiden Darkings

The shadows have been stalking me for days. They come and go without warning, and flood my head with images, as fleeting as they are irritating. When I wake up, the little dark haired witch is here, her eyes desperate, beseeching me with tears and frantic gestures to listen to her. The painful beating begins as I push her away. It's only scant curiosity that allows her to linger briefly. I'm still in control of something.

The shadows never leave me alone. They infect me, no matter what I'm doing. When I eat I'm reminded of dark nights around a wishing well. When I hear laughter, I smell smoke from the fire and feel the warmth of the people around about me, but it leaves me untouched. I tell myself I don't miss kindness or love and I push it away.

As I pull my blade out of another dead Knight, I'm suddenly flooded with the memory of being a child, cocooned within the arms of a woman with long, curly, sweet-smelling hair. She gently dabs ointment on my bloody knee, wipes away my tears and whispers that everything will be okay. I push the memory away, but she returns. This time, her face is older and contorted with pain as I walk towards her with my sword outstretched. The guilt is fleeting. She's not the first or the last person I will kill.

My transformation into a Black Knight is nearly complete. My story is the same as many others. We are chosen because we are strong. We are plucked from whatever unfortunate village we were born in. We discard our birthplaces, leaving only bones and burnt ashes in our wake. We are trained to fight and kill without mercy. Finally, we are tested. If we win, we lose our souls. You cannot survive in this environment unless you are willing to give up your humanity. It cannot survive in this environment. It physically hurts to remember so I disregard the past and concentrating on surviving in the present. It is the only way I can go on. I don't remember my family or my village. I only know my purpose was to join. The shadows tease pictures of my origins. Then there is silence as they are pushed away by the black that has become my very existence.

I remember my initiation clearly. Luther led me to a clearing in a village, surrounded by a circle of men. He pushed me into the middle and I found myself facing another man the same age as me, with a blackened eye and a bloodied arm. I knew what Luther was going to say before he said it. "Gentlemen, whoever lives, wins," he declared.

My opponent and I looked at each other, aware of what this meant. Aware that this decision was one that would define us forever. If I obeyed, I was choosing to kill another human being for no other reason than to please the man who had decreed it. Then a voice whispered, "Do whatever you have to do to get him to trust you." Making my decision, I unsheathed my sword and walked towards the weaker man. I don't remember the fight itself. I only remember standing above his broken body, my sword and hands sticky with his blood, my body slick with sweat, and my heart beating ferociously with adrenalin. In making my choice, I have surrendered my humanity and sold my soul. And from that moment, the shadows started. I used to know why I left the village. I used to know who I lived with and who I loved. Now I can't remember my mother's name. I avoid looking in the mirror. The last time I saw my reflection I didn't recognise the person who looked back. My eyes, always a clear warm brown, had turned a macabre black. I haven't looked at myself again.

But despite what I do, despite how hard I try, remnants of my soul still survive. I know that's what the shadows are. I know that's why they plague me. And I also know that if I don't kill them off forever, I won't survive.

My thoughts are interrupted by a guttural, blood-curling scream. Screams in this camp aren't unusual; we are a band of killers; of the serial nature. Between bouts of extreme violence on unsuspecting villages, the more psychotic among us start fights just to experience the high of killing. But this scream is different, it's animal-like, desperate and I recognise the voice behind it.

I walk into the tent to look, the screams are now reduced to a muffled murmur. Through the worn material, the bright sun bled through illuminating the inhabitants and their actions. Three men are holding a woman on the ground. Two held her flailing arms, as one pressed a meaty hand over her mouth and nose while the other clawed her shirt away. The largest male moves himself between her legs and all laugh at her feeble attempts to escape. She looks like a wounded animal trapped in a snare, vulnerable, unable to move and desperately crying for help. She looks up at me, pleading. Sierra. She's been sharing my bed for months now. I treated her as kindly as I could, given the situation we both found ourselves in.

Without thinking, I unsheathe my small blade and slit the throat of the would-be rapist. His blood spurts over Sierra's naked body and clothes. I kick him off her. As his hand tries to cover the wound, blood seeped through his fingers before foam bubbled from his mouth as he fell to the floor. I finish off the remaining two and pull Sierra up from the ground. She is shaking uncontrollably with shock, her blue eyes are pools of liquid. I pick up her clothes and dress her gently, as I would a child. These men were known for their cruelty to women. Even losing Amber and getting a hiding from Luther hadn't stopped their attempts. If I had saved Sierra today, they would've attacked her again tomorrow. I had to kill them.

I walk through the camp, pulling Sierra behind me. This isn't unusual. People are used to seeing us in each other's company and make crude jokes and innuendos as we pass. Normally that irritates me, but not today. Their assumptions give me time to carry out my plan. We carry on walking until we reach the edge of the dense forest and I look back to check that nobody has noticed us leaving. They're too busy eating and drinking. I quicken the pace and we walk for miles, listening intently for any sign we have been followed.

Dusk falls. We come to a clearing and I stop and give Sierra food and water from the supplies in my pack. She looks at me, wary, I can hardly blame her. I point ahead.

"The Alliance camp is about five miles north of here. Seek

sanctuary with them. Don't return here. I can explain killing those men, you can't."

"Why have you helped me?" she asks.

"I don't know." I answered, at a loss to explain the madness in my head.

"Thank you," she says, as she turns and walks away.

I watch her as she disappears into the distance, the blood dried on her skin and dotted like a leopard, her thin shoulder blades jutting out of her dirty blouse, the beacon of her blonde hair becoming smaller and smaller until it's finally engulfed by the darkness. I walk back to the camp. I'm on the periphery when I hear voices. I hide behind a tree to watch and listen.

Two figures are discussing something animatedly. I can identify Luther by his usual gold and black armour. I don't recognise the other man. He ends the conversations and walks back towards a unicorn, which is tethered to a tree. I'm so surprised by the unicorn that I lean forward to get a closer look and stand on a twig. It snaps. Immediately, the men both turn around and look in my direction. Cursing silently, I use my elements to generate a small whirlwind of leaves. It spooks the unicorn and forces its rider to turn him around and calm him down. He pulls roughly at the gold and blue reins, waves a salute to Luther and rides away. Luther watches him go. I've seen that expression on his face before. He's coming to a decision. Then he turns and heads back to the camp.

While I'm waiting in the darkness to give him time and me

distance, I also come to my own decision. I'm no longer sure about why I'm a Black Knight. I can't give myself over to the darkness completely – that is clear after I rescued Sierra. I kill for a purpose I no longer remember. So I'm choosing to save myself. Redemption might be lost to me but I choose to seek it regardless of the consequences. I have nothing left to lose. I try to hold onto this last thought as I walk back to the camp, before it escapes and my darkness descends once more.

THE ALLIANCE
Amber Lockwood

Last night I had a nightmare. I've not had one in so long that it completely unnerved me. Lauren looked as I last saw her – in pain, her lifeblood flowing from her body. She was begging Daniel to take me away and Duncan lifts my body up, kicking and screaming. I woke up covered in sweat and gasping for air. It's been a year since Lauren died. My life has changed completely since then and I couldn't change it no matter how much I wished it.

When I woke up this morning, shocked and disorientated, I would have given anything for some caffeine. I miss coffee. It sounds like a silly thing to miss, but it was part of my routine when I lived on Earth. I had a cup to kick-start my body every morning before a run. I looked forward to it. But since I've lived in Sensio, a lack of coffee is the least of my worries.

So when Marcus hands me with a cup of hot black liquid with a distinct smell of caffeine and describes it as his 'waking up potion' I could cheerfully hug him. It's not my usual French brand but it's close enough and helps calm my frayed nerves.

I warm my hands on the cup as I walk around The Alliance camp, where I've been living for the past two weeks. It's spread over a large area of forest starting at an huge, ancient oak, the base so large and limbs so heavy it weighs on the surrounding trees, creating a camouflage of dense foliage. I walk along the pathway through a village of tents and reach a small bridge the crosses the brook where we get some, but not all of our water. To get to the main supply, you have to walk over a makeshift rickety bridge, through more tents to a large loch. At one time, this was all forest too, until the white water reclaimed it. You can still see the tips of the trees just under the surface, like some underwater Atlantis forest. In the sunlight, the loch is dappled with a myriad of rainbow colours, played against the thundering roar of white foaming water. It's awe-inspiring and reminds me of what we're fighting to save. In the darkness, it looks too daunting to cross and will hopefully dissuade those who wish to attack.

I nod respectfully to the fierce looking warrior who is on guard duty. They're still wary of me, just like the people of Greenwood when I first arrived. My constant companion has been Fingle who has appointed himself as my mentor until such time as "Boon decides to get himself here".

The Alliance has many supporters, not just from Greenwood but from Kingston and Hopestead. So far, I've met Claudio Alfario and his mate Pearl, a determined couple, who like so many here, have lost family to the Black Knights. Most people in the camp, Fingle included, are reluctant to discuss the reasons that brought them here and seeing the strain and shadows on their faces. I keep my curiosity to myself.

There is an undercurrent, an energy bubbling through the camp. We can all feel it. It's fuelled by a mixture of hate, grief and a thirst for revenge, the determination to get on with the fight before us. So although The Alliance appears to work in harmony on the surface, underneath the tension snaps and crackles desperately looking for the element it will need to ignite.

I stop at the edge of the loch and remember my conversation with Fingle a few days earlier.

"Why are they called Black Knights?" I asked, guessing it was due to their armour.

Fingle told me of their history.

"After the last revolt an army of Sensio's best soldiers was established by the old King. The purpose was to keep the peace and impartially refer lawbreakers to the Kings court. At that time they were known simply as the Knights. But then Luther joined and moved through the ranks, people noticed the violence spiralled and the colour of the Knights eyes changed. No matter what colour of eyes they had been born with they all became black."

I think about this as I drain the last of my coffee, shivering as I remember Luther's dead black eyes and his psychotic stare. Turning back to camp, I walk past Duncan and Daniel on the way. I hold Duncan's gaze and our souls speak without words. My belly flips and I feel my heart turn over, but I hold my head high and carry on walking, determined that one day I will look at him and my heart won't ache. The Alliance was formed to bring the Black Knights to justice but we're all here for our own reasons. We have all lost someone. I'm here for the woman who raised me and my brother who needs me.

I've never belonged anywhere more.

CONNECTION

Rora Ravenswood

I really don't know why I'm here. Pushing away the kaleidoscope of emotions simmering inside me, I walk out of the clearing into the thick of the forest. Branches caress me softly on my head, arms and legs as I walk through the trees. The air is dry with a touch of humidity and the sweet smell of the forest dances around my nostrils teasing my senses. The early morning sun hangs low in the sky, covering everything in coquettish half-light. When I finally made up my mind I was coming today I became settled. I only know the indecision made me anxious. I usually weigh up the pros and cons of every situation before I make a decision. I'm logical and cautious. The decision to come here today is based solely on emotion. All I know is that I have to be with him.

No one knows I'm here. My secret is more one of circumstance than of intention. Maggie's mum, Primrose, fusses over me like a surrogate, but trusts me and gives me freedom. Maggie is blissfully mated and unaware of anyone else apart from Daniel. Boon is shortly to be mated with Dot, so his mentoring duties have fallen by the wayside recently.

I'm entangled in something I yearn for but don't understand. Since that first night, Will has come to Greenwood every couple of weeks to conduct business with Warwick and The High Council. He always arrives, trotting in on his unicorn, when I'm in the midst of the village, like our meetings are planned on a preordained sundial. On the surface, I'm the same person; calm, collected and going about my business but underneath I'm a mass of precarious, unstable emotions about to bubble over. Whenever I see him, my heart turns over and I remember his words: "You're mine. We're Mates."

I used to hate the very idea of belonging to someone, of needing someone, of relying on anyone apart from myself. Now I feel him before I see him. He makes my heart race and my face flush, making me clumsy as I desperately try to ignore his presence. But he also protects me and makes me feel safe.

Ruth Gentles seeks him out every time he visits. Yesterday, she spoke to him as soon as he arrived, laughing and looking gorgeous, blonde and willowy. I tried to look away, pushing at the stabbing jealousy that hit me, hastily pushing back my auburn hair, conscious of my curves. Then Will looked up, stared into my eyes and shook his head, slowly and deliberately. Realising he wasn't listening to her anymore turned, Ruth turned, looked me up and down, her face twisting into a hideous mess and marched off.

He walked over and murmured, "I've never encouraged her." "Meet me tomorrow morning, two miles north at the large oak."

I nodded, feeling vulnerable; exposed and naked before him. Unable to speak sensibly as his hot breath caressed my earlobe causing me to shiver, draw away and towards him all at once. I nodded and felt him watching me as I walked away. Hiding at home, the nerves bit at me until I gradually feel asleep in the early hours and woke up intent on my journey.

I finally see the large oak. Will is standing there. Waiting and stroking his unicorn's long, dark, shiny mane and neck. He doesn't know I'm here and I drink my fill of him, his back muscles flex as he moves his hand lifting his shirt to reveal soft hair on his taut torso. His dark hair shines a soft cocoa brown in the morning light and his eyes light up as he interacts with the animal, a deep unequivocal trust obvious between them. He is truly beautiful.

I leave my hiding place and walk towards him. He smiles, genuinely happy to see me. He takes my face in his hands and kisses my cheek, leaving a trail of heat along my skin. He gently pulls the reins, guiding the unicorn around to face me.

"Clover, this is Rora," he says.

I smile at the unicorn and it looks back at me warily. I lift my hand up hesitantly to stroke it, but it steps back nervously, so Will covers my hand with his and tenderly strokes the silky, coal-black coat.

"I didn't know they existed," I whisper.

"Yes, they do, but they're wary and you hardly ever see them."

He grasps my waist and lifts me up onto the saddle before vaulting up behind me. I feel the heat and hardness of his body behind mine as the unicorn canters along a well-worn path. I need to distract myself from the feel of him so I ask him lots of questions, which he cleverly deflects, encouraging me instead to tell him about my parents, Nana, Lauren and meeting Maggie. All the while his hot breath teases the skin on my neck, his beard soft as he leans into my hair and his lips trail over my cheek. The erotic sensations build inside me. Fuelled by the memory of the dream I had last night, the one Maggie promised I would have one day. Believing that I was brought to her and Sensio to meet the man who was destined to be my Mate.

We come to a cottage in a clearing. Will lifts me down and removing her saddle and bridle, let's Clover graze freely. He takes my hand and we walk up some stairs onto wooden decking pilled with firewood and a rocking chair. Inside the cottage is rustic and simply furnished with a small living room and kitchen. Will stands looking at me quietly as I take in my surroundings. I feel comfortable. I feel at home.

"Welcome to Rowan Cottage, Rora."

Looking up, my breath shot out raggedly as Will places his hands on my hips and drew me against him. I look up at him, caught, the emotions swirling inside me settle as he takes my lips in a kiss that consumes me. I give myself willingly. The time has come to surrender. He is mine, just as much as I am his.

"Is he worthy of my complete & utter surrender?

Something I have never given to another, *ever*,

Will he love me with all his heart?

Will he honor me, till death do us part?"

...Rora

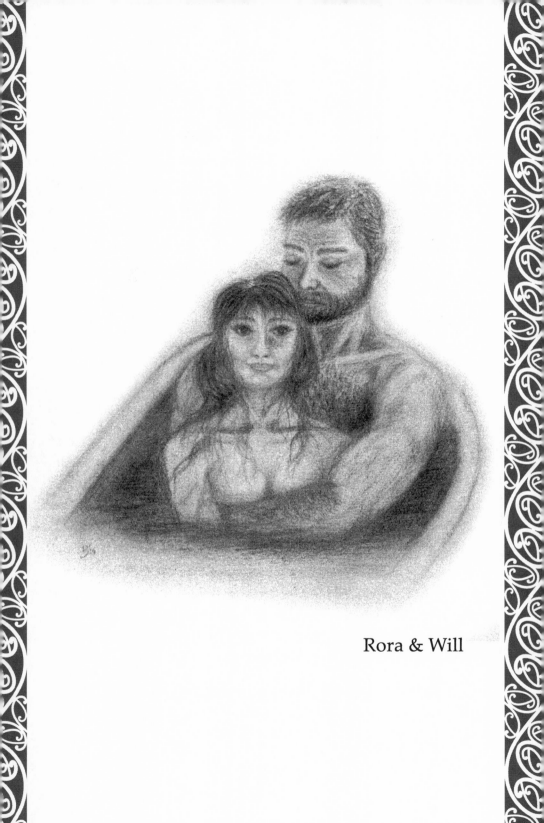

Rora & Will

SEEDS

Rose Darkings

The doubts have followed me from Greenwood. They begin when I wake to the burgeoning light of the dawn and follow me to sleep in the darkness. Trying to wipe the destructive images from my head, I initially welcome the breeze as it sidles up to me, caresses my face and moves my hair and begins the insidious whisper in my ear.

"Aiden can't be saved."

"He already told you he's doesn't want you. What if he really meant it?"

"Do you really think you have the power to save Sensio?"

The doubts have tormented me through the endless days of travel, past the forests, the villages, the bone-dry dust paths and the wet marshlands. Sometimes, if Bramble and I can find an abandoned building or cave, I manage to get some sleep, but then I relive the vision of destruction, violence and death that Warwick showed me. I see the elements finally taking revenge on us for assuming we had control over them in the first place. Then I wake up in the morning and the silent torture begins again. The invisible evil follows, keeping my pace without concerted effort and torments me with doubts I fear will come true if I admit to its presence.

I wonder if this is the price of having second sight. Mum warned me that each talent comes with a catch. Mum can influence stone, but her talent is spasmodic and comes and goes as it pleases. Dad, like Duncan, can influence fire, but while Dad's talent has diminished, Duncan's has flourished. I have seen the potential destruction of Sensio and I have to save it. I have to save Aiden. I have to save my family and myself. If I don't, then what's it all been for?

I haven't spoken to Bramble about what I've seen. I don't want to add to her sorrow. The chatty fey, who always laughs with me is now consumed by grief and longing for her Mate Fingle, just as I am for Aiden. We speak briefly about food and shelter and then only as little as possible. I'm so glad she's here. Perhaps by pulling together we'll give each other the strength to go on.

Bramble and I have spoken about my talent of second sight. It's a rare talent and once in a while, there are rumours that someone has the gift. But as gossip is regarded as unlucky, rumours become a mythical tale floating on the wind between villages, so I'm not sure how many others there are in Sensio. Warwick has never made his gift well known. I remember asking Bramble when I was a child about the stories where faeries replaced newborn babies with a faerie child or changeling. The changeling was born with a caul or a soft layer of skin. Once this was removed, the changeling baby would have the gift of second sight within that world.

Bramble's little cheeks flushed red with temper and she dismissed the stories as fables.

"Faeries are drawn to babies, Rose. They have pure souls and our instinct is to protect them."

I know this is true from my own experience. I had wandered into the woods when I was around four years old, trying to keep up with Duncan and Aiden. I kept on walking until the dark green ferns towered over me and I couldn't see my way out. I wanted to go home and I started to cry. Moments later, I heard a buzzing around my head and I saw two little figures, surrounded by a white crystallised light. I forgot my tears and watched them, entranced. They had small, elfin-like faces and pointy ears that stuck out from their long, curly hair.

"Little lady, what are you doing out in the forest on your own?" said one of the figures, with a small but distinctively masculine voice.

They floated near my face, no bigger than my small hand.

The other figure said, "Fingle, don't scare her. Hello, little girl, I'm Bramble and this is Fingle. We're faeries visiting Greenwood Forest."

Within minutes, I was walking back to the village with Bramble on one side of me and Fingle on the other. They guided me along the right path and reassured me I would soon be safely home.

Since then, I've come to know and love them and I've no doubt that they would do whatever is necessary to protect me. But I don't know what those talents are. Faeries whilst being unpredictable, charming and mischievous are also very secretive.

In Sensio, we don't boast about our talents because they are an intrinsic part of us. And we are taught never, ever to abuse them. So if we have the choice between building a fire and using our talent to create one, we are expected to build the fire. My talent seems to be unpredictable. Usually a vision will appear to me for a reason – as a way of protecting or preventing harm. They arrive like a tidal wave in my head making me cold, fearful and exhilarated all at the same time.

We hear footsteps and stop. Someone is stumbling along, making hiccupping, whimpering noises.

"Be careful, Rose. It could be an aggressor," Bramble whispers.

I nod, shivering, as I remember our encounter two days before. I watch carefully as the stumbling and hiccupping materialised into human form. My first impression is of someone who is traumatised. Her eyes are bloodshot and puffed up from crying so its hard to tell what colour they are. They are smudged underneath by deep, purple shadows. She has high cheekbones, but they jut out unhealthily from a face that is too gaunt. Her pallor is waxy white. She has gnawed her generous mouth until it has bled. And she has been sprayed with blood, which has dried and turned brown.

I come out of my hiding place and stand in front of her. She wants to run but doesn't physically have the strength to do it. I take a step forward and hold up my hands as a sign of surrender. She falls into a heap on the ground, trying to scramble away, but is too exhausted.

I kneel down in front of her, and whisper, "I won't hurt you. I promise."

"What's happened to her?" Bramble asks, buzzing about.

The girl looks up, puzzled, trying to find the source of the noise.

"Was it the Black Knights?" I ask her.

The girl nods, looks away and hugs herself. Bramble explains to her that we are travelling to The Alliance camp and would be happy to take her with us. She nods again, relief flooding her features and I can see that underneath she is a real beauty. I hold out my hand and help her off the ground and we continue on our journey.

After walking for a few hours, I sense that the camp is close. I can feel the heat given off the crowd of people. I see the beacons of light flickering through the trees. A circle of burning torches forms a sort of stockade around the tents and in the distance, I see a huge oak. I hear the murmur of voices and the trickle of water. My throat felt dry and ached for some moisture.

"Who goes there?" a voice barks and a group of armed men walk towards us.

The girl starts to shiver uncontrollably and I take her hand to comfort her. Suddenly, I'm knocked aside by an older woman. She throws her arms around the girl and rocks her as if she were a baby.

"Sierra! We didn't think we would ever see you again," she sobs. A man joins her, who grabs his wife and daughter tightly, as if he'll never let them go.

"Rose?"

I turned round and Amber is looking at me in disbelief

before she smothers me with a hug. Duncan and Dad are close behind, their bodies sagging with relief.

Then as the images begin to play in my head I move swiftly from the reunion with my family to the excruciating pain of jagged cut glass as it tears away at my heart. I bleed lifeblood as I'm assailed by images of Sierra and Aiden, writhing and twisting naked on a bed. I'm flooded by his unmistakeable, masculine scent. The bile rises in my throat and I heave up the contents of my stomach on the ground.

As Amber comforts me, I hear Sierra walk away with her family, aware I won't be able to look at her again. I should have trusted my instincts, my talent. I was right to doubt. But there is no righteousness to find here, only a singular truth.

He's broken my heart all over again. But unfortunately, it still carries on beating.

BRANDED

Rora Ravenswood

My life has changed forever. I had no expectations
on my first day at Rowan Cottage. All I wanted
was for Will to take me in his arms. Months
later, the memory of it still makes me shiver. We lay
afterwards on the bed, the room dappled with light and as
our sweat slicked bodies parted, I knew my life had been
changed forever. His lips lingered on mine, like the whisper
of a butterfly floating over my face, my closed eyelids and
down my cheek before settling at the sensitive place
between my shoulder and neck. His breath tickled and I
shifted closer as my nerves squeezed and I shivered. Will
got up and I missed him, wanting him near me again.
Sunlight seeped through the cracks in the wood and
illuminated the trail of clothes that lay between the chair in
the corner and the bedroom door. It warmed my body and I
buried my face in the pillow, my feet seeking purchase in the
twisted sheets, happy in the moment.

Will walked back through the door and lifted me gently off
the bed. I giggled as he carried me through to the bathroom
and slid me into a bath filled with honey-scented water. He
got in behind me and began to wash me gently. I relaxed and
lay back against him. Feeling the warmth rising in my
cheeks and towards my neck, I felt shy and exposed and
could not stop myself from squirming against him. He
nuzzled my neck and in that moment, that exact moment, I
knew I had fallen in love with him. Feeling vulnerable, I
turned to hide myself from him. He wouldn't let me, he

tightened an arm around me whilst the other took my hand threading our fingers together. I wasn't getting to go anywhere. Placing his lips on my cheek he breathed out "I love you too."

I've never felt such pure, unadulterated happiness. I clung onto him as he pulled us from the bath, dripping a trail of soppy water back to the bed.

Since then I've existed in a haze of euphoria, like a balloon tethered to Sensio by a loose string, only the anchor of Will keeping me from floating away. My world revolves around Will and Rowan Cottage and I spend every moment I can there, living in a world where only the two of us exist. We meet at the cottage every few days, when Will is released from his duties at the King's court. The connection between us strengthening all the time.

I can feel him when we're apart and instinctively know when it's time to begin walking to the cottage. Nobody seems to pay too much attention to these absences. Primrose is used to my days away and Maggie has her hands full with baby Duncan, giving me a stay of execution from her questions. Boon is newly mated to Dot and oblivious. The only difficulty has been Ruth Gentles who makes the occasional nasty remark, despite being formally mated to a High Council member recently. My instinct tells me to remain wary of her.

So while there's no reason why I shouldn't tell everybody. I've done nothing to feel ashamed about. I'm just not ready to share what has become precious and ours alone yet. That is, until a few days ago, when I visited Maggie. I was cuddling and tickling Duncan and as I stroked his soft, dark hair and listened to his shrieks and gurgles, I allowed myself to fantasise about my own child – a child with Will's dark hair and my eyes ...

"Will you ever tell me who is behind that look Rora?" Maggie asked.

Surprised, I looked up at her. But before I could think of what to say Daniel came back home.

I don't know how I would have answered Maggie if we hadn't been interrupted. I was hugging my secret to me while it lasted.

I hear footsteps on the decking and Will shouting my name outside the door. I snap out of my reverie, rush out of the bedroom and jump into his arms. He holds me tight and breathes out as he rests his chin on the top of my head. My nose teases the soft hairs that peak from his shirt and I start to gently kiss his neck, before he nuzzles my cheek and captures my lips.

At night in the flickering firelight, he holds me in his arms while he reads aloud in his deep, rich voice from one of the books I've brought to the cottage. He enjoys poetry and has read Invictus so often that he knows it off by heart. He particularly loves the lines:

"I am the master of my fate:

I am the captain of my soul."

I know that this precious time must end for a few days while Will has to go back to court. My heart sinks. I love our time at the cottage and feel anxious as the time comes nearer for us to part, if only for a few days. I feel like a string pulled too taut the further he is away from me. Rowan Cottage has become our haven, our home and the centre of our existence.

I sit on the decking, watching Will as he tends to Clover. The purple sky has given way to darkness pinned only by hundreds of stars studded into the sky. He puts her in the stable, then walks over and kneels down on one knee in front of me.

"I know this isn't how a man would propose in your world, but these belonged to my father. Now they are ours, if you'll have me."

He opens a black silk box to reveal two identical amulets. Each is a rope of bronze with a circle attached to the bottom, punctuated by four precious stones: black, white, red and rose. The amulet feels warm and comfortable around my neck as if it belongs there, as if it's always been there. Words are inadequate. I kiss him, giving him everything I have, wanting him to know I will love him forever. In the darkness of the bedroom, we hold each other and talk into the night, determined not to waste a moment of our time together, making plans for Will to return briefly to the King's court before we announce our intentions in Greenwood.

It's morning and we have to part. But now I have the amulet. And now I know why it all happened: why my parents died; why I went to live with Nana; why I met Maggie and why I was destined to live in Sensio. To bring me here to the exact time and place where I would meet him. To go back to who I was before is unthinkable. I wear his amulet.

He is mine and I am branded as his, till death do us part.

COMBAT

Amber Lockwood

As the last rays of sun hit the water, they refract into a thousand shimmering, opalescent diamonds, hypnotic and mesmerising to watch. I like this time of day at the water's edge. The slow lull moves to the tide's command, ebbing and flowing, giving instruction and letting me breathe. It calms, soothes and takes me far away from the campfire, where the men talk every night. On the first night, I listened to the male voices, light and deep octaves mixing to speak of plans for battle, revenge against the Black Knights and tales from the King's court. At first, I listened intently interested in the intricacies of The Alliance, my concentration lapsing when I heard his voice, deep and purposeful. His words caressed my body and lulled me into moving, my mind unconsciously rubbing against them like a purring cat. I was halfway to the tent opening before I realised what I was doing. It never seems so difficult during the day when there are plenty of distractions. But when it's quiet and still in the darkness, I yearn for him, so to avoid temptation, I come to the water at sunset.

We've not spoken directly to each other since I came here, but we look at each other and a thousand words leap silently into the air between us and I have to look away. He looks as he did that first morning after he arrived at Rowan Cottage, his hair mussed and flopping on his forehead and I have to physically stop myself from gently pushing it back and smoothing his brow. I'm so relieved to have Fingle's company to distract me and he's rarely left my side. Because it's only now that I understand what Maggie meant about the difficulties of being separated from your Mate. It physically hurts. Without him, I feel as if I'm a piano wire that's been stretched too tight and I can't move without feeling his loss. Then I wonder by what design we were mated in the first place, if we're destined to be Mates, then why is everything so hard?

In the dark of the night I surrender to tears. I dream of him, and then when I wake up and reach for him, but he's not there and I'm slammed by the memories keeping us apart. One part of me tries to convince myself that it's for the best that I'm not meant to be with Duncan. I've brought pain and suffering to his family and his village and he can't accept me the way I am. So it's best we're not together. But the other part of me aches for him, loves him so desperately that I would do anything for him, would wither and die if he turned to someone else.

The night darkens as I watch the flowing river wishing I could mimic its natural flow. I feel hot breath behind me and the warmth of his body as it merges with mine. His hands land on my hips, branding me and bring me back against him. I close my eyes consuming the warmth. My body pushes for surrender and drip drops slowly into molten lava.

"You did not want to come near me when I first arrived Duncan, what's changed?"

"Nothing's changed," he whispers, "if I touched you, I wouldn't have stopped." His hand moved to my stomach and his fingers caressed the sliver of bare skin between my trousers and shirt. His fingers blaze a trail of fire, the fluttering nerves under my skin seeking it.

I feel myself weakened before a thought clicks sharply into place. "Is this why no one will train me in combat?"

My request for assistance round the camp was unsuccessful. I had asked but nobody would help. I'd assumed it was because everybody was too busy doing their own training. I pull away from him and turn around to face him. He faltered, confirming my suspicions as he searched for the right words.

"I wanted you to have no choice but to come to me."

I whirled away, hurt and bravado fighting for first place. I could see his indecision as the battle to please and protect me fought for supremacy.

"What do you want from me, Duncan? Because this is it, this is who I am. I'm impulsive, emotional and a pain in the arse and I can't and won't change for you or anyone else. I will try to save Aiden even though you believe he's lost."

He steps toward, holding his hands out to me.

"I couldn't bear for you to be disappointed. The Black Knights turn honourable men into ruthless killers. He was cruel the day he taunted me about you," he says, running his hands through his hair in agitation. "He could already be lost to us."

He moved forward threading his cool fingers into my hot cheeks tilting my head up so his eyes held mine. There is no mistaking the intent in his dark azure gaze.

"I want you, Amber. I can't watch you walk away ever again. Please come back to me."

I surrender against the impact of his words and gave up the fight. The opposing desires that had separated my mind and body slowly merged into one. The tautness of the wire yielded as I surrender the combat within me. Then we are kissing, wildly, passionately and without control. His hands move into my hair and anchored me as our lips meet and our kiss deepens. My hands move from his waist and follow the taut muscles to his shoulders as I sought to get closer to him. He brings me closer squeezing away all the space between us until I feel every part of him against me. Releasing my swollen lips, he trails his mouth softly down my neck pulling my t-shirt away, his hand caressing my sides until they rested on my hips holding me in place against him. Pulling at the buttons on his shirt I pushed it away before moving my palm up his stomach to his chest where I lay it against his heart feeling the beat thud against my palm.

"Yes, Duncan. I'm yours." I whisper.

He lowers and pushes me softly onto the soft, long grass. The sky is black, but I can still see his features by the light of the stars and the moons. The green thatch trees are wrapped around us, locking us into a world where we only existed. The mossy undergrowth moulds to my back like a soft feather mattress and droplets of moisture from the swollen river dust over our hot skin. He bites my bottom lip gently and the taste of him swirls over from my lips, seared onto my tongue and burned into my soul. My hands flail out and cling to the strands of long grass in an attempt to anchor myself. His eyes darken and losing patience he links our fingers and rests them at each side of my head caging his body around mine. His eyes were darkened with desire; only for me. He takes me, possessing my mouth and body in one motion. Bowing against him we fell away where no one else existed.

Instinctively, I know there is no going back from this moment. He will never let me go. I trace his face with my fingers and kiss his swollen lips. His stubble bites against my fingers and I know my body will bear his mark tomorrow.

I wake up in the still of the night, I move and whimper as my body hums from the memory of his touch, my skin hot and sensitive and I ache for him again, worrying it's the same dream and he's not really there. I relax as he growls, "Come here, woman" and pulls me back towards him. I nuzzle against his chest and put my ear against his heart, it beats steadily and its rhythm lulls me back to sleep. I'm finally at peace.

I'm finally home.

"Unsure of herself, two worlds collide,

Fear chases, she fights for life,

Can her Mate return her faith?

Love is a chance we all must take"

...Amber

Duncan & Amber

GONE

Rora Ravenswood

I can't feel him. The moon casts an eerie glow across the bedroom as I wake and see all the outlines of familiar shapes. The wooden frame peeking at the bottom of my bed, the ornate dressing table, the mirror in the corner showing the two moons within its frame. Alone in the darkness, I feel like I am suspended between my two worlds, with the ability to solve the problem if only I could remember the question. Confusion stirs and I reach out to Will for reassurance but he's not there. Seconds merge into minutes and then to hours. Most nights, it's only a few seconds before I feel him, his warmth curling around my limbs just as his body does when we're together. Then I feel settled like a compass that's found the way home. I can't rest and no matter how many times I reach out, I get no response.

As the birds signal sunrise, my anger and frustration give way to panic and despair. I feel like I'm throwing rocks against thick, unbreakable glass and while they ricochet back at me, Will stays silent. Has he abandoned me? Is he ignoring me for my own safety? Or worse, is he hurt? Is he unconscious and unaware I'm trying to reach him. To distract myself, I begin walking to the cottage. The drizzle of the foggy sky drifts and covers my clothes and hair with a film of moisture and my legs are aching. I usually love the walk to the cottage and butterflies float in my belly in anticipation of seeing Will after a few days apart. I hold my breath as the green thicket of trees comes into view and I try to push through its hidden gate. The branches stay rigid fighting me, pushing me away from where I don't belong. In frustration I push forward violently snapping branches in my haste. In panic, I smash against it, breaking branches until it finally relents.

The cavern leading towards the cottage is eerily quiet, and when I try to open the door, it's stuck too. It suddenly gives way against my weight and I find myself thrown into the middle of the room. Frantically, I turn in a circle looking for any indication that Will's been here. Feeling dizzy, I still and walk into our bedroom, back to the living room, the kitchen and into the centre of the room again. The cottage looks as if it hasn't been inhabited for months instead of days. It's covered in dust and cobwebs. The little table in the kitchen is missing the decorative glass bottle and flowers I'd placed there three days before, as is the one at the window. The shelves above the fireplace, usually full with our books, is empty. Running back to the bedroom, I wrench open the wardrobe looking for clothes. A lone, empty hanger swings on the rail. There is no sign of the life that Will and I share here, all of our things have gone, like they never existed in the first place.

I'm struck with ice-cold fear and feeling dizzy, I sit down on the bed. Even the covers aren't ours. I'm frantic. My head is whirling. Tears blur my vision as I look around the room, frantically searching for a clue to confirm what I knew in my heart. This had all happened, hadn't it? It had been real? Had losing Nana traumatised me so much I've invented a relationship with a figment of my imagination? Upset gives way to despair and I curl up on the bed, hugging myself, rocking backwards and forwards trying to comfort myself.

Tears clog the corner of my eyes and run down the length of my nose blocking it as I take hulking sobbing breaths. In the shattering silence of our home, I mourn for us. My breath, body and heart hurts. Exhausted, I finally surrender to sleep, imagining the warmth of his body next to mine.

When I wake up, my body is aching, my eyes are gritty and my skin is sensitive and sore to the touch. I have a dull headache that comes from upset and lack of food. I get off the bed and stand on something with my bare foot. It's the little book of poetry that Will loved. Sitting back on the bed, I prop it on my knees as my heart pulses a staccato, frantic beat. I look for Will's favourite: Invictus. Opening the page, I study the elegant scroll he has drawn all around his favourite lines "I am the master of my fate. I am the captain of my soul." I breathe out slowly and smile with relief. I haven't made him up. He's real. It was all real.

I hold the book in front of me like a talisman, open the door to the cottage and turn around to take one last look, remembering it as it was. On the way back I torment myself with questions. What's happened to Will? Why have all traces of our lives been removed? By the time I arrive back, the village is busy and I push determinedly through the throng of people to Maggie's home, envying them as they go about their business without a care in the world. I see Boon and Dot out of the corner of my eye, walking hand in hand, happiness all over their faces, I turn away as my heart clenches. Today, of all days, I wish Will and I could experience that simple pleasure.

I knock briefly and walk in. She's delighted to see me as usual. Duncan, now 18 months old, holds out his chubby little arms for a cuddle. Placing the book on the table, I take him in my arms and touch my lips against his soft, baby-scented hair.

"What's happened Rora?" Maggie asks getting up from the table. I sit opposite and put Duncan on my knee. She studies me and I wonder if she's already guessed my secret, for Maggie knows me better than I know myself. I've caught her trying to read my face, her head tilted to the side, waiting for my confession. Lately, the expression has softened, as if she understands my distraction. Maggie knows what it's like to be madly in love. But today, she isn't smiling. She can see my unruly hair and my red-rimmed eyes.

I take a gulp "It's ..."

The door opens and Daniel comes in and he stills when he picks up on the tension in the room. Duncan gurgles "Dada!" and stretches his hands out to his father. Daniel smiles and picks him up, tickling him and making him giggle. I smile at them and then take a deep breath.

"Both of you need to hear this."

Daniel sits at the table with Duncan on his knee and Maggie takes my hand, waiting for me to begin. I try to tell them what happened today in a way that they can understand, but it's hard. I stumble over my words, falling over them in a haste to make them understand and because I want to cry, but I know if I do, I'll never stop. As I describe the scene at the cottage this morning, Daniel visibly tenses. Heart thudding, I give him Will's book and after he's examined it in great detail, he goes without saying anything into the next room and returns with a scroll, which he hands to me.

"Will wanted you to have this, if anything happened," he says, gruffly.

I break the seal and the first thing I see is my name, written in his distinctive handwriting. For a moment, I feel close to him. I look up at Daniel, his gaze is hooded, giving nothing away. Maggie clearly knows nothing about the scroll.

I read his words and I try to take in their full implications. My mind searched desperately for other alternatives but kept being assailed by emotion. I try frantically to think of other options, but there are none. I imagine myself back at Rowan Cottage, lying with his arms around me and I'm panic-stricken. How can I go on without him? How can I still breathe when my heart is breaking? The tears I've held back finally fall.

I look in bewilderment at Daniel and ask, "Is there no hope?"

"There's always hope" he replies.

I close my eyes and grimace. I need more than hope to protect those I love. I walk to the fire and hesitate for a moment before I take the scroll and throw it in, watching as the flames lick around and consume it. "Rora. What are you doing?" Daniel shouts, jumping up from the table and throwing up his hand in disbelief. "That's your only proof..."

I put a hand on my belly and merged my touch with that of our child. A soft butterfly fluttered within and followed the movement of my hand in answer. In that moment, I felt Will with me. I look steadily at my friends and answered their unspoken question. "I have no other choice. I'm pregnant."

CHARGES

Rose Darkings

It hasn't taken me long to understand that The Alliance is made up of people with different agendas. Three days have passed since Bramble and I arrived at camp with ... her. If I were feeling rational, I would admit that she's done nothing wrong. I haven't been formally mated with Aiden. But I can't get the pictures out of my head. They torment me, embers burning, ready to ignite at any moment.

She smiled tentatively at me this morning. The simple salutation only served to scrape over my already exposed nerves and I swung away suddenly away trying in vain to hide the raw emotion on my face. As I heard her steps fade away, I felt guilty. She has no idea that she's done anything to hurt me. As far as she's concerned, I'm the person who rescued her and she'll always be grateful to me. But I have no idea of how to deal with this jealousy. My reverent wish with every fibre of my being is that it had been me instead of her.

The high emotion of the last two days has left me exposed. Before my talent was triggered by closeness. Now I am fully open and can sense or hear what everyone around me is feeling or thinking. I walk past families from Hopestead and I feel their grief. I talk to the people and I sense their despondency turning to despair. Claudio Alfario is angry and yearns for a past unbidden by death and destruction and he is determined that no further harm will come to Sierra. But despite everything they have suffered, they carry on, united and determined to purge the evil around us. Amongst the crowd I feel overwhelmed. Emotions bounce to me from one person and then another without a second's notice and completely at their mercy I wince at their silent assault.

I watch Dad stand before the crowd, ready to make an announcement and I sense his weariness and desperation. He's tired from the weight of hope these people have placed on his shoulders. It's clear in the deep lines and grooves that have aged his face, in the grey streaks that have appeared in his hair. He misses Mum desperately. His eyes scan the crowd and I feel his yearning as he looks for her knowing she's not there but vainly searching anyway. Their separation hurts him.

"The Black Knights will be here in two days," he announces, and the crowd stiffens.

We all know the fear and devastation that these black-eyed men have caused, but while we seek revenge, we also fear the inevitable battle we're going to have to fight to exact it.

"How do you know?" a voice rings out. Claudio Alfario stands forward and answers. "My daughter let herself be taken by the Black Knights. She confirmed this information."

Pearl stands behind Claudio, holding Sierra protectively to her. A hush descends on the crowd and then the whispers begin. Claudio and Pearl look around them defiantly, but Sierra shrinks away from the accusing stares. Her shoulders sink and grief rolls from her in waves and a little boy with blonde hair and brown eyes pops into her head for a moment before she pushes him away. Looking around, I feel disappointed and irrationally angry. I know what she went through.

"It's true." I shout out, shouldering my way from the back of the crowd. "Bramble and I found Sierra on our way here. She was traumatised, spattered in blood and lucky to be alive. Don't judge her. Thank her." I feel Dad's hand on my shoulder. The whispering has stopped and the atmosphere shifted like a dust storm called back to the earth.

"Well thank her." I demand again.

Claudio chuckles "By god, young Rose, you're your mother's daughter."

The tension breaks and everyone starts to laugh. I look at him gratefully and Sierra looks at me with brimming eyes and mouths 'thank you'. Dad addresses the crowd once more. "Our role's is to restrain the Black Knights by whatever talents and skills we possess and present them to the King's court for justice."

The crowd mutters discontentedly and someone at the back shouts, "They kill every person who crosses their path and you want us to restrain them? You're making no sense, Daniel. They killed my mate. I want justice."

The angry cries rang out from the crowd and I could understand their frustration all too well. They'd taken my Mate too, stealing precious moments that couldn't be replaced. But I stayed silent. Dad takes a deep, steadying breath, and says, more quietly. "This is the decree of The Alliance. We must respect the Natural Laws even if the

Knights don't."

I know that the crowd don't care about the decree. These people wanted revenge. They want their enemy to pay for the pain they have suffered. I can hear the vows of revenge and death filling their heads and they fill me with despair.

"Listen to me." I call out. The crowd quietened. "If in two days you take the revenge you seek you'll bring about our end. I have seen our villages swept with fire. Our homes crushed to dust. Our forests ravaged. I have seen the tsunami waves. Sensio will be gone. We will all be gone. Hate only breeds more hate. If we don't restore the natural balance, nature will do it for us."

Dad takes hold of my shoulders, turns me around to face him and looks at me as if I've gone mad.

"Dad it's true, I know our world is going to end if we carry on down this path. I've seen it. This is my talent. I've got second sight. Please believe me."

He stares at me, momentarily stunned.

"She's right Daniel." Fingle appears at his shoulder, his small wings whirring frantically. "We need to go to the Hill of the Faeries."

Bramble appears beside him. "We can't lead the evil there Fingle, it's sacred."

Her agitation is evident from the shakiness of her voice. A look passes between the two and Fingle's eyes darken and look out past me into the crowd.

"We must to do this. It's our price for the past."

"Everything young Rose says is true." A deep voice rings out of the shadows.

Turning around, we all look towards the three shadows emerging from the trees at the periphery of the camp. First a tall, lean man emerges with long blonde hair tinged with an edge of grey. Amber shouts, "Boon," and runs towards him. Dot materialises next to him. Dad stares at the final figure to emerge from the shadow, then sprints off like a bow from an arrow and scoops Mum up, whirling her round and kissing her as if they were newly mated.

"What are you doing here woman?" he half shouts, half sobs. Mum smiles and laughs, strokes his face and hair over and over, as if she can't believe he's there. Duncan gives them some time and runs over to hug Mum and I follow a bit more hesitantly, knowing that leaving so suddenly must have hurt her. She says nothing, but envelopes me in a huge hug, her scent bringing back a flood of childhood memories and I know everything is alright.

"I'm sorry Mum," I whisper into her shoulder.

"It's okay, sweetheart. We're back together now."

"Here lass," Boon says as he opens his bag and Peck's beak pops out curiously. I grab him as he jumps from the bag. I've missed him too. Dad puts his arms around Mum and me, turns around and faces the crowd once more.

"At some point in the next two days you will question why you're here. Why this is your fight. Why you shouldn't just pack up and go home. I'm here because I want to save my family. I want to save my son, who's under the influence of the Knights. I want to return home with my Maggie and see my children happy with their Mates. I believe in our people. I believe in the Natural Laws. I believe in Sensio."

I start to cry as the crowd begins to quietly to chant "Sensio, Sensio," quietly at first, then louder and louder, until they break into a loud cheer. Neighbour shakes hands with neighbour and there's a feeling of energy, of strength and purpose as everyone goes back to their tents. Who knows what will happen in two days' time? Who knows our fate? All that matters is what we believe right here, right now. We believe that we will win the battle and go back to our families and friends. We believe that Sensio will be saved. And I believe that I will get my Mate back and, if I am very lucky, his love.

REUNION

Amber Lockwood

I live in the moment. For as long as I can remember, I've always worried about the past and the secrets lurking there. Secrets lingering in the shadows ready to jump out at me, when I'm weak and unable to deal with the consequences. And then, when I found out about my past, I started to worry about the future. How could I anticipate what was going to happen and deal with it? How could I cope? I've finally come to realise that my life has been so unpredictable that no plan or set of rules would have changed where I am now.

Tonight, as I watch the people in the camp gather around their fires at dusk, that conviction is strengthened. Plans and strategies have no place here. The past is gone and I can't worry about the future. Not tonight. I want to live now. I need to live now. All the people I care about are around me.

I watch Rose walking around the camp. Although she appears to have recovered from her self-induced coma, she seems older than her 18 years. She's unobtrusive, reticent, even, yet she misses nothing and I wonder if the reticence is how she copes with her talent. Duncan explained that second sight is a talent that is as rare on Sensio as it is on Earth. Those who possess it keep their own counsel due to suspicion and fear. Those who are brave enough to embrace and disclose it are usually ridiculed for it.

Her description of the destruction of Sensio sent a shiver

down my spine, reminding me of my nightmares. The responsibility that comes with this talent must be immense. I can see that Rose feels the full weight of it, her skin is pale and there are dark coloured shadows under her eyes. But there's something else weighing down on her. I sense it's less to do with circumstance and more to do with Aiden. She hasn't spoken his name since she got here, like the act of whispering the sound could splinter the bloody wound around her heart and cause more pain. Maggie keeps a constant eye on her daughter, afraid she'll disappear again. She was traumatised by Rose's sudden departure and couldn't rest until she set out to find her. Boon and Dot refused to let her leave without them. Truth be told, they were glad to leave. Greenwood is infected and it's only the battle for power between Ruth Gentles and Warwick that holds it on the precipice. I have a feeling it won't be long before he joins us here.

The trio made light of their journey here, Maggie and Dot joked about finally having "some fun of their own" but they obviously had some difficulties. Boon admitted what happened when they stopped briefly at a village to rest one night. An elderly woman had offered them accommodation and they were just about to sit down by the fire when her body suddenly contorted and cracked open to reveal an Aggressor, a shape-changing demon with a soul of pure evil. In Sensio, everyone knows them as mythical creatures from children's fables, but nobody really thought they existed, until now. Thanks to Boon's quick reflexes and presence of mind, they used their talents to fight it off, and they managed to escape. Given my last encounter with Maggie, I was nervous about how she would react to me last night.

Maggie is like a mother to me. She's been in the background, providing constant and silent support for a year. Her good opinion means everything to me. As I stood in front of her, trying to find the right words to say, she just smiled and pulled me into her arms, whispering how glad she was to see me, stroking my hair just as Lauren did when I was a child.

She glanced at Duncan and said, "I'm so glad that you two have sorted out your differences."

It's heartening to see how much Maggie and Daniel mean to each other. Daniel walks around purposely, conducting his business as leader of The Alliance but he can't go five minutes without touching Maggie, or pushing her hair gently behind her ear, or running his hand down her slender back, their intimacy almost too private for us to witness. It reminded us of what we are fighting for.

The tension of last night has dissipated. Everyone is visibly happier, united in their loyalty and commitment to The Alliance and what it represents. Tonight, I'm not just part of the Darkings family, I belong to The Alliance and tonight we choose to celebrate life instead of fearing it. We all understand our mission tomorrow and what it might bring, so we are all making the most of today. Looking around me, my thoughts stray to Aiden and I wonder where he is and what he's doing just now. When I asked Boon if he could have been infected by an Aggressor, he looked at me sympathetically, understanding that I'm looking for an excuse for his behaviour. I feel for my twin, he sacrificed himself to keep me safe, only to lose himself in the process. We have to save him now.

Boon and Dot are resting upon an upturned tree trunk. Boon sits upright, poking the fire with a stick in an attempt to get it to smoulder. Dot holds onto him tightly as if she can't bear to be physically parted from him, and he, understanding this, holds her hand and rests his chin on the top of her head. I sit opposite them, click my fingers and the fire bursts into lively flames. Boon looks at me with an emotion akin to paternal pride and laughs. I raise my eyebrows and smile cheekily back at him. The murmur of conversation surrounds us, cocooning our trio in a bubble of warmth around the firelight. Dot smiles at me contentedly and sinks closer into Boon.

I break the silence. "You kept me safe at Rowan Cottage. I've never thanked you properly for that."

Boon looks up from the fire in surprise. "I'm your mentor Amber. It's my job to keep you safe."

Dot blushes and nods in agreement. I smile and wonder if they know I see them as substitute parents. Every time I visit their home, Dot fusses over me like a mother hen, while Boon is the father I always wished I had. I'll always treasure the memory of our walks around Greenwood when he introduced me as Amber his student, with more pride than the title deserved. He patiently explained the Natural Laws to me and was genuinely delighted when I understood his lessons. He had been so proud of me when I used my talent for water against his on that last walk. I've discovered under the brittle, harsh exterior, he hides a vulnerability that he reveals only to those he trusts. Boon trusts me.

He frowns deeply as he throws another branch into the fire.

"I'm worried about tomorrow Amber. The natural balance is obliterated and there will be a price to pay." In that moment, he suddenly looks years older. Dot reaches her arm across and rests her hand on his, looking at me in concern. I consider his statement and remember his lessons.

"You taught me the Natural Laws; the balance will always restore itself. Look around you Boon," I add, gesturing towards all the people. There is good all around us. We must believe it will all work out."

Catching the outline of Duncan in the shadows, I don't just know it, I believe it with every beat of my heart. "We must live."

I get up and hug them both before I walk off into the shadows. I hear Boon murmur "The pupil has become the mentor," and I smile, my heart clenching with emotion.

I look for Duncan and find him deep in conversation. He is oblivious to me, so I steal a moment to look at him. I feel my body begin to melt as I remember digging my nails into those broad shoulders as he took me this morning. How did I land this gorgeous demi-god of a man as my Mate?

Since the night at the loch, we've embarked on a new relationship. Without question, I am his equal. He's taught me how to fight and protect myself, how to catch my opponent unaware and growling at Marcus when he's offered to help. Now, after weeks of exercise, I'm fit and ready to do what I must. Duncan has made me believe in myself and in exchange I have all of him. We have no secrets; he shares every part of himself with me.

Leaving the shadows, I put my arms around his hips, stroking him. I plant little kisses and rest the side of my face against his back and he threads his fingers through mine. I feel him clench and I smile, aware I'm teasing him. He quickly excuses us and we walk quickly back to our tent. I wonder if the passion we feel will ever burn out but as Duncan pulls me onto our bed and kisses me, I get my answer. I feel it from his hands on my body, as he drags the clothes off me and catches my hips. I feel it as I pull him into me, as I give him my body, my heart and my soul.

I choose now. I choose to live.

THE FRAY

Amber Lockwood

The mist is haunted. We stand together at the mouth of the loch. The light will have to fight to be seen today. Mist rises towards us like a ghost, sweeping weightlessly, whispering stories of our past and the possibilities of our future, if we survive today.

My feet are planted firmly on the ground, every part of my body taut and centred. It's eerily still. I strain my eyes through the shadows looking for Black Knights. I want to run from what's to come, but I know we have to face it. I yearn for yesterday. I ache to feel Duncan's naked body over mine. He appears at my side and I immediately feel the comfort that only he can bring. He's rigid with concentration, thinking solely of what's ahead. I remember our kiss this morning and pray it won't be our last. Without him, I no longer exist.

Rose is trying to control her anxiety by exhaling long, slow breaths like a runner preparing for a race. Marcus stands beside her. He too is focused, his usual easy smile gone and replaced with a frosty stillness that the warmest sun couldn't thaw. If he, a former Knight is wary, how will I - a mere girl from Earth - fare? Feeling the negativity feed like a hungry serpent, I squash it before it has the chance to take hold. I have to believe. I have to keep faith.

I touch the amulets under my shirt, Aiden's and mine. Aiden's burns me: he's close by and the amulet wants to return to its master.

Duncan releases a long, slow breath as the bow of the boat becomes visible through the mist and moves steadily towards the shore. The figure on board is gradually revealed. His body is skeletal, cheeks hollowed, dark hair long and lacklustre. As he draws closer, I see a ghost of a smile playing on his lips, like he is party to a secret joke. His eyes are shut. It's Aiden, but it's not Aiden. Grief overwhelms me as I realise he has become the physical manifestation of what he tried so hard to prevent. He is a shadow of his former self.

The strength of our line winces in indecision. Do we wait? Or do we attack? Then he opens hate-filled, black, soulless eyes and the decision is made. Rose shouts and Marcus holds her back. I fight to stay focused. We must save him. The sky is eclipsed with screaming crows and as each one lands on the shore, it transforms into a Black Knight. Within seconds, an army is standing on the shoreline before us. It has begun.

Swords clash, bows are released and the shouts and screams are deafening. A Black Knight appears in front of me and laughs heartily. Remembering Duncan's training, I throw up a layer of sand and momentarily blind him. He stumbles backwards, swearing and I slash his belly with my sword. He cries out and doubles over. Stiffening my resolve, I lift a brick from the ground into the air and scream out as it rushes towards his head, bursting the skin at his temple with a large pop. Blood spurts onto the ground, followed seconds later by his body. I stagger back in shock and disbelief, the adrenalin is pumping through me as I realise. I've just killed someone. Then Duncan's words echo in my head, "Don't hesitate. Keep going."

I look around for Aiden, adrenalin burning through my veins. My eyes fall on the lonely figure partially obscured on the other side of the loch. A man with dark hair watches the proceedings dispassionately. He sits astride a black unicorn, that tosses its head agitatedly, an unwilling witness to our brutality. Green and blue shades hit against his backdrop, alternatively hiding and revealing the witness to our fray. The sky is growing black and the wind picks up. Aiden suddenly materialises a few feet away from me.

"Sister." he drawls sarcastically, "How good it is to see you again." Surveying me like a prize already won.

Slowly, he removes his black gloves and I can see that his large hands are thin and wasted and covered with dried blood. He slowly unsheathes his sword and settles it in his hand, ready to strike.

Refusing to be intimidated, I loosen my arms and smile back at him and reply, tauntingly, "You want me brother? Then come and get me..." as I lift up my hand and let loose an arrow of fire.

As he ducks out of the way to avoid the flames, I turn around to run and find myself sucked into and carried along by a flood of screaming, fighting, bleeding humanity moving towards the Hill of the Faeries. Duncan has obviously given the signal to flee. Wind and hailstones push me back as I follow Fingle and Bramble at the front, leading the way. They leave a trail of light for us to follow, it stays bright even as it fades and it gives me hope, helps me to keep going. I see the Hill just ahead, an undeniable feat of nature, flanked by a mass of solid oaks and a group of smaller trees and reaching the foothill I begin the steep climb. I slip on mud and wet leaves, but I keep pushing on, thighs and chest burning, fighting off dizziness, each breath becoming increasingly difficult. I hear shouts and screams around me and I'm aware of Aiden's crazy laughter, but I keep climbing higher and higher, refusing to give up, going round the next corner and the next until I heave myself onto the top of the hill. Chaos reigns. The elements themselves are raging against us, with rain and hailstones battering us and the wind howling. Maggie and Dot are there already, heaving stones down onto the Knights below. Rose suddenly screams and I turn round and see Aiden walking nonchalantly towards me.

Rose and Marcus flank me. "Are you ready for this Amber?" Marcus says. I grimace, shake my head but step forward anyway.

Aiden opens his arms and exclaims, "It's a family reunion." when he sees Maggie try to pull Rose away.

I harness the wind's power and use it to throw him on his back. He's covered in mud and leaves. Within seconds, he's back on his feet. In my peripheral vision, I can see Duncan and Luther. Luther's body strains and bulges against his armour as he moves towards Duncan like they're engaged in an intricate choreographed dance. They turn and Luther catches my eye and winks at me. Everywhere I turn, everyone I care about is in danger. Marcus is defending Rose and Maggie from a Black Knight, while Boon pummels another into the ground with his fists.

I force Aiden onto his back again, this time making him drop his sword. He leaps up and backhands me. For a second I'm blinded and my cheek explodes in pain, but Marcus scrambles over and pins him down. Maggie sees what's happening and sits on his shoulders and pulls his hair. Aiden fights like a man possessed but I press the amulet against his skin and hold it there. His screams are anguished and gut-wrenching, but I don't let go. All the hate, all the evil, all the blackness is being exorcised from his body and his soul. Suddenly, the screaming stops and there's an unearthly hush. The air is rendered still, electricity tingles and crackles, the atmosphere holding us in place, in peril and breaking.

Aiden sits up, dazed, and looks around him. He lifts and studies his hands, looks at the grime, the nails clogged with dirt and the skin covered in dried blood.

He whispers brokenly, "What have I done?"

Rose takes him in her arms and rocks him gently, her face blazing with love and determination. I watch her in awe. I hadn't realised how strong she was. The nature of the shouts and screams around us change.

Rose looks up and murmurs, "It's time."

Down in the valley below, a tsunami is coming towards us, getting closer and closer, swallowing Black Knights, buildings, trees and weapons in its wake. It's like a vision of the apocalypse. Hearing Luther cry, I dismiss the sound, instead choosing what mattered. I take Aiden's hands and cover them with mine, taking away the sight that hurts him. Duncan holds me and his cold cheek rests against mine. I automatically nuzzle into him, seeking the reassurance of his heartbeat, our fingers thread tightly.

He whispers, "I would do it all again to be with you."

I nod, tears rolling down my cheeks, hoping my touch communicates the words I cannot say. Closing my eyes, I feel the spray of the water and prepare myself. If it's my time to go, I do so willingly, surrounded by those I love.

We all fall together into the mist.

FATED

Rora Ravenswood

Everything that's happened in my life has led me here. At home in Ravenswood, I clutch the bed as another contraction overwhelms me and I try to breathe through it. I try to focus and remember the night I confessed to Maggie that I was pregnant. She made me stay that night. My mind raced for hours, tormented by images of the empty cottage, the desperate fruitless search, the heartbreak, the book and the words in the letter.

Then, when I finally found sleep, he came to me. He looked tortured, his eyes haunted and his hair awry. I clutched at him desperately, needing to hold him, crying when my hands passed through a shadow. Was he a cruel figment of my imagination?

"I can't break free Rora." he cried out, anguish marring his features.

"Tell me what to do, Will," I pleaded. "I can't live without you. Please don't make me."

His face whitened at my distress, but he continued, "You must leave Sensio Rora, it's not safe anymore. Please do this for me."

For a second, I could feel his breath, see the ocean move in the blue of his eyes, taste his lips. He was here with me.

"I love you Rora," he murmured, kissing my eyelids.

I say the words back to him, pressing closer, I opened my

eyes, as the heat from his body receded to ice. His eyes stayed with mine, frantic, then deathly still as he moved back into shadow then faded into nothing but air. I screamed out in grief and pain.

"I'm having our baby Will. Please don't leave me."

Then there were arms around me, shaking me awake and I looked up to see Maggie standing over the bed, calling my name. I fell into her arms and sobbed out my grief.

"He's dead, Maggie, he's gone. I don't want to live without him." Reaching out frantically, I try to connect with him but feel nothing. In death, he'd gone where I couldn't follow, leaving me torn, severed in half and bleeding.

Eventually, exhausted, I fell into a deep, dreamless sleep. When I woke up, Maggie was sitting in the faded wicker chair next to the bed, a blanket wrapped around her to keep off the chill in the room.

She looked over at me and held out her hand. "You feel nothing?"

I nodded, checking my amulet. I felt as if time had frozen and I couldn't breathe. I didn't just have one amulet around my throat. I now had two. Somehow, Will had passed on his amulet, his soul, for me to take care of. If I needed confirmation my fears were real - this was it. I stilled the urge to wrench them from my neck and throw it across the room. I wanted none of it - not without him. I remember the last time I saw him and I'm glad I didn't know what was to come. We were happy and in love, my happiness so complete it was limitless. If I knew that was our last moment together it would have been marred with sadness. Every moment with him was everything.

I'm forced back to Earth and the present by another contraction. Lauren encourages me to keep going. I'm so glad she's here. I just don't think I could have done this on my own. I miss Maggie too. I can just imagine her here shouting at me to keep going, just as I did when Duncan was born, while Daniel paced patiently outside the bedroom.

Our goodbye was hard. She knew the moment I gave her Will's amulet to keep safe that we wouldn't see each other again. When I left Greenwood, I turned back and took one last look at Maggie silhouetted in the doorframe and I felt her with me as I disappeared from her view, into the forest and back to my own world.

I removed my own amulet a month ago. It became cold and I knew I was meant to let it go. A few days ago, I went for a walk in the village and was approached by an elderly neighbour with a charity bag. I handed the amulet over. I only hope it brings its new owner more luck than it has brought me.

My body is telling me to push. I roar through the next contraction, pushing, pushing until I hear my baby's loud, quavering cries. Our baby. Our boy. Daniel helps me to sit up and hold him and I look down at him with wonder. In that moment, the pain, the grief, almost seemed worthy of the love replacing it. Another contraction comes and Lauren confirms what I already knew, we've been blessed twice. Our beautiful girl is smaller than her brother and cries quietly. I lie back, exhausted. I've kept my promise.

I try to explain to Lauren but I'm too breathless, too tired, as my soul leaves my dying body. Nana smiles as she holds out her hand to me. I take it and look one last time at our babies. I hope Lauren understands that it wasn't anything she did or didn't do. I haven't died from a complication or an infection. I died of a broken heart, that splintered in half eight months ago when he left this world without me. I kept my promise to live until our babies arrived safely. Will didn't realise that when he asked me to go home, I thought only of him. Nana tugs my hand and I follow her into the bright, warm light.

I'm going home. I'm going home to him.

"I have lost my Will and my will to live,

My heart beats only for love yet to give,

In my journal I write teardrops with ink,

Why can't I sense him? I daren't think...

I have lost my Will and my will to live,

To my unborn babies,

I am so sorry, please forgive..."

...Rora

Rora

WITNESS

The Observer

I watch the scene with bored detachment. The Black Knights fly through the air and descend en masse onto the shore transforming mid-flight from crows back to their human form, before beginning their assault on The Alliance.

Luther is particularly enthusiastic about this mode of attack because he thinks it will completely disorientate our opponents and it uses Aiden to reinforce the point that he's one of ours.

Luther loves to play these mental games, disarming and weakening his enemy prior to completing the actual physical act. For him the pleasure comes from the anticipation, the act of killing itself is in actual fact anticlimactic. He's killed so many times that it's become meaningless to him. The people change but the game stays the same.

As for me, all I'm interested in is the end result. This business needs to be settled, as it should have been many years ago. It's now a matter of honour - my honour. My allegiance demands it.

Pulling on the reigns, I turn the unicorn away. I don't feel the need to watch the proceedings. I have sent men to their deaths before and will do so again without hesitation. And if the outcome isn't what we planned, then I'll put my own plan into action, the one that Luther doesn't know about.

My liege will be happy. That's my only concern.

AFTERMATH

Amber Lockwood

The rain falls steadily and persistently on the coffin as it's lowered into the ground. It drips onto our clothes, slowly working through the material and settles on our skin, turning us from scant warmth to bitter ice cold. Warm breath forms large puff balls of air that converge inside our circle migrating towards the coffin, wishing air back into the body within. The rain hangs heavy, weighing me down, pushing me towards the ground and silently encouraging me to follow the departed. Duncan's hand holds mine, his thumb stroking my palm, the heat from his finger warming and comforting me. Moving closer, I tighten my grip and trail a finger over his skin. Duncan grieves too; in fact, he is probably more entitled to the emotion than I.

This is our second day back in Greenwood and it feels like a lifetime has passed since I was here last. I look around me with a new perspective, feeling as if my past life was lived by another version of me: someone much younger and more naïve. It's seems like an imaginary existence to the adult standing here at the graveside. Our journey back was completed in muted silence; words punctuating the quiet only when necessary.

We were all stunned by the events at the Hill of the Faeries – and we're still too upset to talk about them. This place, protected by faerie magic had stopped the tsunami from consuming us. Somehow, it sent the huge waves back to from where they came from.

Clods of earth fall on top of the coffin. The staccato strikes punctuate against the muffled cries around me, the grief so tangible, I wince against its closeness. We can all hardly bear to witness the burial. Has our liberty come at too high a cost? We are unwilling witnesses to this ritual; unable to accept the aftermath.

Aiden stands reluctantly beside Rose. He hasn't uttered a single word since he returned to himself. He looks haunted, his black eyes ringed with dark shadows. His black hair is overgrown and streaked with strands of grey and white, making him seem closer to middle age than a man of 19. I feel guilty knowing how easily it could have been me instead of him, while part of me is relieved. I don't think I'd have survived it.

Daniel stands beside Maggie, his arm in a sling. While everyone else just watched as Luther was being sucked under the water, he and Boon alone pulled the Black Knight to safety. Daniel has to leave soon for the King's court to act as a witness against Luther, who is being put on trial for his crimes. Duncan has been appointed Village Protector until he returns.

Claudio Alfario was given the task of escorting Luther to court and took on the role of gaoler with great relish as they departed. We watched as he pulled then dragged Luther along behind him, yanking the rope so fiercely that Luther fell flat on his face, admonishing him.

"Come on lad, let's not linger now," as he half-heartedly helped him upright again before they began to walk over the hill, two dark shadows silhouetted against the sun.

As they disappeared over the brow of the hill, we watched them with mixed feelings. Angry shouts punched the air, tension shimmered, some cried, whether through grief or relief that the battle was finally over. As they disappeared, we saw Claudio push Luther over once more and I allowed myself a wry smile. This man, who had caused so much devastation and heartache, was finally at our mercy. The rest of the Black Knights had perished in the waves or had fled.

Warwick speaks quietly as the ritual ends, his voice gruff, and his words sombre. I can't process them. Words seem inadequate. We stand in silence unwilling to accept this end, unwilling to accept the truth, unwilling to face the grief.

A cry pierces the air and Dot's soft gentle features contort in an anguish I can't begin to imagine. She sobs out her rage and despair, barely able to stand. Maggie tries to hold her up before she falls to her knees and her hands clench into tight fists, her red-rimmed eyes never once leaving Boon's coffin. Finally, she quietens, her mouth attempting the physical act but her voice coming out as silence as she clutched the dirty earth now holding her Mate. We all look away, intruding on a moment, so private and painful, we had no right to be there.

In that instant, I'm transported back again to the Hill. Holding Aiden's hands as Duncan held me, waiting for the worst, when we slowly became aware of the euphoric cheers around us. Realising the Hill of the Faeries had saved us and we joined in the cheering. Then we heard the screams.

"No. No." Dot yelled frantically, pulling Boon to her chest and rocking him back and forth in anguish, as Daniel shouted and kicked a blood covered knife out of Luther's hands and knocked him unconscious. I stumbled over to where Boon lay, and put my hand on his arm. Dot murmured softly to him, "You'll be fine, my love, you'll be fine."

I looked frantically around for somebody to help and seeing Fingle, I shouted, "Please do something." He shook his head and looked down. Maggie covered her face with her hands. Boon opened his eyes and looked at Dot and then at me. He smiled, and whispered "my girls," before closing his eyes for the last time.

The silence became absolute as everyone realised that he had gone. Dot wailed like an animal in pain for her Mate, the cry torn from her heart, so painful to hear, even in memory. I open my eyes as Maggie tries to help Dot get up from the graveside.

I can't bear this. Wrenching my hand from Duncan's I turn to go back to Greenwood, ignoring my name as it's called.

I remember our walks around the village. I feel Boon walking with me now, watching me with pride as I reiterate his teachings of the Natural Laws. I'll never understand the Natural Law of death. Not today. Not ever.

I come to the shore, where the white water is calm and still and without a ripple in a way I've never seen before. I sit down and shut my eyes. I remember Boon's concerns the night before the battle. Now I feel guilty for dismissing them so easily. Did he know? Could he feel death coming for him and wanted to prepare us? I'll never know. I didn't linger long enough to listen. I've never had a chance to say goodbye to or grieve for the people I've loved and lost. Today, for the first time, I got the chance to say goodbye and it's devastating. For this man, my mentor and my friend became something I've never had before.

I feel Duncan pull me back against him and rest his head on my shoulder. It was then I gave in and finally cried as I said goodbye to the only father I've ever known.

REDEMPTION
Aiden Darkings

I see the faces of everyone I've murdered. They haunt me day and night. I hear their screams, see their torn flesh, smell their burning homes and all the time my sword blade is dripping with blood and I'm looking for my next victim. I cannot recall my time with the Black Knights at will, instead the memories overwhelm me when I least expect them.

In the first few moments after I woke up and saw Amber, I felt like I used to feel. I felt like myself, the good Aiden. Then I started to get the flashbacks. They come at me like a flood of vengeful insects prying at my skin, burning me with every sick vile act I've ever committed. They linger in the corners of my mind and steal any chance I have of forgetting what I have done. A murderer of men.

Warwick came to see me today, his eyes sunken, his face gaunt and his hair grey. I wait for his censure. What could I say to defend my actions, my choices and their consequences?

"You did what was needed lad, don't forget that. You did what you had to do to survive. It's the nature of war."

Did I? I'm not sure. Isn't it wrong to kill another, whatever the justification? Because it's war, does it mean that I'm forgiven and can forgive myself for my actions? Warwick is a man of magic. If he wants to inflict damage on another he uses a spell or a potion. He doesn't have to twist his sword into flesh, muscle and watch the wound spurt with blood, hear the cries as they plead in the last moments of their life, the shuddering final breaths and then the silence when it is finally over - until the next time.

All I know is that I'm living in a hell that only exists inside my head. I'm so traumatised that I can't even form a coherent sentence. The one thing I'm sure about is that I don't want to hurt another human being for as long as I live.

Then I think of Amber and I remember why I did what I did. It was for her. I pushed my twin away from the day she came to Sensio, but she refused to give up on me when others did. She came after me and I owe her my life - such as it is.

When she came to visit yesterday, she sat on the bed beside me and studied me with such concentration that I thought she could read my mind. Placing her hand on mine, she squeezed it until I looked up from the floor to her clear eyes, guileless and determined.

"You are still you Aiden. You just forgot for a while. You saved me."

I winced. All I remember was leaving her to defend herself against those beasts.

"You released my bonds. You tried instinctively to protect me."

She leaned against my shoulder and said. "You joined them so that they wouldn't take me. You survived. I wouldn't have."

She kissed my cheek and passed a brown journal to me, worn with use and bound together with brown twine.

"When I was lost, Rora was there. Maybe she can help you too."

I wonder if she fully understands the danger I put her in that day. Duncan understands perfectly well and still snarls whenever we are in close proximity, before being quietly admonished by Maggie. I understand his anger and I know I deserve the punch that's coming my way. I would feel the same if it was my Mate.

My Rose… What have I done to her? I pushed her away after she declared her love for me. I betrayed her with another woman over and over again. In Sensio, the trust you have with your Mate is sacred and once that bond is established it's never betrayed. Duncan and I both had our youthful indiscretions. Most young men here do. But these were short lived and discreet. Women have the same right although they seldom assert it. Sierra was … a pleasurable diversion and Rose and I haven't brought up the betrayal that lies between us. It stands between us like a huge brick wall. I killed her trust before it had a chance to grow. She is kind, despite the circumstances, fussing over me as she did when we were children, when I would retreat into silence and linger on the edge of the crowd. Then she would walk up to me, place her little hand in mine and pull me determinedly towards people and life and make me take part. I want so badly to take her in my arms and ask her to be my Mate, but how can I? I don't deserve her. I'm not worthy.

Sometimes, I see her laughing with Marcus, happy and

relaxed, her laughter fluttering in the air like the song of a baby bird and I feel angry because she can't laugh like that with me. I shouldn't resent their friendship. I have no right. I haven' earned the right to be happy. Under the circumstances, I'm lucky to be alive.

I await my sentence. I am no different from Luther and like him, I must also pay for my crimes.

INSTINCT

Rose Darkings

The storm is coming. I look up at the sky, and it's angry with patches of darkness waxing against it, like oil refusing to mix with the rest of the colour. The rain falls relentlessly, looking soft to the eyes but once you're within its element, it leaves cold prickly imprints along your body and chills you to the bone. It makes me uneasy like a sense of foreboding is waiting in the wings to appear at the opportune moment.

On a day like today, the village is quiet. Everyone is at home gathered around the fire. In times past, a dark sky and a bit of rain wouldn't have stopped people being out and about. But the Greenwood of those days is long gone. Replaced by a stillness that refuses to speak. We're all afraid of the future – too afraid to talk about it in case our fears become real.

We all miss Boon. When I'm out in the village I still automatically look for him, walking around at his steady pace, pushing his long hair back behind his ears impatiently, his eyes taking in every details of what's going on around him. I miss his teasing. When I was younger and Megan and I were laughing about something silly, he would always walk towards me with a stern expression on his face, as if he was going to give me a row. Then, as he was walking past he would give me a huge smile and a wink and that always made us collapse in a heap of giggles. He was the backbone of our village and we never realised it until he was gone.

I knock on Warwick's door and wait briefly before entering.

His home is silent apart from the snap and crackle of logs on the fire. The smoke teases my nose, heat clashing against the dust on the table, the cocktail mix making the air humid and cold all at once. The firelight makes the room look warm and welcoming, but if you look closely, it hasn't been used in some time.

Making my way into the bowels of the building, I reach the bottom of the stairs, firelight from the sconces cast an ethereal glow over Warwick, sitting alone, nursing a cup of brew. The lines and shadows on his face are exaggerated by the candlelight from large, thick taper candles fused onto a silver plate, used so much, the dripping wax had frozen in time by its sides. I hear chirping from the corner and the tap of claws along the stone floor, and Peck emerges from the shadows, making little clucks of recognition. Now over a metre tall, he lifts his grey head regally and pokes his yellow beak into my hand. I take a slice of apple from my pocket and feed it to him.

"Honestly, Rose, you spoil him." Warwick says, smiling sadly.

His attention is on the cup of brew in his hand, his fingers caress the grooves in the wood, seeking comfort not given to him by the mead, his eyes on the other filled cup of brew placed near an empty seat. Boon's seat. Lifting his cup, he knocks it unsteadily against the other, making the liquid swirl and overflow. He fusses, cleaning it up, trying to cover the grief and loneliness and something else. Guilt…

"You knew this would happen," I said.

He looks up and for the first time since I've arrived, he meets my eyes. They are anguished, his face twisted in sorrow and I can see the weight of it hang off him. I look away and watch Peck ruffle his feathers and sit back down on a worn rug, near enough to be aware of us, but far enough away to settle comfortably. No responsibility. Not a care in the world. For a moment, I envy him and his simple existence.

We stay silent. I look at the shadows and remember being in the Great Hall with Aiden's hot body pressing my back against the cold stone, as his mouth violently took mine. I shiver at the memory. A girl never forgets her first kiss and as much as I savour it, I also put it away, as I try to shut out what happened afterwards.

I look at Warwick and wonder about his Mate. Everybody knows about her, but hardly anybody has seen her. Perhaps that's why Boon's death has hurt him so badly: he not only lost a friend that day he lost family, too.

I take a deep breath and broach the subject I came to discuss. I came here encouraged by the hush of whispers, the sounds and songs of the ancient tribes and cultures that live on the periphery of our society. They tell me that the fight isn't over and that the natural balance was far from restored.

"There's more to come, isn't there?" I whisper the question, part of me hoping, praying I'm wrong.

Warwick nods slowly in agreement, swirling the liquid in his cup before looking up at me.

"You've an important part to play, young Rose, but first you need help with your talent, just as I did." Warwick continued. "Fingle will take you where you need to go. The

Empress will help you." He stops, suddenly, as an emotion I can't describe flickers across his face.

"When?" I ask, standing up, my limbs sparked with adrenalin and my mind seeking the next step.

"You'll know when the time is right, Rose. Trust your instincts."

He looked back into his cup of brew and I knew our conversation was over. I gave Peck a goodbye ruffle and climbed up the stairs, leaving Warwick to his thoughts.

Outside, the wind had picked up and it whipped my hair about my face as I walked back home.

Warwick was right. It's time I listened to the whispers. It's time I trusted my instincts. It's time I trusted me.

CONTENTMENT

Amber Lockwood

I feel almost guilty being so happy. The mid-day sun floods through the window and makes the bowls and glassware on the kitchen wink and sparkle. The room is filled with chatter and laughter as we bake for the village. We are listening as Rose finishes a story about Daniel that she remembers from her childhood. Maggie looks at her daughter fondly and smiles at Dot. She laughs along with us, her hair neatly pulled back in a bun, a dusting of flour smeared across her cheek. It's her first visit since she lost Boon and we're trying to make it happy. We're trying to help her forget for a little while.

I feel guilty being so happy. Out of everyone in the room, I have exactly who I want in my life. I couldn't ask for anymore.

Maggie worries constantly about Aiden. He's retreated to his room, only coming out to eat and walk around the village when it's dark, when nobody can see him. She worries about the estrangement between him and Duncan, but I've every faith they'll sort out their differences because if I can understand and forgive, so can he. Duncan can't quite supress his overwhelming need to protect me, even knowing that I'm here and safe. In those moments, around the table when I feel the tension, Maggie reaches over and squeezes my arm and smiles at me, rolling her eyes dramatically at the ways of men and I'm so happy to know her that my heart squeezes with happiness.

Rose also worries, but I know it goes much deeper. I've seen how she and Aiden watch each other, always when the other is distracted and completely unaware. Their expressions so intense, so laden with private emotion, I feel like I'm intruding and have to look away. But despite the tension, they rarely exchange words. There is a huge chiasm between them, that they don't seem able to bridge.

Rose often hangs out with Marcus, who is helping Daniel during his sabbatical. Though they laugh and tease one another, I suspect it's only harmless banter, because behind the mirth in her eyes there is caution, she won't let anyone close until she's ready.

I look at Dot and my happiness stills.

Her face has been ravaged by grief to the extent you would hardly recognise her. Her rosy cheeks are now sunken and black triangles shadow her eyes that are dull and faded. Her clothes are hanging from her because she forgets to eat. She listens to us speak but then falls away from the conversation, her eyes glazing over and you know that she's thinking of him, losing herself in memories that both comfort and hurt her. She breathes deeply, trying to calm herself, before listening and laughing once more. Their separation so painful she needs to take a moment to process it. I'm only grateful that she's here, if only for a few hours and trying to go on without her Mate.

I look round all these women, who mean so much to me in their own special way. I realise there is no other place in the world I'd rather be. I'm finally where I belong.

We separate the bread and begin delivering it to the

villagers. Maggie glances at Dot as we walk away and I nod quickly, understanding that she wants me to keep an eye on her. It's so reminiscent of my walks around the village with Boon that it seemed only fitting that now I would be in the company of his widow. For the most part she is fine, nodding and smiling as required. But if anyone tries to comfort her with words or gestures, she visibly freezes and walks off.

When the bread is delivered, we say goodbye and she walks away, her shoulders slumped, her body exhausted from pretending she's fine. I hope there will come a time when she genuinely feels good again.

Returning to the home I now share with Duncan, I head to the bedroom to change my clothes for a run. I can't find them at first and when I see them twisted up in the sheets, I smile, remembering this morning. The sun had just peeked through the curtains when I stretched and got up to leave the bed, only to find myself restrained by a muscled arm.

"And where exactly do you think you're going?" Duncan asked, moving over me and placing soft kisses from my neck to my collarbone.

I breathed in the scent from his thick, dark hair, my skin both awoken and tickled by the stubble on his cheeks. "Well, I was going to go for a run." I began to say. Duncan smiled, shook his head and kissed away the rest of my words.

I pick up the pace as I run round the buildings, past the wishing well and head out of the village. I spot Duncan at the treeline, speaking with his father and Marcus and we exchange a smirk, each of us thinking about why I'm later than usual for my run. Smiling at our private joke, Marcus has to punch Duncan on the arm to get his attention back.

It's finally official and has been for some time: Duncan Darkings rocks my world. I never believed it could be possible to be so utterly consumed by another person, to the point where I feel such a part of him that I don't know where he ends and I begin. He's my everything.

The air changes from breezy to humid when I reach the forest and I follow the winding path and stop to cool down at the cluster of trees. When I'm stretching my legs, something hard presses into my foot and I laugh as I pick up the battered fragments of the mobile phone I threw against the tree over a year ago. For a moment, I think about my former life, knowing I will always miss Lauren and Elaine. But Sensio is now my home, my true home.

The air suddenly turns bitterly cold and the wind rushes through the trees, tearing leaves from their branches and tossing them high into the air and back down onto the forest floor. I hear a familiar buzzing and look around for my faerie friends.

"Amber, you've to come with us." Fingle says urgently.

His words tail off as a drumbeat begins, staccato, steady and relentless. Bramble calls my name, but I ignore her and run back to the treeline towards Duncan. I've never seen him looking so angry. His blue eyes are flashing, his cheeks flushed red with temper and his hands are clenched into fists at his side. He reaches out his hand to me and is visibly calmer when I take it.

"You're not going anywhere," he says, determinedly.

We walk back through the trees into the village and a crowd is assembling around an elegantly dressed man on a black unicorn, flanked by four guards. He smiles when he sees me. Instinctively, I know what he wants before he utters a word.

"I've come for Amber Lockwood," he declares.

JURISDICTION

Amber Lockwood

The stranger locks eyes with me. He is tall, with dark hair and eyes and a mouth that could be seductive or cruel, depending on the occasion. His voice is cultured, the octaves rising from generous lips and his green outfit is tailored, with a white shirt, waistcoat and new, shiny leather boots. Then he turned his neck and reveals a faded, thick, white scar at his neck, at odds with his cultured appearance. He sits astride a beautiful, black unicorn, who moves nervously below him. He's flanked by four large, burly guards with muscles straining from bronzed armour, their bodies still, waiting for his command.

"Amber Lockwood?" he repeats, taking in my sweat riddled face, tee-shirt and shorts with a grimace.

I nod, feeling the stares of everyone around me. Duncan's hand tightens in mine and I can feel the tension building in his body. The man takes out a scroll, and opens it. He reads it slowly and clearly.

"Amber Lockwood, you are ordered in the name of King Garrick and Queen Andora to appear before the King's Court. Your testimony is required at the trial of Knight Luther Barton. As Povack Templeton, Lord to the King and Queen Consort, I hereby order you to accompany me."

I digest the words and try to think of a suitable reply, but I can't, so I stay silent. Then Daniel steps forward, Maggie at his side.

"By what right do you summon my ward?"

Maggie takes my hand and I realise I'm shaking. Povack leisurely replaces the scroll in the sack at his hip before looking disdainfully at Daniel.

"Who addresses me, Sir?"

Daniel's tone is arctic. "Daniel Darkings, Protector of Greenwood. Amber Lockwood is the Mate of my son Duncan and is under my protection."

The crowd murmurs its support. Povack sighs, in exasperation, as though addressing an unruly child.

"The girl is summoned at our Sovereign's decree. All crimes reported to the crown are under the King's own jurisdiction as you should well know...Protector."

The unicorn's hooves clip-clop on the cobbles as the animal moves around nervously, sensing its master's impatience to be off. Claudio Alfario steps out from behind the guards.

"Daniel, man, there's no need for this. Amber lass, you know why you need to go, don't you?"

His question rings out and the crowd looks at me expectantly, wanting an easy solution to another fine mess I've got them into. Maggie sighs and I see her taking in Claudio with his new court clothes and elegant haircut. I look back at Povack. A memory flickered, a hairs breath out of reach then returned crystal clear.

"It was you on the bank watching us ... You were there just before the attack. I saw you." I say with growing conviction.

The pleasant mask slips on Povack's face to reveal an ugly sneer. "Take her!" he commands the guards.

Duncan pushes me behind him and unsheathes his sword, his father at his side. The crowd parts and the guards advance, raising their swords. I see the fight like it had already taken place and knew what was at stake. I can't let this happen again.

"Stop." I scream from the very depths of my soul. "Stop, please. I'll go with you."

Duncan turns around to look at me, sword still in his hand. Povack calls the guards to a halt. Daniel remains still, watching them warily. I walk towards Duncan and take his face between my hands. I can see his chest rising and falling with emotion and I can feel his heart thundering.

I whisper in his ear, "I have to go Duncan. I can't let this happen again."

He shakes his head at my words and his jaw clenches. "You can't go Amber. You need to stay here where you belong."

My eyes fill with tears. I didn't want to leave him. His eyes held mine, determined and ready to fight for me, no matter what the cost. Instead, I place my lips gently on his and kiss him. While he's distracted, I command a stone to rise up from the ground and knock it against the side of his head. He slumps against me, unconscious, and Maggie rushes forward to help me lower him to the ground. His eyes flicker and then close. I caress his temple, my thumb rubbing away the blood trickling from his wound.

"I can't let you get hurt Duncan," I whisper. I grab Maggie's hand and beg her, "You have to make him understand. Please, Maggie."

She nods, cradling her son's head in her arms, her eyes agonised.

The guards take me by the arms and walk me towards Povack. His eyes rake over me, the brown irises darken and I know I've made an enemy.

Daniel approaches Povack and says, "As my ward I'm entitled to accompany Amber and I now assert that right." Povack sighs and waves his hand at him dismissively. The tension dissolves as it looks as if trouble has been avoided. I am marched to our house and told to change and pack as quickly as possible. I look for a moment at the bed, sheet crumpled and twisted from this morning and I remember the feel of his body against mine. Looking around the room, I try to imprint our home into my memory for fear I never see it again.

Leaving the house, the crowd part for us. Maggie and Duncan are nowhere to be seen and I focus on the face of one person. Dot looks at me with love and pain in her face, wringing her hands in the apron and I know I'm not only saving Duncan. I'm leaving because it's my duty. It is what Boon would have expected of me.

CROSSROADS
Rose Darkings

I hear screaming as I run towards the bedroom. Opening the door, I hear the muffled moans as Aiden nuzzles his face into the pillow, his limbs thrashing in protest as he fights against the nightmare keeping hold of him. Sweat is pouring from his face and body.

"Aiden." I shake him urgently, trying to pull him out of his nightmare. "Aiden, wake up."

He snaps awake and peers at me in confusion, before he realises where he is. I sit beside him on the bed and take his hand.

"Another bad dream?" I ask, knowing the answer and hoping he'll want to talk about it.

Nodding, his voice husky with sleep, he says, "It was strange Rose, there was a baby being taken away from me. I try to move towards it, try to lift my arms but I'm so weak. He shudders. "Is Amber here? I think the baby was her ... us."

I grimace and look away, wondering how to explain the scene I'd witnessed a few hours ago. He knows immediately, of course, we're keenly attuned to each other no matter how much we try to ignore it. He gets out of bed and runs downstairs. I can hear the conversation from the bedroom door.

"She's gone Aiden. You're too late," Duncan bites out.

He's sitting on the chair by the hearth, staring intensely at the unmade fire, like focusing could bring it to life, seconds later he did exactly that. The flames smoked licking along the cold wood before being consumed and eaten. It was then I knew how angry he was. Duncan rarely uses his talent outside battle and never, ever in our home. He's holding a cold cloth to his swollen face. It looks painful. He's angrier than I've ever seen him. His blue eyes crystallise to sapphire, hard and unreachable.

"I didn't know Duncan. Don't you think I would've done something if I had." Aiden yelled, looking challengingly at my brother.

"And what exactly would that be, Aiden? You're too busy sitting in your room feeling sorry for yourself. That's all you've done since we got back from saving your arse."

Duncan stands up and throws the cloth against the chair. I skirt past them into the kitchen, where Mum is watching them warily, rubbing the back of her neck with stress. She's missing Dad badly already.

"You're right, Duncan. But I can't change the past. When do we leave?"

Duncan stalks towards him shouting, "I don't need your help lad. Amber's my Mate. I'll bring her back and she won't be going anywhere ... ever again."

His voice dips, revealing the hurt coursing through him. Since they moved into their own home, Duncan and Amber's happiness had been obvious to everyone. Their separation hurt him already.

Aiden tries to placate him. "She's my sister Duncan. I owe her. I'm coming with you."

Duncan clenches his fist and is about to take a swing at Aiden when stones are flung past their heads and smash against the wall. Then Mum steps between them, using her small body as a barrier between her two large sons.

"That's enough." Her voice is icy cold but she is shaking with anger. "You're family and that means you'll do whatever is needed to ensure we stay together. You'll both go to get Amber and your father and you'll both bring them back home."

This time it's Mum's voice that breaks at the mention of Dad's name with the tension and anger dissipate as Duncan and Aiden both try to comfort her. I look out of the window towards the village square, now mostly empty. Ruth Gentles walks across the square, looking elegant, as usual. I'd heard she was missing her daughter Caroline now she'd left Greenwood to live with her Mate. In the distance, I can see Warwick and Marcus talking near the wishing well. Marcus and I had struck up an easy friendship with each other at The Alliance camp. Sensing vulnerability in each other, we couldn't talk or acknowledge. He's funny and makes me laugh, but I know he has shadows from his past that he doesn't want to think about. Our friendship has attracted curious stares, the girl with the strange talent and the former Black Knight. But I don't want to put a label on what we have, all I know is that he's my friend and I trust him.

I go outside and sit at the table, closing my eyes and enjoying the feeling of the sun and fresh air on my skin. Feeling movement behind me, I fight the desire to turn round. I know it's Aiden without looking.

"We're leaving soon," he says quietly.

I nod. His finger grazes mine, searing heat into my skin and I pull my hand away from the burn. I glance over at simple, uncomplicated Marcus, who'd never ever hurt me and for a whisper of a breath I wished I felt more than friendship for him.

"You're close to Marcus," Aiden states, the suggestion lingers in the air.

"Like you were to Sierra?" I ask, watching the colour flood his cheeks. Wanting to hurt him, but only gaining a smattering of satisfaction I'd hoped.

"I wasn't myself, Rose," he whispers, looking down.

I start to feel sorry for him, but then I remember the day we packed up The Alliance camp. I saw Sierra and Aiden standing together, her arm on his, whispering words into his ear. The encounter only lasted a minute. But what I remember most is the look we shared as she walked away. He saw it all on my face: the pain, betrayal, and the anger and the knowledge that even as his Mate, I was the interloper in the relationship. That look only lasted seconds, before he had to look away.

Now a month later, he's accusing me of similar deception. I'm so angry; I wish Duncan had hit him.

"So that means I'm free, then. I have no Mate?" I challenge

him, seeking the closure I need. He growls, turns his back on me, his shoulders stiff and looks out over the village. He's silent and a small part of me that fosters hope flourishes. His answer when it comes is calm and certain

"Yes," he says.

I get up shaking and start to walk away. He grabs my arm. "I need to do this Rose," he says gently, stroking my cheek.

It doesn't matter any more. I'm done.

"Take care Aiden," I say as I walk away.

Mum and I say goodbye to Duncan and we watch them both walk away. Marcus comes over and squeezes my arm. Just at that moment, Aiden turns around and an expression that I can't describe flickers across his face before he turns and walks away quickly. Is it wrong to get a perverse pleasure from letting him draw his own conclusions about Marcus to protect my wounded pride? If it is, I accept it.

"Mum, it's time for me to go too," I tell her. She nods, her face resigned.

On the night that I'd returned from seeing Warwick I told her everything. I knew how upset she was the last time I left without explaining and I swore I would never do that to her again.

"I'll look after her Maggie, I promise," Marcus says and I'm relieved I'm going and that he's coming with me. Although I have absolutely no idea of what lies before me, my childhood dreams of romance and a family had just walked away from me. But I'm still standing with my friends and family by my side.

It's not a bad place to start.

BROTHERS

Aiden Darkings

Blood drips from my nose and I shake my head, trying to clear my blurred vision and focus on the forest floor. Gradually, the mist clears and I can see each blade of grass and pin needle clearly again. The forest floor is covered with my blood.

"You were due that, Aiden and you know it," Duncan says, looking at me unflinchingly.

I nod in agreement, as the sting simmered and I waited for it to abate. I knew it was coming and I'm glad it's finally over. When we left the village, we walked for hours before speaking. Knowing Duncan as well as I do, I respected his need for silence, knowing full well that he would say his piece when he was good and ready and not a minute before. Meanwhile, he punished me by setting a crippling walking pace as we tried to catch up with Amber and Daniel.

Duncan has always kept his temper in check, only giving into it at the precise moment he wants and not a second before. Even as a boy he had an edge that he kept well concealed. At six years old, the other children constantly reminded me of my beginnings on Earth, particularly in Boon's Natural Laws class. He noticed the teasing and put a quick stop to it in the classroom, but outside, I was teased mercilessly by Robin Tricken. It didn't take Duncan long to work out why I came home regularly with dirty cheeks and red rimmed eyes. This went on for a few weeks until one day in class, Robin turned up with a black eye and a completely different attitude to me. I knew then that Duncan had taken matters into his own hands.

Duncan is the perfect combination of Daniel's calm and Maggie's spark: he presents an aura of calm to the world while kicking the arse of anyone who messes with his own. It's appropriate that his particular talent is for fire. On the surface, he's even-tempered and determined to keep it under control as Daniel has taught him. But when the fuse is lit, his temper explodes with epic proportions.

The punch finally came when we reached the small clearing and prepared to make camp for the night. To be fair, I'd been half expecting it for weeks. He's lost his temper more since being mated, it's as if Amber pulls at places he didn't know he had. The highs are euphoric but the lows are devastating. Given the irrationality, I have been plagued with recently I can well understand. Still holding my nose, I sit down with my back against a tree and lift my head as far back as it will go. The blood flow starts to slow down.

"You used to be better at defending yourself, brother. Did the Black Knights soften you up?"

This is the question I've dreaded Duncan asking me, not knowing how I would answer it. I stall for time taking off my backpack, push past Rora's journal and pull out a blanket.

"Do you remember anything at all about your time with them?" he persists.

I finally work up the courage to meet his eyes. "I remember every single person I killed," I say, my face turning red with shame, waiting in silence for his judgement.

"You did what you had to Aiden. I remember the first time I killed," he says.

He looked at me steadily, obviously understanding the conflict that comes when you try to justify the kill but still feel sick about it. But I wonder if it was more. I took to the life of a Black Knight with passionate gusto. The violence, the women and the killing gave me an exhilaration and freedom I never anticipated. I enjoyed my confrontation with him using my new persona to say the words that I always thought but never said out loud. Do I have a propensity for evil that I didn't realise?

"You're not a Black Knight Aiden," he says quietly, reading my thoughts.

Despite his reassurance, the thought still torments me. We lapse into silence and gather wood, light a fire in the clearing and make camp for the night. I lie watching the sky change from dusky purple to black. Pinpricks of stars gradually appear and two moons shine over us.

"Why didn't you tell me of Warwick's plans for you?" Duncan asks.

I think about how to answer this very carefully. There was no reason why I shouldn't have confided in my brother, but I didn't because, quite honestly, I wanted something for myself. I've always been seen as Daniel's ward, the unofficial second son of the Darkings family and when Warwick approached me, not Duncan, I felt special. I wanted to make a difference – just me and me alone. How could I put this into words without hurting him or my adopted family? I know they view me and treat me as son, brother and friend, but despite their best efforts, I've always felt isolated. I had hoped this feeling would disappear when Amber arrived. It faded, but it never completely went away.

"He asked me not to tell anyone."

Duncan nods, understanding the importance of a man keeping his word. I sit up, pulling a clump of grass into my hand and throwing it into the fire, suddenly thinking of Rose. I ache for her so much, I feel a compulsion to talk about it.

"Rose is my Mate, Duncan" I confess.

"Ah, that explains a lot," he says, looking at me, curious, but waiting for me to continue.

"I've set her free. I'm not right for her," I mutter, picking up another clump of grass and throwing it into the fire. I look up and study the totem poles just beyond our camp, firelight revealing the intricately carved wood, a part of our landscape for so long, we had forgotten their origins. Wryly, I wondered if the men of that era had suffered similar heartache with their Mates.

Laughter bubbles from Duncan's chest, ending with huge guffaws reverberating around the clearing.

"Best of luck with that, Aiden. Having a Mate doesn't work like that," he says, narrowing his eyes and looking over at me. "Hurts already, doesn't it?" he asks and I nod, the pain obviously apparent on my face.

"Does it hurt being away from Amber?" I ask him, wanting more information, but not really wanting to know too much about my sister.

Duncan, the definitive alpha male, actually sighs at the thought of her.

"She's just part of me. I can't stand being away from her. Hell, I don't want too." He smiles, touching his swollen temple. "I can't believe she knocked me out." He says proudly, his smile broadening into a grin. "She'll make it up to me, though," he looks off into the dark night, like sheer will alone could bring her out of the darkness towards him.

Changing the subject quickly, I ask him, "It's not just Luther is it? There's someone else pushing this,"

The suggestion lingers in the air, catching life and breeding possibilities. Duncan looks up from the fire, his eyes focused and determined, light years away from the romantic sap of moments ago.

"What's the number one rule in battle?" he asks.

Instantly, I hear Daniel's mantra from our childhood cleverly disguised as lessons in battle strategy and tactics, my heart pounding from running, my eyes darting everywhere, loving my time with my brother and father. We repeated the words out loud together.

"Distract them in one area, win the battle in another."

We talk far into the night until the moons have faded and the fire has died out and the darkness has completely engulfed us. My nose still throbs, but despite the ache, I'm very happy to have my brother back.

All my life I've felt like I'm meant for something else, some other role that would make all the jigsaw pieces fit together. Amber is part of it and I need to save her as she's saved me. But I need to go for myself too, I need to find what I've always been looking for.

I need to find my destiny.

STORM

Amber Lockwood

I take five steps forward then stumble four backwards. My head is muddy and aching. Words swirl around my head and shout in the silence. Pictures filled with hopes and dreams tease, fading away before I can grab them. I feel like an animal trapped in a cage, teased by the fresh air filtering through the gilded bars but never fully able to absorb it into my lungs. I can only breathe shallowly past the hard lump cemented in my throat, the physical manifestation of my imprisonment. We tramp through the forest, purple sprays of colour from the sky push through the canopy provided by the large trees, the branches hunkering under the weight of the sun. I resent it and wish for rain or thunder to mirror the torrid emotions travelling through me. I feel angry at the world. I've been wrenched away from the life in Greenwood that I know is meant for me at the whim of some King and Queen I have no knowledge or interest in. The anger and resentment froths and bubbles over leaving me exhausted, then guilt swamps when I remember Boon and let it go. Then the cycle begins again.

I miss Duncan so much it hurts, our separation assimilating into a physical presence within my soul, kinetically aware of when I think of him, pulling my nerves past the ridge of exquisite pleasure to where unbearable pain only exists. From my rootless existence, I finally found a home in his arms. This is the life I want, but fate seems intent on preventing it from happening. A year ago, I would have crawled underneath the covers and hidden from the world.

Now I'm angry and ready to fight for what's mine.

Since we left Greenwood, we have walked south-west or "towards the sea" as Daniel says. This is the longest amount of time I've ever spent in Daniel's company, through circumstance rather than choice and I've learned a lot about him. He is a stoic man with little tolerance for wasted words, speaking only when necessary and lapsing into a comfortable silence the rest of the time. He has been a lynchpin, intertwined with the significant events of my life. Daniel was at my birth, took Aiden in and made sure I was safe; he saved me when Lauren died and brought me to Sensio. Now when I find myself on the cusp of another unknown experience, he's there for me again. His separation from Maggie must be painful for him but yet he stays and he's so physically like Duncan it's scary. Sometimes, out of the corner of my eye, I'll catch him with a particular expression on his face, or pushing his hands through his hair in frustration and just for a second I think it's him.

It's the third day of travelling and we've camped for the night. Povack has taken up residence in his cream castellated tent, with two turrets pointing to the sky. Despite the fact we camp on grass, leaves, moss or mud every night, the canvas castle is erected every evening without a blemish. It never ceases to amaze me. Povack retires for the night and two guards assume their position at either side of the tent flap. We are camped in the trees, the distance subtle yet significant.

"I don't trust him," I mutter to Daniel. My gut clenches, reinforcing my instincts.

Daniel looks up from the tree he is leaning back against. The last two nights he has placed his cloth bed between them and me, just as he places his body between us when we walk or stop to eat briefly or rest. He nodded his head, agreeing with me.

"Keep your talents to yourself Amber. He saw you move stone, so stick with that."

I take his warning on board; realising my emotions have simmered closer to the surface than I'd realised. Daniel watches my expression and chuckles. "I've been a soldier too long. It's hard to switch it off."

We lapsed into a comfortable silence and I wondered if now is a good time to ask the questions burning since I read Rora's journal.

"Can I ask you about my mother Daniel?" I ask.

Instantly, his expression becomes wary. "What do you want to know about Rora?" he asks.

A thousand questions race through my head. Who was our father? Was her hair long and curly like mine? Did she like jam on her toast? Why did she have to leave us?

"I read a bit of her journal and now Aiden has it." I hesitate and he nods, encouragingly. "Did she want to leave us? Did something go wrong when we were born?" My voice grows husky and I came right out and asked him the question that has haunted me since I learned of her existence. "Did we kill her?"

Daniel's face immediately softens. He holds my hand

tightly, as he says to me earnestly, "Your mother's soul died the moment she lost your father. She lived for another eight months to make sure you both arrived safely."

He let me digest this for a minute and then went on, "Your Mate is part of who you are Amber. When they leave, you have a choice of whether you want to leave with them or stay behind."

I thought of a world without Duncan and a despair I couldn't fathom overwhelmed me. Then I remembered Dot and Boon.

"So Dot has a choice to make?" I whisper.

"Yes," he says solemnly.

"But … I still don't … Rora knew she would have us…" I falter.

Daniel shakes his head, his voice low but hard, and says, "Your mother died of a broken heart Amber. You must respect her decision, even if you don't understand it."

Turning away, he lies down on the blanket and turns towards our hosts, signalling the end of the topic and our conversation. I lie on my back and let the revelations sink in. The secret fear that had lingered around the edge of the consciousness for over a year settled, dissipated and disappeared into the atmosphere. Picking up my hand, I study my finger with a small stain of Duncan's blood left there when I hit him. I hope he understands I wanted to save him as much as he did me.

The next day the scenery began to alter from the rich green of the woodland to structured stone buildings. Woodlands disappears and is replaced by stone roads. Making me think of the effect the Romans must have had when they first arrived in a country and began to civilise it by building their roads and towns and bathhouses.

Without the usual canopy of green, it's as if I can see the purple sky for the first time. The closer we get to Sea Cliff, the more curiously the villagers look at us and the more curiously I look back at their elegant clothing.   I am increasingly self-conscious of my dirty, sweaty clothes and wild, curly hair. The women are beautifully dressed in rich red, blue and yellow gowns, their hair styled tidily but with enough panache to indicate that time had been spent on it. The men grow increasingly dapper, with trousers and jackets in rich and vibrantly coloured fabrics. This is the one side of Sensio I had never been aware of before.   Then in the distance I see the turrets of Storm Castle, a construction that, according to Sensio folklore, was created by a fierce, land-changing storm.

As we get closer, Daniel explains that the original castle was a third of the size, but that it had been expanded and added to in the intervening years. It looks to me like a medieval fantasy come to life. Each corner of the square structure is flanked by pointed turrets, and the windows are elongated, big enough to get a spear out, but not throw one in. There is one flag flying from the pole on top of the roof and it sports the same emblem as the one that Povack wears on his jacket. In the distance, I can hear the roar of the waves from the sea beyond.

The castle is even more magnificent at close range and as we finally climb the steep path to the gateway, a guard raises the portcullis to let us enter. He watches us curiously as we troop past him, and whispers a comment to his colleague, who bursts out laughing. I blush uncomfortably, knowing I'm the subject of their humour. The portcullis is lowered behind us and I feel trapped. Whirling round, I debate whether or not to try for an escape. Daniel senses this and grips my hand. Povack rides alongside and I look up to find him watching me, his eyes crinkled at the corners and smiling broadly, showing sharp white teeth. Thinking he has succeeded, trapping me like an animal in a cage, I feel irrational, wondering if I will wither and die here without the freedom to leave. But I know that I have power over him if I choose to unleash my talents. With that thought in mind, I smile back at him. Furious, he stabs his spurs sharply into the unicorn's flanks and gallops on ahead.

I reluctantly follow, swearing I will make him pay, not only for taking me away from my Mate, but for his cruel treatment of the unicorn too.

DOORWAY

Rose Darkings

I say goodbye to Greenwood once again. I'm only grateful this parting is less fraught than last time. There's been no sneaking about in the early morning darkness and Mum only let us leave once we had a proper breakfast. As we walk through the village our departure is noted, whether through our demeanour, our travelling clothes or the serious expression on our faces. I hear their thoughts. I can hear them all wondering where we are going.

As we walk to the edge of the village and begin to head southwest, I stop for a final look, and catch my breath. The village sparkles in the morning sun, shifting hazy shadows as light fights through the tree canopy overhead. I have never seen Greenwood look so beautiful. I shade my eyes against the low, early morning sun and see Warwick's tall, distinct figure standing by the wishing well. He raises his hand in farewell. We spoke yesterday, when I told him I was leaving.

"How will I find The Empress?" I asked.

His lips tilted in a ghost of a smile, and answered enigmatically. "You won't need to, she'll find you."

After I came back from Warwick's Mum insisted we spent the night alone together after dinner, fastidiously escorting Marcus, Fingle and Bramble to the door before locking it behind them to ward away any potential interruptions. We sat in front of the fire, chatting before she finally brought up the subject I'd been desperately avoiding.

"When did you find out that Aiden is your Mate?" she asked quietly.

Feeling her gaze upon me I looked into the flames watching them dance up and consume the fresh wood that lay there and for a moment, I wanted to be taken away by it. I took a deep drink of brew and whispered, "The day the Black Knights came."

Mum sat beside me and stroked my hair back from my face.

"Rose," she sighed, "I can't help you if you don't tell me where it hurts."

Wrenching myself upwards, I threw the brew into the fire and it splutters and sparks sending flames high into the hearth. Crying out, I move away from the warmth of the fire and towards the coolness of the kitchen, pacing out against the emotions fighting to break free.

"He set me free, Mum. He doesn't want me. And I can't... breathe without him. I'll tell you where it hurts Mum. It hurts everywhere. I can't breathe. I can't move past him."

I sat back down, suddenly exhausted. Mum's eyes shone in the light and I caught a whisper of tears that were pushed back quickly. Mum feels deeply, with every inch of her small body, so much so that her emotion constantly escapes and affects those around her. At that moment, I was fully aware of how much she loved me and how much she felt my pain.

"Piffle." she snorted. "Of course he wants you, lass. It's his hard head that's having trouble catching up with his heart."

"He seemed pretty determined about it," I said, remembering how easily he seemed to walk away. "And then there's Sierra," I added. Her name lingered in the air, unwelcome and my stomach churned in response.

Mum's sigh told me that I didn't have to explain.

"Why's it so different with men? Why can't they remain true until they are mated?"

Mum sighed again and shrugged her shoulder. We both know that women find their mates in their teens. Once you know who your Mate is, it's impossible to want another. Men reach maturity and find their Mates in their twenties. Until then they indulge in discreet affairs on the understanding that once they know who their Mate is, the affairs come to an end. Once you're formally mated that's it. You can only ever have a family with your Mate.

"You know how I met Rora, don't you?" she asked and I nodded, knowing how much Mum still missed her friend.

"I was 13 years old and had gone to tell your Dad he was my Mate, only I came across him kissing someone else."

She winced at the memory and I could only guess how much that hurt. I suddenly realised why she had been in the clearing at the same time as Rora.

"I won't lie to you, it hurt whenever I saw him speaking to another girl. Then one day he knew and he came to me," she said, smiling. "It was just... us and that moment was so perfect that what went on before no longer mattered."

She looked around with pride and love at the home she had created with Dad and for us. "Have faith in him, Rose. Aiden is trying to do the right thing after he knows he's done so much wrong."

I nodded fortified and tried to hold onto her conviction. I'm not ready to let him go. Aiden walks beside me, no matter where I go. I turn around and begin the journey, with Fingle and Bramble float ahead, leading the way to our unknown destination. For all I know of my faerie friends, I knew little of where they came from. We walk mainly in silence for the next couple of hours until we reach a pool of water. Pushing back my hair, I tighten up my ponytail and reach into the clear water to cool my hands. I trail the water up the back of my neck, over my cheeks to my forehead, cooling as it permeates my hot skin. Faintly, I heard the rush of water and look up to see a waterfall beyond a thicket of trees. The rush of white water bubbled into the pond causing a burst of spray to rise up back from where it came. Apart from that movement, the pond remained still; separate from life, separate from any interference, free to be what it was meant to. I wished, for a moment, that I could escape into the water and away from the responsibilities befalling me. Instead I rise when Fingle calls us to begin walking again.

As we walk on, the forest changes and softens. Everything takes on a magical, ethereal glow. Birds song and gentle wind soothe our senses and the grass parts to reveal a path, flanked on either side by a glorious profusion of poppies, buttercups and cornflowers, rising at points against aged tree trunks, wearing away where they'd fallen. We are not far from our destination. It is close. We are about to enter another realm.

We follow the path into another forest, where the trees are dense and shut out the sunlight, but instead of making us feel intimidated, it protects us and keeps us safe, like Mother Nature herself knew our destination and was helping to hide us from anyone who would follow and cause us harm. We continue silently along the path, the sun sparkles along the forest floor, easing the weariness of my feet, sinking them into the earth and massaging them, against the kitten soft grass. We come to a huge oak, that dominates the rest of the trees surrounding it, its trunk so thick it would take three men to cover its circumference. We know, without having to be told, that this is our destination. At that moment, a shaft of sunlight hits the base of the tree and reveals a tiny door with a bell. I look to Fingle for guidance.

"You've to go through the doorway, Rose" he says patiently. I look at him, speechless. He watches and waits, before huffing with exasperation and folding his arms.

"How can I get through there Fingle? The door's the size of my hand."

"You've no imagination, Rose Darkings," he mutters.

"Ignore him Rose," Bramble says, flashing Fingle an impatient glance. "He's grumpy."

She smiles and explains, "It's a magical doorway. You have to visualise it."

I look at Marcus, then back at the doorway and shake my head. His eyes are fixed on the entrance as though concentration will solve the problem. I take a breath, close my eyes and push away the sunlight straining through my eyelids until it gradually fades. I fix the picture of the doorway in my head and begin to change its dimensions until it's the correct shape and size for me to go through. I imagine myself walking up the path to the door and leaning forward to ring the bell. It sounds like a combination of children's laughter and the whisper of faerie wings. Slowly the door creaks open, revealing a light so spectacular it bathes my cheeks with warmth. Together we all walk forward.

Bramble laughs, her voice ticking my senses and whispers in my ear, "Arcadia welcomes you."

REVELATION

Amber Lockwood

I feel like I've entered another world. We follow Povack and the guards into a circular courtyard and wait as he dismounts the unicorn and it's led away by a stable hand. There are two guards in front of us and two behind, holding us and my breath shallows as my body accepts the trap around it, tightening. We walk from the courtyard into the vestibule of the castle where the only light comes from elongated windows within the walls. We stop abruptly in front of a large wooden door decorated with squares of gold studs. I wonder if the designer was threatened with punishment if the shapes weren't measured exactly.

We are ushered through the door and a key turns loudly in the lock and we are left in silence, underlying how precarious our circumstances are. We are prisoners. I walk towards an opening and look out onto the courtyard and stables, drawing the fresh air filtering through deeply into my lungs and steadying my breath. There is a clear view of the paddock where six unicorns run around a square patch of grass that is much too cramped for them. They range in size from foals, skittish and almost wobbly, to the large magnificent unicorn that Povack rode from Greenwood. His unicorn is the largest, almost large enough to jump beyond the confines of the paddock if it wanted to, but its head is lowered and spirit broken. Its large, grey lashes sweep upward revealing large dark pupils and the contents of its soul, before they closed again. My heart aches for the animal and I have to turn away from the acute pain in its eyes. I look away wondering if this is my future, whether I am destined to be a prisoner forever.

"What are we facing out there?" I ask, watching Daniel sitting with his back against the wall, deep in thought.

"We'll be brought in front of the King and Queen and the rest of the court and asked to make a statement against Luther."

I start to feel nervous and my gut churns at the thought of facing a King and Queen and a large crowd who would judge me on my scruffy appearance. But most of all, I feel nervous about seeing Luther, who had hurt so many people to get to me. The thought of seeing him makes adrenalin course through my veins.

The key turns and grates loudly in the lock and Povack stands at the door and crooks a finger, commanding us to follow him. He's changed into a beautifully cut cream tunic and trousers with matching gloves and shiny black riding boots. He looks disdainfully at my almost-week old trousers and jacket, worn walking boots and my grimy hair and I feel like a speck of dust in comparison, but of course, that's all part of his game.

As we walk out of the door, the light catches the elaborate thick gold chain that Povack is wearing on his neck. It's decorated with symbols and studded with precious and semi-precious stones that scream wealth and power. An image of the simple pleasure of baking bread in Greenwood flashes into my head. We don't do it for coin, wealth or power, but simply to help each other because it is the way we choose to live. I wonder what act Povack has done to deserve such a reward.

Povack turns round and stands in front of us and with the guards behind us, we walk back out into the vestibule. Daniel is holding tightly onto my arm, giving me support. A crowd gathers to watch us with undisguised curiosity. We follow Povack down a staircase covered with a plush red runner and I look in awe at the huge, grand room that is revealed at the bottom. A series of tall, coloured-glass windows decorated with beautiful symbols and designs diffuse the light, rainbow-like, around the room, The main colours, similar to the emblem I had seen before are royal blue and gold, the colours swirling together and spinning in my head, making me almost stumble in my study of them. There are sconces on the wall between each window, shaped like unicorn horns.

There is a wide aisle running from the bottom of the stairs to the platform at the opposite end of the room, where two ornate thrones sit, made of a deep, dark wood and etched in symbols and designs, created to tell a long-forgotten story. On either side of the aisle are rows of polished mahogany pews with red velvet cushions. This room is meant for an audience and it has one today. The pews are crammed with exquisitely dressed ladies and gentlemen who are chatting excitedly, the acoustics of the room making their voices reverberate loudly.

Povack walks up to the steps in front of the thrones and turns to face the crowd, still and alert as they wait for their next instruction. There is immediate silence. The guards stand to attention on either side of the thrones. The influx of the crowd moves closer, eager to see and hear more. Povack surveys his audience with pleasure and waits in silence, relishing his power over so many others.

"Stand for King Garrick and Queen Andora" he calls out.

The people in the pews, rise in unison, clasping their hands in front of them and lowering their heads as though they are praying. Daniel and I copy the gesture and as we do so a woman enters the room from a side door and sits down on one of the thrones. I study Queen Andora. She is tall, slim and elegant in her blue silk dress. She wears a delicate silver crown in her grey hair and a large diamond amulet at her neck. Diamonds sparkle at her ears and on her finger. Her pale blue eyes are unnerving: I watch her take in every person in the audience and when she finds someone wanting, her rouged lips, thin and twist in distaste. She studies me haughtily for a moment, then grimaces and looks away. Feeling the weight of her distain without seeking it, my insides clench in response.

A minute later, a younger man comes through the door. His face was gaunt and his moustache and beard are peppered with grey. His crown is bigger and heavier than the Queen's with three vertical crosses and four stones embedded in the band. His tunic and trousers are made of gold cloth, and his red velvet cloak is lined with cream satin. Whereas Queen Andora looks proud and disdainful, his brown eyes are glazed with exhaustion. He sits down on the bigger throne, paying no mind to the crowd, sitting down, his chest rising with the effort.

Povack bows deeply to the King and Queen. The Queen smirks for a half second before sobering. We stand in silence as the Queen speaks, quietly but decisively to the King, who looks down at his feet and appears to utter monosyllabic answers.

If I was looking for an explanation of the structure of Sensio society, then it was here at Storm Castle. The King and Queen are at the head, with Lord Povack coming a close second. The affluent people in the benches are courtiers followed by merchants and residents of Sea Cliff and then at the bottom - Daniel and I. Whilst I understood, my mind rejected the notion, unwilling to be pigeonholed, wishing I could return to Greenwood, where none of this mattered.

The King and Queen finish their conversation, and Queen Andora calls out, "Bring out the accused Lord Luther Barton," her voice ringing around the walls.

As the door opens, a hush descends on the room and Luther walks in proudly his shoulders erect, his normally greasy hair now as shiny as the armour he is wearing. I wonder angrily what kind of society would treat a witness more harshly than a prisoner, when I feel a hand sharply smack my bottom. I whip my head round to see Duncan smiling broadly, his eyes twinkling.

"Turn round" he whispers and I do as he says, my heart thumping wildly in my chest. His hand lingers near the waistband of my trousers and he moves his fingers underneath my shirt and against my skin. His nearness and his touch immediately calm me.

Daniel looks to the side, but keeps his body stock-still. "What took you boys so long?"

"Duncan's getting slow," Aiden whispers, his deep voice coming from my right.

He grabs my wrist, squeezes it and lets it go. I let out a breath I didn't know I'd been holding as I feel the strength surrounding me. We are not alone. Luther is standing to the right of the platform, with a solitary guard at his side. Povack steps in front of him, elegantly rolls out a scroll and reads the charges against him. Luther's face remains stoic throughout, apart from the slight smirk, as if he and Povack are rehearsing a comedy act with a punch line that only they are only aware of.

"Stop Lord Povack." Queen Andora suddenly commands.

He stops speaking immediately, steps back and rolls the scroll back up, before bowing deeply.

"I have heard enough. Knight Luther has been a loyal servant to the crown."

Swirling emotions, quelled since we were forced from Greenwood erupts inside me.

"No." I scream. "No. This isn't right."

In the blur that follows, everyone is shouting, the guards have drawn their swords and there is utter mayhem. I close my eyes and wait for the worst when suddenly I am pushed away from the guards by some unknown force and a woman's voice shouts, 'Stop!"

The figure belonging to the voice shimmers, solidifies and becomes clearer. The guard's retreat at the sight of her and the crowd moves back in awe. She is small and has waist-length auburn hair that hangs down her back in heavy thick strands. Her green eyes dance as she looks at Aiden and I with a loving expression and winks.

Daniel utters "Rora" in disbelief.

She walks confidently towards the platform to stand in front of the King. He straightens immediately, his stare changing from glazed to sharp. Rora held her skirt and curtseyed to him before extending her arm forward. Leaping out of his throne, he pulls her roughly against him, his hand gripping her hair than stroking her face before he kisses her deeply. The man and the shadow merge for long moments before separating.

When he pulls away from her at last, he holds her face and cries out his voice full of emotion, "Rora. Believe me, I never wanted to leave you."

"I know that Will," she says, pulling his hand she moved backwards pulling their bodies into an intricate elegant dance across the stone floor.

"I didn't want to let you go," he cries and his features soften and he looked years younger than the man who had entered the room only a short time ago.

"But I was always here, Will" she says, gently, putting her hand on his heart. "You must redress the balance."

She shimmers away from the King and holds her hands out to Aiden and me, smiling at us. I take her hand and it feels small and warm, but so fragile I daren't press too hard in case it disappears. Rora put her arms around us.

"Will, you must protect our children. Promise me." she begs.

We are all stunned. The King looks in amazement from Rora to Aiden and me and we look back in disbelief at him. Rora joins our hands together, before she shimmers away from us, her smile ethereal and satisfied, as she becomes fainter and fainter, until she disappears completely.

The silence around us is absolute. The King gazes at us and then at our amulets, with their black, white, red and pink stones and I realise that they are exactly the same as the stones on his crown. My breath shallows as I look at my brother and my father. My father, the King.

I've finally found my family.

THE KINSHIP CHRONICLES

The Binding Veil

CASSIE KENNEDY

Air

Earth

Fire

Water

4 elements
3 parts
2 sides
1 last chance
0 the time is now

Illustrations & Poetry by
BRIGID

ARCADIA

Rose Darkings

I feel invisible. The warm sunlight bathes my closed eyelids, penetrating my skin. The heat overwhelms but is then chased away by a cool wind, making me comfortable. Opening my eyes, I look around me and gasp in wonder. Everywhere there's rich, glorious colour. Green grass carpets the ground and as I step forward, my boots sink and mould into it. As we walk, the greenery shifts in an array of shades from dark green to long grass that's been dipped in pale apple.

Lifeless tree trunks adorn the pathways, some sticking out, others swallowed by grass. Their bark bitten away by time, revealing a now white core, the hidden sap long since drained and returned to nature. Even in death, the tree still serves a purpose, indicating the natural path ahead. Flowers peek through the greenery and merge with the grass. There are white summon spells, rich red poppies and soft yellow buttercups studded along as far as the eye can see. They move at the will of a soft breeze, fluttering along the top of the canopy, pulling the flowers petals to the left and right without threat of destruction, like a wave born to tease the foliage.

Tree trunks swing up from the grass, the green and yellow leaves of their branches shimmering and dancing against the light and wind.

As we walk on, the pathway becomes flanked by more familiar plants: shades of blue dune lyme grass and a sea of pussy willows, with their little catkins scattered over the grass like a pillow opened by nature. Occasionally, I see a thistle peeking through the grass and I realise the plants are the ones that Mum planted around our house and I wonder if Arcadia can somehow access your memories. I look to Marcus and see the surprise on his face as he does his own inventory of the plants and my suspicions are proved correct.

We reach the end of the grass pathway and turn towards two large stone pillars, faded and eroded with age and embedded with green moss. Two large stone spheres sit on pillars, supported by a low-slung wall. As a doorway, it's vulnerable to anyone who wishes to breach its borders, then I see Fingle stop in front of it and say in a loud, clear voice:

'Fingle, Prince of the Faeries. I wish to enter Arcadia.'

He waits for a moment and walks forward. Bramble does the same. Marcus and I walk forward until we are stopped by an invisible force field that flexes against our entry, stiffens and bounces us backwards. Curious, I extend my hand forward. It is pushed back by a white-gloved hand that emerges from the force field, slaps my wrist and wags a finger from side to side in displeasure. Marcus and I grin at each other like two naughty children, before Fingle shouts, 'Rose' disapprovingly. Giggling, I walk towards the door and say,

'Rose Darkings of Greenwood. I wish to enter Arcadia.'

I walk on, waiting briefly for Marcus before we follow yet another green pathway flanked on either side by large dense firs. Until now, Arcadia has provided a visual smorgasbord.

Now allowed entry, it fully engaged our senses. My nostrils were teased by a warm scent, the perfect combination between the sweetest coconut and the tartness of fresh rhubarb. Tweets tripped through the air, the sky filled with a thousand small birds, some brown with flecked gold, some tipped blue and yellow and black with orange beaks. They fly around us, merging and separating into different flocks and pairs, while others sit solo on a tree branch, like we are here purely for their entertainment. Birdsong fills the air, as if each is competing in a contest for the most expressive song. Bees and butterflies circle the firs, their outlines clear against the sky, the shade of purple so soft, so clear and so beautiful, I gasp at its clarity. The sun glows a deep beetroot red, its outer edge blurred and in the distance, the two moons sit waiting in the background eager for their chance to shine.

Looking around me, I feel more at peace than I can ever remember, happy to be part of this haven that nature has created.

At the end of the pathway we reach a wishing well, a common sight in Sensio as they're believed to foster positivity and luck. The ground around the base is circled with dandelions, their seed heads just waiting to be released.

Sensing my curiosity Bramble says, "You pick one and make a wish."

Looking at the multitude of dandelions I promise myself I'll do this one day. In my heart I already know what I want.

We follow Fingle and Bramble into the woods, the thicket of trees filters out a lot of the light, but there are still enough diamond-shaped shards to light the way and hide our progress. Steam rises from the ground like after a thunderstorm and the air is humid. It warms me and then, just as I begin to feel uncomfortable, a light breeze cools me down. Arcadia appears to be aware of your thoughts, feelings and comfort levels at all times.

Around us, hundreds of faeries weave in and out of the trees, then flutter around Marcus and me. Greeting our companions in hushed tones before returning to their business. In this part of the wood, the trees cluster close together and there are small doorways with a bell in each of tree trunks. Bright white stones line the pathway to each door. In the middle of the trees there are what appears to be several meeting places.

Here, in this secret Faerie Glen, I feel light and happy. My mind is not invaded by the unwelcome thoughts of other people. Like my life before the Black Knights came. I feel boundless and uninhibited by the limitations and demands I place upon myself. I feel like a droplet of water shimmering through the atmosphere, without obligations or demands, my purpose to be only what I was meant to. I feel a hand on my arm and when I turn around, I'm surprised to see that Marcus's black eyes have returned to their natural warm brown. We smile at each other but stay silent, scared to break the spell by talking.

A silent question pops into my head and Bramble answers it. "Of course you're invisible Rose. You're beyond the veil."

I look at her, trying to grasp what she meant. In this enchanted place, her small voice sounds like a musical flute.

Her skin is luminous, sparkling clearer in the sun; unconsciously I touch my cheek, feeling a ripple of energy against my fingers. I wish Aiden could experience this peace.

A hush descends gradually, as the wind stops, the sun sets, the moisture in the air dissipates and the birds become quiet. Everything stills. I look around me and all the faeries have turned towards the fading sun and are kneeling, their eyes closed and their hands clasped reverently, their thumbs resting on their breast bone, pointing straight to their hearts. We copy them and I close my eyes, only for my mind to see what my eyes can't.

A glowing mass of energy emerges from the dying light and takes the shape of a petite woman with rich dark hair that hangs like silk past her shoulders. She is wearing a large tiara decorated with a variety of strands and sparkling stones of graduating sizes and sapphires that sparkle against her blue-black hair. It frames a heart-shaped face dominated by dark blue eyes with thick black lashes. Her skin is clear and luminous and her lips are full and red. It's impossible to tell what age she is. A royal blue gown with silver circular swirls that twinkle as she walks covers her petite figure and each side of her cape is embroidered with the outline of a dragon. I can feel immense power and serenity radiating from her. I feel a warm hand touching my hair and when I lift up my head and open my eyes, I see the images in my head are real. Vitality and kindness shine from every pore of her skin, making the jewels on her tiara twinkle. I take a steady breath and clear my throat, now dry with nerves. I am about to meet The Empress.

"The magic of Arcadia,

Opens the door to thee...

How true your heart, wonders you will see,

Faerie Glen & Sanctuary welcomes you within,

The secrets of binding, for all our scattered kin"

...Arcadia

Arcadia

FATHER

Amber Lockwood

I don't know who's more shocked. Aiden, our father or me. The King recovers his nerves quickly. He walks slowly back to sit on his throne and I can't help but wonder if it's for thinking time rather than the desire to sit there. Murmurs of conversation in the crowd build to a crescendo, providing a soundtrack to our family drama.

I sense Duncan and Daniel moving closer, offering silent support. I turn around to look at Daniel, but instead of shock, I see resignation on his face. He knows. A glance at Duncan's face confirms my instincts. He looks back at me without remorse, his jaw clenched. Silently, I curse him, anger and betrayal rolling around my stomach. I push nausea away and I pull back from his touch. He lied. But Duncan doesn't regret his decision, if given the choice he would do the same again. He's not even sorry he got caught in the lie. The truth of another secret slams me.

"Take away the prisoner," the King says loudly. The guards obey, and Luther looks both satisfied and amused as he's led away.

"Garrick." The name rings loud in the silence. The King stiffens at the sudden interruption. The Queen sits regally on her throne, austere and elegant, only the tone of her voice revealing a quiver of emotion - one I couldn't place.

He looks at her without answering, before turning to Povack and commanding him, "Take my children and their guests to my quarters." He then stands up and leaves the room. The Queen sits for a moment and then she rises, acknowledges Povack's bow and leaves the room after her son. The background conversation, temporarily lulled, escalates, as the door shuts behind them.

Povack escorts us along a corridor lit by flickering sconces, scrolls and shields decorate the walls and I wonder what achievements they were put up to commemorate. The corridor twists and turns until we finally reach a large door with a familiar emblem, held within a long forgotten memory. The door creaks open into an opulent sitting room, with elegant rosewood and powder blue Georgian chairs that gleam in the light of a log fire. In the corner sits a large ornate desk, littered with papers and scrolls piled on top of each other without care for their priority. Beside it is a worn, wooden chair. The shelves above the desk are covered with artefacts and ornaments, all tinted in either blue or gold. There's a large table in the middle of the room with a long-handled jug and cups. I become aware of the dust in the room and how dry my throat is. The room may have been created for a King, but he certainly didn't use it.

The door suddenly opens and the King walks into the room, his eyes probing as he looks at us intently. Under his scrutiny, I self-consciously push my hair behind my ear; all too aware of my shabby clothes, feeling inadequately prepared to face this man. His expression softens as he takes in the gesture.

"Leave us," he says to Povack, who lingers for a moment, obviously unused to taking orders from his King. The King looks at him pointedly, waiting. No further words are spoken, but a look I don't understand passes between them before Povack leaves reluctantly.

The King indicates to the chairs. "Sit," he murmurs softly, then pulls the desk chair out and sits down. I edge my chair closer to Aiden's, making the wood scrape along the floor. He puts his hand on my arm and looks at me reassuringly, his black eyes shimmering to his natural brown in the firelight. I am glad he's here. If there is a moment when I need my twin, this is it.

The silence stretches out uncomfortably. I glance up nervously at the King. His eyes are drinking us in as if we might disappear into thin air. Here, away from the splendour of the Throne Room, he looks like an ordinary, vulnerable man. He finally speaks, his deep voice gruff, "I didn't know. If I had known for one moment that our children were out there... I would've done anything to find you."

My body sags in relief. I don't know what I expected our father to say to us, but I had been scared of rejection.

"I don't remember much. My memories are in bits and pieces," he continues. "I just thought they were bad dreams. I've been taking a potion for years to get rid of them. Now I know why they persisted. What did Rora name you both?"

We say our names quietly in hushed tones. The King smiles and turns to me. "You're named after your grandmother, Rora's mum," and then he turns to Aiden and says, "You are named after my father."

He then turns to Daniel, sitting uncomfortably in an elegant chair. "Danny, how are you?" he asks, extending his hand.

"I'm fine, Will," says Daniel, shaking it.

Seeing my confusion, the King explains, "My name is Garrick William Thorgood. Danny always called me by my nickname."

Suddenly, scenes from Rora's journal and the nuances of my father's personality came to life in front of me.

There's a loud knock on the door, and Povack re-enters. "Your Highness, the Queen has arranged accommodation for your guests."

King Garrick nods and rises from his chair, looking weary. "My children and friends will stay as long as they wish, Lord Povack. See they have every comfort offered to them."

Povack bows deferentially to the King and then makes a sweeping gesture towards the door to indicate that we are to leave.

Just as we reach the door, the King stops us. "Aiden, Amber, you are now a Prince and Princess of Sensio. You answer to no-one but me." Turning away, he pushes his hair back in a weary gesture and for a moment I see Aiden in him.

We are led along a maze of corridors and shown into separate rooms. As I'm about to walk into mine, I turn around and see the shadow of the Queen out of the corner of my eye, stiff-backed, haughty and a shiver runs through me. Walking towards the glass window, I look out of the narrow opening and in the distance I see lush, green forests. Despite having found the father I always wished for, I also desperately wanted to be back in Greenwood where I was Amber Lockwood, nothing more and nothing less. I look around the huge room at the opulent four-poster bed, the large dressing table and mirror, the chairs around a lit fire and the ornate rugs covering the stone floor. Catching my silhouette in the mirror, my face looks pale. Once again, I am trapped between two worlds and despite the gilded cage, I still feel like a prisoner.

THE EMPRESS

Rose Darkings

Sanctuary. Walking towards the white building, the word pops into my head as I drink in the sight before me. The building rises up against the abundant greenery and rainbow foliage, so white it looks almost translucent like your hand could pass through its mirage, but as we draw closer I can see that it's made of solid bricks and mortar. There is a turret at the centre of the building that reaches two stories high, with two elongated windows that allow the occupier to see out clearly, but keeps any visitors curious. The turret is flanked on either side by one storey, the square markers of the brown bricks are only just perceptible to the naked eye, making the building as wide as it is tall. The entire construction straddles the middle of a lake. The water so crystal clear that it appears at first as if the building has been placed on a piece of glass by the hand of a mighty God. But then you see the ripple of the water lapping, white water against white brick, and then you realise that the building is at one with the elements, earth and water working in harmony.

We have followed The Empress from Faerie Glen and she stays silent as we approach the building, entranced by the sight before us. We circle the lake, the grass and water mixing to produce a clean fresh scent that cleanses our nostrils and slows my breath. As we get closer, I can see that most of the water is covered by huge lily pads that float just below the surface. The circular green pads stretch out, surrendering to the water, the veins within reaching wide and swollen red as they drink their fill. The pink and yellow flowers form a canopy, the outer petals resting in the water, the inner petals pointing up to the hot sun, their carpels stretched ripe for re-birth. I notice that the flowers strain towards The Empress as she passes, like only she could provide the sustenance they need.

We reach a sturdy brick drawbridge and the mist that has been rolling along behind us, covering our tracks, comes to a halt here. It seems that even in Arcadia, nature is wary. The large square door, decorated with gold studs, opens in welcome before we reach it. We walk into a stone vestibule and I feel enveloped in the building, safe within its walls. As the door closes behind us, I look back towards the drawbridge, which disappears in front of my eyes.

"It's Sanctuary," I say, my voice echoing in the large space.

"Yes Rose," The Empress nods "it certainly is."

We follow her along the corridor past a set of stone steps and stop in front of a room. "Young man, you'll need to rest after your journey?" Marcus, habitually quiet except in the company of those he trusts, went from sharp alertness to gradual exhaustion. He makes an attempt to fight sleep, but succumbs and allows the Empress to show him into the room. Instinctively, I know that The Empress had used some power to persuade him to sleep. She wants to speak to me privately.

She walks on and I follow. The outline of the dragons on her cloak sparkle in the darkness, their outlines move into the air, attempting to take flight, before returning to the material and fighting for freedom once more. We move deeper and deeper into the building until we come to a door that creaks open to reveal a large room, dominated by a crackling fire. The fireplace is flanked by two chairs and to the left is a long, square wooden table overflowing with worn scrolls, open faded books, half-burned candle stubs and crystals that glitter in the firelight. The only space available is taken by a small black cat curled up and fast asleep, its white-tipped tail and paws resting on an open book. Lazily, it opens one eye, examines me, and then shuts it again. Turning, I see The Empress sit and notice in the hazy light that her eyes are cat-shaped too.

The shimmer of her blue-black hair sparkles against the tiara, a line of diamonds rest there, overlain by a row of square sapphires, the band curled, closely resembling two dragon heads. The tiara was dominated by seven large sapphires, sparkling against the firelight, igniting the azure of her eyes making her appear all-seeing, all-knowing. This headdress could only belong to The Empress. Noticing my interest, she answers my silent question. "This is my kokoshnik," she says "It belonged to another Empress on the Earth plane who was unable to fulfil her Blueprint. I live this life not just to realise mine, but also hers."

She offers me a cup, and I gulp the honey and ginger concoction greedily. The drink has an immediate effect: the room is immediately bathed with light and everything around me becomes crystal clear, as if it was blurred before.

The Empress looks at me with satisfaction.

"I'm a changeling, Rose," she finally says. "I was born a faerie and was chosen to be raised as a human." She looks at me curiously, and asks. "Were you born with a caul ... skin over your face?"

How does she know this? Remembering Mum's story about how I was so snug in her womb, I fought to stay there. Taken aback, I can only look at her and nod.

She continues, "My human mother was suspicious especially when I began to develop my abilities very early on."

"How old were you when you first realised?" I ask, remembering how long I was unaware of my own talent.

"I was five years old. I was sixteen when I was asked to leave my village."

I gasp, shocked and concerned for the girl-woman left to fend for herself. She raises a hand to stop me from speaking. "It all worked out the way it was meant to. Then, some years later, I met Warwick." Her face softens at the memory and a half smile tugs on her lips.

"Our gifts can be used to heal people, but we must learn to control and appreciate them before we can do that. We all have a Blueprint Rose. That's the reason why you are here," she says, opening her arms in a wide circle. The dragons sparkling on her cloak fly off the fabric and into the air. Her face is vibrant, her eyes dancing.

"What's my Blueprint?" I ask, anxious for her answer.

The Empress smiles approvingly. "I helped Warwick to find his and now it's my turn to help you." She got up, her petite frame bouncing with energy, meandered over to the door, looked over her shoulder and said, "You may call me Empress," before she walked out.

I leaned back in the chair, my brain trying to assimilate all the information it's just been given. Information is shared freely here. While on Sensio it stays a secret, held by others, but never by the people who need it. Despite the overflow, I still feel at peace. There are no silent conversations around me vying for my attention. I take a deep breath and just enjoy being here. Aiden pops into my mind, but for once and without pain, I breathe him out easily and let him go. My place is in the here and now, in Arcadia. This is Sanctuary – for now.

"The gift of foresight, my blessing, my calling,

To see all before me,

Free will can bring mourning,

Your blueprint, the divine purpose of your soul,

Forsake it & you shall never live at all. "

…The Empress

The Empress

CONFUSION

Aiden Darkings

It's been a month since we arrived at Storm Castle and confusion still hangs in the air. Whenever I used to think of my origins, they were a separate part of my existence. As soon as I could walk and talk, Daniel and Maggie told me about Rora, keen I should have memories of my birth mother from a young age. But they never mentioned my father, and because of this, I followed their lead. As their ward, I didn't want to displease them or give them a chance to regret their choice to raise me. So my parents were unreal, like characters from a story I was aware of but never knew intimately.

The reality of my life is that I'm a ward of the Darkings family, although they never set me apart or made me feel any different. Maggie would go out of her way to fuss and hold me as a child, trying to compensate for Rora not being there. A grief she never fully recovered from. I was exempt from the expectations placed upon Duncan and Rose. Both were expected to use their talents to help Greenwood. As a boy, Duncan once said he was envious of my choices. He was expected to follow Daniel as Village Protector but when I asked what he would rather do, he just grinned and shrugged, as if he was not against the idea but just wanted the choice available to him.

I was never expected to have a talent, and when I found I could manipulate all of the elements as a child I kept quiet about it, until Warwick found me in the clearing one day throwing water and stones into the air. He took me under his wing, helping me control my talents and keeping my secret until Amber arrived. I was relieved when Boon confirmed that she had the same abilities. As a teenager, I was tempted to show them off, to perform some physical feat near the wishing well to prove I was more than the ward of the family. Then I would listen to the gut feeling that told me I should keep them a secret. That's when I did wonder about my origins and solved a mystery - my father was from Sensio.

Regret is a wasted emotion. How can you grieve for what you never had in the first place? I spent months hiding from the world and regretting the choices I made as a Black Knight and to what end? I can't do anything to change what I did. I can't replace the lives I stole. But I can live a better life and I've made this my purpose at Storm Castle. I've tried to repair my relationship with Amber. I still don't understand why I listened to the voice that told me to loosen her bindings and leave her near the trees that day. I felt like I had a dual personality. The evil Aiden part of me was gleeful at her dilemma, knowing that the giant oaf who had expressed interest in her would take her as soon as we reached camp. While the good Aiden part of me desperately wanted to help her escape. I watched, helpless, as she ran into the woods chased by not one but five men. With hindsight, I look back with clear eyes and see the scene in its full-scale horror and I'm forever grateful she was able to escape. If she hadn't, I wouldn't have been able to live with myself. Duncan would have made sure of it.

Despite this, she came after me to save me at the Hill of the

Faeries. I will never be able to truly thank her. I can only try and be the best brother I can. We have grown closer, our relationship cemented by our confusion at the situation we find ourselves in. We've been thrust into royal roles within a society that neither welcomes nor wants us. It doesn't matter. I'm only grateful that she's turned back to me for comfort and support.

But while she welcomes me, Amber has pushed away Duncan. She uses her new status to put a wall between them whenever he gets too close. But of course Duncan just pushes against it, as he has always done. He flaunts the conventions of Sea Cliff and unapologetically pushes into her personal space, determined to assert his place as her Mate.

I still believe Rose and I are better apart. Despite my attempt at redemption, I know I'm tainted. What do I have to offer a Mate? Rose has the purest soul I know, always seeing the good in others. Although my mind is resolute, my heart cheats. She lingers on the edge of my consciousness, never fully taking her leave. In my mind's eye I see her tossing her long dark hair over her shoulder and daring me to send her away. But I don't. I can't. Every day, I wake up with the resolve to banish her then go to sleep making the same promise. If my new-found status does serve a purpose then the Prince of Sensio should be able to do as he wishes. But I don't. I can't. I wonder where she is. I wonder how she's getting on with Marcus. Then I bristle. For now, she stays, even if it's only in my mind.

I walk down the dark corridor, I'm determined to try and clear up the confusion lingering and affecting us all. The guard steps aside and knocks on the door on my behalf. As I wait for the door to open, I inwardly grimace. As a Prince, a simple door knock is deemed beneath me. At times like this the absurdity of my status hits me. Daniel opens the door and welcomes me in. Since we arrived, the King has appointed him his informal advisor. Like myself, he is dressed to Sea Cliff convention; black trousers, loose white shirt and jacket all constructed of a material so soft it caresses your skin as you move. We move into the inner sanctum of the King's quarters, beyond the room where Amber and I met him on that first day. A lit fire warms the room, floor to ceiling bookcases cover one wall, and a large, faded desk is also covered with books. A few comfortable chairs are grouped around the fire, the largest occupied by the King. His crown is missing and his hair is mussed as if he has been running his hand through it in frustration. His beard is unkempt, the rich brown mixed with shards of grey and his clothes are rumpled. When he turns to me, his stare is blank and I wait in silence. On the few occasions I've been in his company, I still refer to him as the King. We've not reached the informality of Garrick, never mind father. His expression slowly changes from blank to confused; his dark eyebrows meet to draw a straight line across his forehead.

"Who is our guest?" he asks, gruffly. Daniel and I exchange a look of alarm. Seconds pass and I wonder if it would be better if I just left. Then the King shakes his head and clears his throat loudly before saying, "Aiden, please forgive me, take a seat."

I sit down and he asks how I am settling in at the castle. "Fine, thank you," I reply, not yet comfortable enough in his presence to speak frankly. The silence becomes uncomfortable and I try to explain the reason for my visit.

"Sir, I've something for you," I say, extending my hand to him.

The King takes the package from me and unwraps it carefully. He runs his fingers over the worn cover, now softened by age, before opening the journal.

"It's Rora's journal," I say, breaking the silence. He suddenly stands up and tosses the book to the floor as if it's burnt his fingers.

Anger and pain contort his face, and he cries out, "Do you think I need to be reminded of what I've lost? Every time I close my eyes, I see her."

I sit, immobile, unsure of what to say, wondering what I've done. "I thought..." I stammer.

Daniel watches the King nervously and says, "Aiden, I think you should leave now."

The King begins to mutter and pace around the room, his hands clenching and unclenching and dragging through his hair. I get up and leave the room quickly, this time relieved that the guard opens the door for me.

As I walk back down the corridor, I pray that Rora's words can save our father and release him from the hell he's trapped in, just as they saved us, his children, when we needed them most.

PEACE

Rose Darkings

In Arcadia, nothing is quite what it seems. It's been a couple of months since we arrived and each day, I discover a new facet to this magical and intriguing place. The world I now inhabit exists on the promise that if it lives within the imagination, then it can happen. The feeling of anything being possible is alive within me now.

I pull a brush through my newly dried hair and I look out of the window at the lake surrounding us. The morning suns glints on the water, sparking diamond shaped lights that spiral and radiate like a myriad of rainbows between sky and water. It laps gently against the grassy knoll, caressing the long grass surrendering to the water. Leaving my room, I peek into the main room, a low fire crackles in the hearth, sparking against the dry wood, reminding me of toes curling against a warm blanket; comfortable and soothing. Marcus is sitting at the long table, surrounded by open books, his brow furrowed with concentration as he reads. Tibs, The Empress's black and white tabby, not getting the attention he thinks he deserves, sticks his claws gently into Marcus's arm. Until he lifts a hand and strokes the cat's head and Tibs leans into the touch and purrs with pleasure.

I study Marcus unchecked. His blonde hair is longer, thicker and curls around his neck. My stomach flutters. Lately, when he stares at me with those black eyes framed by thick blonde eyelashes, I feel like he can see into my very soul. The secret part of me; briefly exposed to Aiden, before

I locked it away again for safekeeping. Marcus makes me wonder about... possibilities. Unspoken words hang in the air between us and I anticipate and resist them, knowing that if they are spoken out loud it would change everything and I'm not ready for that.

Licking my dry lips, I look away from him and catch The Empress watching me silently with her shrewd, cat-like eyes picking up my emotions and dilemma, she sweeps her hand into the air and I acknowledge her wish for me to calm down. We've grown close since I arrived. She knows everything I'm thinking and feeling. She understands the burden of hearing everybody else's thoughts. I wave and press a finger to my lips and she lets me leave undetected. I trust her to keep my counsel.

Moving along the corridor, the large door opens and I walk across the brick bridge. In the first few days in Arcadia, I moved gingerly over the walkway, conscious it was disappearing at the back of me. Now, I think it's magical.

Reaching the grass, I move towards the woods. The thickets of branches part as I move between them into the midst of the forest. Bright light dims to hazy darkness. The sun penetrates through the leaves, making paisley-patterned shapes against the mossy floor. The leaves crunch below my boots, making my presence known to those around me. Then I hear the first loud, distinctive knock, cutting against the silence. I walk on, unafraid. They know I'm here. I first saw the inhabitants of these woods on the second night after I arrived. I'd gone outside for a walk after another dream about Aiden and walked outside to cool my fevered heart and imagination.   Standing on the bridge, I looked out into the night.   I could see a purple glow, a magical force field coating the woods, protecting them from harm.   I was about to turn to face the water when out of the corner of my eyes I caught a movement.   I focused on the area of the movement to see if it was a trick of the light.   The foliage moved again and I caught a glimpse of muscles rippling under fur.   I strained my eyes, leaned forward and found myself the subject of similar scrutiny by a pair of large eyes, glowing red in the darkness.

"What is it?" I thought to myself, my mind seeking to provide an answer to the puzzle before me.   "It's a sasquatch," a voice whispered behind me and I whirled round to see The Empress standing there.   I calmed immediately, knowing that no one would hurt me while she was near.   "He won't hurt you," she said, reading me easily. "He's protecting his family."

The creature watched us for a few more minutes before retreating into the trees and disappearing completely from our view, followed by a swift, sharp knock.   I received the message loud and clear, our encounter was over.

"What is it?" I asked again curiously.

"They are you Rose, they just developed differently" she smiled indulgently, delighting in the quirks of nature around her.   "They protect the woods.   They won't harm anyone whose intentions are true.   No creature in Arcadia will."

Now I walk through the woods without concern, feeling the eyes of the sasquatch escorting me as I enter and leave its home.

I make my way towards Faerie Glen, inhaling the fresh air, permeated with the sweetness of the honeyed flowers. The wind caresses my hair with soft, whispering fingers. Everything here speaks. Everything lives. Everything has a spirit. From the seeds falling from the poppy that are welcomed into the soil to regenerate once more, to the ancient tree spirits that speak to The Empress, keeping her abreast of all that transpires within her sphere. All animals live in harmony and food is provided by nature, not by violence. A deer that is meant to die will fall so a sasquatch can find it.

Moving from the edge of the woods, past the wishing well and into Faerie Glen, my nostrils are assailed by the scent of sweet smelling berries. Nearing the well, I pick a wild raspberry and eat it, savouring the way the tartness bursts against my tongue before it gives way to sweetness. I lick the juice from my fingers and I'm flooded with happiness. Arcadia is pure pleasure in nature wrapped together in harmony.

When I reach Faerie Glen, I notice a stillness in the air that's not been there before. The atmosphere here is always fevered, decisions made in a snap second and the ensuing tasks completed moments later. Today, there's only silence. I catch the murmur of voices and follow them until I come to the meeting place. The circle of wood stumps is literally covered with faeries speaking quickly, rising upwards and flying around before settling down once more. Whatever the subject matter, it is of great concern. I don't want to interrupt them, so I stay still. The voices become louder and clearer.

"I can feel it."

"It's as dark as we are light."

"The evil is getting closer"

A sudden flash of gold light scatters the faeries in every direction. The Empress appears in the middle of the circle, her petite frame breathing in agitation. Her eyes glow luminous green and the dragons on her cloak fight for release. Behind her lurks the shadow of a terrifying, fire-breathing dragon, its tongue lolling around razor sharp teeth, its wings flapping as it prepares to take flight. The shadow looms over us all menacingly, blotting out the light, before it rises up into the darkness and recedes. I shiver, shaking with fear. The Empress is fighting to stay calm and in control.

Arcadia is silent, holding its breath, waiting for its mentor to speak.

"As your Empress, I command you not to speak of it. You will attract it here."

In her there is such turmoil that I am able to do what I had never done before; read the thoughts of someone infinitely more powerful than myself. I hear just one word repeated over and over again in a voice so filled with panic and fear it chills me to the bone and I step back to hide from it. Abaddon.

SOCIETY

Amber Lockwood

Looking at my reflection, I no longer recognise myself. I'm so far removed from the dirty-haired girl who first arrived at Storm Castle a few months ago. Sitting at the dressing table, in front of a three-sided mirror, I see myself at every angle. My complexion is clear after hot, perfumed baths filled with rose petals and scented cream so luxurious it melts into my skin on application. My hair has been cut so it falls into shining curls midway down my back, another submission to my new status. It is styled into three plaits that are held tightly by a purple silk bow and hangs loosely down my back making me wonder what the purpose was in the first place, and a thick fringe now frames my face. My features remain the same, but my cheeks are more prominent, on account of the weight I've lost along with the healthy glow that used to dust my cheeks. The soft silk of the deep purple dress is dark against my pale skin. Cap sleeves drift off from a too tight bodice that straightens and lifts, giving me a proud, erect stance even while sitting. From the waist down the dress is a mass of black netting and silk and covers purple satin slippers so light I don't feel as if I'm wearing them. I have never missed denim more.

I stick my tongue out at my reflection. Then my eyes fall upon the tiara and I feel contrite, remembering the night it was gifted to me. A week after we arrived, Aiden and I were summoned to visit the King late one night. We were taken to his inner sanctum, a room filled with books, treasures and adornments that gave me a much clearer insight into this stranger, my father.

Looking nervous, he bade us to sit down and passed us a wooden box each. When I opened mine, I was stilled to silence. Nestling against black silk, a headpiece rested. Strands of lustrous pink gems, woven into an intricate, never-ending pattern and crafted to form a triangular shaped peak, sat on a thick silver headband. The pattern was without beginning or end. It made a statement yet, when I picked it up, it felt delicate and light. I looked up and the King was watching me closely to gauge my reaction. How can you describe the indescribable? I just murmured thank you. Aiden, equally quiet, followed my example.

"It was for your mother. It is made from rose quartz," the King whispered.

I traced the outline of the stones with my fingers, and looked over to Aiden. In his crown three turrets rose vertically from the silver band, each one featuring a pink gem at its peak.

"Are they matching crowns?" I asked hesitantly, unsure of my place, unsure of what I could ask this man, the King.

"I intended to bring Rora here ... this was to be my Mating gift. I wanted to declare my feelings for all of Sensio to see so she knew we'd never be separated." He stopped for a second, sad and lost in the memory, before he pulled himself back. "You'll need to wear them when you're presented formally to Queen Andora."

The King carried on talking, but I was entranced, my attention absorbed by the tiara I was holding. Since I've developed my talent, I'm more open to the environment around me. People, places and objects call to me imprinting the emotions assailing them. Heat from the stone penetrated my fingers and spread along my nerve endings. My stomach dipped as wild emotion tangled within me; a passionate love, with a faith so deep and fathomless it filled an infinite cavern. Followed by a hope, so new and pure it first appeared naïve until it filtered through my limbs and left me peaceful. As the two emotions battled for supremacy, they fell back helplessly against the regret and loss that easily overwhelmed them. A yearning to live the life that had been cruelly denied to them so long ago but is still mourned to this day. All of this was imprinted in these precious stones, searching for an outlet. The King was not just gifting us a tiara and a crown, he was giving us a precious part of himself that he'd lost and was yet to grieve for, never mind come to terms with.

Whilst the tiara was real and alive, I wasn't. My lifeless eyes reflect back at me, the green always lively and piercing is now faded. Faint shadows darken them. I've discovered the father I've always wanted, but now I feel more lost then ever. I always imagined that having a father would provide me with a steady compass pushing away all the previous uncertainty and doubt. But while I'm happy that I know him, it's not what I hoped for. Our present relationship is tentative at best, the three of us circling each other warily for fear of causing further upset. But it's more than that, it's this situation, it's this environment. A Princess - how can I get my head around that? I feel like a bad actress in a black and white film, depicting the dramatic capers of royalty. I don't have a clue what I'm doing.

A scream shocks me from my introspection. Moving towards the window, I stand shocked at the sight before me. Then another scream jolts me to action. Moving towards the door, I walk into the maze of corridors navigating them quickly in my haste. Servants bow as I pass and I acknowledge them, trying to move as fast as possible without doing what I really want to, pick up my skirt and run. Aiden and Duncan walk past me in the opposite direction and I know I have moments before they follow me. I finally reach the corridor adjacent to the Great Hall and I hear the murmur of the courtiers, attending the Queen. I'm forced to slow down and move serenely through the corridor past the small cliques hiding in corners. I'm the subject of undisguised curiosity. In this space, I am part of the hierarchy, given respect due to my bloodline rather than because I've earned it.

Once I'm out the door, I break into a run, the sun temporarily blinding me as I move from the darkness of the stone cavern into the light of the courtyard. The scream radiates through me here, still people arriving at Court move about as though it's silent. Reaching the stables, I see Povack pulling violently at the bridle of a unicorn. He swears at the animal, the reins flailing into the air. The unicorn is panic stricken as she tries to buck away from him. A young boy with an angry red mark on his cheek looks on in horror. As if in slow motion, I watch as Povack lifts one of his shiny black boots and begins to kick out at the animal. I've seen enough. Screaming at the top of my lungs I shout out "Stop!"

Povack straightens up, drops the reins and turns to face me, a vein throbbing dangerously on his forehead in time with his laboured breath.

"Lord Povack." I interrupted. "What are you doing?"

The unicorn immediately calms down and nuzzles into the young boy, who strokes its slick black coat reassuringly and murmurs to it softly. Povack looks confused for a moment, as if I've asked a silly question.

"She's mine. I'll treat her how I please," he retorts.

"Not anymore." I bite out.

"By whose right do you order me, Princess?" he snarls the title out at me, furious anger spilling out of him.

I'm aware of the murmurs behind me, of the unicorns running nervously in circles in the paddock, their stomping hoofs tapping against the awkward silence. The tension is palpable. Then I feel warmth spread through me and I know Duncan and Aiden are behind me, supporting me. I raise a hand warning them not to interfere. This is my fight.

"I am Princess of Sensio; I answer only to King Garrick. If I wish to take control of the stables and all those who work within it, I will do exactly that. You'll never mistreat another animal or a person here again."

I turn my back on Povack, and move towards the stable boy, anger coursing through my veins, licking along my arms and straining from my fingers. He steps back as does the unicorn and I soften my gaze and take a calming breath. Behind me, I hear Povack stomp away. His boots clipping loudly against the stone, determined to lead my attention back to him. His actions reminding me of a child in a temper tantrum. I kneel down on my haunches and smile at the young boy. "What's your name?" I ask gently.

"T... T... Thomas, Ma'am" he stutters and pointing to the unicorn he adds, "and this is Clover." I study him; he's small for his age with a thatch of thick, blonde hair and brown eyes so large they almost drown his face. His cheek has began to swell and merged with a dirty smear already there. Threadbare clothes cover his slight body and I can see his ribs protruding. I ask him to get his master and he gives the unicorn a reassuring pat, then runs off in the direction of a wood hut.

I turn around and everyone has gone apart from Aiden and Duncan. "Will you help me?" I ask. Now the tense situation has passed I am myself again and uncertain.

"Of course we will," Aiden says softly. The unicorn snorts and rears back in fear as Aiden and Duncan try to remove the bridle. When they finally succeed, I see the cuts and sores around its mouth and understand why it reacted so violently.

Looking around the stables I take in the dilapidated buildings, worn tack and lack of food. The man and young boy move quickly towards us, dirtied, clothes in rags and obviously malnourished.

"What's going on here?" I ask aloud, not expecting an answer. There is no sense in cruelty towards a child or an animal. The unicorn, boy and I may be a reluctant part of this society but as Princess I have the power and an obligation to make a difference. I had an opportunity to help another less fortunate than myself. I intended to see it through.

HEADSPACE

Rose Darkings

The voices have started again. They creep upon me in the darkness of the night when I'm vulnerable, invading my senses and leading me where they want me to go. A week ago they began as a gradual whisper, insinuating themselves into my psyche in the form of friendly dreams. The next night, they became persistent when my mind wandered away and back to dreamless sleep. Now they scream into my ear, uncaring of my naivety. They make me remember hazy memories of being four years old, of waking up in the early dawn to find Granny Primrose stroking my hair and smiling down at me, only to be told the next morning she'd passed away the night before.

Other memories stood out. The ease by which I could guess what chore Mum wanted me to help with in the kitchen or who the person knocking at the door was. It got worse during my waking coma; the bubble I'd unknowingly surrounded myself with couldn't protect me any longer. Despite my silence the voices never stopped, staccato beats penetrated while I tried to string a coherent sentence together. Is that why Aiden hurt me so much? When he stalked towards me at Warwick's I knew what he wanted. I had already seen the pictures in his head. He wanted to hurt me, leave his touch so embedded into my skin the outlines of his fingers would linger afterwards. He wanted to paint my skin black and blue with bruises. He wanted to take me, branding my body as his possession. My innocence, instead of a gift, would be a prize he'd take from me. My love meant even less. That's why I was so ill after he left. The evil that had overtaken him had tried to take me as well. I know that if I had not been warned, if I had not run when I had the chance, my fate would have been as I saw it.

My talent has lingered within me since I was a child and saved me when I needed it most. Now with hindsight, I can see what I refused to accept before. I have had second sight since I was born.

On the fifth night of dreams, I give up trying to sleep and leave my bedroom. My head is muddled, sore and dull shadows linger in the background, never fully taking their leave. My limbs are sore and stiff with tension and my hopeful spirit of recent days has fled. When I first arrived in Arcadia, the voices were silenced and I was left undisturbed; I was able to accustom myself to my fairy tale surroundings without fear of what was coming next. This is now over. Walking into the main room, I see The Empress is sitting in a chair, her eyes focused on the flames dancing in the hearth. Taking the large chair beside her, I sink into the soft material and watch the fire dance against the wood. I became hypnotised by the shape of the flames as they merged together and split apart forming indiscernible shapes that almost become recognisable before disappearing once more. Then the colours smoothed the vibrant red, a smooth orange, a dulled yellow then out of nowhere came a cold, sharp black that lingered longer than the others before the colours began their sequence again. Then the black returned beating like a drum. It became hypnotic, making my eyes close as exhaustion threatened to shut me down.

Just as I was about to give in, I'm thrust into sharp alertness. The black flame becomes prominent, reacting to my attention.

The Empress breaks the silence. "The voices have returned?" she says softly.

I smile ruefully, "Is there anything you don't miss Empress?"

She turns away from the fire. Her smile is forced, her blue eyes troubled. "I couldn't keep them away any longer Rose. I'm sorry."

Surprised, I study her, noticing how pale her skin is against the richness of her blue-black hair. Her kindness to me had taken a toll on her. Reaching over, I put a hand over hers and thank her.

"Rose," she says, getting up and indicating that I should follow her. "It's time you learned how to work with your talent."

Following The Empress, I push my tangled hair behind my ears. Her rich apple green gown cascades, its material looking soft to the touch, fitting perfectly around her petite figure. Her long hair curls softly down her black and her crown twinkles pink and purple against the sun as we leave Sanctuary and walk over the bridge. In my worn trousers and top, I feel like a rumpled mess in comparison. Just before we get to the lake, she takes off her slippers, sits down, crosses her legs and lays her hands on her knees gently. Hesitantly, I copy her.

She sits serenely for a few minutes and then smiles,

appearing relaxed for the first time that morning and says, "Rose, our gift straddles two worlds. You see what is in front of your eyes but also what is invisible to others. The natural balance is in everything. Good and bad. To keep yourself safe you need to be able to remove yourself. Meditation helps you do this."

Bringing her palms together, The Empress placed her thumbs against her heart. "Nature helps us create our balance. Close your eyes and listen."

Heeding her request, I close my eyes and hide from the dawn. The light pushes against my eyelids, sending colours through the darkness that dance before receding and finally disappearing.

"Take full breaths in and out," she whispers. "Let it pull you in."

I concentrate on my breathing, on what my senses are telling me. The wind whispers softly against my cheeks, picking up my hair with its fingers before settling it down again. The lap of water pulls towards the edge of the lake before it retreats. The smell of damp dew on clean fresh grass creates an incense that curls beneath and around me like a blanket. The sun rises heating my body to the perfect temperature to echo comfort just shy of awareness. Gradually, my mind fades into oblivion and the voices, always there, fade to a still utter silence, bringing the sounds of nature calming me to the forefront.

I keep breathing in and out, aware of what is around me. I rise out of my body and look over Arcadia and I can see everything below me. I see Marcus wander out of the bridge and watch us sitting by the lake, curiosity furrowing his brow. I hear the sounds of the sasquatch's footsteps echoing against the woodland floor. I see the faeries mischievously weaving magic in Faerie Glen.

Eventually I retreat back into the comforting darkness around me. A light emerges from its very core. It forms a silhouette as it moves closer and curves into a tall thin woman emerging with beautiful green feline eyes, and shining black hair that hangs to her waist. She stands regally before me, her presence inhabiting the space around us with ease and expectation. She raises a pencil thin eyebrow at me, waiting to be acknowledged.

"Do you see your spirit guide Rose?" the Empress whispers.

Looking up, I see the figure in my head. The woman looks pointedly at me, her gaze taking in my still sitting body, cocking her head to the side, waiting. Rising up, my limbs feel relaxed, seeped of the tension that had invaded them and I knew only I can see her. Looking at The Empress, I see her murmur to an invisible presence and I know she has a spirit guide too.

The voices receded to the background were banished by the woman in front of me. She speaks to me, with a soft, melodic voice that trickles over my skin, and for the first time everything makes sense.

"I'm Imperia, your spirit guide. I'm glad to finally meet you." I'm immediately flooded with images of this woman at key moment in my life. Kneeling on the ground that day as Aiden walked away, gently stroking my hair and assuring me everything would be alright. Imperia had always been there. I just didn't know it until this moment.

She smiles, her red lips curving with pleasure at my epiphany, at my realisation and acceptance. I step forward unsure of what to do next. She takes a step towards me with her arms outstretched and asks the question reverberating in my head.

"Rose, are you ready to follow your Blueprint?"

INFECTED

Aiden Darkings

I snap awake as a high-pitched scream pierces the air followed by loud, angry shouting. I jump out of bed blinking to clear my vision, pull on my clothes and run into the corridor. The cold air of the hallway and still silence confirm it's the early hours of the morning. Daniel and Duncan are standing outside the King's room, their clothes rumpled. Daniel looks frustrated, his dark eyebrows knitting as one across his brow as he pulls a hand through his hair. He walks towards me and says in a low voice, "Povack is refusing us entry."

Nodding, I look around the corridor. The odd servant is milling around, despite the hour.

"That was the King?" I ask, knowing the answer but hardly believing it.

The door to the King's room opens and Povack walks out holding a silver tray with a small bottle. He steps from the room with a smile on his face, his body swaying as he walks past us, enjoying our attention but refusing to acknowledge it.

"What's wrong with the King?" a voice asks and I turn to see Amber. Dressed tidily in an elegant gown like she is attending court, her long hair is pulled into a ponytail at an attempt at decorum. She focused her attention solely on Povack, waiting for an answer. Povack remains silent, making us wait, his lips curving into the hint of a smile as he enjoys the game. Amber lifts her head, purses her lips and looks even more regal. Despite the calm veneer, I've known her long enough to understand that she's simmering with anger underneath.

"How is my son?" a voice rings out from the other end of the corridor. We turn to see Queen Andora join us. We rise from our bows and curtseys, to see Povack whispering in her ear, smiling broadly. Her lips twitch and she moves towards us. In full regalia, hair coiffed, crown perfectly placed on her head, Queen Andora looked like a shiny silver pin. Her blue eyes; scan our appearance, her lips flattening in displeasure.

"Go back to your rooms," she commands. "My son has experienced enough upset since you arrived." She sniffs loudly, turns her back on us and walks into the King's rooms, pulling a silk handkerchief between the diamond-clustered fingers. Povack follows her slowly, looking triumphantly over his shoulder at us as he closes the door.

"What's wrong with this place?" Amber bursts out, pacing backwards and forwards in frustration, her eyes focusing on the door, willing it to open and allow us entry. I agree with her. Since our arrival, Storm Castle has created more questions than offered answers. Luther remains within the castle, still a prisoner, yet to be tried. Our father is ill, but we don't know him well enough to help him.

What we found in the stables still makes me furious. Jack, an elderly man and former Knight, has been left in charge and has taken in Thomas, an orphan. They live in a ruined building, the ceiling open to all the elements. The man, boy and the herd of unicorns all poorly provided for. Jack and

Thomas openly admitted they often go without food to give the animals extra nourishment. Amber offered them a room in the castle but they refused to leave the animals. When I asked why the unicorns didn't just leave. Thomas said sadly "Clover won't leave him. Her loyalty will never wane." My heart aches for him and the unicorns. It helps to salve my conscience that Jack, Thomas and the unicorns now have better accommodation and a surplus of food. Two weeks on, they look healthier. Thomas's small ribs are now covered with new clothes and his healthy glow testifies to a proper diet.

This would never have been allowed to happen in Greenwood. In our small, seemingly insignificant village, we share our food. No one is left to starve, never mind a boy or an animal. It makes me incandescent with rage to pass the Throne Room at suppertime and see the tables groaning with meat, bread and brew, too plentiful to ever be depleted. At Storm Castle, a veneer must be maintained. The colour of silk and the sparkle of jewels are more important. People are subject to starvation based on status alone. The polished veneer of the royal court barely hides the ugliness hiding beneath the surface. I'm shaking with anger and then Rose's image comes into my head and calms me immediately.

The door opens and Povack locks it behind him with a large silver key, which he hides in his black leather glove. The Queen laughs, sparing us an impatient glance, as they pass us and stroll back along the corridor out of view.

Then I understand as the jigsaw pieces slide into place. I know why the Queen is so jovial. She has got what she has always wanted. The crown is now hers.

FAERIE GLEN

Rose Darkings

Never, in my entire life, have I met a faerie that is so stubborn. "No!" Indigo shouts loudly, drawing the attention of every other faerie in the Glen. Fingle's mouth sets in a straight line as he folds his arms and waits for his younger sibling to calm down. I watch the interaction with interest, still coming to terms with the intricacies of faerie society. Indigo giggles, holding the berry between her fingers making the juice from the fruit squirt all over her hand. Instead of putting her off, it only succeeds in delighting her as she laughs, the sound tinkling in the air, before saying "No" once more. Moving back, I sit on the tree stump behind me and wait for the debate to be settled.

I first met Indigo a few weeks ago. At The Empress's encouragement, I've been practising meditation every day. The voices, always there, have reduced to a volume that I'm able to handle. I was sitting beside the lake feeling calm and serene when I slowly became aware of a buzzing around my ears and without opening my eyes I could see a dot of light flitting around me. Thinking it was a curious bee or a butterfly, I stayed focused accepting another part of nature around me. Then I found myself abruptly wrestled from my peace by a shower of ice-cold water that covered me from head to toe. Gasping, I sucked in a breath and found myself looking at a faerie with a delighted expression on her face. Bemused, I went to speak and was soaked again. Her laughter rang out loudly against the quiet, misty grey blue eyes fringed with long blonde lashes that sparkled with delight. Wispy blonde hair fell to her shoulders, little ears barely peeking from the curls on her head. Wings so fast they formed a blur at her back as she flew and disappeared as quickly as she'd arrived.

The next morning, whilst meditating, I heard the buzzing again, opened my eyes and moved back at the same time, only to see Imperia standing beside me, wagging a finger at Indigo as she moved surreptitiously towards the lake. A little minx personified and I couldn't resist smiling. The faerie had an element of fearlessness she revelled in. Imperia stepped back and faded away, content Indigo had obeyed her wishes, at least for the time being.

My spirit guide appears whenever she wishes. Demanding my attention the moment she arrives until she wishes to leave. The Empress encouraged me to establish boundaries quickly. "You need to live Rose; while our gift is precious and we're grateful for it, we need to experience life too. We need to live."

We all have a spirit guide; whether we live on Earth, on Sensio or in the mysterious Abaddon. It is their job to protect us and help us to follow our Blueprint, the very reason we exist in the first place. The Empress said my Blueprint would be revealed when the time is right.

Since the day we met, Indigo has become my shadow. She follows me into Sanctuary and comes into my room uninvited. Despite her size, Indigo doesn't get pushed around and does exactly what she wants. She studies any given situation closely, works out the best course of action and then, and only then, she makes her move. She's quiet most of the time, indicating her wishes with direct action rather than whispered tones. Shouting and making a fuss until she gets what she demands, at this particular time, she wants to play with the berry rather than contribute it to the supper feast.

The berry has disintegrated into pulp and Fingle throws up his hands in disgust and turns away. Immediately, Indigo drops the berry and chases after him, nuzzling her face in his back before pushing him away. He moves away, a reluctant smile spreading over his face as he enjoys the antics of his sister whilst wanting to tell her off. Indigo is a little minx but when she wishes she can be the epitome of sweetness, representing the very best of this magical existence.

When I try to get up from the tree stump, I feel sick and faint. Pushing it back, I feel the dizziness of a headache descend and begin to floor me. My limbs soften and I fight to hold myself up, finally catching myself on the tree stump, the nearest solid foundation and surrender to the ailments working against me. A metallic taste fills my mouth and I spit it out quickly. Wiping my mouth, I stare mesmerised at the black stain it leaves. Then I remember the black flame and the cold feeling it gave me. Gradually, I return to myself, becoming aware of Indigo directly in front of my face, shouting my name impatiently. Before I can reassure her, the wind picks up, whipping my hair impairing my vision. The tree spirits wake and begin to mutter in frantic low tones, moaning and moving from side to side, trying to disembowel their roots from the ground and move away. Their murmurs become louder and I sense danger. Here.

Now. Just as Fingle reaches us, it becomes dark and thunder rumbles in the distance. As we look out towards the path of trees a massive, black, whirling tornado comes crashing and swirling towards us. Throwing up everything in its path as it consumes the ground towards the wishing well.

Then miraculously, The Empress appears in front of us, emerging as an apparition into solid form within a matter of seconds. She stands regal, fearless and courageous, between us and certain death. She extends a branch in front of her with shapes carved into the pale bark of the wood. The large, oval diamond at the top radiates a blinding light. I stand frozen, transfixed as the tornado morphs into a faceless, featureless black figure in front of our eyes. Lightning erupts from it, hitting trees at either side of the path, and they groan and scream as smoke and flames engulf them.

Indigo shouts and moves forward to help The Empress and I grab her just in time and hold her tightly in my palm. She stings me again and again, trying to break free, but I grit my teeth and hold on, listening to her shout at the top of her lungs.

There is a huge bang and we're all flung to the ground. When we look up, The Empress stands firm holding the branch in front of her. The diamond at its point, shining so brightly, it hurts to look at it. The shadowy figure has gone, defeated by The Empress, leaving a falling mist and the devastation of destroyed trees. Looking at the wasteland around us, I well up, studying the ancient stumps, broken and ringed with age and I knew they'd foreseen their own deaths. Lowering her hand, The Empress tilts before slumping to the ground. Moving forward quickly, I berate myself for being of little help when needed. Pulling her petite body upwards, I take in the blue black circles under her eyes and her almost white, translucent skin. She looks at me helplessly, a shadow of her former self, and places a cold hand on my arm and says. "I don't know how much longer I can keep the balance here. This is only the start. Abaddon is coming for us."

"The crown is now mine,

Unveiled for all to see,

My purpose finally fulfilled,

My throne, my destiny."

...Queen Andora

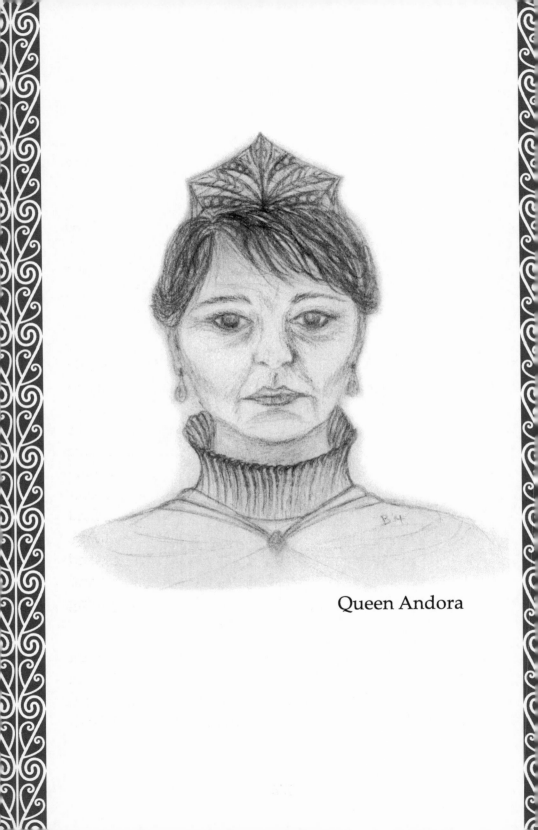

Queen Andora

AUDIENCE

Amber Lockwood

From the outside, I'm serene and calm. Inside, my stomach churns and I'm shaking like a leaf as we wait in the corridor to be formally presented to Queen Andora in the Throne Room. I take a calming breath as Aiden gives me a hug and kisses the top of my head, whispering, "What are you so nervous about Amber? It's only our grandmother ... The Queen." he wiggles his dark eyebrows theatrically, teasing me. Despite the seriousness of our situation, I burst out laughing and hug him back.

Before our stay at Storm Castle, I never anticipated this side of Aiden. He was always so serious, so weighed down by an invisible responsibility that none of us could see or understand. Here at Storm Castle, there's a sardonic, sarcastic edge to his humour that I can't get enough of. Our stay here has been intense, but my twin seems to have made it his mission to make a light-hearted comment whenever the atmosphere gets too serious. Before we were banished from visiting him, Aiden even had the King laughing, obviously a rare experience for him. Between here and Greenwood, Aiden and I seem to have swapped roles and now I'm the more serious twin, who thinks everything through, while he only lives for the moment.

I've even begun to confide in him about my estrangement from Duncan now even wider because of my new status. In one conversation, I speak of the doubts burning in my chest. "If it's not Black Knights chasing me, my unusual talents now he's been told not to approach me without permission. He's better off without me."

Aiden looked at me, a quizzical expression on his face and said, 'Do you know your Mate at all, Amber?"

Aiden bears no grudge against Daniel and Duncan for keeping our true father's identity a secret. Instead, he gave voice to the question I'd been asking myself since we came here. "Can you imagine growing up here Amber?" he said quietly.

Yes, I could imagine. My instincts told me, despite the King's burgeoning affection for us, it would have been very difficult.

The only time I've seen Aiden display any negative emotion was when he saw how thin Jack, Thomas and the unicorns were. The black of his eyes kindled a storm as he exchanged a silent, disgusted look with Duncan. Later that night, I saw him walk out of his room carrying the large bowl of fruit that's replenished every day in our rooms. When he returned half an hour later, I knew he had given the food to Jack and Thomas, staying long enough so it was considered a gift from a visitor rather than an insult to their pride. He's visited every night since showing a quiet kindness without expectation of praise, encouraging myself, Daniel and Duncan to follow his example.

The only subject he won't talk of is Rose. Once when I mentioned her, a look of such stark pain flew across his face and I felt so guilty that I've never mentioned her again.

The door to the Throne Room opens and Povack steps out in

front of us, and greets us with a barely perceptible bow. The gold chain around his neck glints against the sunlight and he touches it deliberately with his leather gloved hand trying to bring our attention to his confirmed status. His hair, now longer, is slicked back, and my fingers itch, almost feeling the thick congealed liniment on my fingers. He irritates me. I had an almost irrational urgency to get as far away from him as possible, like a deep routed splinter, stuck deep within the thick of my finger that I can't get rid of, no matter how much I claw the skin to ease it out.

"What an arse." Aiden whispers as we follow him and I fought back a smile, knowing it would be misinterpreted by the interested stares of the courtiers. We stop in front of the steps leading up the royal thrones. Povack bows theatrically, basking in the attention his role gives him. The Queen studies us. There is only one throne, placed in the middle of the dais, and she's sitting on it. There is no sign of the King. It's clear who's in charge.

"Your Majesty, may I present Prince Aiden and Princess Amber, children of King Garrick, for your perusal and acceptance to the court."

The whole court turns and looks at us. I feel naked. The oppressive stares weigh on us, dragging slowly over every piece of clothing and every inch of skin available to their greedy eyes. The Queen stretches the silence, her sharp blue eyes examining both of us. Her silver dress glints against the sun streaming through the glass windows. Around her neck hangs a chunky diamond necklace and large stud earrings matching her crown. She's wearing our father's crown. Inwardly, I grimace.

She turns towards Aiden first and asks, "Your mission with the Black Knights, what was the purpose?"

He stiffens at the question and I know she's pushed him back to that place and time when he was only a fraction of the man he is now. He clears his throat. "The Alliance asked me to infiltrate the Black Knights, find out their plans and to protect my sister."

I leaned into him, thanking him silently and showing my support. The Queen taps her adorned fingers against the intricate carvings on the arms of the throne. "You think killing innocent men was your mission?" she asks incredulously. Instinctively, I knew the censure in her voice is for dramatic effect rather than feeling the actual emotion and anger kindles.

"It was my mission, your Majesty," Aiden snaps out, her title leaving his lips with a sarcastic bite. Her lips curve into the hint of a smile and she nods in acknowledgement of a worthy opponent.

She turns to me and asks solicitously, "You only recently came to Sensio?"

"Yes, your Majesty."

"Mm, I can tell," she says, looking me up and down disdainfully. My mouth dries up. Queen Andora knew my weakness and where to target to inflict the most damage. "I understand you have been approached by a potential Mate?" she continues. I nod, my heart rate picking up at this line of questioning. "The son of a Protector in a small village?"

I nod again, and look at her defiantly. Anger smouldering inside me, my pride rose and I grab it desperately. "I'm nothing but proud to be the Mate of Duncan Darkings."

The Queen shakes her head as though speaking to a silly girl who knew no better. "Come, my child," she chides, "You're not formally mated. Therefore, you have no obligation to this union. This match is not suitable for a Princess of Sensio."

I'm shocked into silence, unaware that my bond with Duncan isn't considered binding.

"Perhaps you should set your sights higher? A Lord, perhaps?" she says, looking pointedly at Povack. His gaze rakes over me like a tiger that'd spied a succulent piece of meat to devour.

I want to cry out, "Hell no," as bile rises in my throat and I swallow frantically to push it away, followed by a cold chill that stretches out from my heart, past my nerve endings, making my body quiver. While my body reacts, I refuse to give in, straighten and declare loudly, "I will accept no other Mate."

The Queen sighs and shakes her head in resignation, giving the impression she'd tried in vain to help us but we had refused. "Then I have no choice but to postpone your acceptance to this court. Prince Aiden, your conduct will be judged at the trial of Lord Luther. Princess Amber, your status will be confirmed when you have an acceptable suitor." She turns away from us indicating Povack forward, and dismissing us before looking up again. "You may leave." she bit out sharply, giving the impression we lingered where we were not wanted. Aiden and I walk as fast as is seemly to the large door. My body gives way as it closes loudly at the back of us leaving us alone in the silent hallway. Finally flagging, I place my hands on my knees as my body flops in reaction to escaping. Aiden is pacing around like a caged animal, pushing his hands through his hair. I look up at him and ask, "Aiden, what on earth are we involved in here?"

His dark eyes are wary and I know the Queen's questions have taken a toll on him. I'm flooded with frustration and anger and a feeling of helplessness. I get up and take his face in my hands. "Don't you dare go back there, Aiden. You're not that person anymore." I pleaded with him, glad to vent some frustration.

There's a noise behind us and I turn to see Daniel and Duncan storming into the vestibule. Instantly I know they have witnessed our audience. Anger bounces off Daniel, red streaked across his cheeks. Duncan's eyes glitter, the blue sparkling with cold anger and something else I can't identify. He stops, grabs my wrist and walks on, pulling me along behind him.

"I'll escort you to your room, Princess," he says, walking so quickly I have to run to catch up with him. The warmth of his hand tingles along my skin as he strides down the maze of tunnels, looking defiantly back at courtiers and servants, who stare at our joined hands in surprise, until we reach my room. Completely ignoring the people milling about, he pins me up against the door and takes my face in his hands. I lick my lips nervously and my heart feels as if it's going to burst. His reaction, his passion, his fever is all for me.

Leaning forward, he dips his tongue into my mouth. Moving my hand up his torso, I smooth my hands over his waist and feel the soft, dark hair on his stomach under my fingers. Pushing myself closer, I lose myself in his kiss. Taking a key from his pocket, he unlocks the door, while still holding me and we stumble inside. Just before the door closes, I catch a glimpse of Povack standing in the corridor, watching us, anger on his face. I dismiss his image and focus on my Mate as he pulls me towards the bed and claimed me as his once more.

"My day of reckoning is coming,

but that day is not today,

So I witness, I watch, and I wait...

Tactics of war to seal every Mate's fate,

The young to right the wrongs of the old,

A tiresome tale forever re-told,

And so I witness, I watch and I wait...

For my day of recking is not this day. "

...Povack

Povack

ATTRACTION
Rose Darkings

The Empress and I sit in silence in the large room, the night sky casting purple shadows, painting a pattern scaling the walls, before it fades away and returns again. The fire crackles and flickers, the dry wood snapping against the element and the quietness. Warmth consumes the room, bathing my tired eyes with an ethereal glow and offering a peace I cant find. The Empress sits gazing into the fire, still pale and exhausted from Abaddon's attack. It's been a day since she saved us, and she's neither slept nor spoken. Her white, drawn face says everything she can't.

I yearn for Greenwood. There are very little demands upon the youngest child of the Village Protector. I was expected to support my family and bond with my Mate when the time came. I yearn to go back to that simple existence. I want to run away from what's coming. Shutting away the image of Aiden, I ask the question that lingers. "Do you have a Mate, Empress?"

She looks up from the fire, focusing her full attention on me, before speaking. "Yes, I do," she says "but I haven't seen him for a long time. He gave me this." She trails a red fingernail over the branch she used to defeat the black shadow. I study it carefully. It's intricately carved with signs and symbols I've never seen before, and the diamond at the top sparkles in the firelight. "My Mate made this for me. It's a runic wand. It was his mating gift to me."

"What did you give him?" I ask, remembering the worn

handkerchief that Dad lovingly places in his pocket every morning. Waving my hand, I dismiss the question fearing it is too personal, mating gifts are sacred between couples.

"He refused one. He said he had waited long enough to meet me and I was the only gift he needed. That's why I defeated the tornado. This wand is made with pure love. Nothing is more powerful." Her eyes fill up at the memory, her blue eyes a stormy ocean, and she looks away. "When was the last time you saw him?" I asked, something pulling at me but I don't know why.

"15th July. Nearly twenty years ago," she whispers. I gasp as shock and grief overwhelms me and she continues without noticing my reaction. "The natural balance was at risk and I had to keep the elements safe. Nobody else could do it, Rose. Nobody else could keep the binding veil intact. I had to do it. It was my Blueprint."

"The binding veil?" I repeat, confused. The Empress continues, "All worlds are bound together. Sensio is infected and so Earth is too. The infestation is seeping through to Arcadia, making us vulnerable to Abaddon."

A shiver ran through me as she said the word aloud, curious but unwilling to ask before now. "What is Abaddon?"

She answers quietly, "It is the darkness to our light. It's where your worst nightmares will come true and try to destroy you." She gets up and moves unsteadily to the door, and says, "Rose, like me, you live between two worlds. Walking between them will require all the strength that you possess."

I sit in silence, trying to digest this new information, my guts queasy and churning with anxiety. The mention of Abaddon has even kept the wilful Indigo in Faerie Glen after Fingle insisted she stay home. Hearing a sound, I turn to see Marcus watching me from the door. The last couple of nights Marcus has taken to escorting The Empress and I to our rooms. I teased him about it, but The Empress agreed it was necessary. Putting the fire grate over the hearth, I walk to the door, greeting him with a tentative smile. I've found his presence unsettling lately. I daren't go near his thoughts again, once catching a large castle and an endless sea and I backed away immediately, feeling contrite for invading his privacy. I feel the tension between us and I try to ignore it, unwilling to confront the feelings behind it. The tension builds as we walk along the corridor, hidden by darkness and judged by the shadows. I try to think of a light heartened comment, to confirm the status of our friendship but my brain is too overloaded to think clearly. Reaching my door, I turn around quickly to thank him and find him a lot closer than I expected. I become lost in his eyes. The blackness, hooded by blonde thick eyelashes is hypnotic. His hair is now longer, curling onto his forehead. His lips are thick, full and sensual and for a second I wonder how they would feel against mine. Would his kiss be hesitant and gentle or would he kiss me passionately, as I'd imagined.

Remembering my conversation with Mum, I'd questioned how couples without a bond began a relationship. Now I have my answer. He leans forward and I felt his breath brush over my lips and I know this moment could change everything. I let out a shuddering breath and I turn my head so that his lips land on my cheek. He groans in frustration and I know he had wanted this kiss as much as I was confused by it. Murmuring goodnight, I slide away from him into my room and quickly close the door behind me. I lean against it, running my hands over my body, feeling the heat dancing on my skin. Part of me had wanted Marcus to kiss me. To kiss me so passionately that he would wipe Aiden from my very existence. But I knew if I let him, Aiden and I would lose our chance of a future together and my heart won't allow that. Not yet.

I climb into bed fully clothed and curl up into a ball. Just before I close my eyes, a memory flashes, and the words 15th July lit on icing on a birthday cake. Mum and I had made it to celebrate a birthday a few months before. That date, twenty years ago, had been the day Aiden and Amber had been born.

CROSS PURPOSES

Amber Lockwood

I have missed him so much. That every part of me has ached for him. Back in Greenwood, in the brief time we lived together, Duncan and I existed within a bubble. Locked willingly within the life we created in the small house the village gifted us. Duncan is a passionate man, but there were moments when I knew he held himself back for fear of scaring me. Here at Storm Castle, he's taken me as he's wanted to for so long. Duncan has given me every part of himself and I've revelled in all of it.

Duncan's fast hot breaths caress the naked skin of my back as he holds my hips to keep me upright. I close my eyes and relive the last few hours, clothes ripped off and tossed to the floor, hot skin and bruising kisses, hands twisting around my hair and pulling me to him so I can't escape his mouth, pulling us together on the bed, against the wall and in front of the mirror.

Pulling me back against him, our eyes meet and he watches my reaction, drinking in every moan, every nuance of pleasure that I utter. I am wanton. My eyes shine, my hair loose and tangled down my back. Months before, I'd looked into the mirror and studied my reflection, trying to discern who I was. Now looking at myself, ravaged by my Mate, I see my true reflection.

We fall back to the bed, the covers awry and kicked to the bottom. Duncan leans on one arm and stares at me wordlessly, trailing his fingers over my cooling skin, lingering, squeezing and driving me back to the line between pleasure and pain, before pulling back and then taking me again and again.

I was so angry with him when we arrived here. I felt he had betrayed me by keeping the secret of who my father was. I pushed him away using my newfound status as an excuse. On the first night here, I woke up in the early hours to the sound of my door handle being tried. Hearing the impatient slap of his hand against the door and my name growled from his throat. My body yearned for me to answer, squirming against the bed sheet as I did against his touch. Then I remembered the expression on his face: unrepentant and unapologetic for the decision he had made for me. Any concession towards my feelings would have been welcomed. But Duncan, the master of the universe, had decided I was too fragile to deal with the news of my parentage. Now today, I learn he had a key in his possession the whole time, but never used it, giving me a choice I never knew I had.

My issue is not with the situation but Duncan's attitude to it. I am only ever his equal when he decides I am. For me, that just isn't enough.

Feeling his hand tighten in my hair, he places a finger under my chin and forces me to meet his eyes. "We need to be formally mated Amber. You are mine and they need to know it."

I think back to Rora's diary and her description of Daniel and Maggie's formal mating. Her beautiful dress, the intimate ceremony performed by Warwick and her blissful joy for her friend. I could see us, in my mind's eye, declaring and celebrating our commitment for all to see. But I only see part of myself there; the rest is faded away, because Duncan doesn't see all of me as I desperately need him too. While I bristle over the Queen's decree regarding my choice of Mate, I'm unconcerned about what action she could take. I want a relationship with my father but I don't want to be a Princess. I have no interest in jewellery, status or power. I want to know what sort of person my father is, what makes him laugh, what interests him and what sort of relationship we can have with him. My Mate is my choice and I need to tell him so.

"I belong to no one but myself Duncan Darkings." His hands move over my skin again, shredding the incremental lie, pulling my body to his. He sighs at my stubbornness, pulling me on top of him and forces me to look at him. "Where does that leave us Amber? You can't hide here. Not now."

He's right. But I can't talk about us, the emotions swirling around me so vibrant and consuming they scare me. I'm so close to surrendering myself fully to him at the loss of myself. Is this true love? But Duncan's right. The gates are closing upon us. It's only a matter of time before Queen Andora is told of our behaviour in the hall and I'm publicly remonstrated for it or trapped in my room like my father. All of a sudden, a thought springs into my head like an apparition and all of my senses came alive once. Instinct urges me to follow the single thought like a lifeline.

"I know what we have to do."

We must leave here and take the King with us."

POISON

Amber Lockwood

I'm back in Greenwood. My eyes adjust to the darkness. Firelight from the sconces throw dancing shadows on the walls as I walk down into the bowels of the building. The murmuring of voices lulls me forward, offering comfort and piquing my curiosity. Reaching the large room, I see the swords and scrolls and I know I'm back in the Great Hall. Two shadows are sitting at the table, their silhouettes moving in and out as I adjust to the dark room, bathed only by firelight. As I get closer, I can see that one of them is Aiden, his eyes coloured their natural brown instead of the soulless, infected black. He looks right through me and I know I'm invisible to him. I'm here to witness the past.

"Are you listening lad? This is important." Warwick tugs Aiden's arm to get his attention back.

"Of course, I am," Aiden says, impatient and weary.

Warwick is holding a bottle in his hand and places it back on the table and studies Aiden. "He's not getting to you? Is he lad?"

Aiden stays silent, studying his hands, they open and clench in agitation. He looks at Warwick, his face open, betraying a vulnerability I've never seen before. "I didn't think so," he says, "but sometimes I find myself believing the promises he makes."

"It's all smoke and mirrors lad, you know that," Warwick sighs. "I think it's the right time to show you this." He picks up the small bottle again and pulls the string around the paper-topped seal. Gingerly, he uses a spoon to tease out a small amount of the small black seeds within. "Have you ever heard of black henbane?" he asks.

"No, but I can tell why," Aiden says, moving back and wrinkling his nose. I sniff curiously and pull back quickly as I catch a whiff of a repugnant bitter smell. It's like burnt tobacco. I cover my nose to ward away the stench.

"When I was a lad, we used it for toothache, but it has other uses."

Hearing Aiden chuckle, I look curiously at him. He laughs again, and Warwick joins in. I want to laugh myself, without knowing why. Warwick picks up the spoon and looks in amusement at the little seeds resting innocently against the silver.

"These can make him ill lad, really ill. The smell alone makes you giddy but if consumed, it could make him sick, blur his vision and make him confused. If taken regularly over a period of time, it will give him hallucinations. You can make him think what you want."

Aiden looks at the seeds and a small smile of satisfaction plays about his lips. "I can distract him without revealing my talents," he says, relief clear in his voice. Warwick puts the seeds back into the bottle and seals it again with the string. He puts it in front of Aiden, who picks it up carefully, too aware of its power to be disrespectful of it.

Then, I'm thrust backwards out of the room and moved forward to another time. The corridors of Storm Castle feel tense and I flatten myself against the wall to get out of the way of the servants going about their business. I watch myself running from my room, distressed, looking at the King's shut door. Then I'm standing beside Duncan, Aiden and Daniel as we wait nervously to find out what's wrong with the King. Then I see Povack leave the room with the empty bottle on a tray and as past and present collide I know what it is. I understand why the King is lucid one moment and confused the next. The smell reaches my nostrils and I cover my mouth to stifle my laughter. My form stuck in the past grins mischievously I burst out laughing, joined by Duncan, Daniel and Aiden. Povack looks around, satisfied and walks towards a smiling Queen Andora who is wearing the King's stolen crown.

I wake up abruptly and sit up in bed. My eyes open to the bright morning light and I breathe deeply, trying to rid myself of the stench embedded from my dream. "Amber?" Duncan's warm hand touches my cool skin. I get up quickly, needing to see Aiden, needing to confirm what I suspect. As I push the bedcovers back there's a loud, impatient knock on the door. It's repeated a few seconds later.

"Wait here," Duncan says gruffly. In the two days since my audience with Queen Andora and our subsequent reunion, Duncan has refused to leave my room, or leave me alone. Accompanying me wherever I go, his concern, his sword always visible, his worry worsening as time passes. He opens the door cautiously and then throws it open. Aiden strides into the room, his clothes ruffled as if he's thrown them on quickly. I pull the soft material of my robe over my bedclothes. We look at each wordlessly and say one word that confirms we both shared the same dream: "Poison."

An hour later we are ready and Aiden has left to speak to Jack and Thomas to convince them to leave with us. I dread to think what could happen if we left them here. Minutes tick slowly until darkness falls and we deliberately stay away from Court, given the importance of acquiesce and the subservience required to survive it. I know it's only a matter of time before I'm called upon by the Queen to choose another Mate. I reverently hope that today is not that day. Since Povack witnessed our reunion, we've not seen him but I can feel him lingering in the shadows. Waiting to take me as he's been promised by the Queen.

Duncan's behaviour only confirms my suspicions. He refuses to leave me alone, even within the confines of my room in case I'm vulnerable in his absence. This only makes me even more determined for him to see me as his equal. I have my talents. I'm more than capable of defending myself if necessary. Despite our emotional distance, he continues to use my desire for him against me and my heart betrays me again and again, demolishing the wall I'd erected to keep myself safe.

Dusk settles across the sky and as I look out of the windows. I fight the desire to run from the castle. The adrenalin pumping through my veins keeps me tilted on an edge, aware of everything around me, but fully focused on my goal to leave with all of my family intact. Darkness fully embraces the sky and Storm Castle settles into still silence. Duncan gets up and I know the time is now. I take one last look around my glamorous accommodation. I'll not miss any of it. I only wish it was possible to change into my comfortable trousers and tank top without Arousing suspicion. I wait in the corridor as the men go to rescue the King. We don't know what physical state he'll be in behind that locked door and guess that two would need to carry him whilst another kept a look out.

Waiting in the corridor alone, I shiver. Duncan has doused four of the sconces leaving the space in relative darkness. Looking back, I will them to come back quickly. Hearing the murmur of steps, I sigh with relief and turn around and come face to face with Povack. I swallow my scream and paste a wan smile on my face. "Good Evening Lord Povack," hoping my voice carries along the stone to alert the others. He smiles arrogantly, but stays silent. Raising my eyebrows, I use it as an opportunity to move past him. His body moves, mirroring mine.

Povack looks around satisfied that we were alone. "Have you thought more about the Queen's suggestion, Princess?" he says, leaning forward, invading my personal space. His breath is hot and sour and I fight the urge to move away. A single droplet of sweat drips down my back beneath the stiff confines of my dress.

Trying to keep him distracted, I speak very slowly. "Yes, I have considered it."

Conceit laces his features as he slowly removes a leather glove. Stretching his bare hand towards me, he caresses the skin at the top of my collarbone, lingeringly, before trailing it slowly down towards the top of my breasts exposed by my dress. Mistaking my shudder for pleasure, he smiles lavishly and says slowly, "I think it will be a very satisfying arrangement for both of us." His fingers now dig painfully into my flesh, bruising me, marking me. I close my eyes, forcing myself to remain calm and ignore the nausea and panic threatening to overwhelm me. I pray that the distraction is enough for them to escape. Then the fingers fall away and I opened my eyes to see Povack falling to the ground and Duncan standing behind him, his eyes smouldering, his body shaking with anger. Daniel is helping the King, who looks weak but aware enough to look down at Povack, now unconscious, in disgust. Duncan gathers me to him, kisses my sweat-slicked forehead and murmurs, "You'll never have to endure that, ever again."

We walk swiftly through the corridors and out of the castle. As the night air hits us, I hear the commotion begin at our backs, followed by shouting and the movement of people. By silent agreement, we break into a run. The moons illuminate Jack and Thomas as they wait beside the herd of unicorn, like carved statues, waiting patiently for us to arrive. As the King gets closer, Clover pulls against her reins excitedly and stamps her feet. The King briefly strokes her neck before Daniel helps him mount her. We all follow clutching the reins tightly as the unicorns stomp back and forth anxious to move. The voices grow louder, until Povack bursts out onto the stone steps behind us.

"Stop them!" he screams and I see the hate in his eyes twinned within the blood running down the side of his face.

"Move! Now!" Daniel shouts and we gallop out of the stables, speed bursting from the unicorns as they are finally given the freedom to run, as they always wanted. We lurch forward and I hear Thomas shout Jack's name. Before us, the gates are barricaded by Black Knights. I grip the reins and turn to see Thomas clutching onto his unicorn, his face burrowed in its neck. Beyond him, I see Jack lying on the ground, bloody and still. Grief and regret hit me as I shout against the wind, telling Thomas to hold on. As we gallop relentlessly towards the gates and the guards and I close my eyes at the inevitable crash. Wincing, I hear only silence as the sounds of hooves disappears and I open my eyes to see the gates and guards fall away below us. The unicorns are snorting and crying out in delight as they flap large black wings that have sprung from their sides. I hear a deep laughter from the King, as he shouts triumphantly as we fly off into the sky. Away from Sea Cliff. Away from the prison that is Storm Castle. Flying away towards the light of the two moons and to our freedom.

THE ELEMENTS

Rose Darkings

I've never felt an affinity with the elements. My family did. Dad and Duncan are comfortable using fire. Mum can throw a stone from one end of Greenwood to the other. Aiden kept us in the dark about his abilities until Amber arrived. Then there is me, completely and utterly talentless. All the emotions that Mum spoke of, of being at one with your element, your talent, was foreign to me. She spoke of walking past a building and feeling the stone harvested within it speak to her. Not as an impartial observer, but as a member of a family forever entwined with the people who lived within its walls. Mum is drawn to stones, picking them up and rubbing her finger over every curve and crevice they possess until it merges with her and she finds it difficult to part with them, so much so, she had a collection in a trunk at home.

I feel for the elements, they are trying to establish a connection with me that I don't understand. Is my second sight secondary to something I've not been privy to before now? I feel Imperia appear beside me, ever aware of my intentions before I have fully considered the implications for myself. Long limbed arms elegantly fold as her eyes take in my movements and I sit and lose myself in the space around me, feeling my mind move away from my body. I feel at peace as I look around without fear or hesitation. Light bursts past the darkness and in the distance I see four silhouettes walking towards me. Their shapes are indiscernible at first until they move against the light revealing a quirk of their personality through a head tilt or a swing of arms. I feel them. I know who they are.

Fire instantly demands my attention, unpredictable and dramatic, gleeful one moment then frustrated the next. Fire wants it all and they want it now.

Earth is next, dogged and determined to do what's necessary. Nothing will distract them from the mission they have set themselves. Any distractions are pushed away in a burst of anger appearing and disappearing so quickly you're not sure it was there to begin with.

Air is free, flirting around the other elements but never allowing itself to be possessed by any as it slips quickly out of their grasp. So charming the others forgive the indiscretion and seek to possess it again.

Water swirls around the others, picking up on their emotions and echoing them. When adversely pushed it sends an epic wave in retribution before retreating and returning to a peaceful tide. It moves constantly, following its own path, refusing to be held back by anything or anyone.

Then I feel it: the air move towards me, through me and merging with me. Feeling hot and cold all at once, I release a breath. I am at one with the element that I never knew was part of me - until now. Opening my eyes to the light, I smile, feeling peace within me. Looking to Imperia, I'm serene, an emotion so calming I never want to be parted from it.

"What's your Blueprint Rose?" Imperia asks knowing my answer but asking me to confirm it.

"I'm here to protect the elements." I reply without hesitation.

She nods regally and I feel her pleasure flow through me and I wink cheekily at her. She nods in confirmation. "Go now. The Empress will take you to them."

The Empress appears and I stretch my arms above my head and pick myself up from the ground, sated as the movements pull at my relaxed muscles. Just as I reach her, a group of people emerge from the forest and walk towards her. She greets them warmly. The group stretches to around twenty, huddled together not for protection, but for comfort. They are the most beautiful creatures I've ever seen. They have sparkling, clear skin, elegant features with bright clear eyes in deep blue and vivid green. The women have long, curling hair that falls to their hips whilst the men's curled upwards in a haze of blondes and blacks. They are wearing clothes of the softest, most delicate fabric, in all shades of deep pinks and purples, looking so soft, it may disintegrate if you touch it. Their bodies are fit with impossibly long, limbs.

"Ero, you and your family are welcome in Arcadia. No harm will come to you here," The Empress says, smiling warmly.

The creatures smile back, and run laughing towards the lake. The men dive bomb into the water as the women submerge themselves gracefully from the shore. When they emerge from the water they reveal their true form, the human masks gone as they touch their tails with a reverence that's breathtaking.

"Are they what you imagined, Rose?" The Empress asks me quietly.

"You mean the mermaids?" I ask.

She shakes her head and I try again. "The elements?" She nods.

"It's strange," I muse, "I never felt part of them until now. I'm air, but I can still feel the others, as if I know them. Like they're old friends."

She nods enthusiastically, clearly pleased with me. We follow the natural pathway through the woods. The air between the trees feels cooler against my skin and instead of wishing it away I embrace it, relishing the fact I now have an element that's mine.

Then against the hushed silence, a thousand screams cut through me. I fall forwards, my knees striking the hard, cold ground. I cover my ears, trying to push the screams away, until I realise they're inside my head. Seconds later, everyone else can hear them and chaos erupts. The faeries run, terrified, back into their tree houses, the mermaids submerge themselves deep into the water and the sasquatch lets out a long desolate howl.

As we cry out against the noise, the leaves on the trees, usually a lush vibrant green, wither to brown. The tree spirits cry with deep hollowed voices, joining the chorus. The bees and the butterflies fly furiously around only to explode into nothing and disintegrate towards the ground. The Empress moves forward and shouts 'No' so loudly everything else becomes silent and we stand still. Then she takes off, her dress and cloak flowing behind her like wings, the dragons on the side of the cloak flying off and flapping their wings upwards into the sky, screaming out naked flames.

Galvanised into action, I run off after her, past the wishing well and into Faerie Glen, realising that all this time, the elements have stayed there, hidden in open sight. I hear Indigo shouting 'No' before I see her flying determinedly towards a woman in a long black dress, with a netted train that should have impeded her movements, but instead echoes and reinforces them. In her hand, she is holding a hessian sack trapping the elements, which are struggling furiously to escape. I feel their agitation and panic as they move against the material binding them, pulling them further away as they try to escape. Bile rises in my throat, as I stand near The Empress who is immobile, her limbs locked in tension but shaking with the desire to move forward and engage with the intruder. Fingle stands by her side, his small face anguished as he watches his sister, his fists clenched in frustration. Indigo weaves around the figure and it ducks and evades her as if they are playing a child's game. Her wings beat more and more slowly as exhaustion overcomes her. We shout at her to move away, but instead she stills, closes her eyes and falls limply into the woman's hand.

The woman in black turns, her red lips curving in pleasure, as she holds Indigo in her fist and raises her upwards like a prize. "If you try to stop me. I will kill her."

Her face is covered in a black feather mask that falls to her cheeks. Her blue eyes are steely and determined. Her fist is tight around Indigo's body and watching her small figure, so vulnerable to a mere squeeze of a fist. I stay still, fearing any movement will encourage her. She laughs and turns away moving almost sensuously towards the wishing well and down the path that bade her entry. The green beneath her withers as she touches it and trees shrink away. Wherever she treads, everything withers and dies. I know what she is. The personification of everything we fear, the evil we dare not speak of. She is Abaddon.

The Empress screams out in rage as Abaddon walks off, unharmed, carrying Indigo in one hand and the Elements in the other. She falls to her knees, her arms wrapped protectively around her petite body. Blood red rain starts to fall, marking our clothes and stinging our skin. The faeries start to fight amongst themselves as I push Marcus away from my side and shout at him in frustration. He shouts back, pulling me into his arms, screaming into my face, his eyes dancing to the evil moving within him and I smile, wanting to respond.

"Stop!" shouts The Empress. Her movements slow and forced like she is in extreme pain. Her face is pale and stained red. She looks at me, as I move towards her to offer comfort, but she retreats holding out her hand to ward me away. Her voice is hollow and defeated as she says. "I'm going to be taken away and I'm never going to be able to come back." "Fingle" she cries out and he flies towards her.

"Tell them what must be done." He nods, sadly.

The Empress gasps out and closes her eyes against what seems like impossible pain and she shakes in an effort to control herself. She turns to me her cat like blue eyes have sunk into her face, the pupils gone and replaced with deep yellow eyes, taking away the woman I know and trust.

"Rose" she cries, her tone rough. "You must protect the veil at all costs."

Turning, she picks up her small body and follows the stranger. Her silhouette fades and merges. Bursting into a dragon, so large it dominates the sky in front of us. It roars loudly as it stretches its wings and takes off into the sky. It circles once and flies roaring, back towards us, skimming so low, I can see the muscles ripple below the burnt red scaled skin and we feel the kick of the wind as the wings stretch out. The dragon releases a roar so loud it vibrates into the air, making my ears ring and my body hum. A burst of fire emerges from its mouth as it disappears taking my mentor with it as it left Arcadia.

The moment she disappears, I feel a grief so profound that I don't know if it's possible to recover from it. The soul and protector of Arcadia is gone. How can we survive without her? Desolation, pure and piercing, strikes my heart as a thousand voices join the others in the background, deafening me temporarily before bringing me back to the present and to the reality. Indigo is gone. The Elements are gone. Fathomless burning anger takes over and I don't know if it will ever leave me. My body gives up and as I fall to the ground.

The sounds of horses and shouts reach me as I became aware of my body lying on the ground and Marcus holding me and calling my name. I look to him and see a dozen unicorns sweep over us. Their hooves grip against the air as if it's solid ground, their black coats shining with sweat but as they lift their heads and cry aloud I know they delight in the effort. Turning, they descend to the ground and I realise the people upon them are shouting gleefully.

I sit, without the strength to rise and greet the riders. One figure moves closer and I sob as I recognise him. Aiden strides forward with a confidence I've never seen before. His head high, his hair coiffed, beard tidy and wearing a crown. He looks years younger, his cheeks flushed with exhilaration. His eyes, still black, drink me in, his scrutiny prickling the nerve endings on my skin, making every pore feel alive. Seeing me in Marcus's arms, his nose flares with agitation and his fists clench as he bends down, extending his hand towards me. He pushes Marcus away with a look and I feel him retreat, leaving me alone on the ground. Aiden sits down beside me. Slowly he trails his thumb down my cheek and over my lips, before smiling and finally speaking. "Hello, my Mate. Have I missed anything?"

DECLARATION

Rose Darkings

I am finally alone and am thankful for it. Given the first opportunity, we retreat from each other like animals to our respective caves. Looking out of the window towards the lake, I lose myself in the dark forest beyond, trying in vain to organise my thoughts into some coherent order before giving up and losing myself to the darkness once more. In desperation, I reach out for The Empress, hoping that her new form will allow me to communicate telepathically. Once again, I hit a brick wall. Defeated, I reach for Imperia, seeking reassurance from a woman who's stronger than I'll ever be. I feel nothing. Did the transformation of The Empress change me too?

Exhausted by the events of yesterday, Fingle bade us back to Sanctuary, telling us he would see us in the morning. After a brief meal, we each retreat to our separate rooms. Needing distance to process everything that's happened and gain strength for what's to come. My thoughts fall to my mischievous little friend Indigo, so helpless and vulnerable to the strength of a fist. Closing my eyes, I send out a wish that she will survive until we reach her. I've no doubt we're going. I can see us walking down a long winding road in the midst of a desert, framed by mountains under an eternal black sky that rolls with thunder and lightning, warning us that the road ahead is treacherous. My stomach dips as my nerves react to what's to come.

My nerves are still taut from seeing Aiden. He moved so

confidently, I knew the person who'd inhibited his body before was a mere shadow of the man before me. His eyes raked over me possessively as I accepted his hand, staring pointedly at Marcus until he lifted his hands in surrender and moved backwards. I couldn't answer his question. Where did he want me to start? He seemed to understand, squeezing my hand silently, before he moved aside for Dad who pulled me into a bear hug before holding me at length. The crinkles around his eyes were deeper than I remember as he smiled wistfully at me and tugged a loose strand of hair like he couldn't quite reconcile the memories of the child in the woman he saw before him now. I feel like I'm in a no man's land in between. I notice his change of expression and I know he was seeing Mum. In my petite frame, my long curly hair and my brown eyes. I felt his pain at their separation.

"Mum was well when I saw her," I said softly.

He nodded quickly and turned to the man behind him. "King Garrick, I would like you to meet my daughter, Rose."

I made an attempt at a curtsey, but he held up his hand to stop me. I studied him, curiously. His clothes hung on his large frame as if he'd lost a lot of weight in a short period of time. His hair and beard were thick and streaked with grey but looked so soft to the touch and I could almost see the rich luxurious colour it had once been before age reached it. Ocean blue eyes, the colour of a stormy sea, study me as if I presented the answer to a puzzle.

"Young Rose, you're the image of your mother. My son's told me all about you." His voice is deep, husky and ably reflects the regal presence radiating from him. Beneath the surface, I feel the jagged emotions so painfully raw I take a shuddering breath.

Looking past the King to Aiden, I acknowledge the crown on his head, the warm tones of the jewels twinkling against the firelight. He moved forward, took my hand, kissed it and said "Now father, don't scare my Mate away."

His voice is different, the inflections within teasing me, so far removed from the boy I knew I wasn't sure of how to deal with him now. The Aiden I knew was serious and withdrawn. An observer, introverted, and not a leader. I always wondered if this was because of his position of ward of the Village Protector. This, Aiden, confident and flirtatious, I have no concept of how to deal with and the fact that he is the son of a King only intimidates me even more.

It's a huge relief when Amber and Duncan join the conversation. Amber scolded her brother, took my arm and pulled me away. Duncan tugged my hair as I left, and I smiled half-heartedly at his childhood habit, wishing to comfort me without making it obvious.

Somebody had lit a fire and Amber and I gravitated toward it. I looked at her. She was beautifully dressed in an elegant gown that showed off her curves to their best advantage. Most of her hair is swept away from her face, wispy tendrils falling about her shoulders and a dainty tiara is pinned in place accenting her regal carriage. In Greenwood, I always thought of Amber as intricately linked to my brother. You rarely saw one without the other. I turn and see Duncan staring at her, his mouth twisting in frustration and I realise she not only saved me from the awkward conversation. She's saved herself too.

She caught me staring at her and said, plucking at the rich fabric of her dress with nervous fingers.

"Rose, this isn't me." Desperate to reveal the old Amber underneath the glamorous exterior, wanting to escape.

"That may be so Amber Lockwood, but it suits you."

She blushed and then leaned forward. "Your brother is driving me nuts, Rose."

I leaned closer and whispered back "I could say the same about yours."

We laughed out loud and I felt the tension drain from my body. The men turned and looked at us like the sound was unfamiliar and I realised life at Storm Castle must have been very serious.

Catching up, Amber and I use our conversation to devise an early exit to our bedrooms but I know no sleep will come to me this night. My world, steady for a brief time, has again been rocked by events I've no control over. Resolve hardens as adrenalin pumps my veins. Whatever is heading our way, I need to know all about it - no more half-truths or faerie tales. I am no longer an innocent girl, but a woman who is in control of her future and I will fight for the life I want.

I'm ready for the knock and when it comes I join the others in the main room. The tension is palpable and fills the silence. Fingle comes in last, looking worn and fragile. His wings usually moving at a rate indiscernible to the naked eye are beating slowly underlying his weariness. The voices silent since the departure of The Empress begin again in earnest and I wince, covering my ears and raising my eyes to meet Fingle's. He looks at me sadly, apology clear on his face. Understanding, I know what he's going to say.

"I, Fingle Hawthorn, take the place of my sister, The Empress, and bring to you the Declaration of The Soothsayer."

THE SOOTHSAYING

Amber Lockwood

The road ahead is unclear. Back in my Greenwood clothing, I follow the others down the long road that circles and bends giving no real idea of when it will end. Given the revelations this morning, I am surprisingly comfortable with what lies ahead of us. Sensio has always demanded a fair toll to pay for your desires. We walk in silence, each absorbed in a myriad of emotions. My brief experience as a Princess developed my ability to see situations clearly, separating the black and white and disregarding the grey. Choices were offered to Aiden and me in short succinct sentences and answers were expected without delay and while at Storm Castle I engaged with the process, too bewildered to question its validity. So now I'm walking down another unfamiliar road, faced with another set of choices, I don't question, baulk or walk away; I accept what's in front of me and move on. It was my choice to stay in Sensio. If I wanted to be anywhere else I would have returned to Earth long ago.

I peek at Duncan from under my eyelashes as he keeps pace beside me. His arm brushes against mine and kicks up heat along my skin. Our relationship power struggle continues. I still want him desperately. My body yearns for him, while my heart winces in indecision.

Aiden and Rose walk ahead, Aiden strides confidently towards what faces us. Rose, walks listlessly at his side, head bent focusing on the stone path ahead, her shoulders slumped in resignation.   It's like Rose and Aiden have swapped personalities in a perverse juxtaposition. She's not been the same since we spoke to Fingle this morning.

"I can't reach The Empress, Fingle. Is she gone forever?"

Fingle moved closer to her, trying to conceal his fear and sadness.   "The Empress is gone, Rose.   She is now immortalised as Brigid.   The true Celtic Goddess of Fire. The dragon of Arcadia. We can only hope she will return to us."

Rose dipped her head in resignation, slowly nodding and accepting the answer. I knew then how much The Empress meant to her.

I thought back to our meeting this morning.

"Have you heard of The Soothsaying?" Fingle asked the room at large.

"Warwick mentioned it before the Hill of the Faeries," Rose said.

Fingle nodded and recited it for us all to hear.

"Binding of Sensio & Earth,

Destined twins shall be born,

To balance the Elements,

Or the veil's forever torn."

"I've never heard this before, Fingle" my father said, resting his chin on his hand.

"You won't have, Sire," Fingle replied. "Your father hoped that The Soothsaying would come to fruition naturally, but circumstances prevented that."

My father turned pale and swallowed, the white in his beard matching his skin. Fingle paused, trying to find for the right words before continuing.

Nerves jangle and I bite out impatiently "Spit it out Fingle. No more secrets." My father shot me a wry smile and I knew I sounded exactly like Rora. Fingle concentrated and began to speak.

"Lord Thorgood was the peaceful Lord of Sea Cliff. He was well respected and cared for his people. He was a happy man until his Mate Teresa died of a fever. Grief stricken and feeling an obligation to his people, he was manoeuvred into making another match with Andora, who bore him a son, Garrick. Andora sought power and control of the elements and convinced Lord Thorgood he should be King of Sensio. Somehow, we still don't know how, Andora gained control of the dragons and harnessed the dark side of our talents. Foreseeing his death, Lord Thorgood came to me and asked me to hide the elements. Only The Empress had the power to bring them here beyond the veil to Arcadia."

Fingle turned to look at the King and continued, "He left two amulets representing the elements for you and your future Mate. He hoped they would save you. We have been waiting since then for The Soothsaying to come to fruition."

We sat in silence and Aiden and I simultaneously touched our amulets. The four stones glowed brightly and warmed around my fingers. Fingle's words had given them power.

My father stayed silent, looking shocked and dumbfounded. Suddenly, he got up and walked out of the room, slamming the door behind him.

"We were too late to save your mother," Fingle said, answering my father's unasked question. "We didn't know the truth until you were born and she was gone."

"What's next Fingle? What are we to do?" I asked, desperate to put a stop on the nerves dancing in my stomach.

Fingle pointed to me. "What is your element? The first one you mastered?" he asked.

"Water" I replied.

He pointed to Duncan "Fire," he said. Next was Aiden, who said, "Earth."

Finally, he came to Rose to looked confused and stayed silent "Second sight harbours the Air, young Rose," he said.

"Fingle, why are we here?" I asked, desperate to get to the crux of the matter. "Have we to help save the elements?"

"No" he replied. "You are the Guardians of the Elements and you must go through Elias to Abaddon to rescue them. You must save us all."

"How will we know how to do that?" I asked.

"That's part of the test," said Daniel, his presence so inconspicuous until now that I was surprised to hear his voice. Releasing a long held breath, I get up, push my nerves away and accept my fate.

Pausing on the long road, I look back to Arcadia and fading in the distance, I notice a tree covered from root to branch in flowers. Narrowing my eyes, I blink and see the tree shimmer, thinking its a reaction to the wind, until it adopts the shape of a curvy female adorned with every colour of flower imaginable, moving sensuously and casting its long branches like long limbs, waving goodbye to me. I feel sad to walk away from Arcadia, a beautiful world, I've not had no chance to linger in.

Before we left, Fingle gave each of us a crystal that represented our element, making each of us promise to keep it with us at all times. I trace the edges of the rose quartz with my fingertips as I look across the mountains at the lightning and fires that rage from the sky to the ground and I keep walking, despite fearing what lies ahead. The quartz calms me and I feel its divination coursing through me and I realise why I'm walking on. I'm doing it for Duncan.

"A dragon's kiss, a breath of fire,

I am the master of all I desire,

Two worlds torn by ravage & sin,

Man must never, ever give in."

…Brigid

Brigid

A LITTLE BOTHER

Indigo Hawthorn

I play the game of being awake but pretend I'm asleep. The light is subdued here and I listen out for the sounds that make Arcadia home. The high-pitched birdsong, the beat of the trees as they move to the wind, the sound of my brother calling my name impatiently over and over. None are here and instinct whispers to me to keep my eyes closed. While my other senses shift forward to help me. The air surges around me reacting to the woman who's carrying me. It feels thick and dense and stinks of sulphur, like peat placed on a fire and left to burn away, underlined by her strong, sickly sweet perfume. Her hand is cold, holding me with confidence as I'm dragged like a rag doll. For what feels like an eternity, I feel weightless, like I'm slipping into the air before her grip tightens. I peek open an eyelid to try and work out where I am, but all I can see is hazy darkness.

The woman moves confidently along a footpath flanked by large jagged boulders. Huge trees shadow the path, the branches hugging each other to form a leaf ceiling. There's no sun here. Where Arcadia offers warmth and coolness as your body craves it, here it's either fiercely hot or bitterly cold. I want to sweat and shiver. I yearn to get away from this evil. For once, I wish I'd listened to my brother.

The woman leaves the woods and ascends up two flights of crumbling, concrete steps, towards a tower, expertly negotiating the cracks without missing a beat. Water thunders in my ear, as cold mist covers us, making discovery of what's coming next impossible. She turns and moves up another set of steps. Here they are covered with moss and dead leaves from the long hanging branches of trees that linger on the brick wall, blackened and lifeless but still clinging onto the structure that conceived them.

When she gets to the top, she opens a black iron door and as we enter the air is so overwhelmingly hot and stuffy and I fight the urge to gasp for breath. The building feels hollow. As she opens a door and goes down another flight of stairs, I can't help thinking that I am descending into Hell.

Finally we reach a room dominated by a large fire that expands and contracts, welcoming her return. A large cage sits on a table in the corner. Black candles are dotted around the room, to give just enough light to see without taking away the darkness permeating it. The woman dumps the bag on the table with a thud and the elements wiggle wildly and pull at the material in an effort to break free.

"Did you get them?" asks a male voice from the corner of the room.

The woman nods, her red lips curving in pleasure. "Yes, of course I did," she replies, smugly. "I also got some insurance."

She hauls me up by my legs and I squeeze my eyes shut as she holds me aloft like a prize. I'm so angry I can feel my body shaking and all I want is to zap her so hard her fingers will drop her and her smile will be forever wiped from her face. Instead, for the first time in my life, I listen to the voice that tells me to stay still and go limp instead, ignoring my impulse to do exactly what I want.

They laugh as I hear a door open and I'm flung into the bottom of the cage. My body shudders as pain rips through it when I land on the freezing cold base. The man and woman are smug and I watch as the man picks up the bag and they both leave the room laughing. They think they have won already. I know this because I'm more like my sister than others imagine. I know what they're thinking. Fingle thinks it's impatience that makes me argue with him, but it's not. It's nothing but boredom. If you know what someone is thinking or planning to do. What's the point in waiting when I could be doing what I want instead?

My sister, The Empress, calls me a crystal child. I'm not sure what that means. If it means I have some of her gifts then so be it. It's our special secret. She says that I reconciled our family and gave her back her brother. Fingle, the silly faerie, felt so guilty that she was taken as a changeling instead of him that he wanted her to have the freedom to live her own life without Arcadian interference. That worked until she was called to protect The Elements. When she became The Empress, she embraced both her human and faerie existence and finally found peace in the one place that not only accepted every part of her but celebrated it.

I knew she was my sister and refused to stay away from her. Fingle has been responsible for looking after me since our parents passed, and when he found me in or around Sanctuary talking to her he would try to pull me away. I argued, zapped him, pushed him away and shouted until he accepted my wish to see her. Gradually, Fingle and The Empress became close, having a relationship he thought was impossible but she always wanted. It's been the three of us ever since. This is the longest time I have ever been away from them. I miss them more than I can say and I'm sorry for my impatience, at least a just little bit.

It may take me time to acclimatise myself to this strange place. In Faerie society our world is truly made up of equality and balance and as such all relationships are accepted. Just like my friends Wilbur and Simon, members of the Faerie Council, who have loved each other since the beginning of time. Who never fail to admonish me for my misbehaviour whilst laughing at my latest adventure. So, I'm sure I'll get on with whatever I'm sharing this cage with. There's movement at the back of the cage and then the flutter of wings. One little figure moves closer to inspect me. She has dark skin, big brown eyes and short brown hair that almost hides her large ears. Dark wings flutter impatiently as she shakes her head, sighs and turns away. I can't believe it. I'm caged with the most annoying creatures ever. Imps. No patience for anyone or anything.

We hear steps and they huddle at the back of the cage. The door is opened and a single berry is thrown in. There is a second before there is a stampede towards the fruit and I wonder if I should join in before the one who greeted me moves forward and takes the berry. Slapping away the other imps that now surround us, mutters and hands out one seed to each. Then, reluctantly, she turns to me and offers me one and I know that by doing so she is telling me that she is in charge. Schooling my face into the look of innocence that has got me out of so many scrapes in the past. I move forward and take the offering from Lora, the leader of this merry band of misfits. There's no point in scaring them right away. They will realise I'm in charge... soon enough.

"It's so tiring having to be so good,

While all I am, is misunderstood,

In my confines, I shall tow the line,

They will know who's in charge,

In my own time"

…Indigo

Indigo

THE MISSION

Will Thorgood

O nce again, I've lost my children. We stand outside the house and I watch the four silhouettes fade into the distance. I feel the others move away but I linger. Keeping my eyes on the shadows, I feel frozen, unable to turn away and sever our delicate, newly formed bond. My chest swelled with pride as they set off confidently, unsure of their mission, aware of the danger but refusing to turn away from their responsibilities. I wonder at the fates of nature that made it possible for Rora and I to create two future Guardians of the Elements. There's magic in there somewhere.

Our parting was awkward. My royal status has always kept me isolated, nobody ever wants to come close, wary of breaching protocol. They stood unsure, until I took the decision for them, enveloping them tightly into my arms before moving my hands through their hair and down their backs. Looking down at the brown and auburn hair, I was flung back to a memory and know that's how Rora and I would have looked. They raised their heads and I studied their faces, their eyes, searing them into my memory. Amber's dark green shone against the morning sun, while Aiden's black pupils briefly teased the brown they once were, reminding me of how Luther nearly destroyed my children and I swore then and there that I would get my revenge.

Danny was holding his own children close, speaking to

them calmly. I smile at young Rose, so uncannily like her mother and offered Duncan my hand. His blue eyes are unwavering and his hand grips mine with the same confidence as his father. "I'll look after them Sir." he promised solemnly. I acknowledge his words, said with the confidence of a man who's used to combat. Then after one last brief glance backwards, exposing their nerves and youth, they walked away.

I hope they understand that I never wanted this. I had no desire to be Lord or King. Neither did my father, but he loved Sea Cliff and his people more than himself and when my grandfather died and the mantle was passed to him, he didn't hesitate to do his duty.

I remember him taking me to Greenwood to visit his friend Arthur when I was a boy. John was Danny's father and the Village Protector at the time. That's when he was at his most relaxed and happiest, away from Sea Cliff.

Danny and I had a wonderful time exploring the woods, climbing trees, rolling around in the mud and fighting mock battles while my father relaxed, talked politics with John, drank brew and smoked his forbidden pipe.

We both mourned when we returned to Sea Cliff and our reality of respectability, where my mother would rage over the smell of pipe smoke and my muddy clothes. In the intervening years, the criticism only got worse, whether it was appearance, behaviour or lack of ambitions. Her voice loud as her words bit at us, leaving indiscriminate bloody cuts on our flesh that stung as they tried to heal. Wounds invisible to anyone else but open and exposed to the woman who caused them. My father and I both shrank from her. We were both strong men, but her constant criticism, the nature of her campaign to foster our ambition to realise hers, broke us both in the end. We must be hopeless. We must be useless without her. But trapped in our royal roles, we couldn't escape. In the end, my father found release through death and I escaped briefly with Rora. I'm glad that Aiden and Amber escaped that existence.

Every day of my life, I have looked at my reflection and wondered what I lacked to incur her wrath. Why she had to have more. Why, she was never satisfied with me as a son. Why I wasn't enough.

I feel Marcus and young Thomas standing near me. "Are you coming back, Sire?" Fingle's voice tugs me back to the present, to the lapping water of the lake and the empty space before us. I turn around and smile wryly at the question, wondering if he knows where I've been and what I was thinking.

He continues, "We're not done. You need to accept your fate as well." Returning to Sanctuary, and the warm fire-lit room, I remain standing and wait. "The Soothsaying also applies to you," he says, and recites clearly.

"The King shall bring the right,

Fortitude needed for the fight,

The Alliance must make a stand,

Restore balance to our land"

My eyes shot to Danny's, remembering his work with the so-called Alliance. He looks back, unwavering and determined, just as he looked when we planned and fought our childhood battles.

I pace as the stress floods through me and I try to release it through exertion.   Expectations flood me and hazy memories of my waking coma strike out at me. My mother standing above me with a small bottle, berating me until I take it and drink it down, giving me the numbness I needed to survive the life I lived. All the while coloured shadows from another life tease me, of my Mate and the family I've always wanted.   In the stress, my body reaches for the familiar. My throat burns, dry as a desert and I feel thirsty for something I can't identify. Anger and frustration bite at me and to control myself I lash out at those near me.

"Do you think I'm capable of leading an army Fingle? Look at me! I am only King because Andora decreed it so."

I wrenched away from them. Young Thomas flinches as I raise my voice and seeing the fear on his face, I hold out a placating hand immediately.

 "No, Will," Danny said in his patient, calm voice. "You're strong: Aiden and Amber get that from you, not just from Rora."

I know he's trying to comfort me, but he only reminds me of what I wanted, of what I have lost. All I have ever wanted was to be my friend Danny. Content with his future as Village Protector and looking forward to finding his Mate and having a family with them. It was all I ever wanted. The moments that should have been mine, he has taken as his.

He was there when my children came into the world and when my Rora left. He saw my son take his first steps and say his first word. He's been there for my daughter when she needed him and while I know he did it for me, I still resent him for it. He has the memories that he can visit anytime, while I can only guess at the precious moments I have missed. Anger and resentment build up a lava of fury I can't control. Why didn't he come and take me away from the living hell I existed in? Why did he not fight for me?

"Why did you leave me there Danny? I missed everything! Why did you not tell me my Rora was gone?" I scream. Bulleting the words at him to land the blows I wanted to strike with my fists. Then a voice, I've not heard in an age, stops my tirade. "Lower your voice when you're speaking to my Mate, Will Thorgood. He did come for you alright, but you sent him away."

"Yearning for a life I almost forgot,

Without her, my lifeblood, stolen & stopped,

The crown, a weight on my soul,

Our children, the salvation of us all"

...Will

Will

BADLANDS

Rose Darkings

We are in a place I never truly believed existed until now. When I was little, Elias or Badlands was a watchword used by our parents to cajole us into completing a task. It tripped off the tongue easily, usually prompted by my daydreaming. "Rose, are you in Elias? Put that bread in the oven." To my juvenile ears, it was just a word, a blank space between the here and now, clinging to you and refusing to let you move forward. It's surreal to exist within the world of your imagination. Now walking in its midst, I have no choice but to believe it's real. My instinct tells me its part of the game. Are we being tricked into danger? Is this a tactic of battle employed to defeat you before they reach Abaddon? I have been the Village Protector's daughter long enough to know that the fight begins before the battlefield. The mental game takes place first and any decisive blow on your enemy's resolve offers an advantage.

Elias is the no-man's-land between Arcadia and Abaddon, and it has the characteristics of both. Following the winding road, I watch the mountains shift away from view then reappear briefly as the blanket of mist folds away. As the sky shifts clear, it's pushed away by black clouds, storms and thunder that give way to light again. Elias is interchangeable, responding to the pulls of Arcadia, the calm offering of sunshine while Abaddon kills it with storms before it can take purchase. If you listen carefully, you can hear whispers, ancient phrases repeated over and over, echoing within this space and I wonder if the people who uttered them were trapped here, too.

I miss The Empress. When uncertainty hit, I was able to reach out and still my awry thoughts with her nearness. I feel Imperia in patches. Turning, I expect to see her clearly behind me, ready to go where I needed her, only to find nothing but the shadow of the white building blinking in the distance with our family in front of it. Turning away, I bite my lip to ward away the tears that threaten to fall. I'm truly on my own. Possessing a talent that tunes in and out at will. My spirit guide and mentor are gone and next step seems too large to take on my own. It's ironic that I can understand the thoughts of strangers, but not of Aiden, Duncan and Amber or my family. It's like the bond of blood and love has placed me on a different frequency that is unique to them. While strangers, that I have no insight of are like an open door. Second sight is like the air element I represent, fleeting in her affections, fickle and impossible to possess.

We all walk silently, focused on the journey ahead. Our minds too busy churning to indulge in idle conversation. I'm constantly aware of Aiden, far enough away that I have my own space but close enough so I could touch him if I wished. Is it a quirk of having a Mate that makes you so aware of them? The heat from them invades the space between you and sears your skin with their branding. My skin tingles at the thought and I want to bury and lose myself within him. I steal a glance at him and feel the heat rise in my cheeks. He clears his throat and I know he feels the same.

Then, suddenly, he stops walking and kneels down in front

of a tiny man with a thick brown beard, who speaks to him in hushed tones. Behind him, Duncan is running in a circle, frantically trying to pick up a black and yellow lizard with two heads that constantly evades him. To his right, Amber is running in a constant figure of eight, chasing a suspended wave of water, like a water dragon following a pre-determined course. I feel a gush of warm air push me up and off the ground. It's almost as if I'm enclosed within two large loving arms. It felt female, flirty and dainty, pushing into me then back again teasing me with its presence before withdrawing. I know it's the air element I seek. I can't capture it and when I look around me, we're all in the same position, each of us is trying frantically but failing to chase and capture our element and one by one they disappear. It's then I remember that Elias is a deceiver. The wind picks up, and freezing raindrops start to thunder down, piercing my skin. Aiden moves closer, his face disappointed. Elias knew what we wanted and was teasing us, taking it away and forcing us to face our reality once more.

The black mass moves silently in the distance until it circles us. The figure is covered in dirty grey hair and reaches seven foot tall, the head sunk into the shoulders. It glides over us like a bird, before its large wings eclipse its body and the sky circles around us. The dark angel moves closer, the wind generated from the movement of the wings pushing us back, as Aiden holds me close. Its eyes transfixed upon us with a blood red, hypnotic stare, caught and held us in place ensuring we received the message. It reverberates in my head over and over. This dark angel is a harbinger of foreboding and it bade us to leave. We were leaving Elias and moving into Abaddon. A hell we may never return from.

CAMPAIGN

Will Thorgood

"Woman, what are you doing here?" Danny cries out, as he runs over to Maggie, picks her up and buries his face in her hair. I watch them, quickened by the sight and catch the eyes of the woman at the back of Maggie. She looks away from them to the ground. When I stood up for Daniel as he and Maggie were formally mated, I enjoyed their displays of affection, glad to see that my childhood friends had finally found each other. Now, it hurts too much to see them together. Happy. The living embodiment of what I've lost. I want to be free from it all. Free from the responsibilities that I never wanted. But first, I need an answer to my question.

Danny turns and the light fades from his eyes, kissing the other woman on the cheek, he pulls Maggie into his side and walks back to me, refusing to be parted from his Mate for even a matter of seconds. Outwardly, I scoff at the gesture until I remembered doing the same with Rora once at Rowan Cottage and her teasing me mercilessly for it. Pushing the memory away, I clench my fists and wait.

"After the twins were born, I brought Aiden back and left him with Maggie and came to Sea Cliff to find you still alive. Not dead as Rora believed. Jack was still in charge of the Knights then and sneaked me past the courtiers to see you."

I shake my head, not remembering, denying the truth I see in his eyes.

"You were dressing. A woman was leaving your chambers. You looked at me like I was a stranger and shouted at me to leave. Before I left, the Queen stopped and warned me to stay away or my family would suffer the consequences."

I shake my head, trying to push the words away.

"I won't apologise for not coming back. I tried my best for you but I draw a line at putting my family in danger. I raised your boy as I did my own. We thought Amber was safe and when we found out otherwise we went to get her. Duncan has protected her since."

Could this be true? I remember existing in a world with the edges smudged; numb and indifferent. Through the shadows, memories persist of the Queen visiting my chambers daily and encouraging me to take a herbal remedy. It was easier to take it than argue and suffer the consequences. I get up and walk outside, away from the past, away from the truth and away from the images that torment me. No one stops or calls me back, understanding I need space to deal with my emotions. Pictures tease of a past that should have been mine and thrust me into the present I now find myself in.

I follow the lake and retreat to the woods. The silence pushes against the thoughts running rampant. My relationships with women have been brief and emotionless. I always wondered why I had never found my Mate. I assumed it was due to my responsibilities and was not meant for me. Despite this resolution, the Queen always told me to a take a Mate, encouraging daughters from far off lands to visit and tempt me into a commitment. But something always held me back; a lone soft whisper at the back of my mind that always stopped me. A voice so seductive and sensuous, that when it insisted I remain with the status quo, I found it easy to agree. Could a simple herb be responsible for wiping my mind of years of childhood memories in Greenwood and my Rora? The presence of her so integrated into my soul, the mere apparition of her brought back everything I had forgotten. In comparison, I can remember my childhood at Sea Cliff in clear, crisp clarity. There was only one answer. My memories have been manipulated for a purpose. What medicine or herb possesses the power to do this this? My knowledge of natural medicine was rudimentary. Perhaps Warwick could provide the answer.

Leaving the edge of the forest, I came to a standstill near the wishing well. The herds of unicorns linger peacefully in the meadow blanketed by the trees still standing. They move on instinct, running and bucking against one another as their mood dictates. Their black coats shine against the sun, sparkling and dimpling until I lifted my hand to shade my eyes, only for it to settle and dim. Thomas stays near Clover, pushing his head into her neck. She leans into the boy, comforting him, before she raises her head and focuses her dazzling eyes fringed with long black lashes on me and dips her head, beckoning me towards her. Thomas, aware he's no longer alone, lifts his hand and noisily wipes his nose on the new clothes that hang from his frail body. Made aware of the boy's history from Aiden, I am suddenly ashamed of my self-pity when he's lost the only person who ever cared for him. Jack, who served my family faithfully, only to die hungry and at the mercy of the swords he once commanded.

I look at him and say, "You must miss him lad."

He nods.

"I understand you looked after Clover and her family when I couldn't. I will never be able to repay my debt to you."

He studies me, not sure how to reply, his warm brown eyes wary and almost too large in his small face. Confronted with the reality of this boy's existence, I'm glad my children missed a childhood at Sea Cliff. The Darkings and Lauren Lockwood raised my children with love and security. I can't change the past, but I can make Thomas's life better from now on. Perhaps by showing him the strength he needs, I can rediscover it for myself.

I loosen the head collar on Clover's head and I remove it carefully, revealing the dull black hair where it had been hidden too long. I look into her eyes and whisper, "It's time to set you free, Clover."

I stand back, pulling Thomas with me. He looks at me and then frantically back to Clover. He's silent, used to being given commands he does not agree with, but is unable to argue with. Marcus joins us and stands beside Thomas.

"You know it's the right thing to do, don't you?" I ask, wanting his blessing. "They should be set free." Thomas nods, sniffing loudly and I put an arm around him. Clover trots backwards and forwards restlessly, not wanting to leave me, but yearning for her freedom.

"You've done everything you could for me Clover and I thank you, but it's time for you and your family now."

The unicorn bends her head in acknowledgement, first to me and then to Thomas, a whisper of contact before turning and racing away and bucking upwards. The sun glows a deep red in reaction like it senses a significant shift. Turning, she leads the herd until their wings emerge and they race into the sky. A dozen sleek black figures float against the vivid purple sky. Their neighing rang out until it receded as the unicorns disappeared into the horizon.

Hearing the chatter behind us, I see Fingle and the faeries watching the display in delight and clapping their hands. I pick up the head collar and ask Thomas, "Did you know your kin?"

The boy nods, his face grave.

"Speak up lad, you're safe with us. No harm will come to you."

He looks at Marcus and me, hesitating before he comes to a decision and says, "Jack was my grandfather." Nodding, we walk him back to Sanctuary. Like all of us, he will need strength to face what's to come.

I nod in acknowledgement, wondering if I could have prevented this if I'd been stronger. But there is no point in recrimination. I can't change the past but I can be master of my fate from this point on and lead by example. I will begin by invoking The Alliance.

ABADDON

Amber Lockwood

W e are in the place I've fear the most. My stomach tightens as the natural road we are following stops abruptly, from an uneven descent onto hard, unforgiving ground. It's strewn with a variety of jagged stones and scattered boulders, like an epic explosion had taken place, so destructive the resulting debris has been left over miles.

The eagle watches our every movement as we enter Abaddon. Its gaze so focused on us, I wonder if it will attack. Watching us from the tree, it tucks its wings into its body and tightens its claw around the white mouse that wriggles frantically to get free. I watch hypnotised as it wriggles refusing to give up the fight for life in the face of obvious defeat. Until finally, it slows and stills and I realise I am the mouse. Struggling to control my fate as the world around me chooses the path I am to be set upon. The eagle is majestic. White feathers cover a regal head, standing tall and proud, dominated by a yellow beak that hooks down pulling the small eyes into a cruel slant. It lowers its head, its eyes never leaving us as it pulls the head off the mouse into its mouth, consuming it ruthlessly and without mercy. Hypnotised by the sight, I'm overwhelmed by the magnetic power emanating from the bird.

A flock of magpies circles, scavenging, weaving in and out of the tree branches, ready to catch any remnants that the eagle was willing to discard. It ignores them intent on finishing its meal.

I'm lost here and overwhelmed by conflicting emotions. If I am the Guardian of the Water element as and Fingle says, I will react to everything around me. I feel it all pouring over and through me like a wave. I feel the anger and frustration from Duncan and embrace it as my own. Fleetingly, I wonder if I am the source of the emotion before my temper riles in response, at his desire to control me, at his lack of trust in my own abilities. Duncan was of the singular opinion that if he didn't do it, it was not going to be done right. But then it turns on a knife's edge, to a ferocious intense vulnerability. I reach for his hand, holding his cool fingers tightly between mine, reassuring him that I need him, when words are beyond me.

Rose is confused. I feel for her, trying to get to grips with who she is just as events, shake her foundations at their will. She is plucky, facing the danger swirling around us with a proud head tilt and a determined stance.

Her confusion focuses on Aiden and his belief that he's not good enough for her. Watching him pull her to him, and band an arm around her waist, I feel her settle and lean into him as her confusion abates, for a while.

My twin feels lost; trying to hold onto the part of him he embraced at Sea Cliff and let go of the horrific past that haunts him. He brought Rose near to him, not only for her sake, but for his own. She anchors him when nothing else will.

Everything we feel is amplified and our surroundings once vibrantly alive have a deadening nightmarish tilt. Grass that was once a lush, crisp green is now blackened and burnt. Turning, I see an image of myself strapped to a bed, covered with slithering snakes. A large python wraps itself around my legs, holding me still as it opens its jaws and bites into my flesh with its sharp fangs. I scream at the pain and the veins on my leg throbs beneath my trousers as the material is bitten away.

I tear myself from my prison, to see parts of Duncan, Aiden and Rose serrated and attached to different parts of each other creating a creature of horror. Rose's head and Aiden's have been stuck onto Duncan's body and the creature is screaming and running in panic. Closing my eyes, I focus on the word spilling from Rose's mouth, as she pants out, "Deceive. Deceive," over and over again.

I return back to myself. Duncan and I are lying against each other on the hard, unforgiving ground, breathing harshly and holding each other. Mist swirls around us, and as it clears, I can see Aiden and Rose, lying in a similar position, not far away. We look up to see a mass of birds above us, everything from small robins to sea eagles, squawking loudly, screaming for us to flee with them as they flew away from Abaddon. But we can't follow them. This battle; the culmination of all that we hold dear, demands we must stay.

The mist shifts and Rose and Aiden have disappeared. We get up, frantically looking around us, but they have vanished into thin air. Then a sharp click penetrates the air and a flame erupts from the frozen ground and pierces the black cloud above, heralding lightning crackling again and again. I cover my ears and Duncan hits the ground, striking his head on a stone, ejecting a spurt of blood rains onto my hand. Leaning over him, I don't register the presence until the shadow falls over me. The woman is covered in black silk, a tight bodice scales her thin ribs and sweeps over her hips to the ground. Her face is covered by a black mask that leaves the lower half of her face exposed, showing generous red lips curved in satisfaction. Smoky blue eyes shine as she removes the mask and shakes out a mass of curly blonde hair. My lips form her name as my mind tries to process why she's here. Caroline, the girl from Duncan's past, surveys my situation and finds it pleasing to her. She looks down at me with satisfaction and says, "Hello, Amber Lockwood. Welcome to Hell."

THE SUMMONS
Will Thorgood

"You let them go where, Daniel Darkings?" The question echoes loudly through Sanctuary and I hear Danny's muffled voice, as he tries to placate Maggie. She repeats the question again as we enter the sitting room, it vibrates out and I wonder if all of Arcadia can hear it. Maggie's cheeks are flushed red with temper, her nerves frayed at the thought of our children going out into the wilderness, unprotected. Remembering the childhood tales of Abaddon, I hope it's not as evil as I imagined. I have to believe they will return to us safe. In this war to control the natural balance, I have to believe it can be restored. I have to believe that Sensio can change for the better, just as I can.

Keeping my own counsel, I move towards Dot. Glancing, I see Marcus looking at Thomas with unguarded curiosity, the boy unaware as he sits cross-legged in front of the fire eating an apple. Noticing my interest, Marcus looks away and outside the window. Stopping in front of Dot, I clasp her delicate hands in mine. Her bird-like fragile body and open face revealing the girl I once knew in the woman before me and I'm back in Greenwood as a boy, playing with my friends. My heart gladdens at the sight of her.

"Dot Cuthbert, as I live and breathe. How are you?" She smiles at the greeting. "How is that Mate of yours?" I ask, looking around for Boon, remembering even in childhood they were rarely apart.

The room falls to a stunned silence and I want the ground to swallow me up realising how much the question must have hurt her. Dot swallows and bites her lip. Her face pale. I put an arm around her, usher her to sit down and take a seat opposite her.

"I'm so sorry Dot. I didn't know..."

"I'm okay, Will." She hesitates, searching for the right words. "Every time I'm asked about him, it takes me a few seconds to remember he's not here anymore. He still lives in here." She puts a hand on her heart.

I ache for her and swallow to keep my emotions at bay because I understand exactly what she means. I can't see Rora, but I can feel her around me. Every morning in the moment between asleep and awake, I sense her lingering flowery scent and imagine her petite body within my arms. Dot and I share a look of understanding and lapse into silence, living in a past that helps us to survive the present.

Maggie comes bustling over with some food and jolts us from our introspection. "Dot, have you told Will about Greenwood?" She gestures to Marcus and Thomas to join us.

Dot shakes her head. Maggie continues, "Greenwood became darker after Daniel left. The villagers started having petty arguments over food, refusing to share, as we always have. Some even came to blows on more than one occasion. Then, at the High Council meeting, Daniel and Boon's positions were given to Ruth Gentles and her allies despite the fact that Dot and I were attending in their place. Ruth claimed that Daniel had chosen an outsider and had

~ 446 ~

abandoned his duties as Village Protector and Warwick's decision not to replace him made him derelict in his duty as Head of the High Council. Ruth has taken over his position."

"She's got what she always wanted," Dot murmurs.

Maggie nods in agreement. "We left the next morning. Warwick planned to leave two days after us. Other families have already left to go to the other villages." She shakes her head sadly, and says, "Greenwood, as we knew it, no longer exists."

My eyes widen at the picture she paints, remembering the vividly coloured village of my memories and finding it difficult to reconcile with the barren village of my imagination.

The door opens and Fingle looks at me pointedly, his arms folded, waiting to hear my answer to The Soothsaying and what I plan to do about it. Every day, the world around us fractures and crumbles into the dust. The evil that permeates Sensio is infecting everything possessing energy, whether it's a living being or a part of nature. It's time to fight back. It's time to invoke The Alliance.

Looking to Thomas listening avidly to the grown up conversation, I lean forward and ask him. "Have you ever heard of 'The Summons,' Thomas?" Shaking his head, I stand and walk towards him. Fingle tilts his head and observes me, a satisfied smile forming across his lips. I'm giving him what he wants.

"Fingle, shall we?" I ask and he leads us out of the room, into the corridor and outside into the light. The grass shimmers with tiny droplets of dew lending a crisp freshness to the air that cleanses my nostrils and gives me energy. The mermaids basking in the sun on the shore of the lake watch us curiously as we walk away. Ero, morphs into her human form and runs to catch up with us, her long curly hair flowing behind her, her elfin features quirking in curiosity. She stops and speaks to Marcus quickly, then gestures to the others to join us. Walking steadily into the woods, I embrace the darkness. The coolness of the breeze between the trees whispers across my cheeks and ruffles my hair like a loving, lingering hand. Leaving the forest, we move towards the wishing well and stop before the summon spells. Blankets of flowers rise from the back of the wishing well towards the tree line. The green stacks stand proudly amongst the red poppies, white daisies, sunflowers and bluebells.

"Isn't Summon Spell's a child's game?" asks Daniel incredulously.

"Do you think that's a coincidence?" replies Fingle smugly, happy to reveal his long kept secret.

His words invoke one of my earliest memories. I'm running around the gardens at Sea Cliff, running away from my father as fast as my legs could carry me as the scent of flowers tease my nose and constant murmur of waves crash against the rocks below. Calling me over, he knelt beside me and asked me to pick a summon spell. I looked down at the flowers, concentrate carefully and grab the one that appeals to me most. My father steadies me to prevent me from falling. "Think about your wish," he says and I close my eyes, squished them together to shut out the light. He squeezes my shoulder. "Okay, now open your eyes and blow out your wish." I open them, grinning at him as I pucker my lips and blow out the seeds with my breath. They float into the air, carried by the wind, some cluttered together and some on their own. I watch until they have all gone and I'm left clutching an empty green stalk. Hearing my father's voice, I remember the rhyme he asked me to say and I repeat it now:

"I send The Summons

Nature to shout it out

Air, Earth, Fire, Water

The Elements will live out."

From the place between the here and now, I return to the present and I can hear the murmur of voices repeat the words, and see a cloud of summons seeds floating off into the air, heading towards the doorway back to Sensio. My father's voice rings out, as if he's with me now. "Remember The Summons, Will, it's very important." His eyes study me in earnest, beseeching and I answer back now, "Yes Dad, I know. I kept my promise."

The wind picks up and the remaining tree branches move like a sensuous dancer. "The tree spirits are joining in," Fingle says, looking around him as they move and we stay silent, as nature uses our elements; air, earth, fire and water to ensure the message is passed to everyone who needs to hear it. The Alliance has been invoked.

"Won't it also warn the others of our plans?" Ero asks Marcus. In our brief acquaintance, I've come to appreciate her strategic ability to view a situation from every angle.

"We have to take that chance," I answer. We lapse into silence as we watch the rest of the seeds float away. Reverently, hoping our wishes will come true, restoring the balance and allowing us all to return home.

Steady footsteps invade the silence and we turn to see a figure emerge from the trees, his movements stiff, his long black and grey hair awry and his skin bruised and bloodied. Warwick reaches us, holds out his arms in relief, and cries out, "I was too late. She let Luther go."

LOST

Aiden Darkings

We're alone and I'm lost. Looking around, I search for Duncan and Amber, finding the vast space around us vacant of anything but a thick barren tree. Instead of sand and scattered broken rock, the grass is covered in a layer of frost spreading an ice blanket that crunches below our feet. The air is cold, vacuumed within this space, punching particles of cold, as our warm breath fights back. Bolts of lightning light up the sky intermittently and thunder growls at me. My knowledge of Abaddon comes from childhood lore and the odd comment from Luther that lingers in my memory. He claimed Abaddon was the only place he felt truly at home. Abaddon accepted his true self, not the polished Lord that was presented at Sea Cliff, but the heart of him that loves inflicting pain and killing in the cruellest, most vicious way possible. He even joked the weather fitted in with his extreme personality and hearing the thunder move towards, I finally understand what he means.

I clutch onto Rose's hand, gripping it tightly, aware I'm digging into her skin to the point of pain but I daren't let go. Rose anchors me in a way she can't understand. For her, I want to be the best version of myself. She deserves no less. Her faith in me has been tested over and over and while I confuse her by pushing her away then pulling her towards me, she stays strong and steadfast, believing that I will come to my senses and be the Mate she deserves. If I let go of her hand, I'm afraid that the man I banished, the murderer within me, will return. I thought I'd banished these thoughts in Sea Cliff, Princedom gave me the belief I need to overcome it. Here, in Abaddon, I fear it's an illusion I've manifested.

Rose gasps and I follow her gaze, my eyes at first only seeing flickers of snow droplets melting from the clouds. Then, I see movement, the shape of a head, then the silhouette of a body, as it emerges from the clouds above and lands on the frozen ground beside us, followed by another, and another, and another, until we are surrounded by them. Their skin is grey, the cuts on their bodies leaking a vivid rich red blood that trickles from dirty and exposed festering cuts. They circle around us, their faces forming a never-ending daisy chain with which we were prevented from escaping. Then I realise why they won't move. These people are within me. I was looking at the faces of every person I've killed. Sucking in a breath, I look at Rose and try to loosen my hand from hers. She stays silent, breathing harshly, her eyes caught by the haunted souls around us. Her mouth opens then closes, unable to form words of censure or comfort. Confronted by the near physical reality of my past, I try again to loosen my grip on her hand but she refuses, shaking her head and closing her eyes unable to face her true Mate.

The lightning gathers ever closer, moving toward the tree until it sparks upwards, lighting up the branches like a decorated tree, highlighting the people around us in their full horror of stark pain before making them disappear. The branches move then, slithering against the background before forming into two large lions that stretch elegantly and jump down onto the ground padding confidently towards us, before stopping stretching and roaring into the sky. Their mouths open wide, revealing long white teeth stained with blood. As their mouths close, they lick their lips. The male shakes his head, standing proud with his mane around his head like a halo, whilst the female sits at his side, looking to him and waiting for direction. I look around frantically but see no stones I can use to defend us if they decide to attack. The male roars again and Rose and I watch, disbelieving, as his body contorts and elongates horrifically until it stands bi-pedal, revealing Luther. In shock, I release my hand from Rose's grip and push it towards Luther to warn him away from her. He grins pleased, his student performing for his mentor. The crack in the sky as our hands touch was so loud and complete, my hearing fades, like a flicked switch returning me to reset mode. Back to evil Aiden. Back to the Black Knight. Back to the killer.

Moving his hand to the lioness, he places a long dirty fingernail on her head and she moves sensuously towards it, before ascending upwards into Sierra. She smiles with pleasure, her blue eyes bright and cheeks flushed with excitement. Taking her arm, I pull her roughly to me and kiss her. Luther laughs, the sound bounces off the caverns in our space. I hear cries in the back of my mind, sounds muffled through a thick glass that I can't make out properly. Ignoring them, I move my hands down Sienna's body, rejecting the words, as she fades into nothing and I open my eyes to see her and Luther gone.

Rose sits on her haunches, tears covering her face, sobbing, shouting at me. "Fight Aiden. Don't let him control you."

I laugh. No one controls me. I am the master of my own

destiny and I mean to take what I've long wanted. Knocking her onto the ground, I lower myself over her, she coughs and watches me, realising my intentions, breath wheezing from her body. Hearing a piercing roar, I'm distracted until I feel a searing streak of pain in my head and feel the hotness of blood, trickling through my hair and marking my skin.

Rose's red-rimmed eyes focus on mine, her voice clearer and shouting. "Please Aiden. You need to fight for us."

The pain gives way to numbness and in the darkness and I'm lost for the final time. Glad I won't hurt her or anyone else ever again. Glad that when I had to die, Rose was the one to kill me.

PREPARATION
Will Thorgood

A week has passed since we sent the Summons and if I hadn't witnessed the result, I wouldn't have believed it myself. People began to arrive the next morning, in families, pairs and on their own. Once they received the Summons, they left their homes and without intention or direction came to Arcadia to join us. They talk of passing others on their way here. Dark shadowy figures making the same journey in the opposite direction. No words were spoken, only the promise of violence to be unleashed at the Battle for Sensio. Amongst The Alliance there is an acceptance of what's to come. There is no bereavement as we face the inevitability of war, that's been twenty years in the making. If anything, The Alliance is impatient to begin.

Conversations in the impromptu camp set around the Wishing Well and Faerie Glen focus on strategy, ideas and, most importantly, our plans for the future. What we dream of doing once the battle is over and we can return to our lives or create better lives to celebrate the freedom we have fought for.

Watching Thomas collect food and walk confidently back to Sanctuary, I'm glad he is here despite the proximity to danger. I'm glad they're away from the talk of battle and strategy but we can't protect them from what's to come. Children by their nature, unburdened by the worries of adulthood, are more aware of what's coming than the rest of us. I'm happy the faeries, sasquatchs and the mermaids distract them, delighting them with simple miracles we have long forgotten. At my behest, Thomas has appointed himself the unofficial authority on Arcadia providing food, entertainment and reassurance to the younger children. His existence at Storm Castle was so dictated by everyone other than himself, he's glad of having control of a task that is his and his alone.

From the East, the Geans came with enough surplus personality to take over the camp. They are giant-like figures with ungainly lops in movement, reaching seven feet tall. Their big, open black faces house dark eyes and a mass of wild straggly hair strewn around their heads. Despite their size, they move confidently missing nothing of what goes on around them. The day they arrived their leader Jackson entered the camp, introducing himself and his family without guile or inhibition. Gaining curious glances not only from their appearance but also from the albino tarsier's that sit on their shoulders and cling onto the thick material of their jackets with their sticky paws. The tarsier on Jackson's shoulder looked around the camp and enlarged his eyes until they bulged out, glowing deep amber with large black pupils that stared unflinchingly at the source of its concerns. Finding myself moving closer. I stopped only when Jackson clutched my shoulder and introduced the tarsier as Fero before pushing me gently back, holding out his meaty palm to Fero who tapped it in recognition of lynching another victim with his charms and settled back on his shoulder bored, bulging eyes returning to normal. "Neat trick" I said. Jackson burst out laughing, his laughter as loud as his personality.

The most humbling addition to The Alliance was the arrival of the ancient tribes, who have lived on Sensio since her inception but have hid on the fringes of our society rather than joining it. Appearing in Arcadia, they walk confidently towards Sanctuary, led by the Maori's. People in the camp stare and I join them. They make an impressive sight, the men are large and muscular, their dignity saved by a loincloth that merged into a pale straw and reached their knees. Their faces are hypnotic, patterned with whirls of black symbols, curling and dotting their faces and flowing onto their bodies. All carry long wooden sticks which look harmless at first but I guessed could inflict great injury depending on the skill of its owner. Instead of withering under our gaze, they are unapologetic and seeing their proud faces and the clear love of their heritage, I feel nothing but admiration for them. Walking to greet them, I'm intercepted by a curious Thomas.

"Who are you?" he asked the man who reached us first.

"My name is Ata, I am the Maori King." The man answered in a booming, commanding voice.

"What does that mean?" Thomas questioned, his brow furrowing as he examined at the stranger, not quite knowing what to make of him.

"My name mean's 'twin', young man."

Disconcerted, I study Ata and he answers my silent question.

"Yes, King Garrick, we've known this has been coming for a long time. We've been waiting for you."

Thomas peppered Ata with more questions and he relaxed, leaning against the bridge overlooking the clear glass water of the lake. Soon, Thomas was joined by the other children and adults around the camp and the mermaids on the shoreline. The Alliance as a whole listened to Ata, telling the tale of Hinewhaitiri, the children of the elements. They understood more than any of us the importance of the balance of the elements. It began with them. Watching Thomas, a natural born diplomat, I knew this was another bond he'd forged that would never be broken.

Next came the Buddhist Monks, who entered Arcadia silently only brokered by the deep red slash of their thick woven robes. Inconspicuous until they were upon us, their leader Tenzin, a petite woman, introduced herself in quiet, respectful tones, refusing refuge inside Sanctuary when offered it. Instead, Tenzin and her group of twenty, sat beside the lake arranged themselves in a circle and began to meditate. Disconcerted, I wondered how this group would fare in battle.

Jackson, in his natural exuberance asked the question for me. "Exactly how are they going to help stop an army of Black Knights without so much as a sword in their hand? Talk them down?" he asked aloud, as confused as I was.

Tenzin, opened her eyes, raised a slim eyebrow and spoke softly. "Our weaponry is within, young man."

Jackson burst out laughing, and placed his huge hands on his legs as his loud guffaws reverberated around the lake and came back again. "Well, I guess that's me bloody well told then."

Tenzin, returned to her meditation, but not before the corner of her mouth curved slightly showing her appreciation for the joke. But I knew it was more, these people knew how to defend themselves, they had voluntarily walked without weapons into a war and despite their peaceful, unassuming demeanour they seemed well prepared for what was to come, perhaps even more than us.

Our move to Elias will take place in the next few days. Not just yet, but I know we'll need to leave before the week is out. It is fate that our future will be decided in the no-man's-land between Arcadia and Abaddon, hidden by the veil. Our fate is tied to the powers that Sensio has bestowed upon us. The swords and bows we carry will only play a small part in our survival. Our talents will determine the rest. During my waking coma at Storm Castle, I only used my talents spasmodically during rare moments of clarity. From childhood, I understood it was unusual to have all the elements at my control. My father feared the consequences of such talents and bade me to keep quiet about it. Whilst my mother relished the power such a gift could offer. She believed that if she could place her son as King she could use his talents to control all the elements and finally have the power she wanted. I never understood her ambition. Why reaching the heady heights of being Queen was never enough. Before the end, I will understand why.

The Summons called not only to all people. It called to all species of Sensio. They answered the summons and are here to play their part. They remain with us but on the periphery of the camp, part of The Alliance, but determined to keep to their identity outwith it. The sasquatchs remain hidden within the woods but have moved closer to the camp. Anywhere between seven to ten feet tall, they are an intimidating sight of Neanderthal muscle covered in tufty thick hair in shades of dark brown and black. Living in small family groups they congregate closer due to necessity rather than choice. They are territorial and at night, we can hear the loud screechy shouts as the males get too close to another's family and hours of male chest beating commences until dominance has been established. While they remain hidden, they venture out to watch us curiously in the daylight as we complete our daily tasks, taking the food we leave near the woods without thanks or acknowledgement. Their engagement with us is unwilling, they are wary of us, but still I'm grateful for their contribution.

Ero and her family of mermaids will leave for the seas when we set out for Elias. Ero has engaged with us, more to satisfy her insatiable curiosity, rather than a need for information. The mermaids, those who chose to leave with Ero, left the seas when they were taken over by the kracken's. She worries over those she left behind, particularly her sister Moren, who refused to leave and the octopus, dolphins and whales families that hunt and live with. They are unguarded only with the children, putting on shows of water aerobatic displays that delight and distract them and speaking to them animatedly as they linger on the shore, until an adult comes closer and they depart into the water for safety.

Fingle and the faeries have concentrated on marshalling their efforts to reinforce the boundaries of Arcadia that were displaced when Indigo and the elements were taken. He looks weary, the responsibilities of The Soothsayer weighing heavily on his small shoulders. This has been lessened by the arrival of Warwick who eases the burden on his body using his medicine and making much-needed brew for the camp whilst still refusing to share the recipe.

We gather each night to discuss what's coming. Whether from a need to connect with others or feel their support propping up our strength, we sit around small fires for hours and discuss what's coming. We talk about my experience of the enemy from my life at Storm Castle and Danny's knowledge from leading The Alliance at the Hill of Faeries.

Warwick is quiet since he came to Arcadia. Seeing the destruction of Greenwood, the village he had tried to keep safe from evil all his life. For him, the final straw was reaching Storm Castle in time to see the Queen reinstating Lord Luther as head of the Black Knights, the murderer, who hunted my daughter and corrupted my son. I'm glad I'll face him in battle. Warwick was beaten and kicked by the guards, only escaping after making out he was a clumsy, old fool. Like me, he suspects that my mother has allied herself with Abaddon for years and that her use of henbane could not have been enough to wipe twenty years of clarity or my Mate from my mind.

At night, Danny, Maggie and I sit and look into the fire and wonder what has become of our children. What fate have they found in Abaddon? Have they triumphed over the creatures of our nightmares living there? Is their faith in themselves as strong as ours is in them? We don't know for sure. From my brief contact with my children I still feel them, for my own heart still beats strong and determined to see them again. Their fate is tied to ours. If they survive, we will too. I have to believe in our future. I have no choice.

CRUEL INTENTIONS

Amber Lockwood

W e are in Hell and they mean to hurt us. Duncan is slung over the shoulder of the Black Knight who carries him, his head lolling from side to side as the he walks up the stairway of the castle. Caroline and I follow. I move reluctantly, wanting to keep Duncan safe but my limbs tighten, resisting our proximity to this building. For if Sanctuary is ethereal in her white castle surrounded by a magical lake, this structure has been fashioned from a sour smelling bog. The castle rides tall against the dark sky, thunder rolling in waves giving the gargoyles trapped on the turrets a maniacal edge. The blackened brick is covered with an abundance of wet moss giving the air a cold, acrid tinge that catches my throat. Violently coughing, I'm pushed roughly in the back with nails that pierce my skin as the Black Knight turns back to seek instructions on my punishment for causing a delay. Then I still, as he looks at me, emotionless, like a zombie, waiting on a prompt from his mistress with empty fathomless holes where eyes once were. "Keep moving slave." she confirms and he turns and I'm pushed to the ground against the stairs, my knees ricocheting against the broken wet stone. She pulls me up roughly and whispers in my ear. "Stop the hysterics, Amber. No one's coming for you this time." She walks past me and climbs gracefully up the stairs. She looks down at me, wearing a beautiful black dress that shines against her pale skin and blonde hair framed against the intimidating building.

"Follow me or face the wolves, it's up to you. I have what I want," she says, turning away haughtily and disappearing through a wrought iron door.

Hearing the howl for the first time, I see a pack of wolves in the shadows, edged between the darkness and the mist rising from the black water. Pure black from nose to tail, they stare at me with a hungry fever that shines from their bright blue eyes. I stay frozen until they advance towards me and I scramble up the slippery steps, stumbling before reaching the top and follow Caroline and Slave through the door into a hallway lit by fire sconces and into a hot, sticky room. I see a table with books open and a large fire generating black smoke. The air feels warm and stodgy and sweat quickly pearls along my skin. Duncan is tied against a wooden bar with thick rope. His head hangs against his bare chest and he moans softly from time to time. I yearn to run over to him but Slave stands between us.

Caroline walks around him, looking at him from every angle then she trails her fingers along his chest and digs her nails painfully into his skin, leaving three lines that well up with dark red beads of blood that slowly join together and trickle down his stomach. Marking my Mate.

Movement catches the corner of my eye, and I notice for the first time that a large wrought iron cage is anchored to the ceiling. On first glance, it looks empty, but on closer inspection I see the movement of wings and a pair of the clearest blue eyes wink at me. Indigo. I gasp out and Caroline, believing my reaction is due to her actions, decides to hurt me even more.

She licks Duncan from his collarbone to the base of his neck and whispers, "Remember how I'd scratch your back when you took me? I was marking you." She laughs, flicking her wrist and a slim gold knife appears. She uses it delicately, trailing it along and cutting his skin.

Swallowing, I wince, and try to distract her. "Caroline Gentles. If you ever cared for him, please don't hurt him."

She smiles coldly at me and raises her eyebrows. I have her complete attention. "I prefer to be known by my new title. I am, Lady Caroline, the Mate of Lord Luther."

Shocked, I try to run past Slave to get to Duncan, but he stops me and pushes me back so forcefully that I'm flung back against the cage, it smashes against the wall. I stop when my hair is roughly pulled back and a large hand holds my waist. I freeze, recoiling, as the fingers nip my skin, not daring to turn around.

Caroline drawls, "Do enjoy yourself, Povack. I'm planning to." I close my eyes and open them to see Duncan, newly conscious and confused. Caroline smiles.

The grip on my hair tightens, and I'm pulled back against his body. I shudder, bucking against him and shouting out as I'm dragged from the room into the corridor as the door clangs shut behind us. The hallway is now in darkness and I hear our breathing match, mine in panic, his in excitement. Pulling me into another room, his grip tightens on my hair. He binds my wrists, looping the rope around a wooden beam above, forcing me to balance on the balls of my feet. I'm powerless. He loosens my jacket, pinching the skin of my stomach as I yell out. He stills for a moment, admiring the bruise he's created. Then he raises his eyes to mine, cruelty clear on the features of his moon-shaped face, and the sneer of his lips. Sweat runs down his forehead from his greasy hair and I try to recoil but can't move. My arms are frozen, my legs are shaking and I'm trapped. He could do what he wants with me. Stepping back, he raises his hand and slaps my face. A lone tear trickles out of the corner of my eye and I curse as it falls down my cheek. He smiles, pleased with his handiwork. Then he moves closer, using his hand to force my chin up to face him.

"You didn't have a life until I met you. I made you a Princess."

Lowering his hand, he pushes apart my jacket, raises my shirt exposes my stomach and places his hand upon it. His touch makes me cringe. His fingers laying a trail of honey for an army of ants to follow, biting, hurting and leaving festering swells that breed poison over my body.

He kisses my ear gently and whispers, "And I have the Queen's blessing to give you my heir."

I scream out, angry and damming the fates. The door opens suddenly banging against the concrete wall. I look up, hair over my face, eyes gritty and try to focus on the person, and for a second hope rises. Dimly, I hear Povack walk away and say, "Hello, little brother." As Povack moves to the side, I realise I know him. It's Marcus.

INVICTUS

Will Thorgood

The time is now. I anticipated how I'd feel when this moment arrived. I guessed fear, my heartbeat frantically jumping out of my chest to fight off the nerves threatening to overwhelm me. Facing the knoll above us and feeling our enemies beyond it, I'm impatient to begin, anticipation and excitement lick along my veins, making me hyperaware of everything and everyone around me.

It feels like more than a week since we left Arcadia and came to Elias and a lifetime since I emerged from my waking coma at Storm Castle. To face our future in Elias is preordained. This no-man's-land is a barren wasteland. Sand and rock covers the ground. Harsh mountains dominate the sky, jagged rock covered in frozen ice. Trees circle the mountains, their leaves appearing lush green at first until you examine them closer and see the trunks are brown and the leaves dead, still they remain, frozen in time, unable to complete their natural journey to back into the ground for regeneration. Elias taunts them giving access to both options while denying either if chosen. The sky is mutinous, shifting shades of grey and black, blending into one another before receding and coming back once more. White clouds push forwards before disappearing and reappearing again. The sky is intercepted by bolts of lightning and tornados that swirl and circle one another like two teenagers in a dance. Elias requires you to be strong, using its power to hold you still, whilst you wrestle, determined to live.

In this land between life and death, I've seen Rora many times. First, it was teases of her, her auburn hair glinting in the crowd, catching and holding her hooded green eyes that turn away, rejecting me. Then finally, calling out my name in a gut wrenching anguish, begging me to help her and never leave her again to suffer. It was then I knew, in my heart, it was not my Rora. My Mate would never maliciously hurt me. Elias is testing me with every teasing glimpse designed with torture in mind. To shatter the fragile equilibrium, I'd established and preciously protected. I wasn't alone in this suffering. Dot confided she has also seen Boon and each time he's asked why she's not chosen to join him. Elias playing on her fear and on-going dilemma. Anger boils as she confided in a wavering voice, pain so etched into her lovely face; I fear it would mar it forever.

Elias is using silence as a weapon, our reluctance of speaking for fear of being seen as mad. How many others have suffered since we arrived here? Curious, I ask the question at our gathering one night.

"How many of you have seen what you shouldn't have here?"

I refuse to say the word aloud not allowing it any more power than it's garnered. Silence greets my question, followed by small nods. Even the exuberant Jackson, pales at my question as Fero leaves his shoulder and hides himself within his jacket. Moments later, the night wind kicks up through the camp, putting out fires and knocking over tents in an attempt to display its temper. I laughed then. Feeling rejuvenated by the empowerment this knowledge has given us as the wind dissipates and fades, chased away by our willingness to confront our fears. Our talents will determine our future, long after our swords have dropped from our hands. We have empathy, love and understanding and a willingness to help each other, gifts bestowed through serendipity. We have hope.

Sitting in the darkness last night, Maggie looked off into the distance towards the violent sky and Abaddon, her teeth dug into her bottom lip until it drew blood and she voiced her worse fear.

"Do you think they're still alive?" she whispered.

The question hit Danny and me hard, as the thought bred life. Pushing it away, I answered.

"We have to believe they are. I have to believe that having missed most of my children's lives, fate wouldn't be so cruel as to separate us before I got the chance to make it up to them. Sensio is fair, that's the natural balance."

In my heart, I know I will survive because the best of human nature will always win over the bad.

In these last minutes before battle, I'm proud to stand shoulder to shoulder with my friends. We have a blood bond that death will not destroy. As a boy arriving from Sea Cliff, they saw the real me underneath the surface. They saw me as Will their friend. Not the son of the Lord of Sea Cliff or the heir to the throne. During my waking coma, I can clearly remember being irritated by the fakery of the courtiers simpering to the crown on my head while knowing nothing of the man who wore it. The Queen, on the other hand, loved the power the crown gave her. Shoulder to shoulder, Mate beside Mate, clans beside clans and species beside species we move forward. Together. Our fates as one. I will never let them go again. These bonds now extend to The Alliance. Just as most of the mermaids left to defend the seas, some stayed to protect Sanctuary and the children within it. Marcus left suddenly to help our children, explaining it was an impulse he felt compelled to follow but promising that he would return to Sanctuary and care for Thomas, taking on responsibility for a child that was not his, but assuming it anyway. I still remember the look of uncertainty on Thomas' face as we left. "Will you keep me safe Will?" he asked. The other children moving about the large room at Sanctuary stilled at the question, as the mermaids and faeries, lingered, fussing and settling them. "Yes. The Alliance will keep you safe." I answered confidently. "You won't have to ever worry again after this day."

The solemn vow shifted something within me and I know in keeping the promise I would be a part of his life from this day forward. Old friends have also returned. Lightly sleeping during the last night before battle, I woke to the ground rumbling. Leaving my tent quickly to inspect the noise, I saw that Clover and her herd of unicorns had returned. Trotting towards me, she moved confidently, her black coat restored to full shining vivacity. Her eyes bouncing and full of life, her thick eyelashes covers them delicately as she nuzzled into my shoulder. By giving Clover her freedom, she acknowledged gift by returning to help us on the day of battle. My lifelong friend returning to help me, when I need her most.

Watching the bluff, I hear the steady march of heavy feet. I remember a story Rora told me about the Declaration of Independence and how the founding fathers of America faced the threat of death to fight for their freedom. Finally, I understand why she told me the story. So I would remember, on this day, on the precipice of our battle for freedom, that those who went before us with hope in their hearts had been victorious.

Rolling my shoulders, I feel restless, adrenalin pumps through me as I brace myself to give the order when the time is right. Standing on the edge, I take a breath, and repeat the words Rora introduced to me at Rowan Cottage, words that have given me strength ever since.

"Out of the night that covers me,

Black as the pit from pole to pole,

I thank whatever Gods may be

For my unconquerable soul.

In the fell clutch of circumstance,

I have not winced or cried aloud.

Under the bludgeonings of chance,

My head is bloody, but unbowed.

Beyond this place of wrath and tears

Looms but the horror of the shade,

And yet the menace of the years

Finds, and shall find me, unafraid.

It matters not have strait the gate,

How charged with punishments the scroll,

I am the Master of my Fate,

I am the Captain of my Soul."

Opening my eyes, I realise I've said the words aloud. Turning to my friends I see them nod and acknowledge them. At that moment, I feel the whisper of soft lips across my cheek, the scent of wildflowers and a feeling of such elusive peace and I know that Rora is thanking me for the words we cherished together so long ago. I move my hand onto my pocket and feel the journal I always keep close. I make a vow to give Sensio back to herself after this day. Just as I vow to live my life as I always intended and love my children and my friends for as long as I'm granted. Today, I say a "no" to the Queen that is so final she'll never ask again. Shouting, I raise my sword and we move forward as one. I take back myself and everything I love, finally, and for the last time.

"A loyalty & trust never to wane,

I chose him freely,

Not all men are the same..."

...Clover

Clover

BATTLE FOR SENSIO

Rose Darkings

I t's begun. I feel the start of battle, like a cannonball launching from my body. Silent, it leaves me scarred and vulnerable to the images swirling around me. In this vacuum of space holding Aiden and I captive. I submit, closing my eyes, leaving my body to become a silent witness to the war raging around us.

Heading towards the vibrant green ground, I see the earth shake and crust upwards, moving the sea of people upon it. Even as the ground tilts below them, making them unsteady, they don't stop, reacting to their new environment and continuing onward. Just as they move into combat they look like two hands, that pool and merge as one. Were it not for the cries, grunts and sharp clash of swords, you could imagine this army of bees working together as their Queen demanded. Instantly, a white flash eclipses the sky and I'm forced to turn away from the sight, before finding myself down on the ground my body astride a black unicorn, my hand moving from side to side as I cut away the Black Knights coming towards me. Feeling the unfamiliar weight of the crown on my head, I recognise who I have become. I am seeing the battle through the eyes of King Garrick. He's no longer the shadow of the man I'd met. Fortitude and strength radiates through his belief that this battle is necessary. Not just for Sensio and her future but for himself. He fights for the life that he wants. The unicorn pulls him upwards and away from danger, the bodies of the animal and the man moving as a working unit. I feel his relief as he pulls the sword back and begins to use his talents. The talents he'd forgotten he possessed. The talents that had lain dormant until the time was right for them to break free. Fire launches from his fingertips into the midst of the enemy, burning a hole through one Black Knight before moving to another. His eyes move through the mass of people strategically planning his next target. Adrenalin courses through his veins, his heartbeat thundering in his chest as he rejoices in being alive. Fighting what for what he believes in. Fighting for all of us so we have the right to live and love as we choose. He laughs as Jackson pushes past him and throws a Black Knight to the ground with one of his meaty hands.

In his periphery he sees Dot, Warwick and my parents just behind him. The movement pushes the crowd back and reveals on the horizon two figures standing watching the battle. Firenado's; long strands of fire coming from the black clouds pierce the ground between us and he catches a glimpse before pushing forward to confirm his suspicious. The Black Knight stands tall and foreboding, watching the battle like a form of entertainment. The small figure stands close, a black velvet covering and concealing an outfit. Then she moves and a glint of diamonds spark against fire creating a flash that highlights the taut features on her face. Anger rolls through Garrick as he shouts at the sight of Queen Andora and Lord Luther. He moves desperately to push through the throng of people between them. Queen Andora surveys the crowd like an eagle studying its prey. Before them, a pack of black wolves stand taut, waiting, anticipating, blue eyes feverish as they watch the violence, their long pink tongues licking over sharp white teeth, desperate to engage in what they see before them, but waiting for permission to move. Leaning forward, the Queen lays a hand on the largest wolf, a large diamond ring stark against the blue blackness of its fur, and she smiles and mouths a single indiscernible word. The wolves surge forward at the command, tearing and biting into the crowd. She watches for a moment before she takes Luther's arm and walks away from the battlefield.

Flung from Garrick's body I'm lifted into the air and pushed to the next place. The wind whips my hair and pushes it until it tugs behind me as I'm moved over ravaged buildings, fire consuming the earth and raping the landscape. The wind shouts and as the white clouds dull to a stale brown, they cut and lower sweeping over the ground, pulling up trees and stones with sharp glass edges. I am pulled through without injury, my presence removed from my body but still with Aiden. Reaching out, I reassure myself he's still there, but his skin feels cold. I have to get back to him. Stopping above the dark billowing sea, I watch the waves rage against the beach, then pull back into the midst before attacking once more. Then, in the next moment, I am under the waves.

Thrust into an alien environment I panic, trying to draw air into my lungs before realising it's impossible. Pulling up my hands, I spread my fingers, studying the webbed skin in between. Before a sixth sense tells me to move quickly. I use my long tail to take me away from danger, just as sharp white teeth snap and moves onto the next target. Its then I realise that I am in the body of Ero. She moves swiftly, elegantly cutting through the water, clutching a fine boned spear in her hand, intricately sharpened and cut to cause damage to any enemy. Under the surface, the water is calm, the darkness lit with ethereal glow that surrounds each entity moving within it as a silhouette. The kracken suddenly spins upwards, as Ero skirts out of the way, and cracks the surface of the water. Ero laughs and plays a game of hide and seek with the huge creature. Then from the kracken tentacles with sharp claws open and release circular disks that cut through the water. A dolphin is attacked, slumps and stills. The seconds later, the dolphins returns to life, leaps forward and starts to attack the other creatures, infected by the kraken's poison. Ero cries into the water, the message bubbling through the water. Her Alliance moves together all at once, using spears, sharp teeth, tentacles and poison to attack it. Even the great white shark, the predator feared most by all sea creatures, joins in to kill the beast that's taken their position at the top of the food chain.

The kracken launches out of the water and takes us up with it and I see the large boat filled with Black Knights holding shields and swords. They rise up with us, the bottom of their boat teetering on a knife-edge. They join us in pushing the sharp points of their swords into the grey rubbery flesh that's emerged from the churning water. Fighting for survival against evil, they've encouraged to fester. The boat moves ever closer to the central mouth, opening and closing in agitation, seeking food without satisfaction. Giving a low roar, it gives up the fight and stills, no longer noticing our insignificant blows to its dead flesh. We all fall back into the water, the kracken floating into the dark fathomless depths followed by the great whites determined to gorge on their prize. The circular teeth discs fall from the kracken, snapping before stilling, before being kicked back and forward like a ball by the other mermaids before they launched them into the depths back to its master. Ero pulls back her head and laughs. The sounds merging into the water as she plays with her family in celebration.

Thrust away from the ocean and into my body above, I look over the land, seeing all the battles through a green tinge. Moving my large body soundlessly through the sky. I see my shadow against the stone-ridden sand below and the shape of a dragon. I am Brigid. Powerful and determined to embrace the future I've created for myself. I look at the darkened building with impatience wanting the one within, eager to get on with the battle that will determine our future. I roar, breathing fire onto the blackened trees below billowing black smoke into the red fog.

Closing my eyes, I will myself back to the no-man's-land holding Aiden and me captive. He's utterly still and his skin is a deathly blue white. Pushing back Aiden's hair from his forehead, I gingerly place my hand near the bruise at the side of his head. His skin feels cool against my numb fingers and his head rolls away from me. I drape myself around him, trying to warm him with my body heat. I study his face and kiss every precious part of it from his thick eyelashes to his sharp, angular nose and his full soft mouth, thinking of all the missed opportunities and stupid moments of pride that time stole from us. My eyes blur and I feel tears roll from the corner of my eyes and wet his cheek. Wiping the tears away with my hand, I beg him. "Don't leave me Aiden. Please don't leave me. I can't live without you."

I hear my name, and I look at Aiden to see him motionless.

Looking to the side, I see a pair of black shiny shoes and I raise my eyes. The man is tall with thick brown hair and dark blue eyes, and he's wearing a tailored suit. His eyes are anguished as he looks at Aiden. I hear his thoughts in my head and I know this man, Harwyn, has walked beside Aiden all of his life as his spirit guide.

He says, quietly, "Do you want to save him Rose? If you accept my help there will be a price to pay." Holding Aiden, I refuse to let him go. "Yes!" I scream. "I'll do anything. Please save him."

Clutching my hand within his, he places a grey stone in my palm. On turning it over it revealed a soft purple centre, and faded into a crevice.

"Place the Amicus on his wound and always keep it with you. Fear the Arous." Then he disappeared into the air.

Placing the stone against Aiden's wound, I waited, hoping he would wake, never taking my eyes from face, praying his features would soften and acknowledge I'm here. Frantically, I look off into the distance for Harwyn, opening my mouth to shout him back. Then I hear my name croaked out and see Aiden looking up at me, his eyes blurry with confusion. The welling sore on the side of his head has begun to heal, the blood flowing back into the wound, the skin sealing before my eyes and leaving only pink scarred skin. Crying out his name, I take the only action my body is capable of. I black out.

FIRE STORM

Amber Lockwood

H is smile is cruel. Povack steps back from me and I release a shuddering breath, embracing the reprieve, terrified it's only temporary.

"It's a bad time brother," Povack murmurs, pointing a gnarled hand towards me and flexing it out slowly.

Marcus says nothing. His skin is pale. His blonde hair creating a bright halo against the dark shadows in the room. His black eyes focus on his brother, but he doesn't speak. The tension is palpable, crackling in the air of the room, making it static, like any movement could trigger a reaction. Looking at the brothers, I can't see a resemblance between the two, until Povack moves his head to the side and I catch the angle of their faces showing a vague similarity. Looking around for any means of escape, I come up with nothing. Anchoring my heels against the ground, I tried to flex my calves against the tight bounds. The slight movement causes Marcus to focus his attention on me. Lowering my face I try to shield my red eyes and exposed skin, in case it encouraged him to use me too. I have no idea whose side he is on. The blackness of his eyes flare and his cheeks flush red. The anger floods from him in waves.

"Is that what you did to my Mate after you told me she was dead?"

Povack's lips twist as he walks nonchalantly towards the table, leans back against it and folds his arms.

"Sierra is dead, Marcus. You need to accept it."

Marcus bursts into movement and grabs his brother by the collar, half strangling him, bringing his face so close to his own they are eyeball to eyeball.

"She gave birth to our son." He screams. "You almost starved him, and our father. What did you do Povack!"

Povack tries to move back but was trapped by the table at the back of him. With a disgusted look on his face, Marcus punches him so violently, his head snaps to the side for a moment before he slumps to the floor. Marcus looks down at him, fists clenched, his chest heaving with anger. I looked at Povack on the ground with satisfaction, out cold, blood sprayed across his cheek. He couldn't hurt me anymore. Marcus walks towards me. I gulp and instinctively flinch away from him, not knowing enough about him to know what he's going to do. Reaching up to my hands, he loosens my bonds and I groan as my legs relax and lower to the ground.

"It's okay, Amber. I hope I was here in time?" He looks at my face, his features asking the question that he doesn't want to voice. I nod, and his shoulders drop in relief.

"Thomas and Jack?" I whisper, the words grazing past my dry throat.

"Jack was our ... my father, and Thomas's grandfather" he explains. Suddenly, I remember the pride on Jack's face as he pushed Thomas onto the unicorn before turning back to the face the Black Knights and his certain death.

"He saved Thomas. He helped us to escape," I whisper.

"Yes," he nods. "You'd better go to Duncan. He's not going anywhere," he says, rolling Povack's body over with his foot.

Turning away, I push a hand into my pocket and feel for the rose quartz, holding onto the calming aura as it moved through me and headed towards the door. The large hall was still in darkness and I move hesitantly towards the other door. Firelight and warmth flow from the small space afforded by the open door. My stomach clenches as I near it. I don't know what's happening inside. Are they naked? Has she seduced him? Is he still alive? Each of the possibilities hit me, breeding vivid coloured flashes into my psyche, burying deep within my subconscious, haunting me at my most vulnerable. I push the door open as quietly as I can and enter the room. The heat seems insufferable at first, searing my skin to the point of pain before it cleared. Then I heard the sound of Duncan moaning. The sound he makes when I push him to the edge and he wants to slow down and take back some control.

I clutch the crystal in my hand and pour all my positive emotions and memories into it. I remember our first meeting before I knew who he was. Our first kiss in the woods. His arrival at Rowan Cottage. Our reunion on the banks of The Alliance camp. Pouring out all of my love, only a singular thought lingers. Would what I was about to see obliterate all that from my mind? The figures are silhouetted in the warm mist and as it fades I see Duncan still imprisoned to the wood. Caroline stands in front of him with a bone-handled knife, the blade glints in the shadows, as she twists it cutting into the skin of his chest. His chest and belly hair is matted with rivulets of dried blood, sweat and dirt. Wasting no more time, I creep up silently behind her and slam the crystal into the back of her head. The crystal instantly burns my palm, and I drop it, smouldering, onto the ground. She groans and tries to get up. We both see the knife at once. I run over, kicking her arm away. I push past her, grab the edge of the blade just as she rears and moves back. I stand defiantly between her and Duncan.

Caroline rises, blood running from the wound on her head into her bright blonde hair. Her eyes are transfixed on me like a predator on its prey. I feel Duncan behind me, my nerves wired to his nearness. Remembering her glee at finding us in Abaddon. Her indifference at handing me over to Povack to be abused. Her hands on my Mate. Her fury stirs and I lick my lips in anticipation. I'm going to enjoy this. Pointing my fingers, I make a come-hither gesture and say, "Try me." Caroline moves forward then stops mid step as her clear blue eyes recede and begin to glow green as they elongate and widen. She screams and pulls at her gown, a shadow leaps within her skin like a foreign body desperate to break free.

"Brenn…" she screams out, "No Luther. You promised!"

Her voice changes from clear human tones to the screams of an animal as her skin transfigures from smooth to scaly. She stares at me for a moment, so lost within the creature she is becoming. Our battle is forgotten. Tears shimmer in her eyes, making the emerald green glow, beautiful and eerie. Picking up the shards of her black silk dress she ran for the door leaving us alone.

Releasing a breath, I finally lower my hand and face Duncan. His eyes are open and alert watching my movements, lingering on the knife in my hand. Stopping before him, I hesitate. Wanting to drop the knife. Looking at my Mate, trying to find the humour, patience and want, normally clear in his dark blue eyes. I can't see it. His body is tense and he fights to burst the ropes binding him. I hesitate for a moment. Should I let him free? Reaching a hand forward, I dig into his pocket and locate the tiger's eye that Fingle gave him at Sanctuary and hold it against his skin, hoping to calm him. He tenses and licks his lips as the crystal grazes his hot skin. Instead the heat leaps through me. Kicking up my heartbeat. He breathes out straining against his binds. His eyes burn. Gulping, I realise that just as Arcadia brings out the best of intentions, Abaddon gives way to baser instincts. My Mate has become a fire storm, a fire out of control and if I let him loose he could hurt me without meaning to. Duncan is trapped in the no-man's-land that's taken him. I have to bring him back.

Stepping away, I put the knife down on the table, take off my jacket and drop it onto the ground. I take a deep breath and pull my tank top over my head, fighting the urge to cover my curves. Holding his eyes, I take off my boots, loosen my trousers and kick them to the ground. Breathing out, I move into the firelight. Naked and vulnerable. His gaze moves over me, taking in every inch of my body. Laying my hand on his chest, I move it gently over his wounds, kissing his chest, looking at him and giving him everything I have.

"Come back to me, Duncan. Take me. Love me."

I sever the ropes binding his hands and the knife clatters to the ground as he pushes me back against the wall. The stone cuts into my back and I embrace the pain as his eyes blaze like sapphires in the darkness. The soft hair of his stubble burns against my cheek as he teases his lips around mine until I undulate against him. Twisting his hand into my hair, he holds me steady as his hips keep mine immobile, moving closer until I feel nothing but him.

He levers back and demands, "Ask me to take you again Amber."

Pressing my nails into the muscles of his back, he laughs and moves his hands down my body, teasing me, then moving them away. Making it clear he is in control of my body. Willingly, I surrender myself to him. He surges forward and I revel as he takes me. Letting me save him, as I need to. Pushing my fingers into his hair, I pull his lips down to mine and wish for a part of him I have never had before.

"He has my heart,

My soul & body too,

If I save him whole,

I know he will save me too...."

...Amber

Amber & Duncan

QUARTET

Aiden Darkings

I snap awake from the dark to the light. The sky above is calm. White clouds trailing through the mist to complete an onward journey. The vacuum trapping us is now clear, free from the ghosts of Luther and Sierra that held us in the past preventing us from moving forward. Bereft, the tension that has held my nerves for so long has dissipated. The other part of me, the murderer, has been banished. Not only to the shadows but also to the expanded horizon of my existence, the other end of nowhere, where it will never return to haunt us again. In this veritable version of Elias, I have found what I thought was lost. I have found my true self.

The scent of wildflowers teases my nostrils and I push back a soft strand of Rose's hair from her face. The strands move through my fingers like warmed honey and I rest my hand on her back and trail my fingers down her spine as she sleeps. The weight of her slight body is slumped upon me like she had given way to exhaustion and I tuck the top of her head below my chin. In my arms, she feels like home. I am in no doubt of what I want. She murmurs in her sleep, then jolts awake and lifts her head. She quickly reaches and presses her fingers against my chest heating my already warm skin before she lifts her eyes to mine. I smile. Rose strokes my cheek and lowers her lips to mine. I met her halfway, pulling her body against mine. The kiss is tentative at first, like we are two shy strangers, and then we lose ourselves to it, as we embrace each other fully. This kiss, passionate and consuming, should have been our first.

The warm droplets touch my skin softly at first. The pattern marks our exposed skin until I open my eyes and notice droplets of red on Rose's arm. Leaning upward, I break our kiss, still holding her as I look around us. The deserted space that had held us has released us into another. Crouched on crunched leaves, we sit before a foreboding castle that reaches high into the black sky. Thunder rolls above us highlighting the broken windows above making it look unkempt and unoccupied. Looking to Rose, the light flashes across her face and as I study the droplets on her skin realising with horror that it is blood. Standing up, I look at the black clouds patched with red dripping into the atmosphere as if Abaddon itself is weeping in celebration. A thunderbolt pierces the ground not far from us. Jolting upright, we run up the stairs, barely keeping our feet on the slippery mossy steps. Just as we reach the top, the wrought iron door is flung open. I reared back fearing what we would face here, only to see Povack, bruised, bloody and unconscious, being pushed roughly through the door with barely concealed vehemence. At the back of him is Marcus, his face tight and his eyes sparking with temper. Pushing him down to the steps, he sees us both and smiles, looking relieved to see Rose. Jealously rears and I push it back, determined to ignore it.

Marcus holds up a rattan sack that wriggles at the behest of its occupants. "I've got them" he grins. "Amber went to save Duncan. They're back there. I'll wait for you here."

Stepping into the dark, cold hallway, we move to the door in the corner with the light behind it. Pushing the door open, the room seems unoccupied, until we see the silhouettes in the corner. Duncan sits propped up against the wall. His chest dotted with wounds and matted blood. Amber's head is tucked into his neck, her long hair nearly covering the marks on his body. His hand is clasped around her shoulder pulling her tight against him, his lips brushing over her hair. Her body is covered with his jacket, wrapped around him, her legs tangled with his, as if they can't bear to be separated. Aware of their estrangement at Sea Cliff and feeling like we were intruding upon the fragility of their intimacy, I hesitate to make a sound. They are twin flame souls, in love and finally reunited. I cough discreetly. Their eyes turn towards us and they shout with relief as they see us. Rose stops to look at the twisted and broken cage on the stone floor near the fire. Peeking inside, she searches frantically, whispering, "Indigo?" The cage is empty.

"Big blue eyes?" Amber asks her.

Rose nods, biting her lip. Putting her hand on Rose's shoulder, she explains, "I did that by accident. She must have escaped."

Rose nods again. "I'm glad she got away."

We wait outside briefly as Duncan and Amber finish dressing. Duncan opens the door and waits for Amber as she stops near the fire. Lifting her hand she douses it with satisfaction before she joins us.

Returning outside, Rose tells us about everything she's seen at Elias, in the sea and all around Sensio. We don't know who's survived and who hasn't. We would sense if we had lost those we loved. Marcus joins us with Povack propped on the edge of the water fountain. He drifts in and out of consciousness murmuring incoherently.

Screams engulf the sky and two dark shadows fall over us. Two enormous dragons dominate the sky above us. The black dragon moves closer and releases fire from its large mouth directly at us, its large tongue flickering in and out of the fire it generated. We run to stand against the castle for shelter. The red dragon screeches and knocks into it, so the fire hits against some trees in the distance. The black dragon snarls at her before turning back and trying to attack us again.

"That's Brenn." Rose said pointing to the large black beast above us, still trying to attack us and only being stopped by the red dragon. "That's Brigid," Rose whispers brokenly, "That's The Empress."

Rose runs from the safety of the building and wrenches the bag from Marcus.

"We have to free The Elements."

Placing the bag between the four of us, we free them. They escape and I instinctively lower myself to the ground to converse with the gnome who embodies earth. The others do the same, embracing their elements in their own unique way. Above us, the battle between the two dragons rages on, heedless to our efforts. The gnome regards me for a moment and extends his small hand with a sigh. I mirror the gesture until he evaporates from a being into vapored mist towards and into me. The change within is instantaneous. I stand upright mirrored by Rose, Amber and Duncan as Marcus stands back, eyes wide and curious. Povack now awake, watches us frustrated. Extending our hands, we form a circle and bow our heads.

The battle above us stops. Looking up, we see Brigid take Brenn's neck into her large mouth and bite down. Blood floods her white teeth as she releases Brenn and shifts backwards. Her enormous wings dip as Brenn falls from the sky shifting from the body of a dragon into a woman encased within a black dress. Povack jumps up and moves as she falls into the black water of the moat and disappears into the black depths, leaving only the small patch of torn black silk floating on top of the water for a moment before it was also taken. The sky fills with the triumphant screams of Brigid as she moves agitated, waiting for something that eludes her, before she sweeps over the castle, pushing against a turret until it gives and crashes, and she roars out load and disappears off into the sky.

"It's not over yet," Rose murmurs and I move closer and nod, feeling stronger and surer than I have ever felt before. Looking around, I see the strength mirrored in the faces around me.

Marcus nods in agreement and says, "Yes, Rose, you're right. The balance must be restored."

He looks at Povack sitting on the steps, a smile twisting on his face. I knew what was coming was necessary. The elements demanded it.

WATER HORSE

Amber Lockwood

Merged with Undine, my water element, I feel stronger than ever. Until now, I've played a game of chance. Letting fate dictate the circumstances upon which I find myself. In hindsight, I know I made my decisions on a myriad of emotions, up until I found myself at Sea Cliff and had to choose based on impartiality; deemed by my royal status. Since then, I've relied on my instincts, trusting them take me where I needed. Duncan pulls me closer reaffirming my belief. I saved him. Not through talent or a weapon, but by trusting the little ghost inside my head that told me that in order to save my Mate I had to trust him with every part of myself. He saved me too, trusting me to lead him back from the hell that Abaddon had sent him to. Duncan is mine and I will not be away from him ever again. Merging with my element has only solidified my thinking. I never saw the other Elements as they escaped from their cloth prison. I only saw Undine the female water spirit, who wrapped herself around me, rejoicing that she was free before she faced me. Her fragile face elfin, so like mine, as she came closer touching her nose to mine, so I could see the sharp gold flecks in her bright green eyes that looked to Duncan and I knew that I have what she's always wanted. Undine dreams of true love. She's dreams of having a Mate. Then she wrapped her water arms around me and became part of me. Merging into my soul until I felt mine accept hers, promising to cherish and keep her safe within my keeping.

Turning to face Povack, he rises defiantly, eyeing the space around us. He could return to the castle, run for the woods and the wolves within or jump into the black water. Seeing the options run through his mind like a picture show, he elects to stay where he is and take his chances. Years as a courtier made him believe that he could handle us without too much effort.

Marcus walks in front of him and says, "I want some answers before your fate is decided, brother."

Povack stares back at him arrogantly and says nothing, believing he can keep the upper hand by choosing silence.

"He won't speak Marcus, but I can tell you what I see," Rose offers.

Marcus smiles at Rose and inclines his head, happy for her to go ahead.

Rose begins. "He hated your closeness with your father. He felt shunned because of it. Rose turns to Povack, "You wanted power to get their attention, to have them under your control didn't you?" Povack's mouth set in a thin line and I knew Rose has hit him in a sensitive area. "When Queen Andora came to power you courted her, you wanted power of your own."

Rose looks at Marcus, "But what your brother was most jealous of was your Mate. He wanted her for himself and if he couldn't have her, then no one could. He arranged her accident and then told you she had been murdered."

Rose looks hesitant for a moment before she continues, "The man you killed to revenge her was innocent Marcus. I'm sorry."

Marcus stills and covers his face with his hands.

Rose continues, "Povack set you up so he could send you to the Black Knights as penance. Your father was stripped of his Knighthood and demoted to the stables in disgrace. Your Mate had your child. She didn't know what had happened to you, believing and trusting in her love for you. She left Thomas in Jack's safekeeping, until she could find you and reunite her family. She always dreamed of you and her blonde haired boy."

Rose stops speaking, pales and steps away from Aiden. "Your Mate is Sierra, Marcus. She's still alive. She never gave up looking for you."

Marcus staggers and sits down, horror and pain etched in his features.

Povack smiles for the first time, relishing instead of denying the details; "I believe she provided an outstanding service to the Black Knights. Am I right Prince Aiden?"

Marcus looks around wildly, conflicted and unable to process so many details within such a small period of time. Tension consumes Rose, now pale, and Aiden is looking at her like she would disappear. The atmosphere responds to the tension. The wind picking up and pushing at our clothes and hair.

"This is not the issue here, am I right Marcus? We were seeking to address the balance?"

Marcus acknowledges my point, smiles sardonically and

bows in my direction. "You must choose, Amber. When I walked in on Povack, he was intent on raping you. His fate is in your hands."

I swallow and nod, as Duncan snarls and begin to stalk towards Povack. Fists clenched, intent on hurting him like he hurt me. He stops only when I tighten my grip on his hand and pull him back towards me. Povack looks at me, arrogant, believing I don't have the guts to make the necessary decision. That may have been true before, but now I'm a Princess of Sensio and a Guardian of the Elements. I am not the first woman he has hit and forced himself upon. If he left alive he would do it again. I had to do this not only for me, not only for the balance but also for his future victims. Marcus watches me, his eyes brimming with the trust he has placed in me.

My eyes linger on the waterfall and moat behind Marcus that had consumed Caroline. The colour of the water has transformed from a murky dirty black to a translucent iridescent white, the transformation against the black castle showcasing how much the water dominated the castle. Instead of a cascading waterfall moving in a seamless rhythm as it flickers a silhouette riding the waterfall continuously. The silhouette moves forward and I see the four legs, a long neck and a horn extending from its head. I hear Undine whispering, 'Water Horse' in my ear. The animal moves again into the water, running in circles protesting, trying to break free, before resuming the movement in frustration. Remembering Povack's cruel treatment of Clover, her cries reverberate in my head and I feel her fear of him. I know this is the correct choice.

Turning back to face Povack, he bows theatrically in front of me and raises his head smiling, "My fate is in your hands, *Princess*."

Povack believes I'm hesitating due to indecision; that I'm not strong enough to discard him and walk away.

"Povack," I command, "Ride the water horse." He turns to look at the waterfall behind us and the unicorn, standing still beside it. Waiting for him. Squaring his shoulders, he moves towards it and pulls its mane roughly before mounting it. The horse rears up, reacting to the man astride her. Always one for a performance, he bows one last time, tightly digging his heels into its side. It picks up pace and gallops towards the moat, disappearing into the depths of the water, weaving in and out of the waves before retracing its journey. We hear a scream, dulled by the roar of the water. The sound fades as Povack clutches onto the Water Horse's mane on its seemingly never-ending journey. His fear only encourages the animal more, its silhouette sparkling.

Then the shouting stops and the Water Horse emerges without Povack. A gnarled hand clings to the side of the wall before it falls and disappears into the black water. The Water Horse escapes from its prison, jumping over the stone wall and runs into the forest neighing and pushing it head up and down in the sheer delight at being free. My heart soars and as I look at the faces around me, I see acceptance and no remorse. I made the right decision. We listened to The Elements. We have restored the balance.

REACTION

Rose Darkings

The emotions bounce around the large room and head towards me. In the confines of Storm Castle, the large dominating building was designed by nature to protect the inhabitants of Sea Cliff. The extreme emotions inhabiting these halls and rooms were never allowed to leave and since we arrived here a week ago, they have used me as a vessel upon which to express themselves. In Storm Castle, the people keep busy, afraid that if they stop they would have to face the storm raging inside them. The burst of violence expressed in the Battle for Sensio dissipated the tension but did not solve the problem. Queen Andora and Lord Luther haven't been seen since they left the battle at Elias. The Alliance arrived at Sea Cliff anticipating another confrontation only to find Storm Castle abandoned.

King Garrick reinstated himself as ruler of Sensio, dismissing the courtiers and ruling as his father had shown him, with compassion, understanding and peace. Under the surface, his need to face the Queen simmers. A confrontation necessary to resolve his past and embrace his future. While the Black Knights fell like pawns, those that had manipulated their loyalty and presence walked away unscathed. Our family survived Elias with no more than bruises. Glad of the small victory but knowing it's not over.

The Alliance has stayed together. Even Eros has returned. Her smile jubilant from her victory against the kracken to stay with us. Only the sasquatchs elected to stay in Arcadia, to be near the children and the mermaids who protect them.

The Empress is still in the form of Brigid. She flies over Sensio, silently, watching, and waiting for something that eludes her. When I reach for her, I still hit an impenetrable brick wall that pushes me back. I'm only allowed a view of her world when she chooses to let me see it.

Standing beside Marcus in the Throne Room, I watch the milling of activity around us. The King is now dressed as we are, his only adherence to his status being the crown on his head. Determined to establish a new order, he has dismissed the remaining courtiers, who lingered anxious to pay homage and replaced them with good, trusted people who, like Jack, had been demoted to servant status under Queen Andora's regime. As a result, everyone in Sea Cliff, Greenwood and beyond now has all the food and shelter they need. When thanked by a grateful subject, he only apologises for not doing it sooner.

Marcus has been quiet since we left Abaddon. His thoughts running rampant as he waits for Sierra to arrive with her parents. He can't wait to see her but I know he is dreading it too.

"Will she ever forgive me?" he asks suddenly, as we sit on the stone steps where the throne used to be. King Garrick destroyed it and ordered it to be distributed for firewood. I know Marcus isn't expecting an answer. My company is enough to salve the rawness knowledge brought.

Despite my tumultuous feelings for Sierra and her relationship with Aiden, I know that her heart was always pure. Her intentions focused upon the image of the blonde haired boy that she gave birth to, dreaming of his growth in her mind. The image of his father. "Marcus," I say, taking his hand, "Whatever she did, it was all for you and Thomas. You were deceived. She never stopped looking for you. It was all for true love."

Squeezing my hand, he gets up, hope leaping within his eyes. "And Aiden?" he asks. I look down but don't reply, wanting to help my friend but not seeking reciprocation. He repeats the question, nodding to my Mate, standing nearby with his father. Marcus kneels down and lifts my chin with a gentle finger and forces me to look at him.

"We all make mistakes Rose," he whispers, "otherwise how do we learn?"

He stands up and walks over to the gate, where he stands every day. Waiting for his Mate to come back to him. My eyes follow Marcus and I admire his hope because mine has shrivelled. Nothing mattered when Aiden returned to me in no-man's-land. He came back. He was alive. He was all that mattered. Then the mention of Sierra places her between us, obliterating the fragile trust and confidence we've gained. I feel like I have been given the life I've craved only to have it taken away from me. Looking up, I see Aiden watching me. His narrowed gaze following Marcus's departure. His mouth tightens as his gaze flickers over my body possessively. Anger stirs. Does he think I will pursue Marcus in some karmatic need for revenge? I love him. But I'm allowed to be angry because he shared himself with another woman. The air element within me rises and thunders. Twined with my second sight, it encourages me to express my emotions, but right now, I need to get away.

Moving from the hall, I make my way towards my room. A flash of a black stone assails me. It is deceptively beautiful with sparkling green and purple sparks and a feeling of danger. I push the image away in frustration, too caught up in my emotions. The coolness of the air jolts my temper and burns as I walk faster. Hearing the footsteps behind me. My heart picks up and I stop before my door. Waiting. They come closer and I feel the warmth of his body as it reaches mine. I start to shake. A low tremor bounces along my skin. My nerves tingle. His hands possessively clasp my hips. For a second, I yearn to use my talent but Aiden like all my loved ones is barred to me, nature deciding my gift should have a fair price to pay. I know what I'm inviting. I know what I want. But I need to say the words. I face him. His eyes are hot and dark as they search my face. The black of his eyes heat before receding to reveal the original brown he was born with. His tongue moves over his lips and I follow the movement remembering how his mouth felt against mine. The darkness of the hallway is intimate. The murmur of voices too far away to intrude. Leaning back against the door, I see his disappointment and frustration as he restrains himself from tugging me back.

"You need to be sure, Aiden. If you walk in here and I give myself to you... That's it. I won't share you with anyone else. Ever."

I turn around, open the door and walk into the room, closing it behind me. I look at the bed bathed in sunlight and I wait. And wait. Closing my eyes as my heart slams in my chest. My breath shudders and I start to shake as reaction sets in. What have I done? Have I pushed him away too many times for the sake of pride?

The back of the doors slams against the walls before it clicks shut. I feel his arms band around me. His lips take my neck, teasing the sensitive skin as his hands trail up my stomach and he cups me in his hands. I feel all of him against me. Turning my head, he takes my lips and within his kiss I receive a gift I never expected. I hear him asking my parents permission to court me at his Mate. I see his nervousness. His determination to be with me. His surprise when Mum and Dad enthusiastically welcomed his request. In his head, I hear my name being called over and over again in hazy wonder in love. In true love. Then I'm back in the room as he releases my lips from his kiss. Then he says the words out loud, "I love you Rose. Be my Mate. Please."

Clasping his hand, I lead him to our bed. Giving him my whole heart. My body. My soul. Trusting him to keep them safe. Forever.

THE MESSAGE

Indigo Hawthorn

"**N**o!" I shout out, stomping my foot mid-air. Lora folds her arms slowly and dips her head. She thinks her stare will intimidate me. Ha! What a silly imp. Were it not for me, we wouldn't have escaped in the first place. I knew Amber recognised me as I did her before she deliberately fell into the cage, causing a wide enough gap for us to escape.

I couldn't believe it when Duncan and Amber arrived at the castle. The pictures I saw in Rose's mind so clear that when they appeared before me, I thought I was dreaming. Caroline has ranted of nothing but their arrival for days. I knew what awaited them and I was going to help them if the opportunity arose.

Lora thinks I have been sitting quietly accepting my fate, locked up in a cage with her and her band of misfits. How misguided is she? I watched and waited for the opportunity to escape, just as my sister taught me. I have my own part to play and being stuck in a cage with a bunch of imps isn't part of it. I take the opportunity to escape when Caroline is distracted with Duncan. The imps linger. Lora gestures to me wildly as I poke my head out of the cage and encourage them to follow me. She hesitates, too accustomed with her captive environment until the other imps push past her leaving her with no choice but to follow. They quickly move towards the open door. I turn and look to Duncan wondering if I should zap Caroline to help him escape.

Caroline, intent on her revenge, was digging the blade into his chest. He looks forward, clenching his jaw to stop from shouting out and giving her what she wants. My movement caught his attention and he locks eyes on me, as I drift forward to try and help him. He shakes his head with a small movement and mouths "Amber" asking me to help his Mate instead. I nod, zapping the fire instead, taking her attention away from his skin for a moment, before making my escape.

The hallway is darkened, only lit by two sconces. Moving to the other door, I peek inside and see Amber tied to a railing, her clothes being loosened by Povack. What a horrible coward he is. Looking around for some sort of weapon. I see a silhouette in the hall, freezing initially, when I see the black eyes looking at me. The eyes fade to a soft brown and I know this man, for his deceptive appearance may have been a Black Knight for a time, but he has made up for it since. The blackness shimmering inside him was anger at Povack. Lingering, I knew how I could save Amber and repay him for his cruel treatment of the imps at the same time. He likes to tease them with food, taking the one berry they had to share between them and placing it on the edge of the cage and when Lora would go to pick it up, he would take it back and place it in his own mouth. Sweeping in front of the man's face, I whisper in his ear and watch him change direction towards Amber and Povack. I wait until I hear the first punch, then I left. I'd done all that I could to help them.

"Indigo, we're going back to Arcadia," Lora insisted.

I ignored her. I had another mission. My sister told me to listen to my instincts and I wasn't meant to go back to

Arcadia. I knew I was needed at Storm Castle. Turning, I see fate has attracted help. A flock of black swans flew over the moat and landed beside us. The only colour indicated by their red becks and webbed feet hidden below the water. I jump upon the first swan I see, followed by the other imps. The swan took my movement as move and kick their webbed feet into the water and take us away from Abaddon. Lora shouts behind us in frustration. I laugh holding onto the swan as it picks up speed. Clinging to its neck, I turn to see Lora in the distance, her fists clenched at her side, as I took charge of her imps. "Get on a swan, you silly imp!" I shout and laugh as the imps join me, relieved to be free and embracing another adventure.

Looking back at the large waterfall, I feel the spots of moisture freezing on my face and see Hell Castle a day in the future. Its shape covered in a mass of snow and ice, frozen solid, every living thing within it trapped for eternity. The lake expands, the swans fanning out keeping close but negotiating the intricacies of the water. I see Lora on the outer edge, holding the neck of her swan and scowling in my direction. Lifting a hand, I smile and wave at her.

The scream is so high pitched and unexpected I duck and cover my ears. The black shadows pass over, turning around with the intention of coming back. Aggressors. Their slim bodies entirely black and so translucent you initially think they are shadows. Their mouths open to scream this time in unison. Their hands and ankles are shackled with black iron cuffs that dig so far into their ankles and wrists they are fused with bone. Shackled to the cuffs are enormous black wings that move confidently against the wind and rain. The wings will endure even when the man within fails. Aggressors are harbingers of hell. Black Knights who have committed so many evil deeds, redemption was no longer an option for them. They pay their price for eternity, used as Abaddon wishes. The screams came not from their love of the pursuit but their never-ending battle for freedom from their shackles. They scream for themselves.

The swans pick up speed, pushing their pace to the extreme, causing the water to froth. The imps around me begin to panic as the aggressors get nearer. Then amongst the wildness, calm descended and I hear my sister sigh, wearily.

"Indigo, why do you always have to get yourself into so much trouble?"

I laugh as the shadow of Brigid falls over the expansive water and faces us. The imps panic and I shout at them to calm down. As Brigid stops in front of my swan, the creature stops, hypnotised by her presence. Then again, I hear the message I'm to deliver to Storm Castle. "Find the Amicus, Indigo. It will save them."

Winking, she lifts her body and smirked at the aggressors chasing after us, the moaning of their captives becoming louder. I feel a moment's pity for them before turning away and urging my swan onto Storm Castle. This is my part. I have to save them.

MASQUERADE

Rose Darkings

We all wear a mask to protect ourselves. My Mum wears a mask each time she endures a separation from Dad. Her mask makes her cheerful, optimistic, hiding the real pain of separation until they are together again. My Dad's is stoic, purposeful and steadfast, crumbling at the first sight of his girl. Amber's is determined, as she left Greenwood to find Aiden. Duncan's mask is frustrated, giving her space whilst never being too far away. Aiden pushed me away, determined, believing he knew what was best for me. I adopted indifference pretending it didn't matter. Dot's mask is her smile. It hides the tears that fall every time she thinks of Boon. The King wears the mask of royalty, using his crown to hide his dreams of the past and what might have been as he tries to accept the present.

But, on this night, our masks are for celebration only. The King, bereft at having missed each of his children's birthday's announced a celebration. So tonight, we celebrate Amber and Aiden's 20th birthday and the triumph of the Battle for Sensio. Furthermore, he decreed a masquerade ball must be held on this anniversary every year so we'll always remember and never return to the dark times.

In the twilight, the Throne Room looks truly beautiful. It is covered with an abundance of fire-lit sconces, candles and fairy lights that cast a romantic and magical glow over the room filled with all the people of Sensio dressed in their finery. Jackson and his Gean family are here, dressed in their best, even though he pulls agitatedly at his collar, indicating his discomfort but embracing the celebration. Fero perches on his shoulder, fascinated with a blue silk ribbon that Dot gave him earlier that he ties and wraps around his neck before taking it off and playing with it again.

Fingle weaves in and out of the crowd, socialising with everyone, but he can't stop his anxiety about his sisters from creasing his face. We know Indigo escaped but I haven't been able to reach either her or Brigid since the battle.

Ero has thrown herself into the celebrations and looks beautiful. She delighted in getting ready with Amber and me this afternoon, dressing her long, curly golden hair in an intricate elegant hairstyle that she loves and wants to keep. Fero is fascinated by her and slaps Jackson on the back of the neck whenever he gets too far away from her.

Dot smiles as she speaks with the King, their bereavement giving them bond that few understand.

Warwick remains subdued, pleased with his contribution at the Battle but still lost. He is attending the masquerade tonight out of respect for the King, but is looking forward to returning to Greenwood tomorrow.

The only rule of this celebration is that guests are dressed in either black or white to acknowledge the existence of good and evil, light and dark, for one cannot exist without the other. The monochrome fuses well within the Throne Room, milling and shifting, coming together in a throng as we did at the Hill of the Faeries, at Elias and once more at the place, yet to be determined.

Turning at the sound of laughter, I see Amber and Duncan dancing. Her gown sparkles white of pearliest silk that moves like a living animal as they twist and turn against the tones of the strings and fiddles. Her green eyes shine from the beneath her black mask, with swirls of white, pink, purple and sparkly black, adorned by angel soft feathers at each side. Once in a while, Duncan stops and moves his thumb across her cheek and she smiles up at him. Happiness shining from every pore. Since Abaddon their bond has been unbreakable. The angst gone, replaced with serenity.

My mask covers the rising blush on my cheeks as Aiden pinches my bottom and I fight to keep myself still. He laughs as he watches my reaction. Debonair with his black mask and clean-shaven face, the shadow of his evil self gone. Forever. Memories from last night assail me. My body aches for his touch. I have no regrets. He is mine and I am his.

A hush quietens the room as the King stands before us, the missing throne symbolic in its absence as he lifts a cup of brew.

"Thank you for attending our celebration this evening." He hesitates before going on. "I have missed all of my children's birthdays. I am in debt to Daniel, Maggie and Lauren for all they did to protect them." He looks over at Amber and Aiden, and says, choked with emotion, "My Rora would be so proud of you."

The crowd claps and cheers and Aiden holds my hand tighter. Amber wipes a tear away and turns her face into Duncan's chest.

He takes a step down before continuing. "This is my last act as King." A stunned gasp lifts into the air. "At the Battle of Sensio, I swore I would return our world to herself. I swore I would restore the balance. From tomorrow, Sensio will be governed by a High Council, with representatives from every community of people, faeries and species of Sensio. I would like you to welcome them."

The twelve representatives step out from the crowd. Fingle, Jackson, Warwick and Ero among them. They smile, as cheers bounce off the high ceiling of the Castle. The King smiles, relieved at the reaction and takes his crown off and walks down the steps, at one with his people. Aiden and Amber follow his lead, removing their crown and tiara. Holding them in their hands, shaking their heads. Finally free of the responsibility they never wanted.

Then a voice pierces the murmurs and we freeze.

"How dare you discard what I fought to give you?"

The King stops in his tracks and searches for the voice. Queen Andora appears in front of him, her face taut, small in stature in comparison to the King. Her crown sparkles against the candlelight, highlighting the steel blue of her eyes. Queen Andora looks with hatred at her son. Her cheeks red with an explosion of temper she wished to free but was so groomed in her status, she held it in check. Barely. The King's brown eyes glitter as he looks at his mother. Anger rolls from every fibre of his soul towards the woman who has taken away the life he was meant to live.

Our attention is so wholly absorbed in the interaction between mother and son, we don't notice the blonde haired woman approaching them from the crowd. She removes her mask to reveal blood shot eyes etched with pain. The lines on her face whisper of her age are now embedded and grooved into her skin. Whatever her former agenda, Ruth Gentles, was a grief stricken now.

Will studies her. His dark eyebrows shoot up making a straight line over his forehead. "Ruth, is that you?" he asks, aghast.

She turns round and points her finger at the Queen and says, sobbing. "Your son used my Caroline and got her killed."

The Queen ignores her completely, never taking her eyes from her son.

"Ruth. You need to explain what happened," says Will, confused.

"My Caroline was mated with Lord Luther. The bastard son of Queen Andora and you." She screams, pointing to the back of the crowd. We follow the path of her gaze, studying the man who pales and places a hand on his forehead to ward away the pain exploding in his head.

It is Warwick.

ANDORA
Rose Darkings

S hock reverberates around the room. Never having been able to read Warwick's thoughts unless he allowed me, I garnered entry as he faced the hostile crowd around him. My body mirrors his. My heart leaps in my chest and my nerves tingle with unease at the condemnation in the stares. "He didn't know," I said to Aiden, "not until he came here to beg the Queen to stop."

"Ruth, what are you talking about?" Will demands. Ruth explains. "Andora came to Greenwood, curious about your visits. She knew about The Soothsaying but wanted to control it, by selecting your Mate herself. She knew I had feelings for you and wanted me to be yours."

The Queen pursed her lips and glared at Ruth, like a predator watching its prey.

"Instead you met your true Mate, Rora." Ruth's face gentled, for a moment looking younger than her features told, adopting the softness of a young woman in love, vulnerable and hopeful. "The day you returned to Storm Castle and told your mother of her, she was incensed. That was the day she used the Arous on you. That's why you couldn't remember Rora. Your father died the same night and the she took control of the throne."

I watch the events as the pictures spring from Ruth's mind, playing the events of the past. The incognito visits to understand why her son visited Greenwood so regularly.

Her belief he'd be taken away from her. I see Andora's manipulation of a young hopeful Ruth, and how she was forced to endure Will and Rora's blossoming love. I see Ruth's jealousy and outrage when the Queen could not deliver what she promised. Her revenge as she cleared Rowan Cottage and watched Rora search desperately for her Mate.

Back in the present I turn and see my mother's face brimming with tears and her memories of Rora trying to connect with her Mate and giving up the fight for life the moment when she no longer felt him. I feel sorrow and futility well up inside me and grip Aiden's hand tighter, realising how lucky I am to have him.

The King turns suddenly and stalks away, tension radiating from him until he raised the crown in his hand and threw it violently it against the hard, stone ground. The harsh clattering ring is almost unbearable.

When it finally stops, Will faces the Queen and asks, with quiet fury. "Why do you need to possess and control every part of me? I was finally happy. She was my Mate. You don't know what you did to me!"

The Queen faces her son, remaining so defiantly regal and in control she garnered my begrudging respect. "I couldn't allow you to leave me the way he did," she says quietly, and she looks over to Warwick, biting her lip. The King walks towards Warwick. The old man watches their interaction, his face grave.

Will says, "Warwick, why didn't you tell me?

"Will, I...." he looks down, shamefaced, then back up at Will. "I didn't know about the child until just before the Battle for Sensio. We knew each other as children, then young adults. We had an affair. It ended when I found my Mate."

He quietened, looking the Queen, defiant, sure of his actions and accepting his part in them.

Watching the Queen, I see the years fall away from her face, replaced by a young girl, madly in love with Warwick, the boy she'd known all her life. Fearful of losing him to his true Mate, she stole the Arous from Arcadia and used it to bargain with Abaddon. She offered the Arous in exchange for control of the Elements. The destruction of Sensio began when young Andora refused to accept the law of Mates.

Before she handed it over, she used the Arous to encourage a pregnancy. This act forever changed the natural laws. The child was conceived not of love but of evil. Arriving in Greenwood to see Warwick happily mated, she left her baby with a family. Paying them, to care for him and when payment stopped they took their anger out on the child with their fists. Then he came of age and she sent for him to replace Jack as leader of the Black Knights. Caroline, rejected by Duncan, sought a more advantageous match and Ruth went to the Queen and asked for her daughter to have the Mate she was owed. Lord Luther and Caroline were mated at Abaddon.

Andora's decline from innocence to evil started the moment she lost Warwick. Her rise to power was strategically planned. The sudden death of Lord Thorgood's true Mate was meticulously executed. Using the Arous, she seduced Lord Thorgood and conceived his son. Then manipulated him tirelessly to seek the status of King. The only way Andora believes she will not get hurt again, as she did as a young girl, is to control those around her using the Arous. Using her power to out manoeuvre them. Using her status to ensure their loyalty. Her control of her acknowledged son twisted from feelings of love to ensure he would follow her carefully laid plans. She felt no remorse in denying his life with his Mate. She felt no shame at killing the King or putting her son on the throne, so she could rule as Queen Consort. Her true son Luther is the mirror image of her, carrying out her instructions with unreserved violence and without remorse. When Warwick arrived at Storm Castle to beg her to stop, she was satisfied to see him coming to her. As he should have so many years before. She commanded him to follow her into the bowels of Storm Castle, and presented him with their son, Luther, in chains in the dungeon. Andora gave him a choice to free him or keep him imprisoned.

I feel Warwick's shock at being presented with the adult child he never knew he had but so wanted with his Mate. He felt the hate-filled stare from the boy within, angry at being abandoned and left to be abused, who hit back at his attackers every time he killed another person, gorging on the violence; the only real time he felt alive. Warwick, having done nothing for his son until now, made the only decision he could in his heart. He set the boy free, barely escaping the torrid violent attack that the adult gave him. Running from Storm Castle the only noise he could hear was Andora's laughter following him as she realised her life's ambition to get even with the man who broke her heart.

I took a gulping breath and came back to myself, aware that everyone is watching me, aware that I am telling them what I see, bringing alive the images in my head to everyone in the room.

Then without warning, Andora lifts the black Arous, the black crystal I'd been warned about and smashes it onto Ruth's head, screaming, "I don't need you, King. I don't need anything but this."

Ruth crumples to the ground, blood pouring from the wound on her head. Her body slamming onto the stone utterly still and lifeless. Despite my reticence towards her, part of me wept for her death. Ruth Gentles sought love and hoped for so much more. Her only consolation that she would join the daughter she grieved for.

Dad and Marcus rush forward to restrain the Queen as the Arous falls from her hand, and splits into four parts, the greens and purples flickering from the black. Voices rise in the room as Will tries to take control. The air within me rises like a hurricane, rolling me back and I feel my element panic, trying desperately to escape. My breath comes out harshly as panic seizes me. Tugging on Aiden's hand, I move closer to Amber and Aiden catching the mirroring panic on their faces.

We hear the flutter of wings and see four crows circling the room, flying lower and lower. Amber murmurs, "The black crow...Aiden."

Luther materialises as a silhouette at the back of Amber,

Duncan and Aiden and plunges a sword into each of them. I feel the blade like its pierced my own skin, the sharp warm trickling of blood as my skin numbs. I feel Aiden's hand fall from mine and turn to see him gulping, the blood spreading around his middle as the image of Luther at his back smiles at me over his shoulder. His eyes lock on mine and I look down, clutching his hand as he falls to ground and pulls me with him. My hand is covered with his blood. The voices around us vibrate, now silent to our ears. I cry silently as I feel Amber and Duncan leave us, and the last moments as Aiden closes his eyes and my heart breaks as I realise I'm the last to leave.

Looking up, I see the faces of Mum, Dad and Will. Imperia stands at the back of them mouthing words I can't understand. In the distance, I see Luther fully formed bowing to Queen Andora who smiles luminously at him. One son having completed the deed she demanded long ago. Closing my eyes, I join my Mate. The voice of Harwyn takes me to the last moments of my life. "There will be a price to pay, young Rose" and I hear myself answering without hesitation, accepting the choice. I had been warned. The Soothsaying told us that we would be Guardians of the Elements, but it never, ever said we would live.

DRAGON

Will Thorgood

I live in a recurring dream. Since I woke from my waking coma, I dream vividly every time I close my eyes. My mind revels in sending images in glorious colour instead of the dense grey of my waking coma. Every night, my heart searches for what I yearn for most. Rora. The dreams start with me searching Rowan Cottage, seeing Rora run away just out of the shadow. My heart beats with excitement as she peeks back at me from the corner of her eyes, her soft ruby lips curve in a teasing smile. Then suddenly she stops and I laugh, grabbing her. I feel her heartbeat, see her cheeks flushed with heat, and her eyes shining at she looks into mine. My heart bursts as the magnitude of my feelings for her rolls through me like a crashing wave onto a deserted moonlit beach.

Before I met Rora I felt I was a shadow that carried out my duties, only ever feeling truly alive when I visited my friends in Greenwood. My existence was stark, blackened with a hint of white, now I see the sharp blends of colour and feel everything. Then, just as I'm about to form the words to voice my feelings, her joy fades and I hear her scream out as she disintegrates from her living form into ash that fall through my fingers. Pain, sharp and fractured, pierces my heart, killing all the hope she helps me cherish. Grief so acute it encompasses me completely, making every breath hurt and every thought clench. Every night, I try to save her only to grieve again, whilst my subconscious fights for me to accept reality.

I can't face this reality. The pain is the same - sharp and unrelenting. My hands touch Aiden and Amber. Their blood overs my hands and I study the sharp red liquid and ask myself how blood can still flow when life no longer exists. Unable to process my thoughts, my mind wanders back to the first time I saw them in this room. The shock on their young faces as Rora declared them ours. Amber's wide green eyes and open face, so like her mother. Aiden's tall and dark like myself, moving with a confidence he inherited not from me but from his grandfather. Why did I never tell them? Why did I not take a moment and utter the words instead of filling the silence with questions. Why did I never tell them that they were my pride and joy, the best of Rora and me and that I loved them so much I couldn't begin to says the words to express it.

My hands merge with Dot's as she lifts a hand to push back a strand of Amber's hair. Dot experiences the same dreams as I did. Every night she tries to save Boon only to lose him again. Now she has to mourn the girl she cherished but never gave birth too. Maggie's cries penetrate my thoughts, their sounds wrenched from her body like an animal in pain. She bends over all the children she mothered, her cries become louder as Danny holds her upright and buries his head into her shoulder.

When our children left Arcadia and walked into Abaddon I accepted they would face danger but chose to believe the natural balance would not accept us being parted again after only having found each other. My naivety has cost me dearly. I cannot accept this. Looking up, I meet Danny's distraught gaze as anger rolls and bursts between us.

Turning I see Luther standing near my mother and realise we have an outlet. Reaching down, I kiss my children's foreheads gently and get up. Daniel follows me and we walk towards our quarry.

The crowd part for us as we stride towards Luther and the Queen, swords drawn. I look at my brother rejecting that we share any blood. Luther has killed too many to feel any remorse even for his niece and nephew. Reaching them, I raise my sword, my body relishing the first violent blow of the blade cutting into his body when someone screams, "No!" and Maggie and Dot come running up behind us.

"You're not leaving me and sending yourself to Abaddon, Daniel Darkings, do you understand me?" she rages at her Mate, her small body quivering.

Dot stands to the side and I look at her and I know she understands all of it, the feeling of hopelessness, the horrific pain and my need for revenge. She looks at me anxiously, and shakes her head. It is enough.

I slump and drop the sword and it clatters loudly to the ground.

Someone murmurs, softly, "I'm sorry." I turned to see a shadowy imprint of Ruth Gentles, standing over her bloodied body. The lines on her face faded, sympathy clear on her face. She turns to look at our children, watching Fingle, Jackson and Ero surrounding them, determined to provide protection even in death and she closes her eyes. Turning back she repeats the words to Maggie again. Maggie stiffens for a moment and nods accepting the words as they were intended, from one mother to another.

She points and whispers, "They're coming."

The castle begins to vibrate and then hundreds of shadows come through the windows, the walls, and the doors filling the building to capacity between the living and the dead until no space is available in between. A beautiful young woman moves towards Ruth, who clasps her face and begins to cry as she brings her close. She murmurs comforting her and I realise this must be Caroline, my sister-in-law and daughter of Ruth. Stepping forward, she walks past us to face Luther.

He looks at her, defiant, "You dare take me, Mate?" he asks his tone dismissive.

"Mate?" she questioned in a confident, sarcastic tone. "I was a body for Brenn, nothing more. I was never your Mate."

Dismissing him, she turns to the Queen, her gaze sweeping over her in desertion. "Ask her about the dragon's egg, Luther. Brigid will."

The Queen's mouth flattened, angry. Turning back to Luther she looks at him, her tongue licking her lips in anticipation. Ruth stepped forward and searched the crowd until she found who she was looking for.

"Maggie ... my May ... please?" Maggie's expression softens and she nods to Ruth, understanding the enormity of the question and trust behind it.

As the shadows move forward to surround him. Luther faced the Queen, waiting just as I had all of my life for her to be there when I needed it. She looks away from him and to the ground before taking a step backwards. I get no pleasure from the rejection and pain that sweeps his face as the ghosts gathered him up, pulling and cutting at his body just as he had enjoyed inflicting pain on so many others. He starts to scream in sharp staccato bursts as they pulled him with them as they left the Castle and dragged Luther to the hell he had imposed on them when he was alive.

The Queen, stands alone, without the Arous, Luther or the Black Knights to help her. But she stands, regal and defiant, even now.

"What about the dragon's egg?" I ask, softly. She lifts her chin using the only power she had available to her. Silence.

Warwick was silent while his son was dragged away, but now he walks purposely through the crowd, his voice strong. "The dragons are the protectors of Sensio; two are needed to represent the balance. When Andora took the Arous, intent on using it for evil, it split their souls and destroyed the balance. The only way to restore the balance and destroy the evil she spawned was to create a dragon's egg with two new dragons. But Luther stole the egg for the Queen, and as long as it was in her possession, she stayed in control, destroying the balance and fighting continued."

As Warwick finishes, ear-shattering cries fill the air. Fingle moves to the entrance and cries out, "It's Brigid," and smiles at Andora. "She's come for you."

The cries continue as I remembered with a jolt, being seven years old. I had sneaked into my mother's study and began to play with a beautiful, smooth, dark brown ornament mounted on crystal. The hard slap to my small head was shocking as the egg was taken from my hands and I was lectured on coming into the Queen's chambers without permission. Unconsciously, I touched my head, even as an adult, feeling the sting of sharp pain.

Moving through the crowd, I ran through the maze of corridors, reaching her chamber door and pushing it open. The egg stood on the desk just as it had all my life. Circumspect in the open and I can feel the pleasure the Queen would have in knowing she held something so precious to another, she concealed it in plain view. Picking it up, I ran my hands over it and made my way back to the Throne room. There is an intake of breath as the dragon lands in the courtyard of the castle. I can hear Brigid crying out again, sensing that her egg is closer. Reaching the still silent Queen, I lift a hand and remove her crown. She moves suddenly trying to reach the symbol of her power as I plucked it out of her reach and threw it out towards the open courtyard. It clattered against the hard stone and came to rest. The Queen ran after it, stopping only when Brigid tracked fire over it, turning the prized gold crown into burnt ashes that blew into dust. Following my mother, I walk out to the courtyard feeling no fear of the giant beast that awaits us. Determined to do right. Determined to end this once and for all.

The giant beast stands above the crushed gate of the castle obliterating the entryway erected to cause separation between a ruler and its people, looking at the bricks strewn over the same. It seems fitting. Her large body breathes in and out, the red scaly skin looking like a giant jigsaw map with pieces too unpredictable to fit together. Her sharp green eyes watched my movement. I hear the crowd move behind us staying back but wanting to witness our interaction. Stepping forward, I extended my hand and showed Brigid the egg, then placed it on the ground in front of her before walking backward at a steady pace. She watches me and the egg intently.

Just as I reached the alcove there's a flurry of movement and the Queen runs screaming past me, intent on grabbing the egg. I turn around and close my eyes as Brigid cries out and lowers her head. I turned away as the crowd screams and know from the crunch of bone that the Queen has died trying to get back the power she always wanted. I feel no sorrow, my grief still with the slain bodies of my children in the Castle. Looking back, I see remnants of blood on the stone ground but no remains.

Brigid nuzzles the egg lovingly and breathes a feather light flame over the egg. It cracks open, revealing two tiny dragons, yelling and breathing fire. Brigid licks them, and then nudges them so that they fly up into the air.

She screams out one last time, showering fire into the sky that drops back down onto us like warm rain and her skin sheds like a snake to reveal a naked woman with bright blue eyes and long, thick blue-black hair. On her back is a tattoo of a red dragon that twists and moves on the skin, alive within her. Warwick pushes past me, removes his cloak and rushes over to cover her up. She stands up and faces us, strong, resolute and the keeper of immense power. She smiles and places her palms onto his grey and white covered cheeks, happiness radiating from her. "My Mate," she whispers, and then she kisses him, sealing them together. Then a small faerie flies breathlessly into the courtyard, followed by a gang of imps, and shouts "Sis, where's Rose? I have a message for her."

SETTLEMENT

Will Thorgood

I stand frozen. Unbidden hope unfurls within me searching for a home. Turning, I look towards Maggie and Daniel our minds as one. Moving towards The Empress, Warwick and the faeries, we stop in front of them. The magic of the faeries has always been sacred. The secrets shared with no one outside Arcadia. The Empress faces us, her eyes all knowing, taking in everything. "Our children," I say, faltering, stopping when I realise she knows. "Take me to them," following us, she quizzes the small faerie. "Indigo, what was the message?"

"Don't you remember anything as Brigid?" Indigo asks, curious.

"Not much" The Empress replies. "Brigid is her own soul."

When we walk into the Throne Room, Jackson and Ero are still guarding our children. Ero sits, her long legs tucked under her, her hands holding Amber's. Tears rained down her cheeks, vivid blue drops of liquid, like the very ocean itself grieves for my daughter. Jackson, hovers, biting his lips, as Fero tucks his head against her shoulder. Seeing us approach, Ero bows before The Empress, but she dismisses the formality with a wave of her hand, and says, "Ero, it's just Denise now. Arcadia is safe and I'm no longer The Empress."

She bends down to study our children, ghostly white in death. She sits down next to Rose first, and gently touches her cheek. Then she trails her hand down her arm and opens her hand to reveal the crystal with her palm.

"Citrine" she says, rubbing her finger over the crystal. She does the same to Aiden, who is clutching amber, then to Duncan, who is holding tiger's eyes and finally to Amber, who holds the rose quartz. "You did the right thing to protect them," she says to Fingle. He moves closer to her, his wings fluttering rapidly, signalling his excitement. "Yes. They've done more than we have ever asked of anyone. They have earned the right to a second chance."

Hope unfurls in my chest as I watch the interaction, my mind warning me not to believe in the impossible whilst my heart grew excited at the possibilities as Denise says, "Find the Amicus. It might save them."

"It's here." Indigo shouts, picking it up from the middle of the crown that I had thrown on the floor. Maggie, Daniel, Dot and I stand in silence, as Denise takes the Amicus in her hand and closes her eyes. Fingle and Indigo stood at either side of her. The imps move closer and we join them. An imp with large brown eyes comes towards me and extends her tiny hand. Extending my forefinger, I felt her warmth touch us as I joined hands with Dot, then Maggie then Daniel until we are all joined together around the room in a large circle. Denise began to speak.

"A message to the Angel above...

They have done all you have asked,

Faced all the challenges and surpassed,

Earned the right to live true love,

Grant my wish from heaven above"

I close my eyes, praying, hoping with every fibre of my being that the words ring true, that I will open my eyes to see my children alive again. Light burst against my eyelids and I resist opening them for fear I will break the spell. I sense movement around me and I opened my eyes to see Denise in front of us. Her face sombre.

"I've done all that I can." She takes Maggie's hand and murmurs, "Your Rose was a blessing to me."

I kneel down beside our children and wait. Their faces are now white, their bodies frozen in movement. I stay still, refusing to leave or give up. Believing in them even when they have gone. That sheer will could give life once more. The others join me on the floor as I sit in silence, until darkness and exhaustion overwhelms me and I close my eyes. The dream came again, to haunt me, except this time as I held Rora I had a chance to say the words I always wanted to. She clenches my arms to move me, shouting "Wake up, Will. Wake up." I'm jolted awake, to see sunrise filtering through the glass windows. The light moves along the floor as I see Aiden's leg give a slight twitch then stop. I gasp out, hardly believing what I'm seeing. Then I notice Amber, Duncan and Rose twitching, slightly at first, then moving and stretching their limbs. Amber is the first to open her eyes. She looks at me, confused, and asks, "Dad?"

Maggie shouts as she and Daniel rush forward, speaking over one another. I turn to Dot and smile in wonder as she rubs Aiden's cheek and shakes her head. In the distance, I see Denise watching us, Fingle and Indigo at each side and I smile. Knowing I'll never be able to thank them for what they've done. What everyone had done for us. Hours later, we're ready. Together, all wounds cleansed, and grateful for the turn of events. We can't stay. The shadows within Storm Castle have existed too long to be eradicated by one day of settlement. So when the first stone fell and the Castle begins to crumble, I was unsurprised. We rise in unison and move towards the courtyard bypassing the scattered stones. Down the hill, I turn to look back at the Castle that has marred and haunted my life and I feel no grief as a turret uproots and falls into the sea below, dismantling on its own will. The jewels, the rich material that was so important at one time no longer matters. What mattered most were the people around me. As lighting strikes the remnants of the Castle, it gave chase to fire, sweeping black smoke into the sky. The last of the evil within saying a final goodbye. "It's over" I say with relief. I turn my back on the past and put my arms around my children, hearing the sounds of the unicorns in the distance and smile as my old friend Clover escorts me back to Greenwood. The only home I have ever known.

THE CHOICE

Aiden Darkings

L ife shines in Greenwood. I was unsure of what to expect on our return. Horror pictures from my fractured past played in my head of a deserted village, black smoke rising from ash wood, burned to the ground. Instead, we return to the burgeoning village of my childhood. Houses are being constructed to accommodate the new families who have arrived and wish to stay with us. Warwick has been reinstated as Head of the High Council and Denise, Daniel, and my father act as his advisers. My father has asked me to help with the reconstruction of Sensio. Every village, tribe or creatures in Sensio has a representative. We will never return to the autocratic ways of the past. The balance that has now been restored must be protected.

Since we were brought back to life, our family is very protective, refusing to let us too far out of their sight, reassuring themselves with our presence that we are not leaving again. Our father was hesitant with Amber and me at first, for fear of crossing the invisible boundary that came from our separation. Now he's demonstrative, always taking the opportunity to put his arm around our shoulders and hugging us before we all separate for the night. Amber and I did not miss out on this as children. Daniel, Maggie and Lauren were tactile and we never doubted their love. But to receive this love from the man who made us, makes us feel like we are being given an unexpected gift.

My time in the no-man's-land, the one between life and death, is like a hazy dream, but what I remember most are my conversations with Harwyn, the man who has looked over me all of my life. We spoke of everything, my separation from Amber, my fractured identity, my immersion into the Black Knights and my shabby treatment of my Mate. Harwyn stayed with me until I came to terms with it all, reaching the balance that's always evaded me. Explaining his role was to keep me here until a decision was made. When I asked what the decision was, he only smiled.

Amber, Duncan and Rose always remained on the periphery of my thoughts, never too far away that I couldn't feel their connection. In those last moments of life when the cold numbness from the mortal wound spread to my limbs and pulled me away, my focus was only on Rose. Harwyn explained that she offered to sacrifice herself for me at Abaddon. She's everything to me. She is my world. They fled the moment I came alive again in her arms and merged fully when I followed her into our bedroom at Storm Castle. Every kiss and touch solidified my instinct that we were meant to be together. We moved in together as soon as we came back to Greenwood. Simple acts such like preparing and sharing a meal together give me such pleasure that I feel I only existed before without her. Sharing a bed, her body curled into an untroubled sleep as I rest my face into her neck and her hair that shares the smell of wildflowers with our pillows. The confusion in her soft brown eyes before she awakens fully and turns in my arms and seeks my lips as I pull her closer. I finally understand what Duncan meant when he tried to describe that possessive, all-consuming pull that you feel towards your Mate. I surrender willingly. I can't stand being away from her.

Tonight we are celebrating by sharing a meal in the village square to signal the beginning of the celebrations for Amber and Duncan's formal mating tomorrow. Laughter rings round the table as Maggie shares stories of mating and her and Rora's over-consumption of brew the night before. Dad joins in speaking of the first time they saw each other in the clearing and her efforts to evade him during the party. The stories bring her alive to Amber and me, and I listen as she peppers Maggie and Dad with questions, making Rora a part of our celebrations. Amber and Duncan announced their intention to have a mating ceremony the night we arrived back in Greenwood. Her eyes shone as she said she didn't want to wait any longer. They glow with happiness and I feel for Rose's hand on the table and take it in mine, knowing that I want this too. The shadows of Sierra are now eradicated. Marcus and Sierra were reunited at Storm Castle and immediately left for Arcadia to collect Thomas and begin a new life together. Ero left with them to meet up with the mermaids still in Arcadia, followed by a besotted Jackson who insisted on escorting her there for her own safety. She assented, not because she felt it was necessary, but because she's as besotted with him as he is with her.

Dusk descends as we speak into the night. Our presence lit by large softened candles around the large table, the darkness cloaking us together. The flap of wings was inconspicuous at first and I dismiss it until I see Warwick and Denise straighten and look towards the darkened shadows of the trees searching for something.

"What is it Denise?" asks Rose.

I stand up and instinctively push her behind me. The crow suddenly emerges from the forest and heads towards our table, drops a scroll in the middle of it, and flies off again. Then we watch as it falls into a burst of fire to the ground turning into a pile of ashes that's blown away by the wind.

My father opens the scroll and examines the words inside. He stays silent for moment. Then he gets up and walks agitatedly in a circle, before he stops, turns and says,

"Follow me to the Great Hall."

We followed silently. I tug Rose's hand into mine and tuck her into my side. She leans into me, needing me as much as I need her. We descended the stairs and the sconces lit as we moved into the large space and take a seat at the large table. The celebratory mood has been replaced by tension. Dad opens the scroll and begins to read.

"These are the last wishes of Queen Andora Thorgood of Sensio. To properly establish the natural balance, a decision must be taken. My last act as Queen Consort is to remind the King that example comes from the throne. Your heir apparent Prince Aiden was returned from natural death after help was sought. Princess Amber was brought to live in Sensio not of her own free will. You must rectify the balance. Son or daughter? The choice is yours."

Dad throws the scroll into the fire in disgust, watching as the flames catch and dismantle the message.

"What does this mean?" Amber asks in a small nervous voice. Her happiness now gone.

"It means there is a price to be paid" Rose replies, "just as

Harwyn warned." She looks at me, distraught.

We turn to Denise for help. She knows more about Sensio than any of us.

"The elements are still within each one of you," she says quietly. "Andora's message is correct. The balance cannot be restored until the choice is made," she pauses. "Rose and I were gifted with powerful second sight encouraged and required by events. This should be receding. Mine hasn't. Rose?" Rose shook her head and bites her lip. "The changes within our world are unprecedented," Denise shakes her head.

"Can I..." Dad falters then goes silent. He wants to intervene but knows he will steal from the future to save our present. It was no way to start our new world.

"Should I be...?" I say, and Rose begins to cry. I pull her closer. The question circles around the large empty space, attempting to hide in the corners unseen before it came back to the table demanding an answer.

"That's not an option Aiden." Amber breathes out. "If I go back, is there a chance I could return to Sensio?"

Denise replies, truth clear in her dark blue eyes. "I truly don't know Amber. It's a game changer. This is a new beginning for all of us. What I do know is that I cannot intervene, and neither can your father. But, remember, there is always hope. And I know this from personal experience," she says, looking at Warwick. She takes his hand and we see the belief that helped her survive their separation.

I'm crucified by guilt as I watch Duncan get up and pull

Amber away. His jaw clenched. Unbelievably, there is no censure in his eyes as they meet mine, only an acceptance of the inevitable. Amber pulls away and hugs me before she leaves. My twin sister I love and finally appreciate. The choice has been made.

AMBER

Duncan Darkings

I have dreamed of this moment for so long I wonder if it's real. She walks down the aisle towards me, luminously beautiful, her green eyes bright and shining, her lips soft and parted in excitement, her cheeks flushed. Her auburn hair is long and curling down her back and entwined with an abundance of daises and she's wearing a pale blue dress that belonged to her mother. It tangles into her curves and sweeps around her small waist. Her bare feet crunch on the leaves underfoot. Her father and Dot stand on either side of her, honoured and proud. Neither assumed that they had the right to escort her down the aisle but my Amber opened her heart and asked what they secretly wanted. Dot and Boon became the parents of her heart and her father, having missed out on so many firsts, deserved the chance to walk his daughter down the aisle. When she reaches me, I bring her closer and kiss her, unable to wait until the end of the ceremony. She chastises me and blushes behind her laughter and sweeps the coldness away. We say the words that bind us together, the binding veil, the love that exists between us is now fully fledged into life. Everyone cheers and smiles. She made us promise that today would be happy. No tears or sadness. Amber said our happiness was our her gift to her. So joviality rules, as she demands it. Aiden's face is strained with guilt but no one blames him. Circumstances have brought us here. We are mere pawns in a game we don't know the rules of and as we fumble in the dark all we can do is thread our fingers together and hope we can stay together.

I look at her and remember it all. My first dream of her. Saving her from the water. Her anger as she woke to find me in her house. How brave she was when she first arrived in Sensio, scared but plucky, defying me until I accepted she would not yield as I wanted. I had to wait to earn that right. I remember our first kiss in the woods. Her soft lips below mine as I fought from tugging her closer and branding her as I wanted. The moment she told she would be mine. Her silhouette in the moonlight against the open door at Rowan Cottage. The frantic pull of her body as I made her mine. Her belief in Aiden even when we had all given up on him. Her determined face when she entered The Alliance camp, mud slicked and proud, as she faced down and knocked Marcus on his arse. Her declaration in the face of the Queen that she was my Mate and would refuse any other. Bringing me back at Abaddon when I was too far gone to save myself. Taking me exactly as I am; fiery, passionate, and possessive and never once asking me to change, only to accept her as she is, as I wanted her. She now knows. I would never fully respect a woman who gave into my every wish. She is my equal in every way.

She leans into my chest and asks me to dance knowing that all I want to do is throw her over my shoulder and take her away. She stays in the now, refusing to think about tomorrow.

Our night together is frantic and bittersweet. The selfish part of me wants to damn the world, keep her close and never let her go. Instead, I imprint myself on her body. Taking her again and again until we collapse into sleep.

Even then I refuse to move away from her, trailing my lips and hands over her body. When dawn comes, she finally gives in to tears, surrendering to the grief of leaving our home and I damn the choice that had to be made. Where is my balance? How will I go on when she leaves me? How will my heart keep beating when half of it leaves with her?

We gather in the clearing in the still of the morning light. There are no more words that can be said. Our family holds her and walks away just as she asked. I can't do that. I have to give her all of me. I give it freely, because without her, I'm nothing. I pull her closer and force her luminous green eyes to focus on mine.

"Do you know, Amber?" I whisper in the quietness.

She shakes her head. I've never uttered the words, telling myself she knew every time I thought of her, every time I looked at her, every single moment I touched her.

"I love you. You're my everything."

She cries out and collapses into me. I close my eyes and envelope her, my Amber, my Mate, in my arms. She pulls away, sobbing. I feel our family close in the shadows of the woods; refusing to leave her even at the end. The air picks up as I close my eyes and bury my head in her soft hair, holding her so close, we become one. Then my arms drop as she fades to back to her own world, until I feel nothing but the empty space around me. Around my heart.

Opening my eyes I panic, searching the mist of the morning for her shadow, knowing she's gone. I can't feel her. My knees give in as I collapse onto the ground, and give into the fire within, screaming her name.

HOME

Amber Darkings

I'm back where it all began. I open my eyes and let out a shuddering breath. The air feels sharp and clean and I look to the ground and find myself standing on soft grass, running water trickles persistently and I turn to see rushing water bounce off the boulders peeking out of it. The water element still within me rises at the sight, swells and then abates, finding peace within its proximity. Looking up, I find myself looking at a circle of Douglas Firs that stretch into the sky and circle my view. They pin the sky above; the bright blue sky. All of a sudden I'm overwhelmed by memories of my old life. Twisting around, I look at a view similar to the Hermitage but not. Memories assault me and I see a grey hazy image of myself on my morning runs. I see myself running a race as Lauren cheers me on to the finish line. I see myself frantically running home to her the day I lost her. I feel removed from it all, as if it happened to another person. Was that really me? My experiences in Sensio have forced me to change from the immature self-indulgent girl to the woman I am now, who fought for her life and those of the people she loves.

I look around me, and my heart aches for Sensio. I miss the purple sky, the vivid array of wild and glorious colours. I miss the faeries and the unicorns. I miss the magic around me. I miss all of it.

I use the river to calm myself down. Panicking won't help. I have to work out what to do next.

An elderly couple walk past me with their dogs and say hello. Looking down at my clothes, I'm glad I chose to wear my worn jeans, tank top and trainers to help me fit in. Pulling at the worn denim, it feels restrictive and I miss the soft fabrics I'm used to in Sensio. One of the dogs barks and I watch him follow the natural path to the stone bridge, and watch the man throw his folded newspaper into the bin as they walk over the bridge and deeper into the woods.

The seed of an idea flashes and I pick up the newspaper. The date is the 4th of July. Shock pulses through me as the breath leaves my lungs. The implications of arriving home today are serendipitous. Today would have been Lauren's birthday. An instinct born from chance galvanises my limbs into movement and I cross the bridge knowing where I needed to go. Circling Ravenswood, I follow the path across fields, admiring the assortment of wildflowers being pushed back and forth against the breeze. The rich reds of the poppies are dotted across the space, with foxgloves and the odd sunflower, reminding me of my first view of Arcadia from the back of a unicorn as the carpet of flowers below swayed toward us in welcome. Stopping, I reach down and pull the stalks from the ground gathering a bunch together as I see the outline of the building that's my destination. Ravenswood Abbey stands proudly in the morning light, the tallest square steeple rising proudly in the sky. Nearing the wood sign, I trace my fingers over the word 'Ravenswood' realising that Rora's family, my family, had been here forever. Walking around the back of the Abbey, I walked slowly, studying the stone squares erected into the ground. The names and years danced below my eyes until I turned and without reason headed towards a sheltered corner. A tall willow tree sat, it's branches leaning over the space to provide protection to all within its shadow. The words are etched in black onto white marble stone. Tears dance as I read them aloud.

"Lauren Lockwood,

Mother and Friend,

Forever Loved."

The words are simple and I knew whoever chose them knew her well. I replace the dying flowers from the stone vase with my wildflowers and smile, remembering Lauren's face when I would surprise her with an impromptu bunch of flowers. I touch the words, glad that I've found her, but sad that it's here.

"Amber?"

I turn around slowly, as I registered the voice, wondering if it could be true. Rising, I turned slowly. Elaine looks at me with wonder and surprise and drops the flowers she is carrying on the ground. She still looks like the fashionista of our teenage years. Her blue eyes sparkle as she studies me, her cheeks pink and expertly made up. Her blonde hair is long, curling into her shoulders and flowing down her back. Her style is unchanged, a shimmering gold silk blouse is teamed with a long black skirt and a wide belt clinches at her waist. Her legs are encased into soft brown boots that speak of comfort and elegance. Where she scoured vintage shops with a passion as a teenager, I could tell these clothes had the effortless cut that marked them as designer. Whatever path Elaine had chosen to follow, it had been successful. I said her name out loud and she picked up the flowers, placing them tenderly inside the vase beside mine. We lapsed into a comfortable silence, despite the years apart.

"You chose the words," I say, and she nods.

Tears spring and I realise my friend had done what I couldn't. She stands beside me, tucking her arm through mine, and whispers, "You would have done the same for me."

We stand for a moment and she gently tugs me away and we walk me towards the gate. As we round the corner, I look back and say the silent goodbye to Lauren I had always yearned for.

Following a maze of streets, I break the silence. Knowing my friend would not force me to talk before I was ready. "So what happened when I left?" I finally ask.

"When Lauren was found and you disappeared. For a few days we thought you had been killed too," her voice broke and she stops for a moment. "Then I broke into the cottage and saw the photograph was gone and I knew you'd left and taken it with you," she smiles, relieved to share her secret.

That photograph had captured a perfect moment on a birthday night. Lauren and I were both happy and the photograph had captured a perfect moment in front of my lit birthday cake, Lauren's arm was looped around my shoulders proudly and we were both smiling into the camera. It now sits on my bedside table in Sensio.

"Lauren named me as a beneficiary in your absence and David offered to help me return her home and organise the funeral. I didn't go to University. Instead, I bought my shop and David is a Policeman. We've been here ever since."

I shake my head at the turn of events and follow Elaine across the street, the sounds of a car horn makes me jump, used to the quietness only intercepted by the sounds of nature in Sensio.

"I'm sorry Elaine.....for everything."

She stops walking and grabs my hand. "No, don't be. You're here now that's all that matters." "Besides, if you hadn't left I wouldn't be with David," she laughs.

Looking ahead, I didn't need to be told which shop belonged to my friend. The building stood proudly in the street making a statement. The soft green wood that held the sign was comforting and I studied the sharp blue lettering of the sign that swept in italics with 'Elestial Unication' written like the design had flowed from a hand. Opening the door, a bell signalled our arrival and I study the space within, covered in books, crystals and ointments. The walls are adorned with art and wall hangings. She has placed sconces with used sunken candles and mirrors to maximise the space and light. A wood burning stove crackles and blazes, encased by a fireplace with a vintage radio resting on the mantelpiece against a large mirror, flanked by two large armchairs. A black Labrador sleeps contentedly in front of it. The window seat beside the bookshelf is covered with pillows and cushions all different shapes and sizes, colours and patterns that somehow meld together. I smile in my mind, imagining Elaine organising her shop exactly how she wanted it. I feel pride settles as I see my friend has realised her dream to be a success with her own business.

"Amber, come and meet my David," she says, dragging me from my reverie. The man behind the counter has dark brown eyes and a warm, friendly smile. He looms tall, with a commanding presence as he stands comfortably behind the counter, like he'd often helped Elaine out when needed. Elaine turns to look at him and her face softens. Her eyes lighting up. His hand reaches for hers and surrounds the large diamond on her left hand. I stifle a giggle as the dots connected. In all her romantic notions in seeking her one true love she never foresaw that the man she ended up marrying would be David Carmichael who sat in front of us in English. Making our introductions, he studies me, questions in his eyes, before he makes excuses himself, going up a wrought iron steps that led upstairs.

Coming round the counter, she bids me into one of the rocking chairs and flicks on the radio. Leaning forward to tug a strand of my hair behind my cheek, she laughs and places a small flower in my middle of my palm. The sight of the daisy brings a sting of pain that's unexpected as I remember how Duncan removed each one patiently last night before he curled his fingers into my hair and pulled me into his kiss.

"You fell in love," Elaine whispers. I wonder how she can tell. I nod, swallowing and unable to say the words. I can't say his name without it tearing at me desperately. I ache for him. She gives my shoulder a squeeze and says something about a pot of tea. I nod my head, still looking at the daisy. A symbol of home. The radio plays in the background. The announcer's tone is low and monosyllabic as he announces

"Fantasia on a Theme" by Vaughan Williams. I try to relax as it starts, beginning on the periphery of my senses until the staccato highs and lows play perfectly with my mood. The snores of the dog at my feet and Elaine's voice on the telephone, lull me away from everything around me.

I open my eyes to hear the music playing in the background bursting with a crescendo that makes my heart beat faster. I sit up straighter and look ahead to see someone sitting opposite me. Boon Cuthbert looks at me with his unflinching blue eyes, as if I'm still the puzzle he needs to solve. Humour laces his features and he takes my hand within his large one, and says gently, "Remember your lessons Amber," and memories flood of our walks around Greenwood and is patience with my curious questions. Then I remember the last lesson, the day before the Black Knights arrived.

"What Law have we missed Amber?" he had asked that day. I thought before I answered his question, placing my finger on my lips, still swollen after Duncan's kisses of the night before.

"Love." I said, putting a word to the emotion that had unfurled and consumed me whenever I was near Duncan.

He nods proudly and explains. "This is the most important Law Amber. It's pure. It's the true love you have for your Mate and what comes from that. It will save you when everything else you believe in is lost."

I wake up to the sounds of the tea tray being placed on the counter, as Elaine pours our drinks. Overwhelmed I excuse myself, to go to the bathroom and splash my face with water.

My eyes are red and ringed with shadows, placing my hands on the sink, I wet a face cloth and pulled it across my neck. Not noticing the tummy flutters until they persist, rising within my belly, until I place a hand on my skin. They began to jump again, like soft kisses from a butterfly whispering against my palm. Looking into the mirror, I release a stunned breath and knew what I had to do.

I run out of the bathroom, "I'm sorry. I have to go back." Elaine smiles and hugs me tight. I hug her back, grateful to my friend, my sister. She nods, accepting my decision and we hug each other again, knowing this will be the last time. Leaving her shop, I run down the street. Passing the walking occupants on the pavements and back through the graveyard and into the forest. My limbs grow comfortable, warmth spreading as my body grew used to a natural movement. I calm as I hear the water and my feet hit the forest floor. I close my eyes and trust to the vision I see before me, believing with every fibre of my being that where I'm going is where I am meant to be. Seeing the white birch, I smile and run faster. I find the runic stepping stones and begin the dance upon them, stepping on one, missing another, moving on pure instinct and trusting what my soul is telling me. As I reach the end of the path, I see the light, and I shout for home.

BLUEPRINT

Amber Darkings

I have done what I was meant to do. I had to go beyond the veil. I had to go away to be able to come back home. In the back of my mind, I worried over the legacy I had left behind me. Worrying if I had left Lauren in some hellish limbo and Elaine forever left to wonder what had become of me. In the end, it didn't matter. The woman who raised me was at peace and Elaine, my sister, only cared that I lived and was happy, unconcerned with the circumstances that took me away. In returning to Earth, I settled the questions that had always haunted me. Finding out the truth had set me free. In all our battles to rectify the balance, I never fully appreciated that it was me that needed it. That my haunted history would never fully disappear until I gathered the strength to face the ghosts of the past. Now I know. The truth can't hurt you and having the courage to face it will give you everything you have ever wanted.

When I broke free into the clearing, I immediately saw his outline. Hypnotic. Beautifully silhouetted against the purple sky and the two moons. He sat on the ground, his arms hunched over his knees. I moved closer, the soft long grass initially masking my advance. His blue gaze swings towards me and I see the shadows around his eyes and the stubble darkening his chin. The hours I have been gone have been days for him. My heart skips and I take a deep breath as I marvel at how lucky I am that this man wants me. Even when hope is gone, he still believes in me. He still believes in us.

I kneel in front of him and he pulls me roughly to him. His blue eyes kindle as he pushes my tangled hair away from my face. Hardly believing that I am really here. He pulls me on top of him and our lips meet. Then he rolls me over onto my back. I laugh out loud sharing my joy with the two worlds that made me. Duncan leans over me and tries to speak, wanting to understand how I got back. Instead I place a finger to his lips and pull him down to me and ask him to show me instead. Choosing to live now, wanting to show him my heart was whole after being split in half during our separation. Explanations are unimportant; the balance has given me back the other half of my heart. It was at that moment the water element within me broke free, as it was meant to.

Blissful normality has blessed our lives in the months since my return. Aiden and Rose were formally mated a month after I arrived home and have happily settled into domestic bliss in Greenwood. They refuse to be separated and whenever Aiden goes anywhere, she goes with him. And where Rose goes, Peck goes too. Knowing his mistress will always carry a slice of apple for him to munch upon. As time passes, the black of Aiden's eyes has begun to recede to the warm brown they once were. My brother has been elected spokesman for The Alliance, which represents all species of Sensio. Even the sasquatchs have been persuaded to participate.

By returning to Rowan Cottage, my father has regained a connection to Rora that has given him the peace of mind he needs. He comes to Greenwood daily, taking such an active interest in our lives that it seems as if he has always been there. He is like a grandparent to young Thomas, which delights Marcus and Sierra and Clover, his faithful friend, is never far away. Daniel and Maggie continue to live happily in Greenwood. Daniel recently passed the responsibility of Village Protector onto Duncan, saying he had done his duty and refused to be parted from 'his girl' again. They care for May Gentles who happily lives with them. Loved and finally encouraged to use her talent to communicate with animals. We are lucky to have her as part of our family.

Warwick and Denise are happily reunited and are often found kissing like teenagers beside the wishing well, happy after so many years apart. Denise and Rose's second sight has reduced to a level that no longer prevents them from embracing life. The dragons are seen once in a while, happy together near Arcadia and beyond.

Fingle has now taken over responsibility for Arcadia from his sister. Indigo still gets into trouble and the stories of her adventures circle around Sensio and then circulate again with another round of legs and arms added. Although, Rose believes that the more extravagant of the tales are actually true.

Ero has returned to the sea with Moren and her family of mermaids, happy to live in peace with the dolphins and whales. Not long after this, the Geans moved near the sea. Jackson says he will not move until Ero speaks to him again but refuses to divulge why she stopped speaking to him in the first place. The truth will out as it always does.

We all grieved over the loss of Dot. Who went to sleep one night and choose not to wake up. She wanted to stay in our time of need, a gift we were unaware of until she left. We will miss her forever but we take comfort from knowing she is happy and reunited with Boon.

The moment my element broke free from me was also the moment when the other three elements broke free from Duncan, Aiden and Rose and were shared around Sensio. They needed to be protected within us and could only be released when the balance was completely restored. I could never have anticipated that I would be the key needed to open the door. The elements are now part of everyone. We all have the talents to work with air, earth, fire and water. Whilst together, sharing the responsibility. But every single person on Sensio is now also responsible for the safe keeping of our environment. We all now carry an invisible sphere, its weight significant to reflect the responsibility we bear. When you hold it up against the sun, you see the movement within. The clouds in the wind, the stones of the earth, the flame of the fire and the waves of the water. We have lived with the results of their abuse and have lost loved ones as a result. We now understand that we are part of something larger than ourselves and it is our job to keep them safe.

Our twins were born nine months after I returned to Sensio on a warm spring morning. Conceived at Hell Castle, when I gave myself completely to Duncan in order to save him. Unaware, he saved me back by giving the most precious gift. The binding true love that brought me home.

Our firstborn, Tanner, has my green eyes and his father's dark hair. Even as a baby he is rambunctious and will use his charms to get his way. His younger sister, Tallis, has her father's blue eyes and my auburn hair. Easy going and a natural peacekeeper she is adept at calming her excitable brother down. I revel in their closeness, even as they rest in their cot they squirm closer to each other. I'm happy that our children can have what Aiden and I missed out on.

The door opens. Duncan puts his arms around me and nuzzles the crook of my neck, as we gaze upon the miracles we made. Our love has given me what I have always wanted. A family of my own. Turning around, I pull Duncan's mouth down to mine and say a silent thank you for all I have been given.

Dreams can come true.

EPILOGUE

"The Feathered Roots fully formed,

Scatter of Kin bound adorned,

A tale of Kinship chronicled for all time,

For Good will always, always shine."

…On Behalf of Archangel Michael

"Three people, living extraordinary dreams,

Following their Blueprints,

To the Love it brings,

Like the Storyteller, Artist & the Psychic,

Dreams can come true,

The world is full of magic"

"Unlock your blueprint, the key is within you..."

With Love,

Cassie
Brigid
The Empress

xxx

SOCIAL MEDIA

We sincerely hope you enjoyed your journey through The Kinship Chronicles Tri-Book®

If you would like to follow our characters you can find them on Twitter.

Special thanks to those already following, your support is much appreciated.

Amber Lockwood	@ambertkc
Aiden Darkings	@aidentkc
Duncan Darkings	@duncan_tkc
Rose Darkings	@rose_tkc
Luther Barton	@luthertkc
Queen Andora	@queenandoratkc
Clover	@clovertkc
Indigo Hawthorn	@indigotkc
Rora Ravenswood	@roratkc
Will Thorgood	@will_tkc

@cassiekennedyw
@brigidartist
@theempresstkc

Courtesy of www.lifetimephotography.co.uk

9193717R00327

Printed in Great Britain
by Amazon.co.uk, Ltd.,
Marston Gate.